Further praise for
and *Nothing T[*

"With a hard, keen eye, Highsmith crafts beautifully warped creatures and dares us to step inside their minds."　　　—Frank Sennett, *Booklist*

"Readers will revel in this fabulous survey of mostly unpublished work."
　　　—*Pages*

"This is a riveting collection of short stories and should not be missed."
　　　—Teresa DeCrescenzo, *Lesbian News*

"Highsmith writes the verbal equivalent of a drug—easy to consume, darkly euphoric, totally addictive. . . . Highsmith belongs in the moody company of Dostoevsky or Angela Carter."　　　—*Time Out*

"Highsmith's writing is wicked . . . it puts a spell on you, after which you feel altered, even tainted. . . . A great American writer is back to stay."
　　　—*Entertainment Weekly*

"In every story, Highsmith demonstrates her inimitable talent for making even the coldest characters galvanizing."　　　—*Publishers Weekly*

"No one has created psychological suspense more densely and deliciously satisfying."　　　—*Vogue*

"Read it at your own risk, knowing that this is not everyone's cup of poisoned tea."　　　—*New York Times*

"These tales will make you shiver and smile."　　　—C.M., *O Magazine*

"Highsmith's gift as a suspense novelist is to show how this secret desire can bridge the normal and abnormal. . . . She seduces us with whisky-smooth surfaces only to lead us blindly into darker terrain."
　　　—*Commercial Appeal*

"Patricia Highsmith's novels are peerlessly disturbing . . . bad dreams that keep us thrashing for the rest of the night."   —*The New Yorker*

"Highsmith had a profound understanding of the human psyche."
—Laura Cassidy, *Seattle Weekly*

"Though Highsmith would no doubt disclaim any kinship with Jonathan Swift or Evelyn Waugh, the best of [her work] is in the same tradition. . . . It is Highsmith's dark and sometimes savage humor, and the intelligence that informs her precise and hard-edged prose, which puts one in mind of those authors."   —*Newsday*

"For eliciting the menace that lurks in familiar surroundings, there's no one like Patricia Highsmith."   —*Time*

"A writer who has created a world of her own—a world claustrophobic and irrational which we enter each time with a sense of personal danger . . . Patricia Highsmith is the poet of apprehension."   —Graham Greene

"Patricia Highsmith is often called a mystery or crime writer, which is a bit like calling Picasso a draftsman."   —*Cleveland Plain Dealer*

"[Highsmith] has an uncanny feeling for the rhythms of terror."
—*Times Literary Supplement*

"To call Patricia Highsmith a thriller writer is true but not the whole truth: her books have stylistic texture, psychological depth, mesmeric readability."   —*The Sunday Times* (London)

ALSO BY PATRICIA HIGHSMITH

NOTHING THAT MEETS THE EYE

The Uncollected Stories of Patricia Highsmith

W. W. Norton & Company
New York   London

For information about permission to reproduce selections from this book, write
to Permissions, W. W. Norton & Company, Inc., 500 Fifth Avenue, New York, NY 10110

Manufacturing by Maple-Vail Book Manufacturing Group

Book design by Blue Shoe Studio

Production manager: Julia Druskin

Library of Congress Cataloging-in-Publication Data

Highsmith, Patricia, 1921–

Nothing that meets the eye : the uncollected stories of Patricia Highsmith.

p. cm.

ISBN 0-393-05187-0

I. Title.

PS3558.I366 N67 2002   2002070121

ISBN 0-393-32500-8 pbk.

W. W. Norton & Company, Inc.

500 Fifth Avenue, New York, N.Y. 10110

www.wwnorton.com

W. W. Norton & Company Ltd.

Castle House, 75/76 Wells Street, London W1T 3QT

2 3 4 5 6 7 8 9 0

CONTENTS

PART II   MIDDLE AND LATER STORIES, 1952–1982

Part I

EARLY STORIES

1938–1949

THE MIGHTIEST MORNINGS

I

The train, which had been following a clean little river for more than an hour, rounded a wooded bend, blew its whistle, and puffed serenely toward a tiny town at the foot of a mountain.

In one of the cars, a man who had been scrutinizing each town along the way thrust his face anxiously to the window. His expression changed, and he left off the nervous nibbling of his nails. A long thrilling shudder of pleasure ran through him, for he knew that this town he had never seen before was the town he sought.

Under the overcast sky the place looked rather drab, he thought, yet friendly and accommodating, too, for it seemed to have established itself at the very edge of the railroad track for the convenience of anyone who wished to debark here. He could see a church, a courthouse, and a main thoroughfare that paralleled the tracks and presented one of every kind of store a person might have need of. And beyond this frank and hospitable facade lay neat two-story houses, sewn upon green that blended into greener and blue-green mountains that might have covered the rest of the earth.

He put his ten fingertips, which were puffed high and clean beyond nearly devoured nails, on the windowsill as though sounding a final chord to a tormented symphony. He was about to throw himself on his knees and murmur, "Thank the blessed God!" when he heard a hoarse "Boa-ad!" from the platform.

With his valise caught up under his arm, he dashed down the aisle and bumped into the conductor on the steps.

"I'm getting off!" he said, and leapt from the slowly moving train.

The train crept on northward, carrying into nowhere the prints of his ten fingers on one of its gritty sills.

A few paces from the station, he came to the edge of the tarred main street whose name was Trevelyan Boulevard. The marquee of the movie theater loomed before him, its bill of fare a delightful prospect for he loved movies, the pole by the barbershop twirled gaily backward, the screen door of a café slapped as a man came out, and two small girls with ice-cream cones, a housewife with shopping bag, and an overalled farmer passed before him, pleasing and appropriate as characters upon a stage. Yet it was not a stage, but a real little town where probably everyone he saw had been born and would live and die. Already he seemed to feel a kinship with them.

It was hard to remember that he had awakened that morning with the shriek of an elevated train in his ears, that he had sat that morning at the wheel of his cab. Had he driven a fare today? He remembered driving slowly, ignoring people who waved and whistled for him, reluctant as always and suddenly unable to plunge into the hysteria of New York. New York that morning! As he looked back from a distance of eight hours, its cramped fury seemed like a disease. He thought of New York now, intensely, and for the last time. Then he cut his thinking off as he might have a radio that blared a football scramble.

Happiness, goodwill, and optimism seemed to lift him from the ground. A new town, virgin, potential, where he might begin again! He felt reborn. Sunday he would go to the church, whose black spire, surmounted by a gilt ball and cross, he could see above some treetops, and would offer thanks to God with the rest of the townspeople.

Just as a grumble of hunger came from his stomach, his eyes alighted on a white structure a few yards away on this side of Trevelyan Boulevard. Big black letters spelled EATS down its side, and small neon signs front and back wrote out THE DANDY DINER.

The door resisted him, and a voice behind its steamy pane called something that sounded like "Sloy dit!"

Aaron slid it, entered, and closed it snugly behind him. The place was warm and fragrant of eggs-in-butter and of fresh-cooked hamburger.

"Eve-nin'!" the same voice said. It belonged to a husky denim-shirted man behind the counter.

"Good evening!" Aaron replied, nodding to everyone. He seated himself on a stool.

His blue eyes moved pleasurably over the pale-crusted homemade pies, the raft of popping hot dogs on the grill, the bowl of bright soft butter, and the novel varieties of sweet buns on plates in the shelves. Ordinarily his eyes bulged, and from the side possessed a catlike translucence, but now they projected farther as they searched out every feature of the shop. He lifted his hat and gave his brown hair a perfunctory smoothing. He watched the counterman extract a waffle from the iron, butter it generously, and set it before a man in the blue-and-white striped overalls of a railroad worker.

"Syrup?"

"Betcha," the man replied, with a rolling inflection that covered several tones.

The counterman set a pitcher of syrup beside his plate, then came to Aaron. "What'll it be?"

Aaron pressed his palms together, raised himself slightly by the footrest, and called for a hot dog, a waffle, a piece of peach pie, one of the sweet buns, and a cup of coffee. While these things were preparing, he listened to the banter of the counterman and the railroad worker, and to the softer talk of two Negroes that was interspersed with laughter.

The pulse of the electric ventilator bound the world within the diner into a perfect whole.

The telephone rang, and the young girl who had been daydreaming beside the cash register sprang to it. "You-ou!" she drawled, smiling. "Mac says I have to wuhk tonight till eight-thuhty."

"Aw, I'll let you off," Mac threw in good-naturedly. "When do you ever wuhk anyway?"

When the waffle was brought to him, Aaron touched his chin self-consciously. "I should have got a shave first, I guess." He smiled at the counterman.

Mac smiled back. "Oh, that's all right. We ain't fussy. Look at me." He laughed. "Where you from?"

"New York." Aaron ducked his head and began eating the waffle. He poured a discreet amount of syrup on it (even if he were from New York, he would not behave like those he had seen in the Automats, so greedy that syrup and cream had to be meted to them in decent portions), and between bites turned his head to read the various placards on the walls.

COME ONE, COME ALL!
WILLIE WALKER'S FAMOUS SEVEN-PIECE BAND
ADMISSION $1.50 PER COUPLE

BRIGHTON RECREATION HALL
BRIGHTON, VERMONT

Its date was a month old. He wondered if the young girl was going to one of these dances tonight. He had not heard of any of the towns mentioned. Then he saw a sign that said:

ROOMS
MRS. HOPLEY'S COMFORTABLY FURNISHED LODGINGS
BY WEEK OR MONTH
17 PLEASANT STREET
CLEMENT, N.H.

"Where's Pleasant Street?" he asked Mac, so apprehensive lest this town was not Clement, he dared not ask that question first.

Finally Mac brought his hand down from the back of his neck, pointed to a corner of the diner, and gave instructions that Aaron was too excited to attend. His mind was forming images of the house, of the room he would have. He was marveling at his good luck to have found a street with the name "Pleasant," while "Clement" itself was sweet enough to the ear, ringing some bell in his memory that conjured up a picture of a sunny landscape and a picnic.

"Goin' to be here awhile?" Mac asked as he handed him the check.

"I hope so." Aaron smiled, and leaving a dollar on the counter, he backed for the door. "Sure enjoyed that."

"Come back again!"

"'Bye!" the girl said.

Following the direction of the pointed finger, Aaron headed for a street around the drugstore corner. At the intersection he stopped to admire a modest war memorial. It was a cement post set in a triangle of grass, bearing a metal plate on which some hundred names were listed, Clement veterans of all the wars. Adams, Barber, Barton, Burke, Child— Hopley? Yes, there was a Zachariah P. and a William J. Hopley. He might mention having seen them to Mrs. Hopley.

He hurried on his way, smiled a greeting to a straggly-haired bare-foot little girl who leaned against a tree, said "Good evening!" to an old bent gentleman in cracked, well-shined shoes and a starched collar that stood out from his neck.

"Howdy do!" the old man replied.

Walking a general uphill way, he arrived at Pleasant Street, which was bordered with large elms that leaned inward, meeting overhead. And no sooner did he enter this tunnel of greenness than the sun came out and fell through the thousands of leaves like golden rain.

Anxiously he watched the numbers grow until he stood before number seventeen, a two-story, yellowish house half hidden by lush green vines that sprang from either end of the front porch. He recognized the house as he had the town. It was what he wanted. Home! There was homeliness in the cracked brown paint, elegance in the spindling black balustrades that supported the porch rail and the banisters of the wooden steps. Two black iron dogs set in profile, one paw raised, symmetrically guarded the casual front lawn that was divided by a cement walk.

"Lookin' for some'an?" a voice called from the porch.

Aaron started up the walk. "I'm looking for a room."

A swing creaked and a short chunky man in glazed manila pants and shirt came toward him. "Think there's one or two," he said, smiling and inspecting Aaron.

"Who wants a room?" This time the voice came from behind the screen door. "Just got one. Y'can come in an' see if y'like it."

He followed her through a hall, up a flight of stairs and down another hall. Finally she opened the door of a generous square room with three enormous windows.

"Y'lucky," she told him. "Fella just moved out yestiddy. Changed his job an' went to Bennington. Rooms haad t'get anywheres in this town."

He nodded, enchanted. "I'll take it."

He paid seven dollars for his week's rent and, left to himself, inspected the view from each window. From one he could see mountains, from the others could just touch the leaves of a big tree that grew on the lawn. With a pleasurable sense of efficiency and orderliness, he began to transfer his things from the valise to the bureau. The deep newspaper-lined drawers put his wardrobe to shame. His four shirts lay flat and lonely in the bottom drawer, and even the loosest sprinkling of his socks and handkerchiefs over them helped little. Having nothing to put in the last drawer, he read a bit in its newspaper. Finally he set the empty valise in the closet, closed the bureau drawers, and surveyed the room with satisfaction, yet thinking that except for the shaving articles he had left out on the round table, his coming had wrought no change at all. Well, he thought, that was what happened when you left all your old clothes behind, all the trinkets gathered over the years to ornament furnished rooms in New York.

There was a knock at the door.

"Come in?"

Mrs. Hopley came in. "Brought y'some towels," she said in a warmer tone than before, almost an intimate, conspiratorial tone, so that Aaron faced her attentively and blinked at her. She laid two bath towels, a face towel, and a washrag separately along the bedside, then straightened up and smiled at him.

"Fine! Just what I need right away," he responded, though it was only that morning he had failed to shave. "I've been a long time on the train."

Mrs. Hopley nodded and regarded him with huge brown eyes behind thick lenses. She fumbled at the slack, somewhat soiled front of her dress, which hung just as slackly behind, over her bony, cowlike rump. "Where d'y' come from?"

"New York," he replied, smiling nervously, for he felt as he had in the diner with Mac, that the people of the small town might look upon him with suspicion.

"Hmm-mm." Her eyes moved slowly and ceaselessly, resting as often on nearby parts of the room as on him. One of her ancient black house slippers with damaged pompon was poised shyly on the toe of the other, as though to mitigate by womanly grace the questionnaire she intended to put to him. "Got business here?"

He hesitated, then smiled. He could not help smiling at anything that had to do with the pleasant town of Clement. "Well, not exactly. You might say I'm in need of a vacation and the town looked good to me."

"Not much doin' here in the way of vacationin'."

"I don't mean an ordinary vacation." He moistened his lips. "See, I was a taxi driver in New York. My nerves got sort of jumpy, so I decided to pull up stakes and come to a new place."

"Permanent?"

"Maybe. I hope so. I sure like this town."

She thought a minute. "Not much call for taxi drivers around here."

"Oh, I wouldn't be a taxi driver! I've had enough of that."

She nodded. "What d'y' think y'll do, then?"

He saw her look at his hands, and he unclenched them and smiled. "I don't know yet, see? I'll have to find out." He added modestly, "I've got a little money saved up."

"Hmm-mm." She scratched her nose roughly with her forefinger. "Wall, wish y' luck."

Despite her dubiousness, the words put heart into him. He smiled and thanked her.

She began to talk more easily, told him the best places to eat, where he might find work, and mentioned a baler for the leather factory who was staying in the house, whom he might like to talk with because he had worked for a while in New York.

Aaron listened, nodded, and resolved to avoid the baler at any cost.

"Yep, we think it's a nice town," Mrs. Hopley agreed in an uninspired voice as she withdrew from the room.

Aaron shook the tension from himself, and after a moment went to the bathroom at the end of the hall, where he shaved himself at a basin with brass taps. Then he donned a clean shirt and socks and set out happily into the twilight.

He spent the evening exploring the town, rambling through new street after new street like a young dog exploring a new home. He committed landmarks to memory and noted details of architecture and terrain, a labor of love, for he felt it his duty to become as familiar with Clement as any native. He peered about more eagerly as the darkness fell and brought forth, sparse and significant as the stars of constellations, the lights in comfortable and ancestral homes.

It was quite dark when he climbed to a hill southeast of the town, between the river and the railroad tracks, and seated himself with a bag of little purchases between his feet. He gazed downward at Clement, which he saw from nearly the same angle as he had from the train. But how familiar it all was now, how much more probable its possibilities! He knew how the church looked, what the tower was that poked up through trees, what the signpost said on the highway north. He had explored a long covered bridge, which he had not even seen from the train, that spanned the river, had stood a long while at one of its windows, listening to the conversations of people who walked through.

Tomorrow what would he do? He need not worry yet about plans. Over four hundred dollars were sewn into the lining of the black valise, and with that he could afford to take his time. He could try his hand at a dozen professions. He might work as a hand on one of the outlying farms for a while, and buy his own farm if he liked it. He might set himself up in a store of some kind, or go into business with someone he would meet in the town. He could spend weeks merely living, until fate dropped instructions into his lap.

The scope of his imagination startled him, and springing up, he pressed his fist hard against his breast. He bent his intense face toward the town, and believed with all his heart that the course of his life would reveal itself within Clement. He felt like one of the figures in a heroic and documentary painting, his posture governed by determination and nobility of purpose.

"Hello," a small voice said.

He turned around, flustered. It was a skinny, barefoot little girl in a dark dress that the wind snapped against her thighs. Even in the dimness, he could discern a big pattern in the hem which did not seem to belong

to the dress. He remembered her. She was the little girl he had seen leaning against the tree that afternoon on the way to Mrs. Hopley's.

"Who are you?" she asked.

Slowly he brought his fist down from his chest. "Who are *you*?" he
retorted, adopting a playful adult tone.

"Freya."

"Freya who?"

"Freya Wolstnom."

"What?"

"Freya Wolstnom."

"*What?*"

She took a deep breath. "Wolstnom. W-o-l-s-t-e-n-h-o-l-m-e."

He pieced together the first few letters, but the rest merely fell on
his ears. As had happened many times in New York, when his fares had
given him addresses, his mind refused to collect what he had heard. The
memory of those times, of questionings, repeatings, final mistakes, the
blare of horns as he turned the cab, rose about him and he writhed in the
darkness. He passed the thumb of one hand near his mouth and brought
it down again.

"Who are you?" she repeated.

"Aaron Bentley."

After a moment the child turned and walked slowly about the hillside, between him and the town. She held back with both hands the lank
black hair that the wind blew over her eyes, and looked at the ground as
though she sought something.

Aaron sat down and clasped his hands over his knees, thinking she
was on her way to the town. But as she lingered, he called out, mainly to
restore his own confidence, "Where do you live?"

She did not look up, but merely brought her arm back. "Over there."

He could see only black forest. He looked back at her.

She was lifting her feet and parting the high grass with graceful sidewise motions like those of a slow dance. There was a stiffness in her figure, not of self-consciousness but of concentration. He felt that she
noticed his least movement.

Finally, she advanced circuitously toward him up the hill. When she stopped, their heads were almost on a level. He returned her glance smilingly, then, straining his eyes in the darkness, he was surprised to see the straight line of her mouth. It seemed sad and tense and old. Behind the moving strands of her hair, her eyes were mere grayish areas, but he felt they regarded him with hostility. A sudden swimming dismay and sense of inferiority came over him, akin to that he had felt in New York, but now intensified and focused upon him by the child and the town behind her. He felt she was too contemptuous to put to him such questions as Mrs. Hopley had, that instead she faced him as an intruder upon her property.

He fumbled to open the paper bag between his feet. "I don't suppose you'd like to share some cake with me, would you?"

"Nope," she said. "I got to go." She walked slowly around the hillside.

He stood up and watched her until her figure, then the pale hem disappeared into the darkness. "Good-bye!" he called out hopefully.

There was no answer.

He pushed the cake back into the bag, and made his way toward the asylum of his room.

II

He washed and dressed with a frenzied impatience, for the mightiest morning he had ever seen was thrusting through his windows.

He rushed again to the window and, gripping the sill, looked out across a green earth to the ponderous sun that staggered throbbingly upward. It blazed on the tops of trees, the ridges of roofs, the wings of flying, singing birds. He put out his hand and fingered the leaves of the tree. He surveyed a world untouched by greed, bitterness, or the smut of commerce. The lost paradise of brotherly love.

Pirouetting on the gray carpet, he clapped his hands above his head and laughed for delight. Refreshed by his sleep in the pure air, he felt strong as an ox, fit as a warrior, free as—as the butterfly which, as he watched gapingly, fluttered in by one window and out by another.

Morning aromas of fresh coffee and of frying ham, the sound of families' voices drifted from open windows as he strode toward Trevelyan Boulevard. In an ecstasy of contentment, he stopped to admire a tightly coiled rosebud that projected over the walk. It was of so delicate a shade of green, he hardly dared raise it with the tip of his finger.

"What will I be doing," he asked himself aloud, "when its petals are unfolded?"

Suddenly, as he filled his lungs, he realized he had not thought of smoking since he had got off the train. Yet in New York, he had smoked all day and even in bed. It was overwhelming proof of the town's purifying power. And beginning today, he decided, he would set himself to grow his nails.

"'Am 'n X?" Mac greeted him over the heads of a noisy row of customers. "Got extra-good ham this mornin'."

Aaron nodded. He did not feel like talking. He was struck by the contrast of this breakfast with those of New York, with the bolted coffee and doughnut taken standing up, one eye on his cab at the curb. He had never succeeded in being indifferent, as other drivers were. Probably, he thought, it was because he had always had to eke the most out of whatever he worked at. Ever since he had left school to support his mother and himself, he had been working like a madman. He had been a soda jerk, bellhop, a waiter in a number of places, and for the last four years a taxi driver—all jobs in which good service meant tips, but the constant jumping had so torn up his nerves, it was a wonder anything was left of him. He had never had time to think of marriage. There had never been an extra quarter to take a girl to a movie! Then, after his mother's death, he supposed the habit of hard work had persisted. And for the last few months, reaching a sort of crisis of loneliness and depression, he had saved his money as though toward some goal. "You've got to have a goal!" he had often muttered to himself, as he slammed the door of his cab for the last time at night. All day he would have been driving people to certain goals, but as for himself he had had none, except a shabby furnished room somewhere. Maybe this was the goal, he thought, a small town and peace of mind. It was enough. At thirty-four, there was still time to make something of his life.

Down the line of stools someone burst into genial guffaws.

Aaron smiled. He felt he had not relaxed in seventeen years. He slipped the fork slowly, with relish, under his scrambled eggs.

After breakfast he strolled along Trevelyan Boulevard, examining store windows as he might have the counters of a museum. He looked at all the sports photographs in the barbershop window, then stepped in to get a shave and a haircut.

Pete McNary, the redheaded barber, was a talkative fellow, and they had exhausted a dozen topics and had begun to talk about themselves before he finished Aaron off with a dusting of white, sweet-smelling powder.

"Say, I know a couple of faams around here might could use somebody," Pete offered, folding Aaron's bib sheet meticulously against his big body. He was an ox of a man, but with pink precise hands and an air of grace in handling his body. "Ain't likely 'll be seein' the faamers soon, but we can get a ride out some afternoon when I close up and talk to 'em. You just let me know."

"All right," Aaron said with enthusiasm. "Thanks."

But he was not done exploring. He would want many more idle days.

Above Trevelyan Boulevard, vanishing into green meadow and forest, lay the most attractive roads Aaron had ever glimpsed. He rambled them till midafternoon, stopping to fondle pet calves tethered in front yards, to chat with a housewife canning blueberries in an open-doored kitchen, to attend the milking of seven goats, as he sat on the hay-littered threshold of the barn. He brought handfuls of fresh grass and distributed the bunches equally among their eager mouths. He learned the best-yielding breeds of goats, the market price, the fat content and by-products of goats' milk.

"You might like a taste now't you know all about it," the goat farmer said, returning from his kitchen with a slab of brown cheese on white bread.

The bread was warm and bent in his hands. Never had he eaten anything so delicious. The moments at the goat farm seemed to complete a transformation. Actually, he was elated beyond the power to think, but he realized one thing, that he had never before enjoyed merely the fact that he existed.

III

The twelve o'clock whistle of the leather factory began a white-breathed scream that carried easily over the entire town, and under its cover, as he walked a quiet road beside the river, Aaron opened his mouth and shouted his happiness. He heard mountain after mountain echo the whistle until its circle expanded beyond his sense.

Five men walked from the dark shadow beneath the factory shed. They wore blue work shirts and blackened trousers and caps. In long slow-climbing strides they came up the greasy slope to the bridge road that led to Trevelyan Boulevard.

"Howdy!" one called to Aaron, and the others followed suit and spoke or waved a greeting.

Aaron leaned against the brick back of the general store and watched them with a kind of envy and awe, these sole representatives of the armies of factory workers that cover the earth. They did not carry lunch pails, nor would they go to a crowded cafeteria for their meal. Their homes were only around the corner, where a woman would now be setting home-cooked food on a table. He blinked his popping eyes at them as they rose like giants at the crest of the road, then dispersed.

IV

"Hello."

Aaron turned from the bridge window and saw Freya standing on the wooden floor. "Hello." He smiled, genuinely glad to see her. "How are you?"

"Okay."

She came on her bare feet into the bar of sunlight to the window at which he stood. He could see fine dark hairs on her delicate arms, and freckles across her thin, pointed nose. Her eyes were large and of a clear milky gray that suggested blindness. She wore the same lavender dress with the broad hem patterned with strawberries.

"Want me to lift you up?" he asked.

"Nope." She boosted herself to the sill, resting her weight on her forearms.

The whistle sounded, from the top of the giant stack, and though it split their ears at this proximity, Freya remained motionless throughout it, staring downstream.

Aaron forgot to watch the five men. He had formed the habit of attending the twelve and four o'clock whistles, for the punctuality of the change of shifts was pleasant to observe in the town where nothing else seemed governed by clocks. But now he could not take his eyes from the little girl. He had forgotten her since the first evening, and now he was grateful she had troubled to stop and speak to him.

"That's my favorite house to visit," she told him.

He looked where she pointed and saw a house he had not noticed before, set back at the edge of the forest. It was white with a purplish roof, and its windows were slaty in the shadow.

"Is it? Who lives there?"

"Nobody."

"Oh."

"Want to go see it?"

"Sure."

She hopped off the sill. He followed her down past the factory and up a grassy slope.

The house seemed brand-new, but the white walls were streaked here and there with rain, and grass grew high as the downstairs windowsills. Aaron tramped contentedly through the grass beside the little girl, who gazed up at the windows as she walked.

Finally she stopped before the red front door. "Now we can go in."

They walked into a bare house that smelt of paint and closeness. The varnished floors were unmarred save for small dusty bare-feet tracks. Freya told him in whispers which room was which. Upstairs, she pointed out the bedroom where, she said, the murderer had killed the beautiful wife who had just come to live in the house with her husband.

"The *murderer* lives here now—in the cellar!" Freya whispered.

"Does he?" Aaron asked softly. For an instant he had believed it.

"That's why we have to be quiet, even though we put three circles around the house."

He followed her into the attic.

"See this window? This is where the husband yelled for help the night his wife got murdered, only he was so scared he couldn't really yell so nobody heard him."

Aaron looked at the window. He could see the frantic husband screaming and making no sound. The husband wore pale-colored pants like riding breeches, and his black hair was tousled over a handsome head. He looked back at Freya.

"Then the husband fell asleep and had awful dreams, and woke up and ran over the mountains and never came back." Her mouth was stern as it had been the night on the hills, and her eyes held the sad memory of tragedy. "Now we better go."

He helped her to close the stiff front door. They walked through deep grass to the road that went into town. She did not talk anymore to him or appear even to notice him, but her acceptance of his company sufficed for Aaron. As they walked, a sense of companionship with her grew in him. And as if to balance some scale in his emotions, a realization of his loneliness came, too. He rejoiced in both sensations. They were an addition to his heart.

On Trevelyan Boulevard, Freya walked more slowly and looked into shop windows.

"See anything you like?" he asked brightly as she stopped before the jewelry shop window.

"Nope."

She moved on and he walked beside her, thinking he might return to the jewelry shop and buy some little thing for her.

She stopped under the marquee of the movie theater and looked at the panels of stills. The stale, organic, and faintly sweetish aroma common to all theaters, which had thrilled Aaron under marquees in New York, came now through the open doors of the Clement-Olympia.

"Let's go in!" he said.

To share with her the excitement of strange locales, the surprises of the unfolding story, now that he was free of the banality to which he had always been compelled to return, seemed the very highest pleasure.

"I don't feel like it," Freya said calmly.

Aaron swallowed, and uncertainly followed her as she moved on.

At the drugstore corner, she stopped and looked up at him. "Well, I'm goin' home."

He was confounded, now that the moment had come. "Wouldn't you like a soda or something first?"

"Nope." She pushed her hair back. "I know a place almost as good as the house to visit."

"Where?"

"It's up the river."

He looked, but could not see any kind of structure beyond the bridge.

"Maybe we'll go there tomorrow." She stepped off the curb. "Goodbye, Arn."

He was so astonished by her use of his name, by the fact she remembered it at all, he could only stand looking after her with a fatuous smile.

When he turned and walked away, a figure strolled into his path.

"Eve-nin'!"

It was George Shmid, the man who had been on the porch the day Aaron came to Mrs. Hopley's.

"Evening," Aaron repeated.

George fell in with him. "Got a new friend," he said.

"What?" Aaron looked down into George's alert blue eyes, which were fixed upon him smilingly.

George repeated the sentence. His thick lower lip, which he moistened continually, curved up at the corners in a lyre shape. "You know, the kid you was with."

"Oh, Freya."

"That's right." George smiled.

They turned onto Pleasant Street. It had begun to rain lightly, but the rain pattered on the leaves as on a roof, and not a drop came through.

"Where'd you go explorin' today?"

Aaron glanced at him again, remembering that he had told Mrs. Hopley, when she asked him how he spent a certain day, that he had "been exploring." Still, he could not make himself listen to George with interest, and he did not care. He was too happy in himself to want company. With a vague, half-polite smile, he turned in at the cement walk, lengthened his steps and left George, still murmuring, behind.

V

From that day forth, Aaron's happiest hours were those he spent with Freya. They encountered each other almost every day somewhere in the town, and because they never arranged a meeting place or time, their encounters were casual surprises. They greeted each other as though they had merely stepped across a room. Clement was the room, filled with heroic furniture, interesting bric-a-brac, and magic carpets. Clement was their entire world.

The place up the river which Freya had mentioned was a deserted knife factory. It was a long, low building made of narrow boards once painted red. The stilts at the rear had given way and those in front had been uprooted, so it seemed the place had been half successful at suicide by plunging into the river. Aaron and Freya used an old ladder to enter through a side door.

"What a magnificent piece of rust!" Aaron often exclaimed, delighted by his own eloquence, as they stepped inside. "What a miracle of ruination!"

They would make their way down sloping, rotten floorboards that were too dead to creak, toward the broken rear wall where imprisoned river water lapped. Here they would sit on a great comfortable rafter jammed crosswise in the corner, and survey the conglomeration of smashed and tangled machinery. Fingers of sunlight came through gaps in roof and wall, pointing at certain spots as though for their attention. It was their private place. Never had anyone encroached upon it by so much as a glance or a word of reference.

Generally Freya was serious and quiet here. Aaron swung his heels on the rafter and stared with bulging eyes and a bemused smile. He would imagine the place humming, bustling, gleaming, men shouting over the din of machinery, the factory reaching a peak of production, then declining, until its owner sold or died of heartbreak, and the building was abandoned to begin its still-progressing delapidation. Sometimes he merely stared at the cracked belts, rusted cogs, knife parts strewn about the floor, and let anything or nothing ramble in and out of his mind.

Freya might point to some rust-riddled object half submerged in the stagnant water below them. "Look!" Her voice would be an articulate gasp. "Could you ever think of anything so old?"

Aaron would look, silently, his train of thought gently merging with hers. Nothing ever, anywhere, was so old as this.

"Can you imagine it when it was snowing?" Aaron once asked excitedly. "All the shiny machines and knives and the snow outside?"

At other times the place would strike them as terribly funny. The evidence of destruction by man and nature would make them giggle as children must sometimes in church or at funerals. It was this way one afternoon, when they came with bags of penny candies Aaron had bought at the general store.

He helped her onto the rafter, and they sat munching message-bearing hearts, licorice sticks, and taffy kisses that were wrapped in brown and yellow papers which floated in the water below their feet.

"Let's dance!" Freya said.

Catching her hands, Aaron swung her around and around as he turned on the broad rafter.

Then Aaron became conscious of someone's presence. Looking toward the raised doorway, he saw a figure silhouetted. He let Freya swing to a stop against him, her slight weight unbalancing him not at all. The man in the doorway was Pete McNary.

"Hello!" Pete said in a voice of muted surprise.

"Hello!" Aaron called out, almost at the same instant. He released Freya and laughed a little, embarrassed and annoyed. "What are you doing out here?"

Pete remained motionless, his face obscured. "Walkin' home. What are you doin'?"

Aaron could not quite realize he was there, that anyone was able to look inside the place and see him and Freya there. "Not much of anything," Aaron replied, still smiling. He glanced at Freya, who stood on the rafter with her hands behind her, leaning against the broken wall in a way that reminded him of how she had leaned against the tree the first afternoon he had seen her.

"I heard voices. I didn't know what was goin' on," Pete went on explanatorily but somewhat self-righteously.

"Oh, we come here now and then," Aaron said.

Pete looked at Aaron, who looked just as steadily at him. Neither had anything to say. "Well, I'll be gettin' on home."

Aaron listened to the slow footfalls on the ladder. He put out his hand and Freya took it.

VI

When Aaron asked her again and again about herself, Freya told him she was ten, that she had never gone to school because she helped her mother, who did washing and ironing. But Aaron never knew her to leave him in order to help her mother, or to spend any time at home except to eat and sleep. A vision of Freya's mother at work over other people's laundry never entered his mind, nor did any actuality of it seem to trouble Freya. They were too occupied with the pictures of their own minds, which far excelled those Aaron had found in movies. Freya would never go to a movie with him and he stopped asking her, having less need of them himself.

Often they sat on the hill where Aaron had climbed his first evening, where they had a fine view of the town. With a few phrases they could create for themselves the world of Clement as it had been in Revolutionary times, or when it was peopled with men in tailcoats and women in tight-waisted dresses, when the knife factory sent durable and handsome knives down the river. And doubtless the daydreams he lived with her, in which they governed the fortunes of the people they imagined, satisfied to some extent Aaron's compunctions to bestir himself. Comfort enveloped him on the sunny hilltop. He watched the few cars and pedestrians on Trevelyan Boulevard as he might have watched a puppet show, and felt in harmony with all he saw. Trains chugged like toys into the station, and brought a sense of the benevolence and perfection of the universe. He would try to explain some of this to Freya, but if she understood, she made no sign as she sat beside him and gazed impassively at the town.

The bond between them was lighter than air itself. It was a bond of complete individual and mutual freedom, for neither knew the burden of a single chore or obligation even to each other. There was an understanding between them, however, that they were somehow the chosen people of Clement, that all they saw was mere scenery set for their amusement. Joy sat on their heads, and they betrayed their awareness of it perhaps only in the way, whether together or apart, they walked and looked at things with a kind of arrogant innocence.

VII

"Been seein' a lot o' that little Wolstenholme girl, ain't yuh?" Aaron blinked at her. He had just come out of the bathroom, and had nearly collided with her in the hall. "Oh, yes," he said, smiling and frank. He had left Freya not half an hour before. "We take walks quite a lot."

Mrs. Hopley nodded, and looked at Aaron's belt buckle, which bore the letter B. "Course there mightn't be no haam in it, but some folks thinks otherwise."

"Harm?" The soap leapt from his hand and flew toward the stairs.

"Might be. Yes. Don't look s'good. A man an' a young child like that." She delivered her words quickly.

Aaron had gone down a few steps to get the soap. It was covered with lint and was disgusting to hold. He blew on it, opened the washrag and put the soap in its center. When he looked up, Mrs. Hopley's eyes were huge and ugly.

"Not that I see why folks should care much," she added contemptuously.

"About what?"

Mrs. Hopley eyed him. Then she glanced to the floor as though casting about for a way to speak. Bitterly, as though voicing an opinion to herself, she said, "Not that people should care what happens to trash like the Wolstenholmes!"

"What?"

"Yes, trash. Faather killed in a baarroom brawl. Mother just as trashy as him. Worthless people an' a disgrace to the town."

"Father killed? Here in Clement?"

"We ain't got no baarrooms in this town."

Aaron was silent.

"You thinkin' o' gettin' work here finally, I s'pose."

Aaron's whirling thoughts were checked suddenly and brought to focus upon his own idleness. "Yes, I am." He wondered if he should explain again, tell her that he had saved his money for just this sort of a vacation.

"I'd set about it, then." Her eyes moved toward the stairs and seemed to draw her after them.

Aaron was rigid with shame and guilt. He would look for work without delay.

VIII

"Morning, Pete!"

Pete turned in at his shop, fumbling with his keys.

Aaron's lips opened to say "Morning" once more, when a shock went over him. Pete had not spoken to him. Of course he had heard him, must even have seen him. Pete had snubbed him!

Aaron walked quickly past the barbershop before Pete should have time to turn around and to look out his window. He had contemplated being shaved that morning before he went to look for work. It was more than likely an accident, he thought, as he walked on slowly. Still, he was disturbed because he found he had not the courage to enter the barbershop.

He wanted to spend the rest of the morning walking over roads he loved, soothing the irritation Mrs. Hopley's remarks had caused, rationalizing Pete's behavior, but instead he set out grimly for the leather factory, simply because it was the closest place where he might find work and because it was ugly and nothing to his liking. What Mrs. Hopley had said had not touched his conscience about his idleness so much as it had suggested the town might think him a ne'er-do-well if he did not soon get something to do. Now, suppose Pete, for instance, had not spoken to him because he was beginning to think him a good-for-nothing?

The foreman, called outside from a job that had left his hands coated with grease, informed Aaron there was no place for anyone in the factory at the moment. "You'd have to know a little about the business before we took you on as anything but a baler anyway."

"Yes, of course."

The foreman said something else and pointed somewhere, but Aaron did not follow him. He could only stare at the foreman's face. The horrible change in their relationship from nodding acquaintances to that of job-seeker and employer fixed Aaron with its torture.

When the foreman paused, Aaron said, "Thank you very much," and fled up the slope.

He entered the covered bridge and went to one of the windows on the side away from the factory. He put his forearms on the sill, bent his head, and began tearing at his thumbnails. He tried to crush himself into as small a space as possible.

In the last two minutes, in the interview with the foreman, he had completely changed the world in which he had been living for four weeks. He had made the relationship between himself and the town ugly, uncomfortable, mercenary. He had banished the sense of the unspoiled paradise. He had not only asked, but he had been refused!

Suddenly, as he huddled in the window, the town seemed to rise up cold and hostile about him. He shuddered as he might have at something supernatural. The familiar riverbank frightened him, and so did the church spire over the trees, the barn whose roof he could just see, where he had often visited the goats. He squirmed farther into the window at the sight of Mrs. Coolidge, the wife of the postmaster, who was entering the bridge from the other end. He wondered if she would speak to him. He remembered she had smiled at him last Sunday in church. Almost everybody smiled at him, and he was handed an open hymnal when they stood up to sing. But couldn't their smiles from the first have been sarcastic or pitying?

Aaron flung himself about and, bowing slightly, forced himself to say, "Good morning, Mrs. Coolidge!"

"Good morning!" she returned in an astonished, cracked voice. She cleared her throat and passed on, without a change in her pace.

Aaron looked after her and a wave of uncertainty passed over him. What had she meant? How had she meant the "Good morning"? He held fast to the sill, barely resisting an impulse to run after her and demand his answers.

He stared and frowned before him and began to rip his nails. He thought of Mrs. Hopley, remembered Pete in the doorway, recalled that Mac had seemed cool last evening. Wally, the switchman, had greeted him with only a wave of the hand. He remembered George Shmid's smiling mouth, asking him questions about Freya. He could recall a dwindling sincerity in people's voices, even times when he might have been snubbed, when he thought he had not been seen. Suppose the whole town suspected evil of him? Of him and *Freya*? Of course, everyone in Clement had seen him with her at one time or another! He tried to remember when anyone had mentioned Freya or the Wolstenholmes to him. Were they so bad that no one spoke of them? Did the town suspect evil of him or not? And if it did, why didn't it come out and say so?

There was a report like a gunshot behind him. Aaron turned around, as a plank of the bridge floor rattled hollowly into place, and a car moved toward him.

IX

With the relief that it was only a car came a kind of snap inside him, and a relaxation. Slowly and without passion, the idea took form in his mind to go and get his things and to leave the town.

Rather than use Trevelyan Boulevard, he chose the quiet road that ran by the railroad tracks and the river, which would bring him to Pleasant Street. He passed an old man, then a young woman, neither of whom he knew nor who paid him any notice. And though the sight of each had caused a little shock inside him, he began to swing his arms in a physical expression of confidence that almost set his mind at rest.

A block away now, George Shmid stepped out from Mrs. Hopley's walk and turned in the other direction. The sight of his squat, odiously familiar back was enough. Aaron realized suddenly that he could not face anyone he knew, Mrs. Hopley, the baler, any of the roomers. And yet, even now he considered running after George and explaining to him, not for Freya or for himself, but for the town's sake. If he explained, though, could he change what had happened to the town that morning? And how could he explain? What was there to explain?

His thoughts foundered in an emotion he could not at once identify. It felt like guilt. But what was he guilty of? Why had he not been good enough? What was so wrong with him that his best efforts had not made him fit in the town? His mysterious fault seemed to date farther back even than New York, and to be something over which he had no control, and could never grasp and cast out of himself. Then, in an instant, his half vision was cut off, and he felt the guilt and its cause both sealed in him once more.

He faced about and began walking with fast weak steps. He went back to the quiet dirt road that led almost to the factory before it turned and went northward beside the river, away from Clement.

What hurt was the sense that it had been almost avoidable, the sense of the destruction in the very act of his leaving. The town was crumbling at every step, the facade of Trevelyan Boulevard, the Dandy Diner, all the fine trees that grew among the houses, Mrs. Hopley's house and his room, all the fine things he had somehow ruined. And Freya, his best friend. The thought of never seeing Freya again made him waggle his head like a drunken man. The river, the railroad, the men climbing in slow strides up the slope from the factory, the noonday whistle, the good meals served by Mac's hands, the mornings in his big room and with them the joy in his existence and the sense of the eternal potential.

He walked until he had lost the river, until the sun changed its position, not knowing where he walked except that the town was at his back. His feet swished dismally through high grass. Then he tripped and was too tired to catch himself. The stillness was delicious. The river, the railroad, the facade of Trevelyan Boulevard passed in pictures before his eyes. The grizzled old men, the church and the hymnals, the railroad, Freya, the knife factory, the bud on the rosebush, the mornings of the eternal potential and the eternal nothing.

UNCERTAIN TREASURE

The khaki utility bag was sitting by itself on the subway platform near a post that had a slot machine. He looked at it for almost a minute over the top of the *Daily News* comic strip, and gave finally a convulsive wriggle that ended in a bobble of his large head. Slowly, ingenuously, he examined each of the seven or eight persons who stood on the platform awaiting their trains. A train pulled in, changed the pattern of the people, but when it was gone, the khaki bag was still unclaimed. He drew closer, limping deeply on his crooked left leg, rising tall again on the other, like a running-down piece of machinery, holding the forgotten newspaper before him.

A soldier strode in front of him, dropped a penny in the gum slot and leaned there, his shoes crossed beside the bag, which was the same color as his trousers. The cripple edged away, shuffling his big feet sideways. When the next train came in, the soldier got on it without a glance at the bag.

Then as the cripple came forward he saw a man strolling toward him, a smallish man in a green felt hat and a polo coat unbuttoned over a royal blue suit. His eyes were small and green, and as they fixed on him, the cripple kept shuffling forward in timid fascination. They passed so closely their sleeves touched, and when the bag lay between them again, both turned, the one slow, the other foxlike, and looked at each other.

The little man's eyes were steady, but around them the wizened, unshaven face turned this way and that. He sized up the cripple, took in the simple, ugly face, the seedy overcoat. He looked straight ahead, sauntered toward the khaki bag, and stopped with one tan shoe touching its side. He bounced on his toes, and the wooden heels made assertive *thock-*

thocks on the cement. The cripple retreated a few feet. The smaller man went quickly to the edge of the platform, looked first into the black tunnel and then at his wristwatch.

When he turned around, the bag was gone, and the cripple was on his way down the platform, rising, falling, scraping toward the Third Street exit. He did not hurry, but his face was bent into the upturned lapels of his coat with the effort of walking, and one arm threshed the air at his side.

The man in the polo coat hesitated, then went after him. The sloping tunnel echoed the high-pitched *thock-thocks* of the wooden-heeled shoes.

The cripple pulled himself energetically up the stairs. Outside it was raining, a tired thin rain. It was about quarter to six, but night was already falling. The cripple made his way up Sixth Avenue, past the wire fence that enclosed the cement handball courts, the grass plots and the row of benches. As the *thock-thocks* behind him continued, he realized with vague uneasiness that the green-eyed man was following him. He lengthened his sloppy steps and caught the bag up under his arm.

After a few yards the green-eyed man called, "Hey!" and stretched forth a crooked finger.

The cripple kept going.

"Hey!" the smaller man said, running up, seizing the wild arm and wrenching the cripple around. "That's my bag you've got there!" His face was bristling and determined.

The cripple looked at the bag under his arm, and kept the same bland expression. His wide, fluted lips opened but no sound came.

The smaller man saw the slow eyes, the nose and mouth that were squeezed absurdly between the doughy forehead and the smooth jaw. One ear bent under the black-and-white checked cap, but where the other ear should have been was a daub of white flesh like the opening of a balloon which is tied with string.

He yanked the bag from under the cripple's arm, ripped the zipper halfway and took a quick look in, then closed it. He shot a glance into the calm eyes. "Thief! . . . Dope!" Then, with a contemptuous movement of his mouth, "I oughta turn you in!" But he walked away with the bag, on up Sixth Avenue.

The cripple looked after him, and at the bag under his arm, watched both become smaller. His figure gave a convulsion, and abruptly he flung himself after the polo coat, up the long block toward Eighth Street. So fast did his long legs cover the ground that he was only some thirty feet behind when the man with the bag turned into a bar and disappeared.

He relaxed his gait and came to a stop outside the bar and grill. He looked meekly from under the cap brim into the mellow interior, and put his hand on the slimy iron pipe of a parking sign. Wisps of white steam came fast from his lips.

Inside, over the mole-colored curtain that hid half the window, the cripple could see the green hat bend now and then as the man sipped his beer. He came closer to the window, and saw the bag sitting on a stool beside the man. After a moment, the man in the bar slid open the zipper and put a hand inside. The cripple felt a leaden throb in his chest. Just as slowly, the man closed the zipper and, standing up, crossed the muffler under his coat, tilting his head to get the smoke stream out of his eyes.

Shyly, the cripple moved a few feet down the sidewalk, stood in the doorway of a haberdashery shop and looked toward the bar.

The man with the khaki bag came out and walked straight across Sixth Avenue, past the House of Detention for Women, up the left side of Greenwich Avenue.

Behind him now came the cripple, exerting himself only enough to match the other's now-moderate pace. First he had to think exactly what to say to the green-eyed man. But his brain seemed to jam. It refused to create the proper picture, the proper words, to imagine one moment beyond the here-and-now. He followed doggedly up the street, his eyes fixed on the khaki bag.

At Seventh Avenue the first man crossed, while the cripple was caught by a stream of traffic. The streetlights came out suddenly, jumping on in groups up the avenue, making the sky darker. The cripple was a block behind when the man turned west onto Jane Street. Though the street was dim, the cripple could see the pale haze of the polo coat, and could hear once or twice the raucous slip of a heel on the slanting sidewalk before a garage.

The polo coat crossed Hudson Street, continued westward, and turned north onto Greenwich Street.

Looking after him, the cripple saw perhaps two blocks away a lighted corner, and into this walked the man with the bag. The cripple pushed on faster, past the jutting stoops, past the ash cans and lids that his dragging foot struck occasionally with unpleasant noise.

The light came from a modern, silver-plated diner which resembled a car from an electric train. The cripple approached this slowly as he had the bar and grill. The diner was perched high, brightly lighted. He could see through the steamy windows the row of black-and-white menus over the big shining coffee urns. Between the black watch cap and a sailor's hat was the green hat. The cripple came to the long side of the diner, where he could see through the glass door. The khaki bag was on the man's lap now, pressed against the underside of the counter. His wet, yellowish shoes were splayed on the footrest of the stool.

The wind howled up from the river, slapped the rain against the metal side of the diner, and tore at the pale smoke that came from the whirling ventilator. He could catch whiffs of frying hamburger meat, bacon, eggs in butter. His stomach gave a thin, sick rattle. The fluted lips under the overhanging nose came together harder and the blue eyes blinked.

A man behind the counter set, with generous swooping gesture, a plate of yellow eggs before the polo coat, the square shoulders bent forward. The right arm working fast forking the eggs in, poking the triangular pieces of buttered toast into the face behind the hat. When the eggs were gone, he pulled a napkin from the container and blew his nose so hard the man outside could hear it faintly. He dropped the napkin below the counter and started eating pie.

The cripple was studying the bag, noticing how the end bulged with something, how the man paid no attention to it. Maybe it was dirty clothes, he thought, his heart contracting, or tin cans, or garbage. No, there must be something better inside, or why would the green-eyed man want it? Maybe it was something nice like oranges, or sandwiches, or socks, or maybe money.

Finally the man at the counter shoved back his plate, and a puff of smoke broke under the brim of his hat. The cigarette was white and clean in the hairy hand. He tossed off the last bit of coffee and, getting up, swung the overcoat back and reached in his trousers pocket.

The cripple felt a sudden desire to run away. He retreated to the end of the diner, where he could see a straight line down the front. He rested his left foot lightly on the sidewalk, poised to turn in any direction.

The man with the bag under his arm came out the door smoking, down one step before he noticed the figure on the corner. The cripple twisted himself, embarrassedly.

The man with the bag stood a long moment, motionless. Then he came down a step and started walking. The jolt of the step he had not seen took the cigarette from his lips. Rattled, he stopped short again, turned his eyes from the cripple and crossed directly over the street, going once more up Greenwich Street. He walked faster than before and in a few seconds was out of sight.

Hearing the cripple in the darkness behind him, he felt the first stirrings of panic. He quickened his steps, and hitched the bag higher under his arm, his mouth twisted on one side, smiling, reassuring himself, because the bag wasn't worth the trouble or the fear, or the man following him, and it would only be three minutes at most until he came to Fourteenth Street where he would turn off to go to the meeting.

The cripple came on with much waste motion, paddling himself by the two long arms, in a gait that was more like falling and catching himself than walking. Seeing his gain, he felt more cheerful, began to think how he would climb the stairs with the bag and take it into his room and open it sitting on the bed. But first he must say to the man, "I was standing on the platform a long time before you was." He tried this sentence, panting it into his upturned collar: "I-I-I wuz standin' thur a long t-t-t befur you wuz. . . ." The big egg of an Adam's apple flowed up and down. "T-t-time befur you wuz!" he gasped.

He must say this right. He needed courage to do it. He recalled one of his rare moments of complete happiness, and the voice and the words that had made him so happy: "*Archie's all right. When he does say something, it comes out sense.*" It was Mr. Hendricks who had said it. Mr. Hendricks, who always smiled at him and spoke to him, too. And he had been talking about *him*, Archie, who pushed the drays around at the newspaper plant. Mr. Hendricks was one of the editors. Archie remembered exactly how he heard it. He was by the elevator shaft and Mr. Hendricks was talking to Ryzek, the foreman. "*Archie's all right. When he does say something, it comes out sense."* He had felt so happy then, he could make himself happy at any time simply by recalling these words, and hearing Mr. Hendricks's voice as he said them. *"Archie's all right . . ."*

He felt strong and very brave. He would catch up with this man with the bag. He would say words that came out sense.

He began to think of the situation as a mistake that a few words could explain. . . . His sole caught on a curb and made a loud report.

The man in the polo coat threw a glance behind him. Fear settled deeper in his spine and shot him forward with supernormal energy. He ran across the intersection of Fourteenth Street, over the flattened cobblestones and trolley tracks. He could see no people on Fourteenth Street, and for a couple of blocks it was as dimly lighted as the street he was on. He darted back into Greenwich. For a while he walked on his toes, hoping the cripple would think he had turned off on Fourteenth Street. Then he kicked something that slid raspingly over the sidewalk.

"Goddamn!" he said, and his dirty teeth chattered. He turned around and held himself taut, listening. The scrap-slap-scrape came on. He started to trot. "Wh-what the hell am I doin' bein' chased by a nut," he whispered, "when I shoulda turned off Fourteen' t'get t'the meetin'. . . ." His feet hardly seemed to touch the ground, yet he had a sense of being dragged from behind. The cripple took fantastic proportions in his mind, became the inescapable, machinelike figure of a nightmare, and he believed he was after him now, not the bag, driven by a crazy desire for revenge. He clutched the bag harder and determined to turn off at the next street, however dark it might be, to get to some place where there were people.

He heard his heart stagger, catch itself up like a pair of heavy feet, and he slowed immediately. He shouldn't be hurrying like this, a guy with a delicate heart. What if he should keel over in the gutter. . . . "Suppose he don't leave me alone all night! Suppose he don't never leave me alone! . . . What would the guys at the hall think if they saw me wit' a lousy bag bein' chased by a nut!"

For he was the bookkeeper of a large fraternal organization, and occasionally made speeches, as he had only two weeks ago tonight made the speech denouncing Putterman, who had sat on the front row hardly six feet away. *"It ain't often I feel called upon to talk like this about a fellow mem-*

ber," he had concluded, wiping his mouth with his handkerchief. "*But my only concern is the organ-eye-zation!* . . . *I say Putterman is a guy who says things are all right to your face an' then* . . . *an' then,*" extending a finger, but the gesture reminded him of hailing the cripple, "*then goes and spills this crap about the organ-eye-zation to someone higher up!* . . . *Gentlemen, I got my facts an' I present them!*" Great applause, Putterman ousted by oral vote. Wh-what would the guys say if they . . .

"Huy!" shouted the cripple, very close. "Huy!" He made a pass at the yellow coat with his gangling hand.

The shorter man bounded. "You want it? Take it!" he screamed.

"Huy! . . . I jus' . . . I jus' . . ."

But the man in the polo coat was far away, and the *thock-thocks* were running now, turning off, running eastward.

The big bony hands came down, groping over the sidewalk. They found the bag, lifted it, nestled it in the lumpy arms of the coat. Archie continued up the street, holding the bag so tightly against him that the affection sprang in him, making him warm and happy. The man in the polo coat faded from his mind. He smelt the damp khaki, redolent of clothiness. The fluted mouth spread serenely.

He kept going for four or five blocks, up to Twentieth Street, where he went east. He did not feel to see what might be in the bag. His face had returned to its usual expression of bland contemplation. He looked straight ahead of him, not noticing his shadow that the lamplights along the curb passed one to the other, the shadow whose head twisted now and again in bizarre design on the sidewalk.

At a certain brownstone he pulled himself up by a broad balustrade, produced a key and let himself in. The foyer was lighted by a small naked bulb at the ceiling. He climbed the stair, tugging at the shaky banister, turning at each landing with a dogged pump of his head. At the fourth floor he stopped at a low squarish door, so kicked and fingerprinted that the brown paint was almost all off. He opened the padlock with another key.

Inside, he went familiarly and turned on the gooseneck lamp that sat on the oilcloth-covered table beside the gas burner. The yellowish light revealed a cube of a room, furnished with a bed that sagged like a hammock, a spool-legged table, a straight chair, a bedtable made of an upended crate, and a battered chest of drawers. All around the walls were tiny notations, so closely and equidistantly written as to make almost a pattern: the names and addresses and telephone numbers of all the people with whom he had anything to do. There were the employees of the newspaper plant down to the scrubwomen, the names and particulars of the grocery men at the corner, of the cigar store and the drugstore, and many addresses of miscellaneous direct mail advertisers who had in past months sent him letters.

He hung his overcoat behind a cloth that made a closet of one corner. His head was quite long and flat on top, seen from the side, like the model profile beside a Mercator projection. The hair was blond and very fine, falling in big haphazard locks around his head. He moved gracefully in his room, as though he were completely at ease and knew the position of every article.

He carried the bag to his bed and sat himself gently on the bumpy quilt. The gold-colored zipper sent a chill of pleasure through his fingers. Its purr was a song of richness, of mechanical beauty. His fluted mouth spread wider, his blond eyebrows arched expectantly. He parted the sides of the bag and in the dim interior saw many columns of glossy blue and gold paper, and red and yellow and green and gray and mauve and white papers, each a block itself, but making one great block together. The regular and immaculate wrappings of hundreds of penny chocolates and chewing gums.

His eagerness subsided to a troubled, uncertain disappointment. The arched eyebrows dropped a little and the mouth hung loose. Then, caught by the spectroscopic colors, he lifted ten or fifteen chocolate pieces from their box, pressed one against the other between his thumb and forefinger, and laughed aloud until the column broke, tumbling over his legs onto the bed and the floor. He put his hand in again, this time drawing forth many green boxes of chewing gum, which he let cascade off his palm onto his pressed-together thighs. He took more chocolates and sifted them through his fingers like coins, dropping them onto the bedspread. And there was also, at one end of the bag, in a drab canvas sack, perhaps two dollars' worth of pennies.

He pulled up the spool-legged table, removed the alarm clock and the pencil stub and made a field of the chocolates on the top, arranging them in rows of dark blue, mauve, and green, squinting from all possible angles at this panoply of color, at these hundreds of pieces of candy which he would have bought only one at a time, and very rarely. Then, luxuriously, indulgently, he chose a certain piece and, unwrapping it, put the black cool candy onto his tongue. He pushed himself back against the wall, turned his flat-topped head to let the light fall on the little paper in his hand and, humming tunelessly, began reading the ingredients of the thing releasing flavor in his mouth.

MAGIC CASEMENTS

I

Hildebrandt knew it was the magic casements that drew him each evening to the deserted bar, but he would have confessed this to no one but himself. The magic casements were only doors, made to look like the windows of the galleon's stern, which, looming absurdly from a wall of red brocade, formed the entrance to the gigantesque Pandora Room. Mid-Victorian was certainly not his style, yet the casements redeemed it all. Their brass-hinged, golden-hazed arms were influng casually, differently each evening, and had a tremulous, suspenseful look of being about to usher forth a miracle.

He turned from his brandy to gaze at them once more, and idly recited to himself, "'That oftimes hath (something) magic casements, Opening on the foam of perilous seas, in faery lands forlorn. Forlorn! The very word is like a bell!'—"

Oh, when would someone, be it man or woman, walk through those magic casements and into his life? Or was he becoming one of those fixtures that had always roused his pity, sometimes his contempt, the brandy-fuddled, rather asinine gentleman-at-the-bar, eternally waiting?

He surveyed the Pandora Room dismally. His somber brown eyes were partially shielded by shriveling lids that drew over their outer corners. Though there was no one but the bartender to see him, he was conscious of the aristocratic lids as he straightened on his stool and inspected the room with an air of thoughtful superiority. Far away amid a cemetery of white-clothed tables, a waiter attended a lone dinner guest. Sources high in the walls, concealed by festoons of gray or red velvet, poured recorded music without cease into the ever-empty chalice lined with tap-estry, Persian rug, and gilt moldings. Background music that back-grounded nothing, Hildebrandt thought. The gargantuan loneliness of the place seemed at times to dwarf his own. He wondered if that might be another reason why he came here.

"Pandora Room," he whispered, "what a mockery of your name!"

He slumped lower on the tall, delicately legged stool and turned the stem of the brandy glass that resembled a mounted thimble. His slight black-suited figure looked insignificant as a candle wick. The amber bar that occupied only a corner of the huge room glowed around him like a fuzzy flame.

He began to stare critically at himself in the mirror behind the bar. The ingenuous hope of deliverance from boredom, which ordinarily only peeked now and then through the jadedness, confronted him plainly like an imprisoned but still spirited child that cried, "What have you done about me? . . . What are you going to do about me?" It was a face hard to notice and easy to forget, a wisp of a face unasserted by the broad, close-clipped mustache. Whatever distinction it possessed was inherited, his own contributions tending to its detriment. The eyelids, for example, might have been old when he got them, for they reminded him now of outworn lace curtains hanging at *oeil-de-boeufs* in a decaying mansion. He admitted that it was, already, the perfect face for a gentleman-at-the-bar of one of New York's largest and most conservative hotels, eternally waiting.

I am not lonely so much as terribly alone, he thought. For though he could honestly say he had many friends, old friends and new friends, to a man and to a woman they bored him and served only to impress upon him that the rut he was in, lest he think it only the sinecure of a job so com-fortable he would never leave it, included the whole of what composed his life.

"Another brandy, sir?"

"If you please."

He wished the bartender were not so attentive, but what else had the miserable fellow to do? Hildebrandt watched chips of bright yellow lemon peel drop from his knife into an old-fashioned glass, looked around the burnished oak curve of the counter and saw other such glasses, and wondered when all the martinis would be drunk and by whom.

Cluck!

Hildebrandt started, though he knew the bartender had merely vanished behind the small brass-latched door and would reappear in a moment bearing a box of sugar cubes or an armful of limes.

"A pretty girl—is like a melody—" the music droned, oversweet with strings.

What pretty girl? thought Hildebrandt. Did he want a pretty girl? Really the thought sickened him. He pulled his cuffs out just beyond the garnet links and turned again to the galleon's stern.

A plump woman in a large black hat came in, scanned the room for her party, fluttered a hand and plowed across the sea of Persian rug toward a distant table.

Cluck!

And the bartender appeared, struggling with an armful of limes. Hildebrandt turned his eyes away.

This was his last brandy. In another quarter hour or so, he should have watched the entry of two or three superannuated inmates come to take a late dinner, perhaps but not likely a pair of middle-aged men, well dressed but of that incredible colorlessness that only the Hotel Hyperion seemed to attract, come and stand a polite distance away from him at the bar and order bourbon old-fashioneds. In a quarter of an hour, he should have paid his check and walked leisurely back through the galleon's stern, not abandoning hope for some unimaginable and unimaginably exciting stranger, until he found himself suddenly on the sidewalk beneath the hotel's marquee. There a gust of desolation should divest him suddenly of poetry, tranquillity and will, and he would debate whether to take a taxi or the subway to his apartment or to walk to the nearest movie or to call up his friend Bracken, who lived just around the corner on Sixth Avenue. As yet he had never called up Bracken, but the possibility offered a modicum of comfort, so the thought always crossed his mind.

Actually, though, he was alone.

In the lobby beyond the galleon a man stopped, looked into the restaurant and walked on. The casements and the chandeliers sparkled like coruscating fireworks. The galleon floated in a blur of golden light. And abashedly realizing that tears had caused the distortion, Hildebrandt threw the brandy into his mouth. It flamed into his nose, and he saw the galleon through deeper tears.

A black line appeared in the center of the goldenness. It was the figure of a woman with hair of the same golden beige as the doors. Suddenly Hildebrandt felt a thrill of happiness beyond that which the magic casements had ever caused, a throb of recognition. It was the way he had expected to feel when the destined one arrived, but now he smiled to himself, afraid to believe. The tremulous, inexpressible promise which for two weeks had emanated from the galleon's stern seemed to have lifted from them and fixed itself on this woman whom the casements presented as its materialization.

He turned back to the bar, unable even to look for her in the mirror. Her presence behind him filled the room. Before he looked at her again he must know how he intended to approach her. And yet it was, somehow, foreordained and accomplished.

He paid his check, turned and walked, with the same leisured grace he would have walked toward the magic casements, toward the woman who sat at a table amid the field of empty tables.

She looked up as he came closer, and all Hildebrandt could realize, dazed as he was by nearness to her, was that she regarded him without surprise, as he had known she would. Surely she would recognize him, too!

He bowed slightly. "If I may, I should like to say good evening to you." She was slim and stately as the casements, the heart of their poem. "My name is Oliver Hildebrandt," he added.

She was older, more reserved than he had thought. He could not take in anything definite about her at once except a straight fall of light brown hair beneath a small hat with a veil. Her silence confused him.

"Are you waiting for someone?" he asked.

"Only for a waiter."

"Would you mind if I sat with you a moment?"

Perhaps her brows went up a little. Then she gestured to an empty chair. "If you like."

He slipped a chair out and sat down. She looked pleasant, he thought, though certainly she failed of the interest in him he had expected. Behind the veil her face was narrow and very pale, and Hildebrandt was shocked to see a thin scar that began under her right eye and curved out of his sight.

"You haven't been here before, have you?"

"No."

Even her voice was as he had known it would be. The brandies bore him along, against her indifference. "Strange you should happen to come."

"Is it? It does look like a very restricted place."

Hildebrandt laughed. "I don't know why anyone comes here, really, but . . ." He hesitated between sophistication and honesty and, not knowing which he chose, said, "I come because of the casements."

He would not have admitted then even to himself how he counted upon a sympathetic answer from her. He watched her gray eyes, which looked tired and not amused like her mouth, move to the entranceway, then back to him.

"They are rather romantic," she said in low musical tones that thrilled him. Yet in a way, she had said it like a plain statement of fact.

"Yes. Absurd—and yet romantic." He carried a match to her cigarette before she could use her lighter, took one of his own for himself and tossed his box of Players on the table. "Won't you tell me your name?"

"Oh"—she smiled—"that's the least important thing."

"But I've told you mine." He looked at the green lizard-bound lighter. "I know your initials—H.C. So I might as well know your name."

"Maybe legion. That might do for both of us."

Hildebrandt laughed uneasily, touched the brandy glass that had somehow appeared before him, and watched her sip at hers. This was the moment at which he should have had a toast to say. Yet more important it seemed to awaken her.

"Look here, I hope you don't think I've been rude," he said, confident he had not been.

"Not at all. I'm glad you came to talk to me."

Hildebrandt's assurance leapt, put him on the edge of his chair, inspired him to fix his eyes dreamily in space for an instant, as he often did before embarking upon a rehearsed story. "You know, it's strange, but

I've so much to talk to you about—of trade winds and lapis lazuli seas, maybe the mosques of ancient Persia—and the way you came into this room tonight."

"Talk to me, then," she said quietly. "I should love it."

She had relaxed and seemed suddenly dependent upon him. Hildebrandt felt enormously tender toward her. "Is something the matter?"

She smiled. "Later. Talk to me about everything or nothing."

It was what he wished. She was delightful. Yet as his mind danced with anticipation of what he would say, he thought first of describing all the hours at the bar, the sense of rotting away, the absence of purpose and savor in all he did, the unwordable dream of the magic casements before she had come. And what else?

"Shall I talk about Austria?"

"I said anything."

Where had Austria fled? He remembered a ski trip with thermos bottles of American black bean soup. The blond girl he had thought he had loved, but not enough to follow her to Hamburg. Or was it Bremen? The foreign scenes he could recall were seen through an atmosphere of drifting and gluttony combined. He could not re-create them in words now for her.

"There is Paris."

"Yes," she said.

The slow kaleidoscope of his past fifteen years revolved around him and the woman beside him like a thin sphere that enclosed them and kept the world out. Whatever he said now would be right, since all within the sphere was perfect.

"No." He laughed. "Shall I tell you of the most terrifying adventure of my life? It was my adventure with aloneness. Here." He glanced at the great coffered ceiling.

She smiled slowly. "I've had those adventures myself."

"Then you know what they're about." He was rather pleased. Then he added, "They're not nice, of course."

"No. When did yours take place?"

"Until you walked in tonight."

She was silent. The kaleidoscope turned slowly, its patterns blurred and forgotten. All that was clear was her narrow face behind the veil that made it seem he saw her at night, in some enclosed garden.

"Are you sure it ended when I walked in?"

"Yes."

"How sure?"

"As sure as I am that you did walk in, that you are sitting here beside me."

"That you are no longer alone?"

"Yes."

She touched her hair with the backs of her fingers, wearily, as though to see if it were there, and looked away. "It's nice to hear. Yet it's hard to believe, because I am so lonely."

"But now it doesn't have to be." He smiled. "We've beaten it, don't you see?"

"Do you think?"

"Oh, absolutely!" Hildebrandt said with the English accent he affected in his most self-assured moments.

She rested her head against her fingers and gazed at him appraisingly.

"What's the matter?"

"I don't know. Perhaps I'm tired. Perhaps I'm already asleep."

"I can guarantee you you're not. How about another brandy?"

She shook her head. Then with her long pale hands she drew her cigarettes and her lighter toward her. "I don't know. Maybe I should be going."

"No, please!"

"Thank you. I really can't stay. I'm glad you spoke to me, though— if you are."

Hildebrandt was standing as soon as she. "But I may see you again? I mean, I must see you again!"

"I don't know," she said vaguely, and moved toward the casements.

The music played "Over the Waves," as though to point out his comic figure floundering beside her across the silent Persian sea. "Really," he stammered, laughing, "this is no way. I *must* see you again!"

She stopped and turned to him. There was no one in all the wide room to see them. Hildebrandt could enjoy as though they had been alone the tilt of her head, the unexpected warmth as she said, "All right, I'll see you, then."

"Tomorrow?"

"All right. Tomorrow."

"Where shall I call for you?—May I see you home now?"

"I'll come here."

"At the same time?"

"All right."

He let her go, back to the casements' wings.

II

He had not wanted their second meeting to be in the Pandora Room, whose one charm, that of the casements, had gone when she had entered. But since it was to be, he waited for her at the bar, wishing to glimpse her once more as he had seen her first. And finally, toward ten o'clock, her image between the casements was the end of a vigil that had begun really when he had stood here the night before, watching her disappear, having nothing but the promise that she would return. He slipped off the stool and walked across the soft rug toward her.

She held her head higher than she had last evening. A green and brown dress brightened her, and made her less tall and thin, though she was almost as tall as he.

"I've a table over here," he said, in his intensity forgetting to greet her.

He led her to the table he had elected during his wait at the bar, where two glasses of brandy, ordered long before as a kind of bet with himself that she would come, stood ready for them. As he seated her carefully, Hildebrandt felt that the miracle of this second meeting made the air quake and shimmer, as though a gloriole were painted about their table. He felt he would babble nonsense unless he was cautious. It might have been for this moment the Pandora Room had been created.

"I have so much to tell you," he began in a burst, for though he had forgot in detail what she looked like, he felt their acquaintance had progressed and only conversation lagged. He had felt for the first time, since last night, that his life had a focus, which was she. He looked at her, his eyes misty with happiness, and suddenly, though she seemed ready to listen, he was afraid to tell her all he felt. He was afraid of exposing himself. It occurred to him she had encountered such men as him before, had evaluated and was already bored by their futile, hardly varying stories. She had suddenly seemed disturbingly intelligent, and though intelligence was what he had wanted, he could not speak.

"You might begin."

"Oh, can't you tell me something about yourself first? You might at least tell me what your name is now. Where you live. Or even just what you are thinking about." He felt more like himself now, and he slipped his cuffs out to the garnet links.

"I don't live here. My home's in San Francisco."

"San Francisco!" Hildebrandt exclaimed, seizing the fact like a nail to fix her to some background, yet almost at the same time he realized he did not want to know about San Francisco. "How long are you staying here?"

"Just a short while. As short as possible."

"Then what luck you happened to wander in here!"

"Is it?"

She was looking down at the tablecloth, running her thumbnail in it as though thinking of something else. It struck Hildebrandt that she regretted having met him here tonight, and the thought kept him silent as he watched her taste her brandy.

She turned to him and set down the half-empty glass. "I'm sorry. You like to linger over your brandies, don't you?"

"Oh, not at all!" Hildebrandt smiled.

"Like a gentleman—the gentleman-at-the-bar."

Hildebrandt's drooping lids quivered a little. He had needed to tell her nothing. She knew. He saw himself perhaps a month from now, perhaps tomorrow evening, slumped on one of the high stools. No, not this bar, however. Some other, at least. But he lifted his head and smiled. "Shouldn't you like dinner?"

In a voice so gentle it hardly seemed an interruption, rather the quiet entrance of an idea, she asked, smiling, "Tell me, aren't you married?"

Hildebrandt leaned back with a feint of surprise. "What prompts you to ask that?"

"Don't you have a wife? Or didn't you?"

He put out his cigarette and slowly lighted another. "Yes, I was married once. Years ago. It's funny you should ask that out of the blue. I've been divorced—going on eleven years."

"But it lingers. Doesn't it?"

"You seem to think so. Though my marriage didn't." There began stirring in him the desire to tell the story of his life, a desire so strong it overruled his fear that she knew it already, that it would bore her and kill whatever affection might have grown in her for him. But also, he reasoned, he wanted her to know. He smiled, captured by memory. "You see, my idea of life was to travel up and down one romantic river after another in Europe, just the two of us and a servant or so, until we got ready to come home." He was making it short, beginning near the end. "We were both very young. I was only twenty-four, with an income from my father, so I saw no reason to work. I hate work anyway, actually. Only—she fell in love with someone a bit richer before we'd even left the States." He laughed a little, sadly and tolerantly, like a gentleman who related sordid facts reluctantly, though they showed him to advantage.

"But you went on to Europe."

"Yes, I did. Went though all the advances I could get on my trust fund and finally went through the principal. Then I came home and sobered up and found a pleasant spot in my father's advertising firm. Which brings you practically up-to-date. Now I drift around, trying to put an edge on a hopelessly dull existence."

She was looking off again, toward the casements now, and suddenly he realized she knew he had said the same thing in the same words many times before. It had never mattered before that he had, but it mattered now because she was different. He looked at her and bit the end of his tongue and cursed himself.

"Not by yourself all the time."

"Oh, yes. Quite," he replied, contritely. "It's not often I meet anyone like you." He puffed nervously on his cigarette. "I mean, I never have. Do you know how it is sometimes," he began again, trying to turn her eyes to him, "when you are lonely for something, you want something and you can't discover what it is? Not friends or lovers or any spot on earth. Something less graspable than any of those." His hand closed with a grasping gesture on nothing. He had not said this to anyone before, and he was pleased with his articulateness and also with his honesty.

"I know."

He nodded, believing she did know. He felt his eyes were stretched wide the way they were sometimes when he looked into bar mirrors and saw the ingenuous hope. But now he did not care. He wanted to go on, to tell her that at the times he wanted this mysterious thing, he sat in bars where he could heighten the sense of its absence and so possibly discover one day what it was he wanted. But remembering her phrase, the gentle-man-at-the-bar, he dared not. He brought his face under control, leaned closer to her and said quietly, "I know it's to meet you that I've wanted."

"I'm sorry," she said, her slow words making it sound somehow final and irreparable, "that you're so lonely!"

"Lonely? I'm never lonely!"

She only smiled at him now, and he did not know what to make of the smile.

"No, I'm not *lonely!*" He laughed, feeling that such an admission would be a weakness, as though loneliness were a disease which even when cured left some unattractive trace.

She said nothing. Now the smile was gone and only the corner of her mouth was drawn up a little, with what expression Hildebrandt could not see, for her head was bent over the table.

"At any rate, *have* you had dinner?"

"Yes, thanks."

"I wish I'd thought to ask you last night."

"But I had an engagement."

"You might have broken it."

"No, a business engagement."

"Business?"

"Legal business."

"Oh?"

"Tell me what you do on Sundays."

Hildebrandt smiled, wanting to embrace her. "But I'm very curious about you."

She reached for a cigarette. "I'm here to settle some accounts—having just got a divorce."

"Oh, I see," he said subduedly, while within he fell into small quiet pieces. He realized he had thought of her as isolated from everyone but himself. If she had had a frame in his mind, it was that of the magic casements and the red and gold lobby beyond. Now all at once she was estranged, and to learn more of her was to risk thrusting her yet farther away.

"Do you have any children?"

"No." She smiled at him. "I'm quite free. I suppose I can't believe it yet."

Hildebrandt relaxed. In the moment of crisis the magic of the casements had all but left her. She had been the divorced wife of another man, the former mistress of a household in San Francisco. He might have ceased to love her, he thought, but instead, his love had metamorphosed to one that loved her as a creature of reality. He felt he had become real himself. He had risen suddenly far above the dreary gentleman-at-the-bar.

He sat upright, solicitous, beside her. "Could I ask you—if I've a right—to tell me about it?"

"No, don't ask me that!" she said with a laugh.

Hildebrandt watched her face return to its poised, somewhat preoccupied expression. He saw, despite his love for her, the distance that separated them now unless he could span it somehow. Yet this was not the time, either, to tell her he loved her. He wondered if her husband had been cruel to her. Or unfaithful. Or if he had given her the scar on her cheek! He wanted to hunt down the monster and kill him!

"Is there nothing I can do?" he asked searchingly. "I do wish you'd tell me even the least important things, if you will."

"The least important things are the least important things—like my name. And the most important thing I think you know."

"No, I don't."

She was silent again, and Hildebrandt continued. "I just can't bear to see you unhappy."

"But I am not so unhappy."

He pondered her reply as though it had been a riddle.

III

She was more than an hour late.

Hildebrandt, scanning the people who walked from right and left on the sidewalk, paced once more across the long cement step. He dared not leave to call the St. Regis, for it had now reached a time at which she, arriving and not finding him, might think he had grown tired of waiting and gone away.

"Of course she will come!" Hildebrandt said to himself. "She has never failed, has she?" He could look back on the one occasion, last evening, when she had kept their appointment in the Pandora Room. And because she had been later than he expected, he told himself she was probably late for all her engagements.

"You may think this is funny," he could still hear her say. "I wanted to go to the Metropolitan while I was here."

And he had assured her he could take the afternoon off and go with her. He had begged her, in fact, to let him see her today, because last night while they had had eggs and toast at midnight in the sandwich shop, she had said something— He could not quite remember it. Something like, "You mustn't think I've cured loneliness in you. Only someone who's never known it can cure it." And while he had laughed at her theory, it had hurt him, because he had realized she might be saying in this way that she knew he was inadequate to cure her own loneliness, to give her what she needed, perhaps in the way that mattered to her was inferior to the man who had been her husband.

But these doubts had vanished before the promise of the afternoon at the Metropolitan, which last night had seemed a gay adventure. He would learn, later when they took tea in some quiet place, all the things it was absurd he did not know already, her name, when she would come back from San Francisco and why she had to go in the first place. He would tell her then that he loved her. He would begin all over again, somewhere besides the Pandora Room, as though he had never been lonely or inadequate.

The museum had been enchanted by her presence when he had run up the steps at three o'clock to search the lobby. Now the place was melancholy. He found himself staring at a man who walked down the steps with a small boy on either hand, and only when they reached the sidewalk did he remember he had seen them go in at three o'clock. He paced slowly back along the broad step.

Even in the outdoors, with the collar of his black overcoat thrown up carelessly, his tapered face below the gray homburg stiffened against the cold twilight, he was the gentleman-at-the-bar, the anxiety of waiting but externalized upon his face by the discomfort of chill. There was a finicalness in the rigidity of his arm, the gloved hand that held the other glove, and in the precise click of his heels. He might have been impatient at having been delayed in reaching his bar at his usual hour.

He could not endure the scene any longer. The gap between three and five on the face of his watch seemed enormous. He ran down the steps and began walking south on Fifth Avenue, still watching both sides of the street, still turning to inspect taxis that drew up.

He tried to outstrip the darkness, for it seemed if he should reach the hotel before dark, it would be still afternoon, still conceivable she had been only delayed. She might, as he walked into the lobby, be coming from an elevator to meet him.

When he turned the corner and saw the hotel, he began running toward it. He expected at every second to see her. He glanced around the lobby, then went to the desk.

"Listen," he said to the clerk, "can you tell me the name of a woman who's staying here whose initials are H.C.? Miss H.C., I think. Matter of fact, I'm not sure of the C." He began to feel embarrassed. "She's from San Francisco."

The clerk came back from the registry. "Would that be Miss Helvetia Cormack?"

"Yes, it might. What room is she in, please?"

"Miss Cormack checked out this afternoon, sir."

"Then it isn't she. Look again." He gestured impatiently to the registry, but suddenly he knew it was she and that she was gone.

"No other from San Francisco by those initials, sir," the clerk said, scanning the book. "Checked out at one P.M."

"A blond woman? Tall and slender?" Hildebrandt persisted.

"Yes, sir. I remember her. Have you got something of hers? She may write us and ask for it."

"No. She left no forwarding address, either?" he asked desperately, on a wild last chance.

"No, sir."

Hildebrandt sank back on his heels and slapped his glove into his palm. "All right. Thank you."

Outside, under the marquee of the hotel, he stood a moment as he did each night beneath the marquee of the Hotel Hyperion, while he decided what direction to take, what to do. And suddenly, realizing it was not the Hotel Hyperion, that the circumstances were quite different, he felt loneliness spring up like a dark forest all around him. The odd thing was, he felt no impulse to hurry after her, to find her somehow. What would he have to offer her except the history of weakness, loneliness, and inadequacy, the decline and fall of himself? He himself was the core of the loneliness around him, and its core was inadequacy. He was inadequate even in love.

His eyelids trembled, but he raised his head indifferently, pushed his gloved hands into his overcoat pockets, and walked toward the avenue.

MISS JUSTE AND THE GREEN ROMPERS

Miss Juste's police whistle rent the air with two awful blasts. The two hundred little girls in green rompers stopped dead in their tracks. Two blasts meant line up. Line up like at the beginning of the period.

Obediently the green rompers milled about and found their appointed places in regular lines the length and breadth of the gymnasium. With grim pleasure Miss Juste watched the girls respond to her command. She had called them back, after once dismissing them, as a master might jerk her dog back on a leash. On musclebound legs she mounted the platform in the front of the gym. The platform was just like those on swimming pools, only without the diving board.

Standing at attention, her shapeless white sneakers side by side, her knees like two cauliflowers below the voluminous serge bloomers, Miss Juste waited till every movement in the lines should cease. As usual, it was Edith Polizetti who could not find her place. Edith Polizetti who, under the terrible eye of Miss Juste, tried to squeeze her way anywhere into a line and was mercilessly shoved out by the other little girls. At last, desperate, she ran to the rear and took shelter at the end of a row.

Miss Juste blew once more for attention and let the whistle fall, with military unconcern, the length of its black ribbon.

"Next Friday," Miss Juste's voice rasped against the bare walls of the gymnasium, "that's day after tomorrow . . . you are all to take home your rompers to be washed. . . . *Washed!* Do you understand? . . . You'll have the whole weekend to do it in, and *no* excuses will be accepted!"

Her blue, fishlike eyes swept the lines as she paused for the words to sink in. She paused so long the line nearest the door showed signs of wavering. It was lunchtime. They were hungry. Miss Juste gave an earsplitting blast on her whistle and glared at the offenders. The line froze into position.

"And also," she continued, "your sneakers *cleaned*! . . . Not with chalk so you leave dust all over the place. . . . But *cleaned* . . . with cleaning fluid! . . . If you can't afford to buy cleaning fluid use soap and water! . . . We're to have visitors Monday!"

Miss Juste took time for the announcement to register. One little girl on the front row was scratching her knee.

"Sophie Stephanopolos!"

Sophie Stephanopolos, the tenth girl in the third line, stiffened and held her breath.

"I want to see that elastic fixed by Friday! . . . I've *warned* you about it . . . you've *neglected* it . . . and it's *disgraceful*!"

Sophie Stephanopolos's fingers worked at her side, drawing up the romper leg that hung below her knee.

"Grace O'Rourk . . . I want to see a belt to those rompers on Friday. . . . If you've lost it, get a new one. . . . I don't care *how*!" A moment of tense silence passed. "And I want that dance perfect on Friday! . . . After six weeks of work, there's no *reason* why it shouldn't be perfect. . . . If you don't know one of the steps, practice it with a friend before Friday!"

The lunch bells were ringing all over the school now. The little girls shuffled miserably in their places.

"And furthermore," Miss Juste said, "if any girl has *not* her rompers washed and her sneakers cleaned on Monday, she needn't come at all! . . . Just don't *bother* coming!" she snarled, as though this were the most awful banishment in the world.

Then she gave the signal to Miss Pendergast at the piano, who launched into a stirring march with emphatic cadence. Miss Juste marked time energetically to start them off. The two lines nearest the wall closed and filed off and were followed by the next. Around the gymnasium they marched, lengthening their steps near the locker door, past the section of wall worn smooth and black with the rubbing of hands, breaking into blissful disorder as they left the gym and Miss Juste's eye. The march out was used only on solemn occasions, like when they had visitors, or like now, when they were to remember Miss Juste's adjurations.

Miss Pendergast's march beat on, over and over until the last couple had gone out and Miss Juste's whistle told her to halt. The hollow, jangling chords stopped in the middle of a phrase. Miss Pendergast's flat figure rose from the piano stool. A hole had been bored in the keyboard cover and the wood below so that a chain might pass through. Holding the chain was a large rusted padlock, which Miss Pendergast now fastened. Then she stacked her music and tiptoed a polite ten feet behind Miss Juste across the wooden floor, out of the gymnasium.

Friday Sophie Stephanopolos's elastic had been repaired, but Grace O'Rourk had been unable to procure a romper belt. She said so, from her place on the floor, when Miss Juste's hawkeye found her.

"Never mind! Never mind! I don't want to hear about it!" Miss Juste interrupted her, at the same time pointing ominously to the door.

Grace O'Rourk, after one humiliating instant, broke and ran tearfully to the exit.

And on this, the last day of rehearsals before the visitors came, Miss Juste's wrath at the state of the dance knew no bounds.

At Miss Pendergast's first sprightly chords they could group themselves into five circles, they could skip around twice, reverse and skip once the other way. They could break into two squares, pirouette, change places diagonally, and form their circles again. But they could not skip to the center of the circle and make a turn and skip backward again to finish in a circle. Invariably there were collisions in the center, violent collisions, or else they did not come in far enough. And when they skipped backward, the result was anything but a circle.

Miss Juste stamped a sneaker on the platform. "No!" she screamed. "No! No! No!"

They had been stuck on the circle now for the entire six weeks. She had seen it from the beginning. The rest of the dance went well enough, but the *circle*!

"Take hands! Take hands when you skip backwards, so you'll at least end together! . . . Again, Miss Pendergast!"

Again Miss Pendergast bent to her work, reading tensely through her horn-rimmed glasses, her eyes only a few inches from the music and her thin arms akimbo as her fingers pounded.

There was a fancy run at the point where the dancers were to skip, in simulated coyness, to the center of the circle. Here poor Miss Pendergast went off, and a few little girls, like Helen Murphy and Teresa Galgano, doubled up with suppressed laughter.

The terrible whistle shrieked again, and Miss Juste glowered on various sections of the class until the faces were recomposed.

"Again!" she commanded.

Miss Pendergast, always with her eye over her shoulder lest she miss a cue from Miss Juste, ventured to ask, nodding her head and smiling, "From the beginning?"

"No, from the skip in, please!"

Miss Pendergast resumed from the phrase marked "skip in" on her music.

Taking hands helped the shape of the circle, but Miss Juste was still not satisfied. "If you could stand up here where I am . . ." (Miss Pendergast's music wilted out at the first sound of Miss Juste's voice.) "It's abominable! . . . Simply abominable! . . . I'm going to give every girl in this class a D unless that circle's perfect right now!"

A shudder passed over the class. The faces grew serious. There was a story that once, long ago, Miss Juste had given a senior a D, which delayed her graduation one year, during which time she had had to take gym all day with Miss Juste. Some little girls believed this story and some did not.

"All right, Miss Pendergast!"

"From the beginning?" Miss Pendergast said timidly.

"Yes!"

Again the sprightly chords. The little girls, in position for the skip in, turned in confusion as they tried to start from the beginning. Some even skipped in.

"Stop!" screamed Miss Juste. "Stop! Stop! Stop!"

Everything stopped. There was not the twitch of a muscle in the whole gymnasium.

Miss Juste sighed. "From the beginning, please."

The circles skipped around and around, reversed and went around again, broke into squares. Each green romper skipped diagonally to her partner's corner.

Miss Juste pounded the beat grimly into her palm. "Lift . . . your feet! . . . Show . . . some . . . life!"

Miss Pendergast halted obediently at the voice, realized suddenly that she was not to have halted, and pounced onto the music again.

There was chaos among the dancers.

Miss Juste was furious. If the class had not been there, she might have vented herself upon Miss Pendergast.

Miss Pendergast's colorless lips formed an apologetic "Oh."

Again from the beginning. "Lift . . . your . . . feet! . . . All . . . of . . . you . . . look dead!" Miss Juste drummed with the beat.

The two hundred pairs of feet, heavy with fatigue and boredom, lifted themselves an inch higher.

"Lighter! Lighter! You sound like a troop of horses!"

The enormous bell over the door broke into the music and the tread of feet with brazen clangs. Gratefully, the green rompers stopped and drew breath. The bell went on for thirty deafening seconds.

The hour was over. Miss Juste expressed complete disgust with the class's performance, and made dire threats lest there be no improvement on Monday when the visitors came. There was not a word of encouragement.

"And I repeat . . . Any girl who does not have her rompers washed and ironed and her sneakers cleaned on Monday just needn't come at all. . . . And she'll get a D for the term!" Miss Juste concluded with her last ounce of vituperation.

The class was dismissed.

"And Miss Pendergast, you will practice some over the weekend, won't you?"

"Oh, yes! . . . Yes, indeed!" Miss Pendergast nodded as she closed the padlock.

When Monday came, the attendance was unusually good. Furthermore, the sneakers and rompers were universally spotless. The class filed in two by two to Miss Pendergast's finest march. A pungent odor of oil and resin came from the shining floor. The familiar stack of dirty canvas mats had been removed from the corner.

The visitors sat at the rear of the gymnasium, against the wall beneath the high windows. They were two large ladies in furs and one large gentleman in a black overcoat with his hat off. The three sat, very attentively, with Mr. Fay, the principal, on small straight chairs. The visitors and the principal himself were so large the chairs could not be seen at all, and they seemed to be suspended in the air.

The visitors were objects of great interest to the little girls, and several couples failed to halt when the march stopped. There was a bumping in the lines like a row of dominoes.

It was a very cold day, but the long windows behind the wire protectors had been flung wide open to show the visitors the fine health habits of the school. The little girls shivered and stood rigidly in their places. Miss Juste pushed her hands deep into the pockets of her big black coat sweater. And the visitors themselves pulled their furs and coat collars closer about them.

To add to the uniqueness of the occasion, Miss Juste was smiling! Actually smiling, in spite of the cold. And she was wearing a bright red tie with her middy blouse, and black-and-red golf hose pulled up to her dappled knees.

When the entire class was in couples all around the gym, Miss Juste, still smiling, blew her whistle, at which signal the couples broke up and took their places in the lines for the attendance.

There were two gaps in the ranks where Grace O'Rourk, who was still without a romper belt, and Concetta Rosasco were to have stood. Concetta's partner for the dance, Lucia DeStephano, darted suddenly out of line and escaped through the door. Miss Juste saw her. Half the class saw her and knew Miss Juste saw her. But Miss Juste continued to smile as she scanned the attendance cards. The class watched her with fascination. Her face looked different. She was like a stranger standing there on the platform.

Then she blew her whistle, Miss Pendergast pounced with enthusiasm onto the Washington Post March, and the lines were miraculously transformed into ranks of four that marched forward, turned the corner smartly, and began a circuit of the gym. The maneuver was not difficult. They had been doing it ever since their first year of gymnasium work. There was no possible chance of mistake, even for people like Edith Polizetti.

Mr. Fay leaned over in his chair and whispered something to one of the large ladies, who nodded and smiled.

After the second lap around the gym, the lines came down the center and stood marking time before Miss Juste. The slender vase of bachelor buttons on Miss Pendergast's piano rocked with her crashing chords. When the music stopped, there was a patter of applause from the three visitors. Several of the little girls snickered self-consciously.

The exercises were over. Miss Juste raised her whistle to signal the positions for the dance.

But just at this moment the three visitors rose simultaneously. Mr. Fay rose, too. Miss Juste did not blow the whistle. The visitors came forward slowly between the first line and the wall. Miss Juste waited, beaming upon them.

Mr. Fay came to the platform while the visitors stood by the door.

"Mrs. Heathwaite, Mrs. Donnelly, and Mr. Sheppard ask me to express their commendations to the class, Miss Juste," said Mr. Fay.

The little girls on the first row across listened with open eyes and mouths.

"And to Miss Pendergast's playing." Miss Pendergast smiled and nodded several times. "They are sorry they must leave so soon, but they want to see the rest of the school, and they have a luncheon at twelve-thirty."

"Why . . . why, yes. . . . That's quite all right, Mr. Fay," Miss Juste said. "And would you please tell them it was a real pleasure to have them!"

Mr. Fay and the visitors left the gymnasium.

Miss Juste stood on the platform, looking at the back of the gym. The class saw her take a deep breath. The class took a deep breath, too. Her smile had disappeared with the visitors, but her mouth had not taken on its usual firmness, nor her eyes their flintlike expression. In fact, Miss Juste's mouth was open and she looked a little blank, as though she were thinking of something else. A frown came between her brows. She tapped the whistle idly in her palm.

Slowly she turned toward the piano.

"All right, Miss Pendergast," she said.

The gay chords jangled through the gymnasium as the little girls skipped in their circles. Across the room, near where the visitors had sat, Grace O'Rourk's partner for the dance was curtsying and locking arms with an imaginary figure.

WHERE THE DOOR IS ALWAYS OPEN AND
THE WELCOME MAT IS OUT

Riding home on the Third Avenue bus, sitting anxiously on the very edge of the seat she had captured, Mildred made rapid calculations for the hundredth time that day.

Her sister Edith was arriving from Cleveland at 6:10 at Penn Station. It was already 5:22, later than she had anticipated, because some letters Mr. Sweeney wanted sent out at the last minute had delayed her at the office. She would have only about twenty-two minutes at home to straighten anything that might have gotten unstraightened since last night's cleaning, lay the table and organize their delicatessen supper, and fix her face a bit before she left for Penn Station. It was lucky she'd done the marketing in her lunch hour. All the last half of the afternoon, though, she had watched the dark spot on the grocery bag grow bigger— the dill pickles leaking—and she'd been too busy at the office to drag all the things out and rearrange them. Now, with her firm, square hand over the wet place, she felt better.

The bus swayed to a stop, and she twisted and ducked her head to see a street marker. Only Thirty-sixth Street.

Dill pickles, pumpernickel bread, rollmops (maybe it was the roll-mops leaking, not the pickles), liverwurst, salami, celery and garlic for the potato salad, coffee ring for dessert, and oranges for breakfast tomorrow. She'd found some gladiolas in her lunch hour, too, and their blossoms still looked as fresh as when she'd bought them. It seemed like everything, but she knew better than to think there wouldn't be *something* at the last minute she'd forgotten.

Edith's telegram last evening had taken her completely by surprise, but Mildred had just pitched in and cleaned everything, spent all last

evening and early this morning at it, washing windows, cleaning out closets, as well as the usual dusting and sweeping and scouring. Her sister Edith
was such a neat housekeeper herself, Mildred knew she would have to
have things in apple pie order, if her sister was to take a good report back
to their Cleveland relations. Well, at least none of the folks in Cleveland
could say she'd lost her hospitality because she'd become a New Yorker.
"The welcome mat is always out," Mildred had written many a time to
friends and members of the family who showed any signs of coming to New
York. Her guests were treated to a home-cooked meal—though she did
depend on the delicatessen quite a bit, she supposed—and to every comfort she could offer for as long as they cared to stay. Edith probably
wouldn't stay more than two or three days, though. She was just passing
through on her way to Ithaca to visit her son Arthur and his wife.

She got off at Twenty-sixth Street. Five twenty-seven, said a clock in
a hardware store window. She certainly would have to rush. Well, wasn't
she always rushing? A lot Edith, with nothing but a household to manage, knew of a life as busy as hers!

Mildred's apartment house was a six-story red brick building on
Third Avenue over a delicatessen. The delicatessen's crowded window
prompted her to go over everything again. The coleslaw! And milk, of
course. How could she have forgotten?

There were two women ahead of her, their shopping bags full of
empty bottles, and they chatted with Mr. Weintraub and had their items
charged in the notebook he kept hanging by the cash register. Mildred
shifted and trembled inwardly with impatience and frustration, regretted
that neighborliness had such a price these days, but her tense smile was a
pleasant one.

"Coleslaw and milk," repeated Mr. Weintraub. "Anything else?"

"No, that's all, thank you," Mildred said quickly, not wanting to
delay the woman who had come in after her.

Some children playing tag on the sidewalk deliberately dragged an
ash can into her path, but Mildred ignored them and fumbled for her
keys. Necessity had taught her the trick of pushing the key with a thumb
as she turned the knob with the same hand, a method she used even on
those rare occasions when both arms were not full. She saw mail in her
box, but she could get it later. No, it might be something from Edith. It

was a beauty parlor advertisement and a postcard about a new dry-cleaning process for rugs.

"Plumber's upstairs, Miss Stratton," said the superintendent, who was on his way down.

"Oh? What's happened?"

"Nothing much. Woman above had her bowl run over, and the plumber thinks the trouble might be in your place."

"But I haven't——" It was quicker to suffer accusation, however, so she plodded up the stairs.

The door of her apartment was ajar. She went into a narrow room whose two close-set windows looked out on the avenue. Crossing her room, she felt a lift of pride at the unaccustomed orderliness of everything. On the coffee table lay the single careless touch: a program of the performance of *Hansel and Gretel* she had attended last Christmas in Brooklyn. She'd found it in cleaning the bookcase, and had put it out for Edith to see.

But the sight of the bathroom made her gasp. There were black smudges on everything, even on the frame of the mirror over the basin. What *didn't* plumbers and superintendents manage to touch, and weren't their hands always black!

"All fixed, ma'am. Here's what the trouble was." The plumber held up something barely recognizable as a toothbrush, and smiled. "Remember it?"

"No, I don't," she said, letting her parcels slide onto a kitchen chair. It wasn't *her* toothbrush, she was sure of that, but the less talk about it, the sooner he would leave.

While she waited to get at the bathroom, she spread her best tablecloth on the gateleg table in the kitchen, pulled the window shade down so the people in the kitchen three feet away across the air chute couldn't see in, then dashed the morning coffee grounds into the garbage pail and stuck the dirty coffeepot into the sink. Keeping one foot on the pedal of the garbage pail, she pivoted in a half dozen directions, reached even the bag of groceries on the chair and began to unload it.

The closing of the door told her the plumber was gone, and crushing the last paper bag into the garbage—she generally saved them for old Sam the greengrocer, but there was no time now—she went into the

bathroom and erased every black fingerprint with rag and scouring powder, and mopped up the floor as she backed her way out. In the minute
she allowed for the floor to dry, she pushed off her medium-heeled
oxfords at the closet door and stepped into identical newer oxfords. But
their laces were tied from a hasty removal, too. She stooped down, and
felt a dart over her bent knee. A run. She mustn't forget to change the
stocking before she left for the station. Or had she another good stocking? Buying stockings was one of the errands she had intended to do
today in her lunch hour.

Twenty-one minutes of six, she saw as she trotted into the bathroom. Eleven minutes before she ought to leave the house.

Even after the brisk scrubbing with a washrag, her squarish face
looked as colorless as her short jacket of black and gray tweed. Her hair,
of which the gray had recently gotten an edge over the brown, was naturally wavy, and now the more wiry gray hairs stood out from her head,
making her look entirely gray, unfortunately, and giving her an air of
harassed untidiness no matter what she did to correct it. But her eyes
made up for the dullness of the rest of her face, she thought. Her round
but rather small gray eyes still looked honest and kind, though sometimes there was a bewildered, almost frightened expression in them that
shocked her. She saw it now. It was because she was hurrying so, she supposed. She must remember to look calm with Edith. Edith was so calm.

She daubed a spot of rouge on one cheek and was spreading it outward with timid strokes when the peal of the doorbell made her jump.

"Miss," said a frail voice in the semidarkness of the hall, "take a ten-cent
chance on the St. Ant'ny School lottery Saturday May twenny-second?"

"No. No, child, I haven't time," Mildred said, closing the door. She
hated to be harsh with the little tykes, but at seventeen minutes of six . . .

As a matter of fact, the alarm clock shouldn't be out on the coffee
table, she thought, it looked too much as if she slept on the living room
couch, which of course she did. She put the clock in a bureau drawer.

For a moment, she stood in the center of the room with her mind a
complete blank. What should she do next? Why was her heart beating so
fast? One would think she'd been running, or at least that she was terribly excited about something, and she wasn't really.

Maybe a bit of whiskey would help. Her father had always said a little nip was good when a person was under a strain, and she was under a slight strain, she supposed. After all, she hadn't seen Edith in nearly two years, not since she'd been to Cleveland on her vacation two summers ago.

Mr. Sweeney had given her the whiskey last Christmas, and she hadn't touched it since she made the eggnog Christmas Day for old Mrs. Chevlov upstairs. The bottle was still almost full. Cautiously, she poured an inch into a small glass that had once contained cheese, then added another half inch, and drank it off at a gulp to save time. The drink landed with a warm explosion inside her.

"Dear old Edith!" she said aloud, and smiled with anticipation.

The doorbell rang.

Those children again, she thought, they always tried twice. Absently, she plucked a piece of thread from the carpet, and rolled it between her thumb and forefinger, wondering if she should answer the door or not. Then the bell came again, with a rap besides, and she plunged toward it. It might be the plumber about something else.

"Miss, take a ten-cent chance on the St. Ant'ny—"

"No," Mildred said with a shudder. "No, thank you, children." But she found a coin in the pocket of her jacket and thrust it at them.

Then she dashed into the kitchen and set out plates, cups and saucers, and paper napkins in buffet style. It looked nice to have everything out, and would save considerable time later. She put the big mixing bowl for the potato salad on the left, and lined up beside it the smaller mixing bowl for the dressing, the salad oil, the vinegar, mustard, paprika, salt and pepper, the jar of stuffed olives—a little moldy, best wash them off—in a militarily straight row. The sugar bowl was low, she noticed, and lumpy, too. And only three minutes left! She hacked at the lumps in the bowl with a teaspoon, but not all of them would dislodge, so finally she gave it up and just added more sugar. Some of it spilled on the floor. She seized broom and dustpan and went after it. Her heart was pounding again. What on earth ailed her?

Thoughtfully, she took down the whiskey and poured another inch or two into the glass. Soothing sensations crept from her stomach in all directions, made their way even into her hands and feet. She swept up the sugar with renewed fortitude and patience, and whisked the remaining grains under the sink so they wouldn't crackle underfoot.

The kitchen curtains caught her eye for the first time in months, but she resolutely refused to worry about their streaks of black grit. A person was allowed *one* fault in a household, she thought.

As she pulled on her coat, it occurred to her she hadn't boiled the eggs for the salad, and she'd meant to do it the first thing when she came home. She put three eggs into a saucepan of water and turned the gas on high. At least she could start them in the few moments she'd be here, and turn them off as she went out the door.

Now. Had she keys? Money? Her hat. She snatched up her hat—a once-stiff pillbox of Persian lamb, much the same color as her hair—and pressed it on with the flat of her hand. Nice to have the kind of hats one didn't have to worry about being straight or crooked, she thought, but she allowed herself one glance in the hall mirror as she passed by, and it was enough to reveal one rouged cheek and one plain one. She hurried back into the bathroom, where the light was best.

It was six minutes to six when she flew downstairs.

She'd better take a taxi to the station after all. She regretted the extravagance, though she felt herself yielding to a gaiety and abandonment that had been plucking at her ever since she thought of taking a nip of whiskey. She didn't really care about eighty-five cents, a dollar with tip. A dollar was just a little more than one-hundredth of her weekly salary. Or a little more than one-thousandth? No, than one-hundredth, of course.

Crossing the lobby of Penn Station toward the information center, she felt the run in her stocking travel upward and was afraid to look. She'd forgotten to change it, but she wouldn't, really wouldn't have had time to look for a good stocking, even if she'd remembered. She could tell Edith she'd gotten the run hurrying to meet her. In fact, she thought brilliantly, Edith didn't have to know she'd been home at all, which would make her house and herself, after some apologies, look very nice indeed.

"Downstairs for incoming train information," the clerk told her.

Mildred trotted downstairs, and was referred to a blackboard, where she learned that the Cleveland Flyer would be twenty minutes late. Suddenly something collapsed in her, and she felt terribly tired. She started for a nearby bench, but she knew she was too restless to sit still. She wandered back upstairs. Her nervous system was not adjusted to waiting. She

could wait in the office for Mr. Sweeney to finish a long telephone conversation and get back to whatever work they were doing together, but
she could not wait on her own time—for an elevator, for a clerk in a
department store, or on a line in the post office—without growing anxious and jumpy. Maybe another touch of whiskey would be a good idea,
she thought, a leisurely one she could sip while she composed herself.

A big, softly lighted, pink and beige bar came into view almost
immediately. And there were several women inside, she was relieved to
see. Feeling strange and somehow very special, Mildred went in through
the revolving door. Every table was in use, so she stood shyly behind two
men at the bar, over whose shoulders she could see the barman now and
then.

"Whiskey," she said, when the barman seemed to be looking at her.
"What kind?"
"Oh, it doesn't matter," she said cheerfully.

Everybody in the place seemed to be having such a good time, it was
fun just to watch them. She never gave such places a thought, yet they
were going full blast all over New York every evening, she supposed. It
occurred to her she was probably a more sophisticated person than she
realized.

She wondered if Edith still wore her hair in those stiff marcel waves.
The last time she had seen Edith, she had looked like one of those dum-
mies with wigs they have in beauty parlor windows. That wasn't a nice
thing to think about one's sister, but Edith really had looked like them.
For the first time now, Mildred realized that Edith was actually coming,
that she would see her within minutes. She could hear Edith's slow voice
as clearly as if she stood beside her, saying, "Well, that's fate, Millie," as she
often did, and as she probably would say about her daughter Phyllis's
marriage. Phyllis's husband was only nineteen and without a job, and,
according to a letter Cousin John in Toledo had written her a few weeks
ago, without ambition, either. "Well, that's fate," Edith would say by way
of passing it off. "Parents can't boss their children anymore, once the
children think they're grown." Mildred's heart went out to her sister.

The square-numeraled clock on the wall said only 6:17. Just about
an hour ago, she had been on the bus going home. The crowded bus
seemed suddenly dismal and hideous. It was as if another person had

been riding on it an hour ago, not herself, not this person who sipped whiskey in a bar where dance music played, this person who awaited a train from Cleveland.

One of the men offered her a high red stool, but she was so short, she decided just to lean against it. Then all at once it was 6:28. She paid her check, clutched her handbag, and dashed off.

Now, really now, her sister was pulling into the station. She giggled excitedly. A bell went *whang-whang-whang!* A metal gate folded back. People rushed up the slope, people rushed down, among them herself. And there was Edith, walking toward her!

"Edith!"

"Millie!"

They fell upon each other. My own flesh and blood, Mildred thought, patting Edith's back and feeling a little weepy. There was confusion for a few minutes while Edith found her suitcase, Mildred asked questions about the family, and they looked for a cab. With a flash of pain, Mildred remembered the eggs on the stove at home. They would be burning now, aflame probably, the gas was so high. How did burning eggs smell? In the taxi, Mildred braced Edith's suitcase against the jump seat with her foot and tried to listen to everything Edith was telling her, but she couldn't keep track of anything for thinking of the eggs.

"How is Arthur?" Mildred asked, one eye out the window to see if the driver was going right.

"Just as well as can be. He has a new baby."

Mildred hoped every child in the neighborhood wasn't cluttering the front steps. Sometimes they played cards right in the doorway. "Oh, a new baby! Oh, has he?"

"Yes, another little girl," said Edith. "Just last week. I was saving it to tell you."

"So now you're twice a grandmother! I'll have to send Arthur and Helen something right away."

Edith protested she shouldn't.

Mildred paid the driver, then struggled out with the suitcase, waving Edith's assistance aside, and not waiting for the driver to help, because drivers usually didn't. She realized too late that she might have added another dime to the tip, and hoped Edith hadn't noticed. Pinching each other's fingers under the suitcase handle, the sisters climbed the three flights. Mildred felt a rough corner of the suitcase tearing at her good stocking.

"Are you hungry?" she asked cheerily as she felt for her keys, trying not to sound out of breath. She sniffed for burning eggs.

"I had a snack on the train about five o'clock," Edith replied, "so I'm bearing up, as they say."

"Well, here it is, such as it is!" Mildred smiled fearfully as she swung the door open for Edith, braced for any kind of odor.

"It's just lovely," Edith said, even before the light was turned on.

Mildred had flown past her into the kitchen. The eggs were turned off, resting quietly in their water. She stared at them incredulously for a second or two. "It's just the one room and a bit of a kitchen this time," Mildred remarked as she returned to her sister, for Edith, standing in the middle of the room, seemed to be expecting her to show her the rest. "But it's much more convenient to the office than the Bronx apartment was. I know you'll want to wash up, Edie, so just have your coat off and I'll show you where everything is."

But Edith did not want to wash up.

"As Father used to say, 'I propose we have a wee nip in honor of the occasion!'" Mildred said a bit wildly, her voice rising over the roar of a passing truck on Third Avenue. She thought Edith looked at her in a funny way, so she added, "Not that I've become a drinking woman, by any means! I did have one while I was waiting for you in the station, though. Could you tell?"

"No. You mean you went in a bar by yourself and had a drink?"

"Why, yes," Mildred replied, wishing now that she hadn't mentioned it. "Women often go into bars in New York, you know. It's not like Cleveland." Mildred turned a little unsteadily and went into the kitchen. She did want another bit of a drink, just to continue feeling as calm as she did now, for it certainly was helping to calm her. She took a quick nip, then fixed a tray with the bottle and glasses and ice. "Well, down the hatch!" Mildred said as she set the tray down on the coffee table.

Edith had refused the maroon-covered easy chair Mildred had offered her, and now she sat tensely on the couch and sipped her whiskey as if it were poison. She gazed off now and then at the windows—the curtains, Mildred admitted, were not so clean as Cleveland curtains, but at least she had brushed them down last night—and at the brown bureau that was her least attractive piece of furniture. Why didn't Edith look over at the kitchen table where everything was lined up as neatly as a color photograph in a magazine?

"The gladiolas are beautiful, Millie," Edith said, looking at the gladiolas Mildred had set in a blue vase atop the bureau. "I grow gladiolas in the backyard."

Mildred lighted up appreciatively at Edith's compliment. "How long am I to have the pleasure of your company, sister?"

"Oh, just till—" Edith broke off and looked at the windows with an expression of annoyance.

A truck or perhaps a cement mixer was rattling and clanking up the avenue. Suddenly Mildred, whose ears had adjusted long ago to the street noises, realized how it must sound to Edith, and writhed with shame. She had quite forgotten the worst feature of her apartment—the noise. The garbage trucks that started grinding around three A.M. were going to be worse.

"It's a nuisance," Mildred said carelessly, "but one gets used to it. What with the housing—" Something else was passing, backfiring like pistol shots, and Mildred realized she couldn't hear her own voice. She waited, then resumed. "What with the housing being—"

But Edith silenced her with a hopeless shake of her head.

A war of horns was going on now, probably a little traffic jam at the corner. That was the way it went, Mildred tried to convey to Edith with a smile and a shrug, all at once or nothing at all. For a few moments their ears, even Mildred's ears, were filled with the cacophony of car horns, of snarling human voices.

"Really, Millie, I don't see how you stand this noise day after day," Edith said.

Mildred shrugged involuntarily, started to say something, and said nothing after all. She felt inexplicably foolish all at once.

"What were you going to say before?" Edith prompted.

"Oh. Well, what with the housing being what it is today, New Yorkers can't be too picky where they live. I have my budget, and I didn't have any choice but this place and something on Tenth Avenue when I wanted to move from the Bronx. Took me three months to find this." She said it with a little pride that was instantly quelled by her sister's troubled regard of the windows. Well, there weren't any trucks passing now, Mildred thought a bit resentfully, and the traffic jam had evidently cleared up. What was she looking at? Self-consciously, Mildred got up and lowered the window, though she knew it would not help much to lessen the noise. She looked at her geranium. The geranium was nothing but a crooked dry stalk in its pot now, at the extreme left of the windowsill where the sun lingered longest. It must have been three weeks since she'd watered it, and now she felt overcome with remorse. Why was she always rushing so, she forgot all about doing the nice things, all the little things that gave her real pleasure? A wave of self-pity brought tears to her eyes. A lot her sister knew about all she had to contend with, the million and one things she had to think of all by herself, not only at home but at the office, too. You could tell just by looking at Edith she never had to worry or rush about anything, even to take a hard-boiled egg off the stove.

With a smile, Mildred turned to Edith, and under cover of a "Hungry yet?" ducked into the kitchen to see about the hard-boiled eggs. She balanced the three hot eggs on top of the block of ice in the icebox, so they would cool as fast as possible.

"Remember the time we took the raw eggs by mistake on the picnic, Edie?" Mildred said, laughing as she came back into the living room. It was an old family joke, and one or the other of them mentioned it almost every time they cooked hard-boiled eggs.

"Will I ever forget!" Edith shrieked, bringing her hands down gently on her knees. "I still say Billy Reed switched them on us. He's the same rascal today he always was."

"Those were happy old days, weren't they?" Mildred said vaguely, wondering if she shouldn't perhaps cook the eggs even longer. She made a start for the kitchen and changed her mind.

"Millie, do you think it's really worth it to live in New York?" Edith asked suddenly.

"Worth it? How do you mean worth it?—I suppose I earn fairly good money." She didn't mean to sound superior to her sister, but she was proud of her independence. "I'm able to save a little, too."

"I mean, it's such a hard life you lead and all, being away from the family. New York's so unfriendly, and no trees to look at or anything. I think you're more nervous than you were two years ago."

Mildred stared at her. Maybe New York had made her more nervous, quicker about things. But wasn't she as happy and healthy as Edith? "They're starting trees right here on Third Avenue. They're pretty small yet, but tomorrow you can see them.—I don't think it's such an unfriendly town," she went on defensively. "Why, just this afternoon, I heard the delicatessen man talking with a woman about— And even the plumber—" She broke off, knowing she wouldn't be able to express what she meant.

"Well, I don't know," Edith said, twiddling her hands limply in her lap. "My last trip here, I asked a policeman where the Radio City Music Hall was, and you'd have thought I was asking him to map me a way to the North Pole or something, he seemed so put out about it. Nobody's got time for anybody else—have they?" Her voice trailed off, and she looked at Mildred for an answer.

Mildred moistened her lips. Something in her struggled slowly and painfully to the surface. "I—I've always found our policemen very courteous. Maybe yours was a traffic officer or something. They're pretty busy, of course. But New York policemen are famous for their courtesy, especially to out-of-towners. Why, they even call them New York's Finest!" A tingle of civic pride swept over her. She remembered the morning she had stood in the rain at Forty-second Street and Fifth Avenue and watched the companies of policemen—*New York's Finest*—march down the avenue. And the mounted policemen! How handsome they had looked, row upon row with their horses' hoofs clattering! She had stood there not caring that she was all by herself then, or that the rain was soaking her, she felt so proud of her big city. A man with a little boy perched on his shoulder had turned around in the crowd and smiled at her, she remembered. "New York's *very* friendly," Mildred protested earnestly.

"Well, maybe, but that's not the way it seems to me." Edith slipped off a shoe and rubbed her instep against the heel of her other foot. "And sister," she continued in a more subdued tone, "I hope you're not indulging more than you should."

Mildred's eyes grew wide. "Do you mean drinking? Goodness, no!

Why, at least I don't think so. I just took these in your honor, Edie. Gracious, you don't think I do this every night, do you?"

"Oh, I didn't mean I thought *that!*" Edith said, forcing a smile.

Mildred chewed her underlip and wondered whether she should think of some other excuse for herself, or let the matter drop.

"You know, Millie, I'd meant to speak to you about maybe coming back to Cleveland to live. Everybody's talking about the interesting new jobs opening up there, and you're not—well, so deep-fixed in this job that you couldn't leave, are you?"

"Of course, I could leave if I wanted to. But Mr. Sweeney depends a great deal on me. At least he says he does." She swallowed, and tried to collect all that clamored inside her for utterance. "It's not a very big job, I suppose, but it's a good one. And we've all been working together for seven years, you know," she asserted, but she knew this by itself couldn't express to Edith how the four of them—she had written Edith many a time about Louise who handled the books and the files, and Carl their salesman, and Mr. Sweeney, of course—were much more of a family than many families were. "Oh, New York's my home now, Edie."

"You've always got a home with us, Millie."

Mildred was about to say that was very sweet of her, but a truck's brakes were mounting to a piercing crescendo outside. She dropped her eyes from Edith's disappointed face.

"I've got some things I ought to put on hangers overnight," Edith said finally. "And do you mind if I wash my white gloves? They'll just about dry by morning. I'll have to leave early."

"What time?" Mildred asked, in order to be cooperative, but, aware that her worried expression might make her seem eager for Edith's departure, she smiled, which was almost worse.

"The train's at eight forty-eight," Edith replied, going to her suitcase.

"That's too bad. I'm sorry you're not staying longer, Edith." She really did feel sorry. They'd hardly have time to talk at all. And Edith probably wouldn't notice half the things she had done around the house, the neat closets, the half of the top drawer she had cleared for her in the bureau, the container of soft drinks Edith liked that she had thought of the first thing last evening.

Mildred wiped the back of her hand across her eyes, and went into the kitchen. She got the stew pan of boiled potatoes from the icebox and dumped them into the salad bowl. She separated the celery under running water, bunched it, and sliced it onto the potatoes. The old habit of rushing, of saving split seconds, caught her up in its machinery as if she no longer possessed a volition of her own, and she surrendered to it with a kind of tortured enjoyment. She hardly breathed except to gasp at intervals, and she moved faster and faster. The jar of olives flew into the bowl at one burst, followed by a shower of onion chips and a cloud of paprika that made her cough. Finally, she seized knife and fork and began to slice everything in the bowl every which way. Her muscles grew so taut, it hurt her even to move to the icebox to get the eggs. The eggs had descended three inches or more into the ice, and she could not extract them with her longest fingers. She peered at their murkily enlarged forms through the ice cake, then burst out laughing.

"Edie!" she cried. "Edie, come here and look!"

But her only reply was the flushing of the toilet. Mildred bent over in silent, paroxysmic hilarity. If her sister only knew about the toilet! The toothbrush the plumber had dragged out that hadn't even *looked* like a toothbrush!

Mildred straightened and grimly wrestled the ice cake from the box. She shook the eggs into the sink, holding the ice with hands and forearms. The eggs had bright, gooey orange centers, but they were fairly cold. She hacked them into the salad, listening the while for Edith's coming out of the bathroom. She was racing to have the supper ready when Edith came out, but what did it matter really whether she was ready or not? Why was she in such a hurry? She giggled at herself, then, with her mouth still smiling, set her teeth and stirred the dressing so fast it rose high up the sides of the mixing bowl.

"Can I help you, Millie?"

"Not a thing to do, thank you, Edie." Mildred dragged the coleslaw out of the icebox so hastily, she dropped it face down on the floor, but Edith had just turned away and didn't see.

Within moments, she was ready, the table laid, the coffee perking, the pumpernickel bread—but there wasn't any butter. She'd forgotten butter for herself yesterday, and forgotten it again today.

"There isn't any butter," Mildred said in an agony of apology as Edith took her place at the table. She thought of running down for some, but felt it would be rude to make Edith wait. "It's the same old-fashioned potato salad Mama used to make at home, though."

"It looks delicious. Don't you ever have hot meals here at home?"

"Why, most of the time. I try to eat a very balanced diet." She knew what her sister was thinking now, that she lived off delicatessen sandwiches, probably. She passed Edith the coleslaw. "Here's something very healthful, if you like." Her throat closed up. She felt ready to cry again. "I'm sorry, Edie. I suppose you'd have preferred a hot meal."

"No, this tastes very nice. Now, don't you worry," Edith said, poking at the potato salad.

At the end of the supper, Mildred realized she had not put out the dill pickles. Or the rollmops.

"Would you like to step out tonight? Take a look at the big city?" Mildred came in from the kitchen, where she had just finished cleaning up.

Edith was lying on the couch. "Well, maybe. I don't think I can nap after all, with all the traffic going. I suppose it lets up at night, though."

"There's a nice movie a few blocks uptown within walking distance," Mildred said, feeling a sink of defeat. How would she ever break it to Edith that there was some kind of noise on Third Avenue all night long?

They went to a shabby little movie house on Thirty-fourth Street, whose gay lights Edith had seen and fixed upon.

"Is this your neighborhood theater?" Edith asked.

"Oh, no. There's any number of better theaters around," Mildred answered rather shortly. Edith had chosen the place. She almost wished Edith had wanted to go up to Broadway. She'd have spent more money, but at least the theater would have been nicer, and Edith couldn't have complained. Mildred was so tired, she dozed during some of the picture.

That night, Mildred was aware that Edith got out of bed several times, to get glasses of water or to stand by the window. Mildred suggested that Edith get some cotton from the medicine cabinet to put in her ears. But Mildred slept so hard herself, even on the too-short sofa, most of her impressions might have come from a great distance.

"Are they mixing cement at this hour?" Edith asked.

"No, that's our garbage disposal, I'm afraid," Mildred said with an automatic little smile, though it was too dark for Edith to see her. She had dreaded this: the clatter of ash cans, the uninterrupted moaning of machinery chewing up cans, bottles, cartons, and anything else that was dumped into the truck's open rear. Mildred bared her set teeth and tried to estimate just how awful it sounded to her sister: the clank of bottles now, the metallic bump of an emptied ash can carelessly dropped on the sidewalk, and under it all the relentless *rrrr-rrrr-rrr-rrr*. Quite bad, she decided, and quite ugly, if one wasn't used to it. "They have their job to do," Mildred added. "I don't know what a big city like this would do without them."

"Um-m. Looks to me like they could do it in the daytime when nobody's trying to sleep," said Edith.

"What?"

Edith repeated it more loudly. "I don't see how you stand it, even with the cotton in your ears."

"I don't use cotton anymore," Mildred murmured.

Mildred did not feel too wide awake the next morning, and Edith said she hadn't slept all night and was dead tired, so neither said very much. At the core of Mildred's silence was both her ignominy at having failed as a hostess and a desire not to waste a second, for despite having gotten up early, they were a bit pressed to get off when they should. At eight o'clock sharp, the pneumatic drill burst out like a fanfare of machine guns: a big apartment house was going up directly across the street. Edith just glanced at Mildred and shook her head, but around 8:15, there was an explosion across the street that made Edith jump and drop something she had in her hands.

Mildred smiled. "They have to blast some. New York has rock foundations, you know. You'd be surprised how fast they build things, though."

Edith's suitcase was not closed for the last time until 8:27, and they arrived at the station with no time to spare.

"I hope you can manage a longer visit on your return trip, Edith," Mildred said.

"Well, Arthur did say something about going back to Cleveland with me for a while, but we'll let you know. I can't thank you enough for the lovely time, Millie."

A pressed hand, a brushed cheek, and that was all. Mildred watched the train doors close down the platform, but she had no time to watch the train pull out. What time was it? Eight forty-nine on the dot, her wristwatch said. If she hurried, she might be at the office by nine as usual. Of course, Mr. Sweeney wouldn't mind her being late on such a special morning, but for that very reason, she thought it would be nice to be prompt.

She darted to the corner of Seventh Avenue and Thirty-fourth Street and caught the crosstown bus. She could catch the Third Avenue bus uptown and be at the office on Second Avenue in no time. At the Third Avenue bus stop, an anxious frown came on her face as she estimated the speed and distance of an oncoming truck, then ran. She mustn't forget to buy stockings today during her lunch hour, she thought. And tonight, she ought to drop a note to Edith in Ithaca, telling her how she had enjoyed her stay, and inviting her again when she could make it. And a note to Arthur, of course, about the new baby. Maybe Edith and Arthur both could stay with her awhile, if they went back to Cleveland together. She'd be able to make them comfortable somehow.

IN THE PLAZA

He was born in a hut made of twigs and mud that leaned against a straw-colored hill. The road to the village went past the door, and at the age of one, he knew that the people who said "Hello" instead of "*Adiós*" were *americanos* and very rich. They gave money away for nothing, his father said. Money bought sweet rolls and candy sticks. So he had no time to play on the dirt floor with his older brother. He had no time to wonder, as his father and grandfather had wondered, sitting on the same wooden doorstep, whether the huddled hills were the backs of giant burros, as an old story told, or if the distant mountains that lay in great golden-tan curves held bubbles of air that might escape at the puncture of a pick and let the whole world down. He had time only to watch for *americanos*. He could tell them by their pale faces and their new clean clothes. When he saw one, he would rush out into the road, naked as he was, grin and say, "Ai-lo!" and hold out his palm. The coins always fell.

At four, he loitered around the smaller plaza in the village, where the buses unloaded. He learned to say, "Can I help you, lady?" and "Can I help you, sir?" and always he was given centavos, because the words meant, Could he carry the suitcases that were as big as he was and weighed a lot more? If he talked fast, he could get money from all the *turistas* before the older boys, his brother Antonio among them, could carry off their suitcases. He learned to say, "That is the best hotel," as he pointed up the road to a big white house, and if people went there, he trotted after them and collected a peso from the hotel manager. The rate at the hotel was one hundred and twenty-five pesos a day, but for the *americanos* this fortune was nothing.

When he saw an American, he did not see a person at all, but centavo pieces and red-and-green peso notes. It fascinated him to watch them buy in the silver shops. They selected things quickly, as if they were eager to get rid of their money, and there was never any back-and-forth talk about the price. The women had even more pesos than the men. Every American was a moneybag he had merely to puncture with a smile and hold his hands out to. His only competition was a loose army of other small boys which roamed the village, but the competition was not serious because he, in distinction from all the rest, was cute. "Cute" was a word nearly all the Americans said when they gave him money. It meant he did not have to carry suitcases as the others did, that all he had to do was smile and hold out his palm. His last name happened to be Palma, but several years were to pass before he learned the English word "palm."

In the evening, he impressed his parents by shouting the *inglés* he had learned. "Easy on that camera!" and "Put that with the rest!"

"*Por dios, Alejandro!*" his pious mother exclaimed. She was beginning to worry about him. He was home only to sleep. Already he did not want to go to the cathedral because, he said, the Americans did not go and were much richer than the Mexicans.

He was supposed to lay the money he had earned on the table every evening, as Antonio did, but Alejandro could always conceal most of it in his pockets, because his father was not clever. He could buy all the ice-cream sodas and chocolates he wanted. He could buy factory-made shirts in the marketplace. Never did he buy anything for his parents, like Antonio. Wasn't it enough that what his father took from him enabled them to have coffee and fresh meat all the time? Without him, they would still be eating nothing but tortillas and frijoles that his father got in exchange for his wooden saddles and his mother's serapes. The cleverest Mexicans, he told his parents, were not farmers of corn or makers of wooden saddles, but guides, silver shop owners and hotel owners, people who did things for the Americans. Therefore his parents were stupid. So was Antonio, who worked like a burro carrying suitcases but did not earn half what he did just by smiling. He taunted Antonio for his stupidity, in English that Antonio could not understand, and in the older boy arose a jealousy that became hatred.

It was true that the town subsisted on money that came from the tourists. The village whored after money. Some of the natives had much money, some hardly any, but all paid the high prices for basic needs which the extravagance of the tourists had brought about. The tourists took the best houses and the best food because they had the money to pay for them, while the natives whose great-great-grandparents had been born here lived on what was left. It was ironic that this had happened to their village simply because the village happened to be so pretty. Beneath a superficial cheerfulness, hatred against the tourists ran like an underground stream that rose in the eyes of bent old men sometimes, and in the faces of small children who had not yet learned to hide it. Most American tourists moved too fast to detect it, but some Americans who had made the village their home detected it and then began to see it everywhere, even in the eyes of the stray dogs in the plaza and behind the smile of the hotel managers who spoke English perfectly. They could never escape it, except by drinking.

Alejandro learned English almost as easily as Spanish and in time the languages were side by side in his mind. He listened for new English words and earned extra centavos if he asked the Americans what a certain word meant. He learned the value of dissembling friendship, of remembering names. If he smiled, waved a hand and called, "Hello, there, Mr. So-and-So!" to a tourist he had got money from before, he would be tossed more money. By tagging after a group of tourists, babbling English, he would be invited sometimes as a kind of court jester to one of the hotel dining rooms to share a meal his parents could not imagine even after he described it.

One day when he was about seven, his offer to help a lady was accepted, and he had to carry a small bag up the longest hill to a hotel. He took his two-peso tip sullenly, and when he had walked back down the hill, he was resolved to become a *guia,* a guide. All the guides did was walk around and talk. So he went past the buses to the main plaza, where under the tall plane trees before the cathedral the guides made up their parties.

"Can I show you the town, ladies and sirs?" he asked with the same winning smile he had used at the bus stop.

He competed with boys much older than he, more capable of supporting the plump, middle-aged women who turned their ankles going down the steep cobblestones, but generally the women would say something to their men with the word "cute" in it; and he would be beckoned to. In the plaza also was his brother Antonio, who at fourteen had just graduated from porter to guide in the town's curriculum. Antonio with his indifferent English and his square, serious face. Alejandro laughed at him and took his customers from under his nose. Antonio had memorized the whole guidebook and did not know how to pronounce the words right, and besides, what American on a holiday wanted such a sad lecture? Antonio and he were real rivals now and seldom spoke to each other. It was hard to believe they were brothers, solemn Antonio and the happy-eyed little Alejandro.

Alejandro had trailed the guides often enough to know the things they pointed at and what they said, such as, "This cathedral costed ten billions of pesos," but he varied the ordinary tour. With the gestures of an experienced host, his small figure led groups of ten and twelve from Silver Shop to A Picturesque Street, to Silver Shop (the guides made commissions on the purchases), to the Cathedral, to A Beautiful View, a tour neither too short nor too long, that ended happily at one of the two high-class bars in the plaza, where a drink made with two jiggers of tequila and mentioned in every guidebook was served. Alejandro became the most popular guide of the village. His age and size were a novelty, his customers told their friends to ask for him, and there were always those tourists who came every year and had known him since he was four, who took pleasure in introducing him to their friends who were seeing the village for the first time.

He made from sixty to seventy pesos a day. The bulge of banknotes so delighted him, he got the habit of walking with one hand in his pocket to feel it, which emphasized his easy, jaunty poise. He bought brilliantine for his softly curling hair to make it shine with blue highlights. He bought trousers like the Americans wore, that sold for forty pesos in the market, kept them freshly washed and pressed and never forgot to close the zipper as many Mexican boys did, an omission he knew was remarked unfavorably by the American women. He struggled to read American magazines. He went to every American movie that came to the two picture houses in the town, and learned new words by comparing them with the Spanish written at the bottom of the screen. He cut and parted his hair after the fashion of American actors and dressed himself as nearly like them as he could.

The word "cute" he heard less often now than "good-looking." He was twelve years old. Already his face was lean and manly, with an astute expression that suggested more years than he had. His body was a lithe five feet five inches and weighed one hundred and fifteen pounds, in American measurements. Of all the young men of the village, he was the most handsome, and he noticed the effect of this on women. It was the furtive embraces of the American women as they caught at him slipping down the lanes, their hasty, shy pecks on his cheeks and lips after their second tequilas that awakened his desires. All the guides were familiar with this nervous lovemaking of the American women and laughed at it. Often they boasted to their comrades, as they pointed out this or that pretty American girl, that it had been she with whom they spent the night, half jokingly, half as if they expected to be believed.

So did Alejandro boast, though he had seduced only one girl and she was a Mexican, Concha, the prettiest *muchacha* in the village. He had been eleven and she thirteen. But this was nothing. One little peck from an American woman, no matter how old or ugly she was, counted more, because she was American. And really, Mexican girls had never attracted him. He liked American girls with blond hair, like those he saw in the movies, and sometimes getting off the buses or driving into the village in their cars. He longed to seduce one. This desire began to be stronger even than his passion for money.

His first American girl was a well-developed blue-eyed young lady of fifteen with blond hair that curled at the ends and hung partway down her back. It was the blond hair that fascinated him, the blank staring blue eyes that encouraged him. Her name was Mary Jane Howell, and she was with her mother. He took them and some other tourists around the village, then was invited to lunch at a hotel by Mrs. Howell, to whom he had been especially courteous. After lunch, Mrs. Howell wanted to go shopping, but Mary Jane said she would stay behind. Having directed Mrs. Howell to a silver shop, Alejandro returned to the hotel just as Mary Jane was stepping from behind a potted palm in the lobby with her eyes even wider, even more fixed.

He gave her his most charming smile, copied from a certain American actor, on the left side of his face with his eyes narrowed to crescents of long black lashes. "I show you that map I told you upstairs, yes? There is much breeze down here, no?"

"Yes!" she said.

He could have spoken better English, but he knew when to use an accent. He followed her into the room, and almost before he could close the door, Mary Jane had locked her arms around his neck and planted a moist warm kiss on his lips.

Hardly half an hour later, he was downstairs, walking automatically, though buoyantly, toward the plaza. His tongue leapt in his mouth to tell of his conquest, and in the next quarter hour he told it four times, in increasing detail, to as many guides and plaza loiterers as would listen. They believed him now, because he believed himself. The realization of his triumph was stronger in the plaza than it had been in Mary Jane's room. A blond American girl! Later, when Mary Jane and her mother walked about the village, they were followed by the eyes of almost the entire male population.

Thereafter came many American girls. There were a few rebuffs, but Alejandro could take success and failure with the same pleasant bow and smile—which often turned matters his way after all. He came to be known as the "bad boy" of the village, and enjoyed a worse reputation than he deserved. His walk was haughty, its tense grace suggestive of a well-cared-for tomcat, and he was always walking, roving the town. He held his narrow head high. Merely the glance of his dark eyes was half the conquest of the women he wanted.

At fifteen, he received two or three letters a week from American girls, schoolteachers, married women, beginning, "Dearest Boy," "Darling," "My Spanish Angel," ending with dirges of their boring existences in the States and a wish that the joys they had known might sometime, somewhere be relived. These letters he read conspicuously, sitting on the benches in the plaza where the plane trees dappled them with rich shadow and glaring sunspots. He put them in his hip pocket with the American stamp showing at the top, and strolled off in quest of more girls. Some of the letters he answered in careful English, most were not worth the trouble. He had found a new ambition. He wanted to marry an

American woman, a wealthy one, and live like the prince he was for the rest of his life. There were many marriages between Mexican boys and American women in the village. One of their homes was the most palatial house he had ever seen. But he was still young, and it was difficult for a Mexican boy to marry an American woman before he was seventeen. He must act older, concentrate on the wealthiest and freest of the American women and charm them out of their senses.

For six months he charmed a score of American women out of their senses, but none seemed to want marriage. American women expected casual romances as part of the village's entertainment. They enjoyed the jealousy of the American men, their nervous anger or their badly pretended boredom, when they made engagements with young Mexicans. The women seemed to play a game just for the pleasure of reconciliation with their men at the end of their stay. Alejandro took his disappointments with a smile and a shrug. American women were not all so elusive. The woman for him would come.

One day, a woman like none Alejandro had seen before strolled into the plaza on the arm of a well-dressed gentleman with red hair. Was she American? Alejandro examined her from head to toe. She held herself as proudly as he did. She carried a long cigarette holder and wore high-heeled green lizard pumps in which she seemed to glide rather than walk over the cobbles that turned other women's ankles even when they wore straw sandals. She looked bored, and it seemed to be the man's idea that they see the town, though it was she who selected him as their guide. She did not look at the things he pointed to, but kept her gray-green eyes on him in a sleepy, thoughtful way that gave Alejandro an odd feeling. She was not attractive and yet she was. At any rate, and the thought gave him his bearings again, there was no doubt she had much money. Earrings of hammered gold circles hung below the lacquered upswept black hair. The pale green tweed skirt had been made for her and the gray silk blouse, too, and perhaps also the green lizard belt that matched her shoes.

She did not want to enter the cantina with the others at the end of the tour. She stopped just outside the door, looking at Alejandro, who hung there, too, as if she were the only member of his party.

"What is your name?" she asked him in a voice like a distant pipe organ and with a smile that revealed interesting teeth, one partially of gold.

"Alejandro Palma, at your service." He could not look back at her face after his bow. Never had he felt like this, and he did not know if it was shyness, attraction, or dislike.

"Alejandro," she repeated, rolling the *r* as easily as he. The gray-green eyes, half shaded by crinkly lids, blinked at him affectionately. "Well, perhaps I see you tomorrow again, Alejandro. Today I was too tired to enjoy your village."

"My pleasure." Alejandro bowed.

Her escort offered his arm with an absentminded resignation, and Alejandro watched her move off in a slinking gait that set one foot in a line with the other. Then he dispatched for fifty centavos a small boy to ascertain at what hotel she was staying, her name and that of the man. The boy reported back that she was a Countess.

The next morning, she was in the plaza before nine o'clock, before Alejandro had begun to make up his first party. She wore flat iguana sandals now that made her feet look even longer and narrower. She said she wanted a drink, so they went to Cesar's Cantina, a tequila-soaked niche in the wall of one of the lanes off the plaza, since the better cantinas were not yet open. In Cesar's, the fleas were so thick one could see them hopping here and there on the red-tile floor in search of a human leg. Two dirty Mexicans slouched over the low bar.

In an open-collared white shirt and white linen trousers, Alejandro sat erectly at a little table with the Countess. He spoke English loudly and distinctly, proud to be seen by Cesar and the two Mexicans with the elegant woman who also spoke English, used a holder for her Russian cigarettes, and was in every respect beyond the iron tradition that forbade women to enter such a cantina. To her questions, Alejandro replied that he was eighteen, though he was only sixteen, and said that he had been educated at the Academia Inglesa in Mexico City.

She lifted the tiny tequila glass in her bony hand, drank it off without salt or lime, and looked at him calmly. "You are very handsome. You appear a little Spanish. Is it so?"

"My father and mother—they were pure Castilian," Alejandro said, lowering his eyes sensitively. One of Cesar's fighting cocks, combless and limping like an old man, was entering the cantina pecking at the floor.

The Countess smiled and blinked her eyes at him, and though it was a tender smile, he felt she knew he lied. "Me, I am nothing. Because I am everything. Do you understand?" She smiled again. "Like you."

He did not understand, and he did. "What about your friend?"

"Robert?" She laughed and waved a hand that drifted back to the silver cigarette case that had initials on it and a crest. "Robert told me yesterday a good-bye forever."

Again Alejandro could not look at her, could not say any of the things it was now time for him to say.

"No, do not walk back with me, Alejandro." With a bored air, she had got up. "Visit me tonight at ten if you care to. You know my name already, don't you? Countess Lomolkov—Paula."

Alejandro was there at ten. He had been unable to work all day for anxiety. In the disorderly room where her possessions obliterated the Mexican decor, the Countess made bewildering love to him, wooed and won him and covered him with heavy, tender kisses, insulted him by laughing at his lovemaking, though she made Alejandro laugh, too. She told him his language of love was more broken than his English. She made him frantic to please her. All he desired was that she let him see her again.

"Of course. Tomorrow we are going to Acapulco." She lay on her back, blowing the smoke of her Russian cigarette toward the ceiling. "Already I have telephoned reservations in an hotel."

In the morning, he packed some of his best shirts and slacks into a valise he had just bought.

"Where are you going?" asked his mother, who was putting on a pot of beans in the outdoor kitchen.

"*Quien sabe?*" he answered sourly, then began to smile as he walked down the hill. His mother would think he was merely going to Mexico City again, and this might be the last time he would see his home! He did not look back. The world spread bigger and bigger before him. The Countess filled it all.

He drove the Countess's shiny black Jaguar out of the village and turned its chromium radiator cap on the road to Acapulco. The Countess was quiet and thoughtful, and kept her eyes on the road even when she took swallows out of the long thin bottle of tequila añeja she had bought "to celebrate."

Alejandro had never felt so happy and so carefree. Though his time had always been his own, his days spent in the out-of-doors, he had always been working to earn money. Now he did not think about money. He did not want money from the Countess. He did not want to marry her unless she wished it. He thought of his marriage to anyone as a fraud, and he did not want to cheat the Countess. Just how he felt, he could not say, because he did not know the meaning of the words *respect, affection,* or *love,* and they did not occur to him now.

In Acapulco they stayed at the favorite hotel of the season, where their suite and meals were three hundred and fifty pesos a day. The Countess bought him a bathing suit consisting of a strip of chartreuse material splotched with vermilion flowers. With this wrapped around his narrow hips he swam at Hornos Beach in the mornings and at Coleta in the afternoons, lolled with the Countess on the sand, while she, marking with her sunglasses her place in the book she never read for gazing at him, stroked the curls back from his forehead or dribbled the white sand down the brown hairless arch of his chest. Often, after tamarind highballs on the hotel terrace, they drove to Pie de la Cuesta, a promontory fifteen kilometers away. Here they lay in hammocks strung only a few feet from the waves' edge, sipped coconuts through straws, and watched the sun drop into the water like a world on fire. They dined at all the hotels for variety, and had whole banquets sent up to their rooms. Generally, they retired early, because the Countess needed much sleep.

She told him of her childhood in Poland on her father's great estate where three hundred serfs tended vast wheat fields, of her narrow escape when Hitler came, of her life afterward in Paris and in New York. Alejandro did not believe a tenth of it, but he listened with the respect he would have demanded of a listener if he had told a comparable story of his life in Mexico. And this was what drew them together, their common habit of lying, their fellowship of falseness, their dependence on the timid man's fascination by the outrageous. Where had she got her money? She had none, she said. She lived on credit.

"When my credit will be gone, then I shall be gone also." And when Alejandro looked alarmed, "I could not live at all if I did not live in danger! Neither can you, Alejandro, even after you marry, you will see. Make a wise marriage, not a stupid one. Marry an ugly woman if you can, or if she is pretty be sure she is stupid, but they usually are. . . . You don't yet understand all, but you will."

She taught him as if she were a school of manners, morals, love, hypocrisy, and opportunism. He was her protégé, son, lover, and husband, because he would finally need to know how to be a husband, quite a different art from that of lover. She supervised the cutting of his hair, dramatizing the ripples in back and at his temples, balancing the curve of his head with an orderly clump that fell partially over his forehead. She imposed an English restraint in his dress, taught him a thousand little graces for different places and occasions, all without embarrassing him, even contriving to flatter him. And Alejandro learned with the ease and pleasure of one whose life is devoted to ease and pleasure and the pleasing of others. He burst into bloom. The Countess and the tropical sun caressed him. He caressed the whole world. Happiness! How could she make him so happy, he wondered, when a thousand times a day she criticized him, caught him in a lie, impressed some trivial matter on his mind like a schoolteacher? Yet he felt that his happiness was traced with every movement of his body like an invisible design in the air. Wasn't that why everyone gazed at him on the beaches? Even men, who always loathed him, took secret pleasure in watching him disport himself. His figure poised for a moment against the bright blue water as he sought the Countess, his flight up the beach to the older woman who was clearly not his mother and to whom he seemed so devoted began many conversations, he knew.

Two blond American women angled for him at the hotel, but Alejandro was not once tempted to be false to the Countess. He spent his evenings close by her side, usually in white linen slacks (the Countess liked him in white linen), a dark green or blue sport shirt with one of her silk handkerchiefs knotted at his throat, listening and talking to her as if she were the only woman in the world. People in the hotel could not figure them out, but how they loved to watch!

Alejandro never stopped to ask himself if he were in love with the Countess, and, probably because his emotions for sixteen years had been so false, he could not have given himself a truthful answer. He dropped postcards to his friends back in the village, telling of his extravagant, carefree life, of how voluptuous was *la condesa,* and of course of how many new conquests he had made. He wrote also to Concha, his first *amor* and now the betrothed of Antonio, and sent her a necklace of small gray seashells that he bought from a peddler for two pesos.

After six weeks, the Countess could find only the most minute faults in Alejandro. The sandpapering was over, she told him. The rest would be with emery dust. Now he learned how to make at least one incontrovertible statement on such subjects as abstract art, Negroes in America, communism in Latin America, and Wagnerian opera.

"I do not want you should anymore be a guide," the Countess said one day in the absent monotone that meant her thoughts were far ahead of her words. "You should be manager of a fine hotel in your village."

Alejandro said something evasive. He was much too busy being happy to think about working or about the future.

The Countess turned from the window in fury. "Do not be lazy! You have in you that stupid laziness of your stupid country, and if you cannot step it down we say good-bye forever this minute! . . . Yes, your country is full of stupid, lazy people! Like your parents—Yes, I know all about your parents, stupid boy! Like you would be without me! *Don't deny it!*" She shook him hard by the shoulders. "You will not grow up to be a lazy, fat bum, you will grow up to be zome—*zing*! Understand?"

Alejandro got up, bowed as she wished him to do, and murmured, "The woman I love can make the impossible possible."

"And this is not even the impossible, my sly one, you know that." The Countess smiled.

The next morning, she did not join him on the beach after her usual letter-writing period after breakfast. Alejandro went back to the hotel and was told she had checked out. Trembling, he opened the envelope the clerk handed him, conscious of the dramatic figure he made before the clerk and the two blond Americans standing nearby, of the tragedy in his young face, of the new blue banknotes he let flutter to his feet. A short letter with many interpolated terms of affection told him she had spoken with the manager of the hotel at which she had stopped in his village, and that it was all but certain he could become the receptionist there—second in importance only to the manager himself, she reminded him. The bill was paid at the Acapulco hotel for the next five days, and he was to enjoy himself and not think of her, forget her with someone else if he wanted to. "How strange I should have found in Mexico one so like myself! Bless you and thank you, my darling! But do not try to thank me except by to remember a few of the things I have told you. Never think you may see me again, never think I forget you. Your Paula. Countess Lomolkov." The last two words were underlined.

Alejandro was too lonely to stay on. Dimly, he realized he cared more for her than he had admitted, and he could not bear to face it, so he caught a bus back to the village. Once more, the world opened itself wide to him on the mountain road. He could face the world more easily than the loss of the Countess. He must turn his eyes outward, live dangerously, as she had said. Before nightfall, he had spoken to Señor Martinez, the manager of the hotel. Alejandro's bearing, his knowledge of English—even Señor Martinez did not know much English—got him the job. Señor Martinez, a shy, serious man eager for the Americanization of the hotel, had agreed with the Countess on the telephone that an English-speaking receptionist would be an advantage. Alejandro then was the likely young man she had promised to send. Alejandro's reputation would have proscribed him, but the manager's monastic habits had kept it from reaching his ears.

In the hotel, Alejandro wore either white or gray flannel with a red flower always in his buttonhole. It was his job to welcome guests, see that their rooms were satisfactory, that their breakfast orders were correctly filled before the trays left the kitchen, to invite lonely women guests out for cocktails occasionally, the bills to be paid by the hotel. He flew smoothly about the two-story patioed building, set a vase of bougainvilleas in a certain room, brought raw meat for the dog in another, replaced small light bulbs with larger ones, and gave every guest the impression that he or she was his favorite. There was never a complaint against Alejandro, and there were many tips, many commendations to Señor Martinez. When some of the *señor*'s friends remarked that Alejandro had reformed, the *señor* did not know what they meant.

Alejandro did not earn quite as much as he had as a guide, but his new position carried greater dignity, and dignity was important, the Countess had told him, to an American woman who considered marrying a Mexican. Since starting his job at the hotel, his ambition to marry a wealthy American woman had returned with new force. He was so much better equipped now. He longed to succeed.

Only the wealthiest women merited his invitations to cocktails. He made engagements with wealthy women staying at other hotels, too. All the bills were sent to Señor Martinez with notations that they were for such and such *señoras* or *señoritas* stopping at the hotel. Often he invited young ladies to the hotel to spend the evening in a room that happened to be free. This deception might have gone on indefinitely, if not for one indiscretion that would certainly have brought the severest tongue-lashing from the Countess.

Concha had married Antonio, who was now twenty-four and still not graduated from the guide class. Alejandro and Concha saw each other every Saturday night, when Antonio was busy taking tourists on a round of the bars until they closed at midnight. Antonio was now trying to teach Pancho, their fourteen-year-old cousin, how to be a guide, so he was quite occupied. Pancho tagged along with him everywhere, even on Saturday nights, and since he was as serious and stupid as Antonio, Alejandro knew he would turn out the same way as his brother—adequate as a guide, perhaps, but without a very interesting future.

Alejandro and Concha were fond of each other, but far from being in love. It was just that they enjoyed reliving the childhood *amor* they had known six years before. Concha liked to laugh, and Alejandro laughed so much more than Antonio. And it amused Alejandro to give horns to his brother.

It was Concha's birthday. Señor Martinez was in Mexico City overnight on business, and the bridal suite in the hotel happened to be free. Alejandro thought it would be fun to bring Concha there. Concha was delighted with the idea. She and Alejandro went to the hotel, telephoned down for rum and tostadas with sour cream, and pretended they were newlyweds. At eleven-thirty when they came downstairs, whom should they see behind the desk but Señor Martinez. Alejandro said, "*Buenas noches, señor,*" like a gentleman, escorted Concha home, but he knew it was the end. Señor Martinez knew that Concha was a married woman who lived in the village. Alejandro could have bribed the help, but not Señor Martinez, who would never forgive him. Alejandro was discharged that same night.

Alejandro was too optimistic to fear that Antonio would hear of the evening through Señor Martinez, but he spent over a thousand pesos bribing the staff. For a few days, Alejandro felt nervous and resentful. He was a little afraid of his brother, though when he watched him in the plaza from time to time, he could see no change in him. And when the idea occurred to him that Antonio might take action, he dismissed it as he dismissed his family—he had lived at the hotel since his return from Acapulco—because Antonio was essentially as stupid and ineffectual as his parents. Meanwhile, Alejandro had moved in with an emotionally starved American woman resident of the village, whose young Mexican husband had just abandoned her. He had often called on her before, and now she welcomed him for as long as he cared to stay.

Not long after his discharge from the hotel, on one of the afternoons he was idling about the village, too proud, still too well off to worry about earning more money so soon, he wandered into a bookshop off the plaza and saw Mrs. Kootz. Mrs. Chester Kootz came every summer to the village and stayed three or four months. Though she was a millionairess and a widow, Alejandro had never considered her because she was so ugly. She wore her hair in a gray bun that could hardly be seen under the strands that escaped it and that hung down like gray rags. Her dresses were uniformly gray, too, and so shapeless they might have been slept in. The joke was, she had been cited year after year as one of the ten wealthiest women of America, and that if she did not look it, then she must be all the wealthier for not spending money on adornment.

In a bitter mood, Alejandro flirted brazenly with Mrs. Kootz in the bookshop. Mrs. Kootz glanced at him, dragged on her cigarette, and chose a book. She had known Alejandro by sight since he had been a little centavo-beggar at the bus stop. Alejandro smiled cockily to himself and strolled out of the bookshop in the tracks of Mrs. Kootz's run-over oxfords. She started up the lane that led to the big house she always rented. But the way was so steep, Alejandro lazily turned back, slouched onto a bench in the shade of the plaza's trees, locked his fingers over his flat waist, and dozed for a while, lulled by the hum of Spanish voices around him, by the squeals of children at play.

The idea took form in the middle of a little dream: he was enjoying some delicious pleasure because he was married to Mrs. Kootz and had money. The dream fell away, but the idea remained. He would court Mrs.

Kootz and try to marry her. It made him snicker now to think about it. But would the Countess laugh? Alejandro quit the shade of the plane tree as Gautama had quit his Bodhi Tree, with a purpose.

At about six that evening, Alejandro glanced up at the balcony of a bar in the plaza and saw Mrs. Kootz at a table alone, drinking one of her brandies. Alejandro went up the stairs without even raking a comb through his hair or pulling his thumbs down the sides of his collar, his habit before going into action. He walked directly to her table, and asked if he might join her.

She drew on her cigarette, squinted up at him, then gestured to the opposite chair.

Alejandro changed his tactics from those of the afternoon. Now he was the gentleman the Countess would have advised him to be. He behaved as if the sleek Countess had been sitting opposite him instead of dowdy Mrs. Kootz. He asked if she was enjoying her stay, and she replied not particularly, that she came every year because of her asthma. She spoke briefly of her ailment and with an unfeminine frankness. She was interested in buying a house in the village but couldn't because she was not a citizen or a permanent resident. This gave an opening for the remark that if she married a Mexican, she could buy it in his name, but even he felt it so pointed he could not say it.

"Do you know the Countess Lomolkov?"

Mrs. Kootz shook her head. "Who's she?"

"A lady who was here in the spring. From New York, too. We spent a month together in Acapulco."

Mrs. Kootz said nothing.

Alejandro talked pleasantly for nearly an hour, but nothing of his charm seemed to penetrate. Mrs. Kootz only drank brandy after brandy, sipping from a glass of Carta Blanca as a chaser. Then she said something about the fleas in her leather chair eating her alive and that she wanted to go. He accompanied her to her house, lending her an arm over the rough spots. He lingered at her door, waiting to be asked in to dinner.

"Good night," she said, without glancing over her shoulder.

Alejandro turned away cheerfully, remembering the hundred-peso bill she had taken out to pay the check, one of many others in her big worn alligator wallet. He had insisted on paying the check, of course.

Appraisingly he looked at her dark green convertible parked in the alley, flecked with Mexican mud, but still showing its thirty-five-thousand-peso lines.

In the plaza he saw Antonio and Pancho. Antonio came toward him with one hand outstretched.

"Is from your mother," Antonio muttered in Spanish as he passed him at arm's length, as if he did not want to befoul himself with touching him. Even Pancho had barely greeted him with a nod.

Alejandro looked at what had been dropped into his hand. It was a rosary with a small silver cross he had seen before. He had not been home in over two months, and evidently his mother was concerned for his soul.

With a big bouquet of red frangipani, Alejandro called on Mrs. Kootz the next morning at eleven. A Mexican girl opened the gate, then went to see if Mrs. Kootz would admit him. Finally Mrs. Kootz herself came slowly down the flagstone walk, frowning against the sun and the smoke from her cigarette, wearing the same dress she had worn yesterday. Her forefinger was in the pages of Guizot's *History of France.*

"What's up?" she asked hoarsely.

"Good morning." He smiled, twiddling the bouquet. "I beg to see you a moment. Inside?"

She looked at him. "Come on in."

He followed her up the steps to the front hall and into a large sunny room with a tile floor and scatter rugs, with comfortable-looking corners that held books and reading lamps and Mexican leather easy chairs. Mrs. Kootz went toward one corner where a laden ashtray and an open bottle of brandy showed she had been sitting.

"Drink?" she asked, refilling her glass.

Alejandro shook his head. "These are for you." He advanced with the bouquet and bowed as he presented it.

She took the flowers as if she had not noticed them before. "Thanks," she said in a tone of surprise. "Juana?" When the girl appeared, she gave her the flowers and made gestures at a nearby vase. "Aq-wah."

The girl started to remove the tamarind pods from the vase she had indicated.

"No, not that one," Mrs. Kootz said impatiently. "Find an empty one."

The girl looked blank.

Alejandro rapped out a sentence or two in Spanish and Juana left the room promptly.

Mrs. Kootz stared after the girl, said "Damn," and tossed off the brandy. She put another cigarette in her mouth, but before Alejandro could get her a light, she had struck on her thumbnail one of the American wooden matches she always carried about her.

"Do you like Wagner?" Alejandro asked, fingering a biography of Wagner that lay on a table.

"Some. His art songs." She sat down heavily in her chair.

"He is too noisy for me," Alejandro said prissily.

Mrs. Kootz looked at him as she had looked at the flowers. "Say, what's your name?"

"Alejandro. Alejandro Palma, at your service." He bowed again, then seated himself gently on the arm of a divan. "Do you know why I came to see you, Mrs. Kootz?"

"Why?"

He stood up. An amused smile had forced itself to his lips and he lowered his head. "Because I am in love with you." He had decided the simple, direct approach was best. "I admire your mind, your . . ." But what could he say about her? The hag!

Mrs. Kootz got up, too, started to pour another brandy, then strolled out onto the side porch, the only move inspired by self-consciousness she could recall ever making.

Alejandro was beside her, insinuating his slight body into her arms. He kissed her before she could recover from her surprise to thrust him away, kissed her again.

A few yards below and in front of them, a girl named Hermalinda Herrera glanced up from her own roofless terrace, where she sat chewing gum and reading the latest issue of *Hoy,* and saw an unbelievable sight: the "bad boy" Alejandro kissing Señora Kootz *muy caliente* and the *señora* liking it, too! That afternoon, the whole village learned of it.

No one would have believed it, if Alejandro and the *señora* had not been seen together so often thereafter. Could they be thinking of getting married? Alejandro's Mexican girlfriends twitted him, and he told them frankly that he was going to marry the *señora* and for her millions of pesos. He told the guides in the plaza and his friends in Cesar's Cantina. Whether it got back to Mrs. Kootz before he clinched the marriage was no worry to him. It would sound like typical gossip, might even be good propaganda: he was having trouble convincing Mrs. Kootz that their getting married was at all possible, that someone could love her and want to make her his wife. Mrs. Kootz had somehow forgotten she was a human being, but he was teaching her to remember. But the bridge between the two languages did not seem likely to be crossed. Only the Mexicans seemed to talk, and Mrs. Kootz had no Mexican friends and only a nodding acquaintance with a few Americans.

They were married in a little chapel of the village with the traditional ceremony of two rings and thirteen pieces of silver money, symbolic of the union of their worldly estates. Antonio would not even look at Alejandro now when they met, and Concha only stole sidelong glances at him. All his Mexican friends were in awe of him, and he could make them comfortable with him only by getting them drunk.

Immediately, Señora Palma bought in the name of Alejandro Palma the house she had rented for so many years from Ysidro Barrera, a gift shop owner in the village. Interior decorators came from New York and Mexico City and argued with one another over the deployment of mountains of furniture and drapes Señora Palma had ordered, and when they at last went to work, each seemed bent on making his or her contribution as hideous as possible in order to blame the others. The house became a famous atrocity of the town, and Señora Palma allowed groups of gaping tourists to shuffle through it twice a day, conducted by guides who told them it was an example of the "luxuriant embellishment" of the Americans who had made the village their permanent home, which it was, and told them it was exquisite, which most of them believed. Señora Palma was flattered, as she had been flattered by Alejandro's attentions. She had grown less introverted, and for a while Gibbon, Toynbee, Guizot, and Prescott were forgotten in the planning of her house and the honeymoon trip she and Alejandro would make in the fall. After the house was running smoothly under the care of three maids who would be paid two hundred pesos each per month, she and Alejandro were going to drive in the green convertible to Mexico City, New Orleans, Charleston, New York, the American West, San Francisco, and home again, enjoying themselves where they found things to enjoy, spending money as they pleased. She had never known what pleasure it was to have money until Alejandro showed her how to spend it. She had never known what pleasure companionship was, or what it was to be loved. And she was proud of him: he was handsome, and his grooming inspired a kind of terror and reverence in her. Most of all, and with her self-analyzing temperament she realized it and admitted it, the novelty of him pleased her, the fact that he was a Mexican, that he was so young, that despite all the odds he had come so far with his ludicrous ambitions, his veneer of cosmopolitan gentleman. And his crumbs of information on the Negro problem, Wagnerian music, and Russian history! In another environment such determination might have made a Napoleon of him, or a Henry Ford. As a historian, she respected his intensity.

While preparations for the American tour went on, Alejandro indulged himself in sprees around the village. He bought drinks for whole cantinas, bought gifts of silver and leather for Mexican girlfriends and many new American girls. How much easier it was to get an American girl now that his tailor-made clothes proclaimed from across the plaza that he was rich! There was really no limit to the money he could spend now. He gazed with a dreamy smile at the five-figured numbers in the *señora*'s account books, at her stock reports, the Mexican bank account that was in his name as well as hers. And he owned the house, too, one of the biggest in the village. At seventeen!

The night before their departure for the honeymoon, Alejandro decided to visit Cesar's for a final tequila with his old cronies. He heard the jukebox from the cantina as he turned up the lane from the plaza. It played a gay ranchero song that he loved, and he sang with it:

> *Quien dijo miedo, muchachos?*
> *Si, para morir nacimo-o-os!*
> *Traigo mi cuarenta y cinco*
> *Con sus cuatro cargadores!*

He stood for a moment on the threshold of the cantina, smiling on everyone. Drunken shouts greeted him, many stood up and opened their arms, because even if he were not everyone's personal friend, he had money and would buy rounds of drinks. As the jukebox stopped, a mariachi in the corner began a fast rollicking song on his guitar.

Then Alejandro saw his brother Antonio sitting at one of the little tables. His was the only unfriendly face. Antonio was drunk, and Pancho was beside him, his solemn face frowning and worried. There was something so unfitting in Antonio's being here, something so frightening in Antonio's being drunk, that Alejandro hesitated to go in.

Then Pancho stood up and, with his hands in his pockets, still frowning, strolled forward, veered toward the jukebox just to the right of Alejandro, then furtively motioned for Alejandro to step back from the door. Alejandro stepped back into the alley.

"Go home!" Pancho whispered. "To the house of your parents! By way of the barranca!"

Alejandro smiled, but Pancho had turned away and was already strolling back to Antonio.

"Alejandro! Coming in?" someone yelled.

Still smiling, Alejandro waved a hand in a general good-bye, and walked back down the alley. Go home to the house of his parents, indeed, and by the back way? Not on the night before the great trip. He didn't care to get into a fight with Antonio, so he'd give up Cesar's tonight, but back to that mud hovel his parents lived in?

It happened at the foot of the steep lane that led to his big house. Two figures stepped out of the shadows only inches away from his shoulders, and simultaneously they struck at his back. The impact nearly pitched him forward on his face, and when he staggered upright again, he felt he was going to faint.

"*Ey!*" he called, but they had already disappeared, on the run.

Then the cobblestones came up and hit him in the face. He crawled around, trying to rise, murmuring for help, for someone, anyone. Then, after a long time, two men came and with loud voices lifted him up and asked him questions.

"To the house of my parents," Alejandro said in a voice as weak as a whisper. He waved a hand in a certain direction, and he spoke in Spanish. He was dying. No doubt of it. Dying, and there would be no more honeymoon, no more pesos to spend, no more American girls. As the men bore him away, he thought of Antonio sitting at the very table in Cesar's where he and *la contesa* . . .

His mother, who undressed him in the hut, found the wounds in his back. Then she called to her husband, who had been standing outside while she did the work of undressing and washing the body. When her husband opened the door, the music of an American dance tune came louder from the hotel on the hill. She pointed to the two tiny spots of blood on either side of Alejandro's spine. He had been killed by the daggers with square, notched blades that close up the flesh when they are withdrawn, so there is almost no bleeding. In between her sobs, the American dance music came. Finally, the man went to the window and closed the shutter against it, but still the music came.

A few minutes later, they heard a hesitant knock at the door. Alejandro's mother opened the door cautiously, a candle in her hand. She saw an American woman, a very ugly American woman of about fifty years.

"What do you wish?" she asked politely.

"Is Alejandro here?" the woman asked in heavily accented Spanish.

The mother hesitated. "He is here. Who are you, if I may ask you?"

She knew how to say it. She remembered it from the day of the wedding. "I am his wife," she said.

Then Alejandro's mother slowly raised her hands, the candle dropped, and she let out a wailing, insane scream that reached all the way to the village, and echoed and reechoed across the black hills.

THE HOLLOW ORACLE

The black mass of the house sprang out of the darkness, and he tripped on the wooden step. He knocked on the screen-door frame, seized the knob and wrenched it back and forth as though he must be let in before a pursuer overtook him. Like a murderer he held the powerful clawhammer straight down at his side, in a grip that made the hammer a part of his arm, welded in the ache of his muscles. He shook the door until the sound grew crazy in the silence, and he stopped, losing then the momentum that had carried him the two miles down the road, the murderer's momentum that had started twenty minutes before, like the beginning of the act itself. In the stillness there was time to hear his own gasping breath, to feel the eyes in the dark behind him. He pressed close to the house, making no sound.

The door pushed against him. He stepped back, his arm shooting up at an awkward angle, like a girl's arm about to throw a stone. But it was several seconds before he could distinguish her figure on the threshold, and her head was inches higher than his hand. His arm dropped slowly, indecisively.

Then the woman said, "Arthur? . . . It's you, Arthur! Come in!" Her voice was hollow in the house, coming from nowhere.

He hesitated, almost turned and fled, but now he feared the night through which he had just come even more than the house. He came in quickly, and in the movement lost her figure in the porch. The stale, yellowish smell of the house invaded him, lifeless, insidious, forcing upon his mind a thousand visits with her. He crouched, breathing shallowly, watching for the woman, who could see him well in the dark.

"I guess it's been all of three weeks since you've come to see me, Arthur."

He said nothing. It had been four months. Almost exactly four months. He cursed himself for remembering now. By now it should have been done! But how could he see her without some light? It would be horrible to miss with the hammer. And yet he wished it might be done without seeing her.

"Come into the kitchen and I'll fix some tea." She glided away from him, and he heard her long cotton skirt rustling faintly over the bare floor.

He came after her, avoiding by old knowledge the porch furniture. "Before the lamp is lit!" he swore. "Before I can really see her!" But he had sworn to the night air, swinging his hammer like Thor in the unresisting air, that he would strike her before she could recognize him, and he had failed. He felt like a diver who has looked too long at the water to make the leap.

The kitchen was large, and he did not find her until the lamp waxed suddenly and filled the place with golden light.

He saw it then. He stared long seconds at the distortion of her figure, stared with his myopic eyes wide in their dark sockets, his thin lips parted in an expression that was strange to his tense face. He watched her until he grew conscious of a kind of hypnosis over himself, a feeling of giddiness and exhaustion. He hid the hammer behind his trouser leg and backed against the sideboard.

Emma did not once look at him. She filled the kettle, struck a match to the gas burner. She moved gracefully, weightlessly, in spite of the bulk of her body. A few gray hairs, escaped from the mottle-brown comb, caught the lamplight like a halo about her smallish head. Her hands, for all their activity, made gentle, uncertain movements. But there was, even in the placing of the lid on the teakettle, an expression of a generous and indiscriminating love.

The man watching her grew afraid. It was the child he was afraid of, not of Emma. It had invested her with a reality that bewildered him and stupefied him. He began to feel that his inertia was willed by Emma, and by the subtle aroma of the house. To strengthen himself he whispered, "It is inevitable! . . . Inevitable!"

As though the words had reminded her he stood there, she turned to him and said, "You must have a great deal to tell me, Arthur, after three weeks."

The trite, courteous words embarrassed him. She was not herself, he thought. But what was herself? Her rapt attention when they read together? The fascination when he talked about the creations of his brain? The intent of his paintings that he could never put on canvas? He cleared his throat. "No, I . . ."

"About what you've been painting, and thinking and reading, about the walks in the woods, and the long nights walking," Emma went on. She stood now in the center of the kitchen, facing him, pale and calm. Her eyes, clear as a young girl's, played without direction about his face like blue mists.

"I haven't painted at all," he said. He noticed a kind of satisfaction in her, a childlike pride, and he wondered if she were waiting for him to mention the child. The thought disgusted him.

"It is not fit for you to create while the child is being created," Emma said.

A sickening thrill went through him.

She came straight toward him, and he slipped aside. She took down the white china cups and saucers from the cabinet over the sideboard. "The air is filled with creation," she remarked.

He recognized with sudden shame that the words were precisely his, that he had said them one night as they stood by the well in the garden. To what exultation had he given voice that night?

"I have told the people again and again that my child is God-given, and how few will believe," she continued, without passion, with only a conviction that flowed like a thin, buried stream in her. "So it has been since the days of Sarah."

He gripped the hammer, but his energy was from shame, wasting itself in the trembling of his fingers. Now he was far from striking her, so far that he did not think to ask himself why he delayed. Her voice like the wind, void and capricious, rose and fell, parroting the words, enchanting him. *Sarah . . . and the creation of the world . . . and the days of Sarah . . .*

Still she stood, holding the cups and saucers in her long hands

upturned before her. "You have always understood such things, Arthur.
. . . You can understand why it is my duty to speak God's word on the
streets."

He said nothing. He drew his upper lip between his teeth, seeking
among many remembered conversations the pieces that had built the
precarious structure of her belief.

"You yourself have told me that those of God's inspiration should
proclaim themselves. I shall tell every living soul unto my last breath and
they will believe finally."

"Oh, hush! Hush!" He stepped forward, but he could not have
brought himself to touch her. He glanced behind him at the window, but
the squares reflected only the scene in the kitchen, the man and the
woman with the golden lamp between them. He looked at it for several
seconds, wondering at the strange sensation he had of not participating
in the action in the room.

"They do believe," Emma continued quietly. "Some have come to
me and bowed down and said they believe . . . and the others . . . they
believe, too. That's why they want me to go away. . . . They would make
my child of mortal man. Their hearts are closed to the spirit and their
eyes bent down to the earth!"

His words! His words, all of them, come back to fill him with shame.
His lean face, sloping back from the finlike nose, thrust forward, parting
the mystic veils around her.

"They were here today. . . . What did they say?" And at the same
time, he was thinking, what did it matter what they said? Or what did it
matter if they knew, since he had come to kill her?

Emma turned her face to the ceiling, closed her eyes. "They said we
are mortal men, and we proclaim our blindness. We proclaim our need to
be saved."

"I mean Roy . . . Roy's men, Emma. The men from the courthouse.
What did they say?"

"The twelve men did come and they said we are humble men before
you and there is a beam in our eye!"

He seized her arm and a cup fell at their feet, breaking like an
eggshell. Emma started. "No! What did they say, Emma! What!" he whispered as desperately as though the answer would free him.

She frowned, looked down on the shards at her feet, confused at the disorder. "They said I must leave the town unless I tell who the man was," she sighed.

He took his hand away. Her words were so clear, he felt suddenly she had been pretending the rest. "But you know there was no man," he said, and the sentence was supplied from some part of his brain that wanted him to live and be saved.

"I said, 'Ask for him and no man will show himself, for there was none.'"

His shoulders relaxed. How sweet would it be to believe! To sit and talk and drink tea and to go home believing, and thinking happily as he walked home of all the multitude of things in the world that he loved and which gave him pleasure.

"They have asked," he whispered, "and you are right, there was no one."

"Oh, no." Emma smiled. "Yes, it is divine. It will be a divine child."

She turned her face toward him, waiting for more beautiful words from his lips, trusting him, and tasting joy in each syllable. But he could not open his mouth. He could think of no beautiful words. "What else did they say, Emma? Do you remember?"

She looked at him, with the suggestion of disappointment in the movement of the eyebrows that lay pale and fine below the handsome forehead. "They said people think it was the Negro Jim Crawford and they'd have to lynch him."

The weight of his guilt lifted suddenly. His head was light. The waters flowed away, into this new channel, where he saw them swirling, catching up another creature. He did not participate. The maelstrom had passed over him. "Lynch him! . . . Will they lynch him? When will they lynch him!"

Emma went into the dining room and set the dishes down on the table, arranging them. "They didn't say."

The flatness of her voice brought him back to his senses. They had told Emma they would lynch the Negro in order that she, in pity, might tell the truth. They didn't think the Negro guilty. Why should they suspect a man who was fifty years old? Who tended his farm by himself and went to church on Sundays? Emma did not realize what she was saying! She was repeating words!

She came back and turned off the gas, poured the water into the teapot, lifting the kettle with difficulty.

"Yes, they should lynch him," he said, confusedly, "and get it off their minds."

"It would be but one more sin to be redeemed," she replied. Then, as if the words first took meaning for her, she shook her head. "Oh, no, Arthur. . . . Oh, no, I don't understand you tonight. I'm sure I don't."

"I mean they will never understand such things as this. They must have blood revenge, and only then will they stop annoying you." And he felt he was two people, one talking about the other, because certainly the blood revenge would be himself.

"They are only children, clamoring for the answer." She took the potholder from the nail by the stove and set the white and gold teapot on it. She went into the dining room. "But they may well lynch him, in spite of all that I say to save him."

"How do you know?"

"Does God save the innocent from their pain? The sins must mount up against the guilty. . . ."

"Did Roy Patterson say they'd definitely lynch him?"

"Oh, no." Emma came back and hung up the potholder. "But Jim Crawford says it was you. He says he's seen you here so much at night."

The blood drained from him, downward to his feet and away, leaving him empty and floating to nowhere. "When—when did he say that?"

"Today. He was here today with the others." Emma got some tea buns from the larder and arranged them on a plate.

"But he only says that to save himself! Anyone can see that!"

"Yes," Emma replied. "That's why I think they will kill him."

"Who thinks it was I? Who!" He strode to her place at the table, where she sat calmly preparing her cup of tea, the gray head bent delicately, the hands busy.

"Come have your tea, Arthur, while it's hot."

"But who? . . . Who believes?"

She did not even look at him. "Arthur, I don't understand you tonight."

"How is it the Negro saw me come here?" he flung at her. "He spied on us! He spies on us!"

He laughed, but choked with fear. "Everybody knows I come here to see you," he whispered. "It's no secret, is it? And nobody but Jim Crawford says it was I. . . . Isn't it so?"

Emma was silent. Then, "Oh, I don't understand you, Arthur!"

He seized her by the shoulders, turned her toward him. "You understand. Say it! . . . You know it wasn't I! . . . Say it, Emma!"

"What wasn't you?"

He relaxed. He wanted to laugh again, wildly to fall into tears, to throttle her, to embrace her. He stood straight and tense. "It wasn't! It wasn't!" he screamed. "No, it wasn't." The hammer clattered to the floor.

Emma looked at him, uncomprehending.

The escape of the hammer from his hand sobered him all at once. Neither of them looked at it, lying on the floor at his feet. Emma had observed it. Her eyes were gentle. How delicate was the balance of her belief! he thought. He calmed himself deliberately. He must not touch those precariously balanced scales behind her eyes. . . . If the Negro were lynched, the town would stop its questionings, the alms of the town would still be given, the suspicions on himself would pass away. . . . Emma would have the child . . . but if the child were alive! How could Emma give birth to a live thing? . . . And suppose the strange processes in her mind one day reassembled the facts and she were to announce them in the church as she had announced her visitation from the angel of God!

The torment seized him once more and he wondered that he had felt those few seconds of freedom. "There is no solution but that the Negro child should die," he said. "I'll see that he does. I'll fix it."

But Emma wasn't listening. She broke a cinnamon bun in half, ate it slowly, dipping portions of it into her tea, turning her smooth, pale face slightly as she took her bites.

Strangely she grew more and more real. She was no longer something artificial, without past or future. The child was a promise of some tomorrow. She was no longer like one of his blank canvases, on which he would paint what he would. She was real. One day she would remember, and speak the truth.

She rose up. "I want to go into the garden. I want to go and talk." She went into the kitchen and turned, waiting for him.

The lamplight put a ring about her head. She was like an angel, transparent, without understanding of deception.

"There is no solution but that he must die!" he repeated.

Emma waited. "I don't understand you. I don't understand what troubles you."

"It wasn't I!" he cried, as if he must fight her accusation. "No one can think it was I when they know how I take care of her. Everyone knows I take care of her like a child! That I treat her better than any other man would. . . . Everyone knows what she means to me . . . alone in that house!" He came close to her, pleading to the hollow oracle. "They know how I feed her and talk to her just as though she could hear me, when any other man would have put her into an institution! Didn't they all say I should put her away or I'd go crazy? Don't they all say what a rare good man I am to keep her? Don't they, Emma?"

"Of course, that's so."

He laughed bitter, falsetto. "I guess Jim Crawford . . . I guess they'll all be surprised to know how we read Blake and Shelley and drink tea and look at paintings and talk about things no one else can understand! . . . I guess they'd be surprised to know that's all we do, wouldn't they, Emma, my darling?"

"Oh, yes . . . yes."

"Isn't it so they call me 'professor'?"

"That's so," Emma replied. And, bored with his tumultuous moods, she turned and continued on her way to the back door.

He followed her, heard the faint rustle of her long dress, the click of the door latch. When Emma went out, he stood on the threshold, listening to hear if anyone was waiting outside.

He stepped down after a moment, hurried after her, and whispered fearfully, "I must go, Emma. I'll be going now!" He was feeble and insignificant in the expanse of the night. But a voice inside him countered, *Where? Where?*

They passed through the grape arbor, whose white trellises showed occasionally through the leaves. Emma was somewhere near him, amorphous, escaping him. He longed for the security of the hammer in his hand. He turned quickly to go back for it, and then he was afraid to enter the house alone.

"It was here I heard the voice," Emma said, leaning back against the post that supported the well roof. "It said, so quietly I could hardly hear, that from this small village my child should cast a beam so fine and strong it would encircle the earth."

He remembered when he had said "from that small village . . ." and what had he said would encircle the earth?

"Wherever men's hearts are closed against one another, they should be opened to see all the workings of the earth and of themselves as a reflection of God's glory . . . all the music, poetry, painting, all creations would be delights doing honor to God. All powers of mind and spirit derived from God."

"Blake!" he whispered. "Blake you were remembering. We read that months ago!"

Emma was silent. He heard her make a little bewildered sound in her throat, could feel all her being reaching trustingly toward him, helplessly toward him, thought he could see only the milky glow of her face in the dark.

He was repulsed by the thought that, overcome as she was now by the hypnosis of her words, she might come to him, her hands groping about his face. He could not have borne it. . . .

"But it was the voice I heard," she declared.

He had stood several seconds near motionless from the anxiety of the darkness. Now he began to regain confidence. "Since the child's conception was a miracle, it is fitting that his birth should be also," he remarked calmly, in the preacherlike tone he knew she loved. She bent forward as though drinking from a spring. His brain worked with clarity, with a detachment that shamed him. He remembered one evening when he had spoken of a crazy whirling picture in his brain which he was going to paint. It would be called *The Creation of the World.* Emma had followed him about the room, savoring the abstractness of his words, and he had retreated, babbling on and on and retreating until he was in a corner, and then he had told her to go back to her chair, and she had gone. And when he said to her, "Come here," she had come. He had sent her back and forth many times, until the game had frightened him and made him ashamed.

He reached his hand out to her. "Come," he said, "tell me about the miracle."

She came around the curve of the well. "Oh, he will be brought forth only with the sweet pain of a revelation, spreading happiness beyond all measure."

"And if he were to appear in his time from the well, like a spirit emerging from the center of God's creation, then his coming would be miracle enough. He could command all the people who would wonder at his birth. . . . Isn't it so, Emma?"

"Yes!" She reached out for his hands. "*That* would be a miracle!"

"Yes." He did not realize how icy his hands were until he felt her warmth. "Destroy yourself, for your presence will make only confusion." He drew her nearer to the well rim, nearer to himself. "Otherwise the people's minds will be divided, for you are mortal. . . . Is it not a fitting thing the child should come forth of his own?"

There was a sharp crack from the road, as of a tree breaking.

He recoiled to the other side of the well. "What was that?" he whispered.

Emma had not taken her eyes from him. She leaned toward him, held to the well stones, and took a step toward him.

"Emma, don't look at me! What was that on the road?"

She turned her head in the direction he pointed, but she was not seeing, not listening for anything but the magic words.

The gate swung in the soil. Steps came slowly, grinding on the ground.

Arthur could hardly breathe. The miracle, the scales, the fantastic theater he had played in, were dispelled. He could not find himself. He was in limbo, and in his mind now was the paralyzing quiet. His brain was seized in the prison of his own evilness. . . . Polluter! destroyer! And no goodness ever! He drew his fingertips along the stones till he felt them bleed. The steps came closer—cautious, flaring eyes somewhere in the darkness.

Emma heard the crack of his head in the column of the well, the impact of his body meeting the water. The air in the well shimmered like the water and settled into silence.

Dumbly Emma stood without stirring, dumb to the Negro's voice which said something to her as from an enormous distance. The thread that had guided her through the labyrinth of her world had been severed. She relaxed suddenly, broke into a wild scream that died like the wail of an animal lost in the woods.

She stumbled toward the house. "Oh, God!" she cried. "Look down on us! Oh, God, save us!"

THE GREAT CARDHOUSE

Lucien Montlehuc started a little when he saw the notice. He read it twice, slowly, and then, as if he finally believed it, put down his newspaper and removed his monocle. A habitual expression of amusement returned to his face, and his lids fluttered over his bright blue eyes. "Imagine Gaston Potin taken in by it!" he said to himself. "Of all people to be fooled!"

This thought made him even more gleeful. It would not be the first time that he had proven Gaston Potin wrong. This particular Giotto was a forgery, and Gaston was putting it up for sale as a genuine. Lucien meant to have it, and the sale was that very afternoon. How fortunate he had been to see the notice in time! The magnificent counterfeit might have slipped through his fingers again.

Lucien put his monocle back in the grip of his slightly protruding brow, summoned François and ordered him to pack their bags for an overnight stay in Aix-en-Provence. While he waited, he turned to *The Revelation to the Shepherds* in his book of Giotto reproductions and studied it. Again he thought how odd it was that poor Gaston Potin would not have suspected it to be a forgery. Perhaps it was the too-rigid faces of the kneeling shepherds that told him the painting was not from Giotto's hand. There was no real religious feeling there. The annunciatory angel's robe was a too-brilliant pink. The composition itself was not right, not Giotto—but it *was* magnificent, as a forgery. Lucien did not need a magnifying glass to detect a forgery. Something within him, some inner sensory apparatus, betrayed the spurious instantly and always. It never failed.

Besides, hadn't an Englishman, Sir Ronald Dunsenny, questioned the authenticity of this *Revelation* around the time of the Fruehlingen purchase? Indeed, Sir Ronald had ventured that the original had been destroyed in a fire in the middle of the eighteenth century! Evidently Gaston Potin didn't know that.

It was Lucien's passion to collect the most perfect imitations, and only the imitations, of the great artists. He did not want genuine paintings. And he prided himself that his sham masterpieces were such fine shams that any could, if presented as the original, fool the eyes of the most astute dealers and critics in the world.

Lucien had played many such tricks during the fifteen years he had been collecting forgeries. He might submit one of his forgeries as a loan from an individual who owned the original, for instance, then attend the exhibition and remark his suspicions publicly, to be proven right in the end, of course. Twice he had subjected Gaston Potin—with his great reputation as an art dealer—to such embarrassment. And once, Lucien had made Gaston uneasy about an original by presenting one of his forgeries that was so good it had taken six experts three days to decide which picture *was* the original. All in all, it had caused Gaston Potin to refer scathingly to Lucien's well-known collection and to his lamentable taste for the bogus. Lamentable to whom? Lucien wondered. And why? His pranks had cost him a few friendships, perhaps, but then he cared as little for friendship as he cared for the true Leonardos, the true Renis, the true anything: friendship and bona fide masterpieces were too natural, too easy, too boring. Not that he actually disliked people, and people liked Lucien well enough, but if friendship threatened, Lucien withdrew.

His six-million-franc Delahaye sped along the Route Napoleon from Paris toward Aix at a hundred kilometers an hour. Plane trees in full leaf, their smooth bark peeling in purplish, pink, and beige patches, flickered by at the edges of the road like picket fences. A landscape of dusky orange and green and tan, the occasional blue of a farmer's cart—a landscape as beautifully composed as a Gobelin tapestry—unfolded continuously on right and left, but Lucien had no eye for it. Nature's creations did not interest him compared to man's, and his stocky body sat deep in the seat of the car. Today there was the Fruehlingen Giotto to think about, and he looked forward to the auction with the keen, single-minded anticipation of a hunter or a lover. Merely for Lucien Montlehuc to bid for a painting meant that the painting was, or most likely was, a counterfeit, and would in this case immediately throw suspicion upon Gaston, who was sponsoring the auction. Some of the audience at Aix might think he was trying to play another trick on Gaston, of course, by bidding. So much the better when the experts confirmed the falsity after the picture was his.

"Excellent snails," Lucien remarked with satisfaction, his pink cheeks glowing after his luncheon. He and François walked quickly to the car.

"Excellent, monsieur," François replied agreeably. His good humor reflected that of his master. François was tall and lean and congenitally lazy, though he never failed to carry out an order from Lucien. He had not forgotten that he had once been earmarked for execution by the Spanish government for being in possession of a false passport. Because François had been amused and cool about the whole thing, he had won Lucien's admiration, and Lucien had managed to buy his freedom. Since then François, actually a Russian who had escaped to Czechoslovakia with a price on his head, had lived in France, safe and content to be alive and in Lucien's employ.

Lucien himself had once lived in Czechoslovakia. In 1926, most European papers had carried an account of a very young Captain Lucas Minchovik, a soldier of fortune who had been severely wounded in a skirmish on the Yugoslav border. Years ago, in Czechoslovakia, people had sometimes asked him about the 1926 report, the young captain's heroism having made the story memorable, but Lucien had always disclaimed any knowledge of it. It had been another soldier of the same name, he said. Finally, he had changed his name and come to France.

In Aix, Lucien and François stopped first at the Hôtel des Étrangers to reserve a three-room suite, then drove on to the Musée de Tapisserie beside the Cathedral Saint-Sauveur. The auction was to be held in the open court of the *musée,* and was scheduled to begin in half an hour, but things in Aix were always late. Cars of all sizes and manufacture cluttered the narrow streets around the cathedral, and the courtyard was a bedlam of hurrying workmen and chattering agents and dealers and private buyers who had not yet begun to seat themselves.

"Do you see M. Potin?" Lucien asked François, who was a good deal taller than Lucien.

"No, monsieur."

An acquaintance of Lucien's, a dealer from Strasbourg, told him that M. Potin was giving a luncheon at his villa just outside the town, and that he had not yet arrived.

Lucien decided to pay Gaston Potin a visit. He was eager to let Gaston know of his interest in the Giotto. As they drew up to Gaston's Villa Madeleine, Lucien heard the treble notes of a piano from within. Faint but bell-like, it was a Scarlatti sonata. He was shown into the hall by a servant. Through the open door of the salon, Lucien saw a slender woman seated at the piano, and a score of men and a few women standing or sitting motionless, listening to her. Lucien paused at the threshold, adjusted his monocle, and espied Gaston just behind the piano, concentrating on the music with an expression of rapt and sentimental enjoyment. Lucien's eyes swept the rest of the company. They were all here—Font-Martigue of the Dauberville Gallery in Paris, Fritz Heber of Vienna, Martin Palmer of London. Certainly the cream.

And they were all listening to the sonata—with the same absorption as Gaston. Lucien's appearance in the doorway had not even been noticed. The fast movement the woman was playing was splendid indeed. The notes sparkled from her fingers like drops of pure springwater. But to Lucien's ear, which was as infallible as his eye, an ingredient was missing—a pleasure in the performance. It was audible to Lucien that she detested Scarlatti, if not music itself. Lucien smiled. Could she really be holding the company as spellbound as it looked? But of course she was. How obtuse people were, even those who professed a knowledge of the arts! There was a perfect crash of applause from the little audience when she finished.

Lucien saw Gaston coming toward him with the pianist on his arm. Gaston smiled at Lucien as if the music had made him forget that there had ever been unpleasantnesses between them.

"Very happy and surprised to see you, Lucien!" Gaston said. "May I present the music teacher of my childhood—Mlle. Claire Duhamel of Aix."

"*Enchanté, mademoiselle,*" said Lucien. He observed with satisfaction the stir of interest his entry into the salon had caused.

"She plays superbly, doesn't she?" Gaston went on. "She has just been asked to give a series of concerts in Paris, but she has refused, *n'est-ce pas*, Mlle. Claire? Aix should not be deprived of your music for so long!"

Lucien smiled politely, then said, "I learned of your sale only this morning, Gaston. Why didn't you send me an announcement?"

"Because I was sure there is nothing here that would interest you. These are all authentic pictures of my own choosing."

"But *The Revelation to the Shepherds* interests me *enormously*!" Lucien told him with a smile. "I don't suppose if it's here you might let me see it now."

Behind Gaston's frank surprise, there was just the least alarm. "But with the greatest pleasure, Lucien. Follow me."

Mlle. Duhamel, who had been gazing at Lucien all the while, checked him with the question, "Are you an admirer of Giotto, too, M. Montlehuc?"

Lucien looked at her. She was a typical *vieille femme*—an old maid—of a Provençal town, drab and shy, yet with an air of tenacious purpose in her own narrow, cramped way of life, a look of wiry vigor that suggested a plant growing at the edge of a wind-whipped cliff. Gentle, sad gray eyes looked out of her small face with such depression of spirit that one wanted to turn away immediately, because of an inability to help her. A less attractive person Lucien could not have imagined. "Yes, mademoiselle," he said, and hurried after Gaston.

Lucien's first sight of the picture brought that leap of excitement and recognition that only the finest forgeries gave him. From the patina, he judged the picture to be more than two hundred years old. And today it would be his.

"You see?" Gaston smiled confidently.

Lucien sighed, in mock defeat. "I see. A beautiful piece indeed. My congratulations, Gaston."

Lucien attended the auction in the subdued manner of one who watches from the outside, a bystander. He waited with impatience while an indifferent Messina and a miserable "Ignoto Veneziano" from the Fruehlingen collection were put up and sold. Apart from the false Giotto, Lucien thought mischievously, the Barons von Fruehlingen did have execrable taste!

Mlle. Duhamel, on a bench against the side wall, was again staring at him, he noticed, with what thoughts behind her quiet gray eyes, he could not guess. Lucien found something disturbing, something arrogantly omniscient in her scrutiny. For an instant, he resented her fiercely and unreasonably. Lucien removed his monocle and passed his fingertips lightly across his lids. When he looked up again, the *Revelation* was on the dais.

A man whom Lucien could not see bid a million new francs.

"A million and a half," said Lucien calmly. He was in the last row.

Heads turned to look at him. There was a murmur as the crowd recognized Lucien Montlehuc.

"Two million!" cried the same unseen bidder.

"Two million ten thousand," replied Lucien, intending to provoke laughter, as he did, by the insultingly small raise. He heard the sibilant whisper of "Lucien" among the crowd. Someone laughed, a sardonic laugh that made a corner of Lucien's mouth go up in response. Lucien knew from the rising hum that people had begun to ask one another if the Giotto were indisputably genuine.

The unseen bidder stood up. It was Font-Martigue of Paris. His bald head turned its eagle profile for a moment to glance at Lucien coldly. "Three million."

Lucien also stood up. "Three million five hundred."

"Three million seven," replied Font-Martigue, more to Lucien than to the auctioneer.

Lucien raised it to three million eight hundred and Font-Martigue to four million.

"And a hundred thousand," added Lucien.

At this rate, the figure might be driven beyond the price of a genuine Giotto, but Lucien did not care. The joke on Gaston would be worth it. And the audience was wavering already. Only Font-Martigue was bidding. Everyone knew that Gaston Potin had been wrong a few times, but Lucien never.

"Four million two hundred thousand," said Font-Martigue.

"Four million three," said Lucien.

The audience tittered. Lucien wished he could see Gaston at this moment, but he couldn't. Gaston was doubtless in the front row with his back to Lucien. A pity. It was no longer a contest of bidding. It had become a contest of faith versus nonfaith, of believer versus nonbeliever. Fifteen meters away on the dais the *Revelation* stood like a reliquary in its golden-leaf frame, a reliquary of the divine fire of art—as each of them saw it.

"Four million four," said Font-Martigue in a tone of finality.

"Four million five," Lucien promptly replied.

Font-Martigue folded his arms and sat down.

The auctioneer rapped. "Four million five hundred thousand new francs?"

Lucien smiled. Who could afford to outbid him when he wanted something?

"Four million six," said a voice on Lucien's left.

A man who looked like a young Charles de Gaulle leaned forward on his knees, focusing his attention on the auctioneer. Lucien knew the type, the de Gaulle type indeed, another believer, an idealist. He was in for five million francs at least.

Five minutes later, the auctioneer pronounced *The Revelation to the Shepherds* the property of Lucien Montlehuc for the sum of five million two hundred and fifty thousand new francs.

Lucien came forward immediately to write his check and to take possession.

"My congratulations, Lucien," Gaston Potin said. His forehead was damp with perspiration, but he managed a bewildered smile. "A genuine work of art at last. The only one in your collection, I'm sure."

"What is genuine?" Lucien asked. "Is art genuine? What is more sincere than imitation, Gaston?"

"Do you mean to say you think this painting is a forgery?"

"If it is not, I shall give it back to you. What would I want with it if it were genuine? You know, though, you should not have represented it as a genuine painting. It ran my price up."

Gaston's face was growing pink. "There are a dozen men here who could prove you wrong, Lucien."

"I invite them to prove me wrong," Lucien said courteously. "Seriously, Gaston, ask them to come to my suite at the Hôtel des Étrangers for aperitifs this afternoon. Let them bring their magnifying glasses and their history books. At six o'clock: May I expect you?"

"You *may*," said Gaston Potin.

Lucien walked out of the courtyard to his waiting car. François had already strapped the *Revelation* carefully between the seat back and the spare tire. Lucien happened to look behind him as he reached the car. He saw Mlle. Duhamel walking slowly from the doorway of the courtyard toward him, and he felt a throb in his chest, a strange premonition. Sunlight, broken into droplets by the trees, played like silent music over her moving figure, light and quick as her own fingers had played in Gaston's salon. He remembered his feeling, as he listened to her Scarlatti sonata, that she loathed playing it. And yet to play so brilliantly! That took a kind of genius, Lucien thought. He was aware suddenly of a great respect for Mlle. Duhamel, and of something else, something he could not identify, perhaps compassion. It pained him that anyone with Mlle. Duhamel's ability should take so little joy in it, that she should look so crushed, so agonizingly self-effacing.

"Do you know that I am receiving some friends at six o'clock this afternoon, Mlle. Duhamel?" Lucien said with an unwonted awkwardness as she came closer. "I should be honored if you would join us."

Mlle. Duhamel accepted with pleasure.

"Come a little early, if you will."

"Five million two hundred and fifty thousand francs for a counterfeit," Mlle. Duhamel whispered with awe. She sat on the edge of a chair in the salon of Lucien's suite, gazing at the picture Lucien had leaned against the divan.

Lucien strolled back and forth before her, smiling, smoking a Turkish cigarette. François had gone out a few moments before to fetch Cinzano and pâté and biscuits, and now they were alone. Mlle. Duhamel had been surprised, but not overly surprised, when he told her the Giotto was a forgery. Her reaction had been exactly right. And now she regarded the picture with the respect that was due it.

"One usually pays more dearly for the false than for the true, mademoiselle," Lucien said, feeling expansive in his hour of triumph. "This hair I touch, for instance," he said, patting the top of his light brown, gently waving hair, "is a toupee, the finest that Paris can make. Grown by nature, it would have cost nothing. Strictly speaking, it would have been worthless. It *is* worthless, to a man with hair of his own. But when I must buy it to hide a deficiency of nature, I must pay a hundred and fifty thousand francs for it. And it is a just price, when one thinks of the skill and labor that went into its creation." Lucien swept off his toupee and held it in his hand, lustrous side uppermost. His bald crown was a healthy pink-tan, like his face, and really detracted little from the liveliness of his appearance, which was extraordinary for his age. The bald head was a surprise, that was all.

"I had no idea you wore a toupee, M. Montlehuc."

Lucien eyed her sharply. He thought he saw amusement in her tilted head. She had one element of charm, he conceded: she had humor. "And applying this same principle to the false Giotto," Lucien continued, inspired by Mlle. Duhamel's attention, "we might say Giotto's genius was a thing of nature, too, a gift of the gods, perhaps, but certainly a faculty which cost him nothing, and in a sense cost him no effort, since he created as every artist creates, out of necessity. But consider the poor mortal who created this almost perfect imitation. Think of his travail in reproducing every stroke of the master exactly! Consider *his* effort!"

Mlle. Duhamel was absorbing every word. "Yes," she said.

"You understand then why I value the imitators so highly, or rather give them their proper value?"

"I understand," she answered.

Lucien felt perhaps she did. "And you, Mlle. Duhamel, may I say that is why I find you so valuable? You have a superb talent for deceiving. Your performance of Scarlatti this afternoon was by no means inferior to the best—technically. It was inferior in only one respect." He hesitated, wondering if he dared go on.

"Yes?" Mlle. Duhamel prompted, a little fearfully.

"Your hated it, didn't you?"

She looked down at her slim, tense hands in her lap, hands that were still as smooth and flexible as a young girl's. "Yes. Yes, I hated it. I hate music. It's——" She stopped. Her eyes had grown shiny with tears, but she held her head up and the tears did not drop.

Lucien smiled nervously. He was not good at comforting people, but he wanted to comfort Mlle. Duhamel and did not know how to begin. "What a silly thing to cry about!" he burst out. "Such a talent! You play exquisitely! Why, if you could endure the boredom—and I really admire you for not being able to endure it—you might play in concerts all over the world! I daresay not a music critic in a thousand would recognize your real feelings. And what would he do if he did? Make some trifling comment that's all. But your playing would enchant millions and millions of people. Just as my forgeries could enchant millions and millions of people." He laughed and, before he realized what he did, put out his hand and pressed her thin shoulder affectionately.

She shuddered under his touch and relaxed in her chair. She seemed to shrink until she was nothing but that small, unhappy core of herself. "You are the only one who has ever known," she said. "It was my father who made me study music as a child and as a young girl, study and study until I had no time to do anything else—even to make a friend. My father was organist of the church here in Aix. He wanted me to be a concert pianist, but I knew I never could be, because I hated music too much. And finally—I was thirty-eight when my father died—it was too late to think of marriage. So I stayed on in the village, earning my living in the only way I could, by teaching music. And how ashamed I am! To pretend to love what I hate! To teach others to love what I hate—the piano!"

Her voice trailed off on "piano" like a plaintive sob itself.

"You fooled Gaston," Lucien reminded her, smiling. An excitement, a joy of life was rising in him. He could not stand still. He wanted—he did not know exactly what he wanted to do, except to convince Mlle. Duhamel that she was wrong to feel ashamed, wrong to torture herself inwardly. "Don't you see it isn't at all logical," he began, "to take seriously something you were never serious about in the first place?—Look, mademoiselle!" With a graceful movement, Lucien removed his right hand. He held the detached and perfectly natural-looking right hand in his left. His right arm ended in an empty white cuff.

Mlle. Duhamel gasped.

"You never suspected that, did you?" asked Lucien, grinning like a schoolboy who has brought off a practical joke with success.

"No." Obviously, Mlle. Duhamel hadn't suspected that.

"You see, it's exactly the mate of the left, and by certain movements which have now become automatic, I can give the impression that my useless hand cooperates with the other." Lucien replaced his hand quickly.

"Why, it's like a miracle!" Mlle. Duhamel said.

"A miracle of modern plastics, that's all. And my right foot, I might add, too." Lucien pulled up his trouser leg a few inches, though there was nothing to be seen but a normal-looking black shoe and sock. "I was wounded once, literally blown apart, but should I have crept about the world like a crab, disgusting everyone, an object of horror and pity? Life is to be enjoyed, is it not? Life is to give and take pleasure, is it not? You give pleasure, Mlle. Duhamel. It remains only for you to take it!" Lucien gave a great laugh that was so truly out of his heart, that rolled so solidly from his broad chest, Mlle. Duhamel began to smile, too.

Then she laughed. At first, her laugh was no more than a feeble crack, like the opening of a door that had been closed for an incalculable length of time. But the laugh grew, seemed to reach out in all directions, like a separate being taking form, taking courage.

"And my ear!" Lucien went on with delight. "It wasn't necessary to have two ears to hear what I heard in your music, mademoiselle. An excellent match, is it not, of my left ear? But not too perfect, because ears are never exactly alike." He could not remove his grafted right ear, but he pinched it and winked at her. "And my right eye—I will spare you that, but suffice it to say that it's made of glass. People often speak of my 'magic monocle' when they mention my uncanny judgments. I wear the monocle as a joke, by way of adding an insult to an injury, as the English would say. Can you tell the difference between my eyes, Mlle. Duhamel?" Lucien bent forward and looked into her gray eyes that were beginning to glow behind the tears.

"Indeed, I cannot," she told him.

Lucien beamed with satisfaction. "Did I say my foot? My entire *leg* is of hollow plastic!" Lucien struck his thigh with a pencil he picked up from the table, and it gave a hollow report. "But does it stop me from dancing? And did anyone ever suggest that I limp? I don't limp. Shall I go on?" His affirmative clap of laughter came again.

Mlle. Duhamel looked at him, fascinated. "I've never——"

"Needless to say, my teeth!" Lucien interrupted her. "I had scarcely three whole teeth left after my injury. I was a young man then. But that doesn't matter, I saved my employer's life, and he rewarded me with a trust fund that enables me to spend my life in luxury. Anyway, my teeth are the product of an artist in deception, a Japanese whose ingenuity and powers of depiction certainly rank him with the great Leonardo. His name is Tao Mishugawa, but few on earth will ever hear of him. My teeth are full of faults, of course, like real ones. Every so often, just to deceive myself, I go to Tao and have some more fillings or an inlay put in. Tell me, mademoiselle, did you suspect?"

"I certainly did not," she assured him sincerely.

"If I could remove every artificial part of myself including the silver shin of my other leg and my plastic ribs, there wouldn't be much left of me, would there? Except the spirit. There would be *that* even more than now, I think! Does it seem strange to you that I speak of the spirit, Mlle. Duhamel?"

"Not at all. Of course it doesn't."

"I knew it wouldn't. There was no need to ask. You, too, are among the great in spirit, who respond to challenge and make nature appear niggardly. Your hours of tortured practice at the piano are not lost, mademoiselle. Not because of these words I say to you, but because you gave pleasure to a score of people this afternoon. Because you are able to give pleasure!"

Mlle. Duhamel looked down at her hands again, but now there was a flush of her own pleasure in her cheeks.

"The critics and the art dealers call me a dilettante, the idiots! That I am an artist escapes them, of course. Let it! They are the real dilettanti, the do-nothings. You understand me because you are like me, Mlle. Duhamel, but all those who sneer, who stare, who laugh at me and envy and admire me at once because I am not ashamed to confess what I love—— And here they are now!"

Someone had rapped on the door.

Lucien glanced at his watch. François was having trouble finding the right kind of pâté, perhaps. Lucien did not like to answer his door himself.

Mlle. Duhamel stood up. "May I open the door for your guests?"

Lucien stared at her. She looked taller than before, and almost—he could hardly believe it—happy. The glow he had seen in her gray eyes seemed to have spread through her entire body. Lucien, too, felt a happiness he had never known before. Perhaps the kind of happiness an artist feels after creating something, he thought, an artist whose talent is given by nature.

"I should be honored," Lucien said.

Gaston had come, and with him four other dealers, one of whom carried a picture which Lucien recognized as Giotto's *Magi in Bethlehem* from a private collection. Lucien greeted them hospitably. Then more people arrived, and finally François with the refreshments. The man with the picture set it next to Lucien's against the divan, and all got out their magnifying glasses.

"I assure you, you possess an original," Gaston said cheerfully to Lucien. "Not that you didn't pay a fitting price for it." All of Gaston's confidence had returned.

Lucien gestured with his false hand at the group beside the divan. "The experts have not said so yet, have they? Let their magnifying glasses discover what I can see with my naked eyes." He strolled off toward Mlle. Duhamel and M. Palissy, who were talking in a corner of the room. How charming she looked, Lucien thought. A half hour ago, she would have been afraid to use her beautiful hands to gesture as she spoke.

Gaston intercepted Lucien before he reached Mlle. Duhamel. "You agree that this picture is genuine, Lucien?" he said, pointing to the picture the dealer had brought.

"Certainly," said Lucien, "That *Magi*—a careless piece of work, I've always thought, but certainly genuine."

"Examine the brushstrokes, Lucien. Compare them with the brushstrokes on your picture. It's so obvious, a child could see it. There is a fault in the brush that he used to paint the backgrounds of both pictures, a couple of bristles that made a scratch here and there. Evidently these pictures were painted at about the same time. It's the general opinion that they were, you know." Gaston stooped down beside the pictures. "One doesn't even need a magnifying glass to see it. But I had some photographs made and enlarged, just to be sure. Here they are, Lucien."

Lucien ignored the photographs on the divan. He could see it, with his good eye; a hair-line scratch here and there with an even finer scratch beside it, the scratches of a single brushstroke, made by the same brush. It was the same in both pictures, like a pattern, obvious enough when one looked for it, yet not obvious enough to be worthy of forging. Lucien's head grew swimmy. For an instant, he felt only a keen discomfort. He was aware that the eyes of everyone in the room were upon him as he bent over the two pictures. Most painfully of all, he was aware of Mlle. Duhamel. He felt he had failed her. He had been proven fallible.

"Now you see," said Gaston calmly, without malice, merely as if he were pointing out something that Lucien might have seen from the first.

Lucien felt as if a house of cards were tumbling down inside him, all that was himself, in fact. He could see now, looking at the picture he had believed to be false, that a misconception—a quick, initial misconception—was possible. Just as it would have been equally possible to judge the picture correctly, as he did now, and to sense that it was genuine. But he had made the misjudgment.

Lucien turned to the room. "I admit my error," he said, his tongue as dry as ashes.

He had expected laughter, but there was only a murmur, a kind of sigh in the room. He would rather they had laughed at him. No, at least there was one exchange of smiles, one nod of satisfaction from Font-Martigue that Lucien Montlehuc could be wrong. Lucien would have felt quite lost if he had not seen it. Yet no one seemed to realize the catastrophe that was taking place inside him. The great cardhouse was still falling. For the first time in his life, he felt near tears. He had a vision of himself without his artifices, without his arrogant faith in his infallibility—a piece of a man, unable even to stand upright, a miserable fragment. For a few moments, Lucien's spirit bore the full weight of reality, and almost broke beneath it.

"If you'd like to sell it back, of course, Lucien," Gaston's voice said kindly, distantly, whispering into the false ear, "I'll pay you the same price—"

"No. No, thank you, Gaston." Now he was being unreasonable to boot! What did he want with a genuine painting? Lucien stumbled toward Mlle. Duhamel. He stumbled on his artificial leg.

Mlle. Duhamel's face was as calm as if nothing had happened. "Why don't you tell them you were pretending?" she asked him, out of hearing of the others. "Why don't you pretend the whole afternoon was a great joke?"

Her face was even victorious, Lucien thought. He looked at it for a long moment, trying to draw strength from it, and failing. "But I wasn't joking," he said.

Then the guests were gone. Only he and Mlle. Duhamel remained. And the genuine Giotto. François, who had witnessed his master's defeat, standing in the background like a silent tragic chorus, had excused himself last of all and gone out.

Lucien sat down heavily on the divan.

"I shall keep the painting," Lucien said slowly, and with quiet, profound bitterness. He did not recognize his own voice, though he recognized that it was his real voice. It was the voice of the fragment of a man. "It will be the one original that will spoil the purity of my forgeries. Nothing in life is pure. Nothing is one thing and nothing more. Nothing is absolute. When I was a young man, I believed no bullet would ever touch me. And then one day I was struck by a grenade. I thought I could never misjudge a painting. And today a public misjudgment!"

"But didn't you know that nothing is absolute? Why, even my kitten knows that much!"

Lucien glanced at Mlle. Duhamel with the fiercest impatience. He had scarcely been aware of her the past few moments. Now he resented her presence as much as he had when she had spoken to him first in Gaston's salon.

She was standing by the little three-legged console table where lay her green string gloves and her big square pocketbook that was as flat as her own body. She looked at him anxiously, as if she were puzzled for a moment as to what to do. Then she came toward him, sat down beside him on the divan, and took his hand in hers. It happened to be his false hand, but she betrayed no surprise, if she felt any. She held his hand affectionately, as if it were real.

Lucien started to take his hand away, but only sighed instead. What did it matter? But then, with the touch he could not feel, he realized another misjudgment, a much older one. He had thought he could never feel close to any human being, never allow himself to be close. But now he did feel close to Mlle. Duhamel. He felt closer to her than François, the only other person who knew of the great cardhouse that was Lucien Montlehuc. François had not suffered as Mlle. Duhamel had suffered, the idiot. It was a tenderness he felt for Mlle. Duhamel, and admiration. She lived within a cardhouse, too. Yet, if nothing was absolute, a cardhouse was not absolute, either. He might rebuild it, but it would never be perfect, and had never been perfect. How stupid he had been! He who had always prided himself that he knew the imperfections of everything, even art. Lucien looked down in wonder at his and Mlle. Duhamel's clasped hands. It had been so many years since he had had a friend.

His heart began to thump like a lover's. How pleasant it would be, Lucien thought suddenly, to have Mlle. Duhamel in his home, to have her play for him and his guests, to give her luxuries that she had never been able to afford. Lucien smiled, for the thought had only flitted across his mind like the shadow of a bird across the grass. Marriage, indeed! Hadn't he just realized that nothing was ever perfect? Why should he try to better what couldn't be bettered—the happiness he felt with Mlle. Duhamel at this instant?

"Mlle. Duhamel, would you consider being my friend?" Lucien asked, more seriously, he realized abashedly, than most men ask women to be their wives. "Would you consider friendship with a man who is sincere only at the core of his ambiguous heart and in the way he wishes to be a friend to you? A man whose very right hand is false?"

Mlle. Duhamel murmured adoringly, "I was just thinking that I held a hero's hand."

Lucien sat up a little. The words had taken him completely by surprise. "A hero's hand," he said sarcastically, but not without contentment.

THE CAR

"I had Carlos wash the car today," Nicky said as he sat down at the table.

"I saw it. It looks beautiful." Covertly, she removed a bewildered ant from the tablecloth. "It was sweet of you to remember."

"Oh, you'll find I have a very good memory."

They smiled at each other, a little shyly, and with the intent concern of newlyweds. Actually, they had been married a year, but they thought of these last two weeks as their real honeymoon. In the last year, their marriage had been a matter of his flying up to San Francisco on rare weekends to see her, and of her going down to Mexico for the summer to see him. But now Florence had given up her teaching job and had come to live with him in San Vicente.

"It's nice I can see the car from the porch," Florence remarked, as she did almost every evening.

She gazed below her, half across the town, at the parking lot behind the Hotel Estrella del Sud. The Estrella del Sud, the best hotel in town, was where she had been staying when she met Nicky a year and a half ago on her summer vacation. The farthest car of the three in the lot, the big aquamarine Pontiac, was hers. It was the first car she had ever owned. She had bought it with her own money, saved over a period of years. The car was more than a year old, but still looked brand-new, because she was meticulous about its weekly washing and she had never gotten a scratch on it.

"I wish you could drive it, too, Nicky."

"Oh, I don't mind. I'll enjoy it enough." He could not drive because of his weak eyes.

"Have more soup, Nicky."

"No, thanks, I couldn't. It's awfully good, though."

She went into the kitchen and came back with a platter on which sat a well-browned roast surrounded by braised potatoes, carrots, and peas. She set it down modestly.

"Boy!" Nicky exclaimed, though he took little interest in food. "You're feeding me much too well, Florence."

"I got the roast yesterday in Mexico City. I wanted to surprise you."

"You certainly did." He began carving.

"The meat markets in this town are a sight, Nicky. They're so smelly, I can't even get through the door. I've decided once a week I'll drive to Mexico City for fresh butter and meat."

"The meat's not as bad as it looks, you know." He smiled at her as he sat down. "The natives look pretty healthy, don't they?"

Florence nodded agreeably. It was what he always said whenever she questioned the cleanliness of anything in Mexico. She gave a start, and under the table drew up one foot and pinched at her ankle. There was a flea inside her sock, but it was foolish to try to kill it by pinching, she knew, because only a pair of thumbnails were of any use. She could tell a flea easily from an ant now. Fleas moved in stealthy jerks, while ants went steadily in one direction, even if it was a wrong one. Compared to fleas, ants were innocent, friendly little creatures.

She helped Nicky to more and more food, despite his protestations, but otherwise they said little to each other. She listened to the tinkling music of the cantinas' jukeboxes that were starting up here and there with the fall of night. From the hill where they lived, they had a splendid view of pink-roofed houses spilling one atop the other down a hillside, of a small, bushy valley just below where pigs and chickens wandered, of the dark green treetops in front of the cathedral's yellow towers, and finally of the mountains that lay in no range but loomed up everywhere, around the full circle of the horizon. She felt very happy here with Nicky.

"Would you like some more tea?" she asked when they were starting on the chocolate layer cake she had baked. Nicky did not drink coffee except in the mornings, and she had adjusted her habits to suit his.

"I would if it's convenient."

While she was in the kitchen, Nicky stood up and strolled to the balustrade of the porch. He was a slightly built man of about forty, hardly taller than Florence, of Belgian birth and Swiss and German descent. Usually his face had an expression of impersonal amiability, an expression sometimes seen on the faces of people whose business it is to be pleasant to everyone. He was manager of the second-best hotel in the town.

He put his lean hands on the porch rail and tested its steadiness. He had built the porch himself the week before Florence arrived. The two-room house he had rented would have been nothing without the porch. They were saving all the money they could to buy a house on the other side of the cathedral. The new house cost twelve thousand pesos in down payment, but they had forty-five thousand now, counting the four thousand dollars Florence was going to draw from her bank in the States. Nicky wanted very much to own a house, because he felt that no one was anything in San Vicente unless one did. He was looking forward to spending the rest of his life in a comfortable house with a comfortable wife.

"Nicky, what's the matter with the water?" Florence called to him. "It won't run."

Nicky came into the little galley of a kitchen. A thin trickle of water wheezed into the dishpan Florence held.

"I've been waiting a long time. It's on full force."

"Couldn't be the drought already," Nicky said, half to himself. "I guess it is the drought starting, all right. It's early yet—but we'd feel it first up here on the hill."

After a few days, the water stopped running in the daytime, but came on mysteriously for a few minutes around ten in the evening. Hearing it belch through the taps they had left open, Nicky and Florence would hurry and fill all the buckets and pans in the house. A week later, there was no more water at any time, and they were forced to haul it, pairs of buckets by pairs of buckets, from the nearest fountain, which was at the foot of the hill. The distance down to the fountain was only a few hundred yards, but the climb back made the chore exhausting and even dangerous. The cobblestone lane was steep, and it was a common thing to see people slip and take bad falls.

Since Nicky had little time to wait in line at the public fountain and Florence was rather weakened by diarrhea, they hired a woman to work half days for them. It was an extra expense, but under the circumstances a necessary one. Nicky knew they would have no water until June when the rains came, and this was only the middle of March.

In saddle oxfords and socks, a blouse and tweed skirt, Florence walked self-consciously past Pepe's Bar into the shade of the plaza's trees. She looked up at the open balcony of Pepe's, where the usual six o'clock crowd jammed the little tables. The balcony was bright with sports clothes, and through the brassy din of the four-piece Mexican band, she could catch American phrases.

"Oh, Freddie, you *didn't*!"

"I did! Lord knows what was in it, but I ate it!"

A shriek of laughter that could only be American laughter.

She longed to be up there with them, and yet she wondered if she would be happy even then. Nicky had taken her up to the balcony one evening, but he hadn't known anyone. "Oh, these are mostly new tourists," he had said. And all of them had been so much better dressed than they that Florence had felt subdued and uncomfortable. Besides, she didn't like to drink, not even beer.

She bought some peanuts in a newspaper cornucopia for fifty centavos, and took them to a bench. She broke the shells slowly, eating the nuts one at a time, watching the balcony with the wistful expression of a child who is there and yet not there, listening at the same time for the car that would come up the narrow street at the corner of the plaza. Nicky had taken the car yesterday with his friend Mr. Sigismundo to drive to Mexico City, as they both had business to do for the hotel. It was the first night she had spent alone in Mexico, and now she was eager for Nicky's return. The peanuts were nearly gone when she heard the familiar motor, and the change to first gear for the climb to the plaza's level.

"Nicky!" She stepped into the road and waved as the car crept toward her. Here was one thing she needn't feel ashamed of before the people on the balcony. Not many of them had a car as beautiful as hers.

"Hi, Florence!"

Florence started to open the door on Nicky's side, when she saw that the backseat was full of Mexicans. They were not Mexicans like Mr. Sigismundo, but Mexicans in sombreros and dirty shirts, four or five of them.

"It's all right. Get in." Nicky made room for her in front.

Then one of the Mexicans opened a rear door, and there was a squawk of chickens. One by one they got out, two with chickens' legs in each hand, one with a tiny white goat in his arms, and with bowing and tipping of hats they bade their adieus to Nicky and Alfredo.

"*Adíos, señor! Muchas gracias!*"

"*Por nada! Adíos!—Adíos, señor!*" Nicky smiled and nodded to each in turn.

"Who are they?" Florence asked.

"Oh, we picked them up this side of Puebla," Nicky replied. "How've you been?"

"All right." Florence twisted around, and inspected the back of the car. There was a swipe of mud on the edge of the seat, marks of dusty feet on the floor, a blob from a chicken. "Nicky, why'd you let them bring a *goat* in here?"

Nicky gave the backseat a glance. "Oh, I'll clean that, Florence."

"Did they mess it?" Alfredo Sigismundo asked. He pulled into the parking lot and stopped.

"Not much," Nicky said. "*Buena noche,* Carlos!" he called to the care-taker.

Florence didn't trust herself to speak until Alfredo left them. Then she said, "Nicky, promise me you'll never pick up people like that in my car again."

Nicky smiled. "Why, Florence, they were stuck on the road with a broken cart axle. You couldn't just pass them by."

Florence sat tensely in the leather chair, her Spanish lesson book open on her lap, watching Maria, the cleaning woman, moving about on the porch. In a minute, Florence thought, Maria would come to the threshold and jabber something about going home, and at that instant something inside her was going to burst in a million pieces.

The woman moved more and more slowly, idly readjusted a plate, whisked an ant off the tablecloth, because everything was ready and had been for nearly an hour. But Nicky had not arrived. Florence knew he was in one of the cantinas, drinking beer, talking on and on with Mr. Sigismundo and a lot of other Mexicans. It was the fifth time he had been very late. The third time, she remembered, she had gone down to get him, but it had been an embarrassing experience. Women were not supposed to set foot in the ordinary cantinas, so she had stood in the street in front of the open door until Mr. Sigismundo had seen her and poked Nicky. Then she had moved into the shadow by the wall and waited until Nicky had come out. Nicky was never really drunk but he could get tipsy enough not to realize or care that he kept her waiting. What annoyed her most was that when he came home on such evenings, he would invite Maria and her dirty little daughter, if they were around, to have dinner with them. Imagine! Mexican help eating their good food at their own table!

She watched Maria seat herself on the porch rail and run her fingers through her long, loose hair. Florence would gladly have dismissed her for the day, but she was not sure of the Spanish, and besides, the woman's presence in the house somehow paralyzed her. Florence hated her. She had haggled forty-five pesos out of Nicky for half-time work, when fifty a month was standard for full-time, she ate their food behind their backs and moreover was lazy and deliberately neglectful of the main thing she had been hired for—to see that there were always three or four buckets of water in the house. And when Florence could get Nicky to speak to her, she would say she hadn't been able to understand a thing that the *señora* told her to do. Just let a servant behave like that in the States and see what would happen!

Florence's face took on a childlike expression of affront as she gazed at Maria. Her face was round, good-natured, and naive. When she was pleased, it broke out in a small, upcurving, wooden-angel smile, and when she was surprised or hurt, these emotions were recorded, not promptly but accurately, in her face and even in her body. Now there was hardly a trace of lipstick on her thin, soft lips, and the powder she had put on an hour before had vanished. Her nose shone as it generally did with a kind of dead whiteness between splotched pink and white cheeks. She had gained weight from lack of exercise (in California she had played a lot of tennis), and there had grown about her an air of no longer caring, of having been defeated, as anyone might have been, by privation and primitive living. She looked older than thirty-one, and even by San Vicente's informal standards she was dowdy.

She twisted around to see the clock, but it was already too dark in the room. The chair creaked loudly as she moved. It was a sprawling, uncomfortable chair that Nicky had inherited from the hotel where he worked. Florence suspected they had got rid of it because it was full of fleas. The back and seat were made of one piece of leather, and though shaped invitingly, it was hard as a rock to sit on. A month ago, she had torn her last pair of silk stockings from the States on the rough edge of the leather. On that day, too, she remembered, she had waited for Nicky to come home to dinner, an especially good dinner, and he had not come until nearly midnight. She swallowed, as though to thrust back the memory of the miserable evening lest she start weeping and the woman see her. The woman was coming.

"All right, all right!" Florence interrupted.

The torrent of shrill, complaining words stopped abruptly.

Then, because her voice had been harsh, Florence said very courteously, with a smile and gestures toward the door, "*Sta beeyen, señora, sta mooey beeyen.*"

With a final shrug and an amused little smile that Florence knew was at her bad accent, the woman ambled off.

She felt better as soon as the woman was gone. The house was all hers again. She no longer wanted to fling herself across the bed and weep, and she almost decided not to scold Nicky. She really hated arguments, and she had held her tongue many times so Nicky might not think he had married a nagger. She slanted her Spanish book toward the light and stared at a declension chart of irregular verbs.

"Concha!—*Concha!*"

It was Maria, calling her daughter in the street. Tomorrow she would tell Nicky she had stayed long overtime, and Nicky would pay her extra, though he would tell Florence that he hadn't. She had once thought Nicky economical, even a little stingy, but these two months had changed her mind. He spent at least seventy pesos a week on beer alone, and as far as she could see let himself be cheated by every tradesman in town.

The cathedral chimes struck, and she got up restlessly. She stood on one foot, debating whether to turn the light on, scratching flea bites on her calf with the laces of her shoe. She listened for Nicky's step, but all she heard were the street sounds that came with startling clarity from just behind the wall, the clatter of a burro's tiny hooves, Mexican men's voices drifting past in pairs and the slap of their sandals on the stones, the whack and slide of the boards the children rode like sleds down the hill, making the cobbles as slick as glass.

The lane beside the house was another thing wrong! It was not only the noisiest, busiest lane in town, but the steepest. She fell on it about twice a week, fell on her face or sat down hard, always amid giggles of children. In the dark, it was risking life and limb to use it unless one went backward on all fours. After dusk, she felt imprisoned in the house. Why they didn't put steps in, she couldn't see. There was enough picturesque about San Vicente without having lanes that broke people's necks.

Every direction her thoughts took led to the same impasses of dis-comfort. Nicky did not seem to realize how hard it was for her, how lonely it was without her friends, how much more confining it was in a Latin country for a woman than for a man. She had thought he would have a few American friends in the town, but all his friends seemed to be Mexicans. The time he had taken her to the Barreras' had been awful. They had tried to be nice, but neither the husband nor the wife had known any English, and she had sat through the whole evening not understanding a word, keeping a pleasant expression on her face until she felt like a ninny.

She walked slowly through the foyer and onto the porch. The light from the Estrella del Sud's dining room fell on the parking lot behind it. She stared at her car and felt better, though the tears rose in her eyes until the twinkles of the rear bumper looked like stars with long points. Often when she was lonely or depressed, she would look at her car for long moments, while all sorts of things ran in her mind, thoughts of home, the voices of her mother and her brother and sisters saying things she had heard them say and had not known she remembered. She would think of the places she had been to in the car last summer with her sister Clara. Yellowstone Park and the geysers. The Black Hills of South Dakota. The roadstands where they had stopped for hamburgers and Cokes. Good American hamburgers, served in clean paper napkins fastened with a toothpick. . . .

There was a thump on the door, followed by three facetious little raps, and she wiped her eyes and mechanically pushed her hair into place before she went to the door and opened it.

"Hello. I forgot my keys," Nicky said, smiling as he came in. His small blue eyes blinked affably, but the lids were pink and swollen as they always were after he had been drinking. "Sorry I'm late."

"Oh, that's all right," Florence replied in an expressionless voice, for at the last minute she had not been able to decide whether to be angry, cool, or to overlook.

Nicky, assured that she was not vexed with him, opened the door again. "Come on in."

Alfredo Sigismundo's aristocratic figure descended the two steps into the foyer. Florence smelt the thin, medicinal aroma of tequila as he bent low over her hand and deposited a moist kiss.

"Ha! Ha!" Nicky laughed, as though both he and Alfredo considered this Latin courtesy a great joke. "You don't mind if Alfredo joins us for dinner, do you, Florence?"

"Why, no."

Alfredo passed a finger over his small black mustache. "Just a moment," his voice vibrated richly, "till I wash my hands." He took two careful strides on tiptoe before his hand went out to support him on a doorjamb. One starched white cuff glowed in the half darkness.

"Oh, there isn't any water in there, Mr. Sigismundo," Florence said, finding her tongue suddenly. She fumbled for the light string in the kitchen, and remembered with sudden pain that the toilet had not been flushed since that morning. "Nicky!" Florence called. She found the light string. Only one bucket of the six held water. The woman had not brought *any* that day. Florence felt ready to cry. "Here, Nicky!" she whispered, thrusting the full bucket into his hands. "Go flush the toilet!"

"Oh, he understands how things are with the drought on," Nicky said with elaborate reassurance.

"Go flush it! Hurry!"

"All right," he whispered back, and went.

Florence, her breath held in shame, walked onto the porch. Then, reminded by the sight of the table, she quickly laid another place and brought a chair from the kitchen. She lighted fires under all the pots, started to put water on for tea, then remembered the water was in the bathroom.

"Don't we have any beer?" Nicky called with his head in the icebox. "Ah, here's some."

"Nicky!" She came and grasped his arm. "Don't let him use all that water. It's all we have for tea."

"Oh," Nicky said, and started off to the bathroom, where Alfredo was singing to himself in a soft baritone.

Florence seized a saucepan and with a hope that never died turned on the faucet. Nothing happened. Not even a wheeze.

"Here it is." Nicky presented her with the bucket in which less than two inches of water remained.

Florence said nothing. She was too near tears.

When Alfredo came back, Nicky said casually, "I thought I might take the car tomorrow, Florence. Alfredo wants to go to Mexico City, and I've got to go anyway to get somebody's typewriter repaired."

"Whose typewriter?" Florence asked vaguely.

"A fellow's who's staying at the hotel. He's a writer and he needs it right away."

"Won't you sit down, Mr. Sigismundo?" Florence gestured toward the table and ducked into the kitchen.

She brought the big china tureen to the table, and Alfredo dragged himself up from his chair. He bowed deeply, an unlighted American cigarette hanging from his lips.

"Oh, please don't get up," Florence said, flattered and laughing a little in spite of herself.

"All right, Florence?" Nicky asked.

"What?"

"If we take the car tomorrow."

"Oh." She looked from him to Mr. Sigismundo, who exhaled a long stream of smoke and stared tiredly into the distance before him. "Well—all right, Nicky. Of course."

Nicky leaned over and laid a hand on Alfredo's shoulder. "See?"

Florence smiled and nodded awkwardly to Mr. Sigismundo as she sat down, for once more he had stood up and bowed, though without looking at her. She had a frozen smile on her lips and it would remain as long as Mr. Sigismundo was in her house. She felt his eyes fixed seriously on the soup as she ladled it into the bowls. She knew he would not say a word to her during the meal, that afterward he and Nicky would sit on the porch talking Spanish until the beer was gone, and then go down the hill to a cantina.

"I don't know what's happened to the car," Nicky said, his voice as calm as ever. "Probably nothing's happened to it at all. Alfredo's a very good driver, you know."

"But—two days ago, you said. Where was he going?"

"I don't know." Nicky removed his leather jacket slowly. "We were both taking a nap in our hotel room about three o'clock, and Alfredo woke me up and said he was going out to visit a friend near Chapultepec."

"Where's that?"

"Oh, that's right in Mexico City. You remember Chapultepec Castle. Where Maximilian and Carlotta lived."

"Didn't you *look* for the car?"

Nicky opened his hands gently. "There's not much use looking for it in a big city, Florence. I wouldn't worry. He'll probably come in with it today." He took his shaving articles out of his valise.

"Oh!" Florence gasped, on the edge of tears. "I just can't understand you, Nicky. I can't—Why you even lower yourself to associate with him, I can't understand!"

Nicky blinked at her. "These things just happen in Mexico," he said soothingly. "Don't forget you're dealing with a different kind of people from Americans."

"I don't forget it! How can I forget it, when you're getting just as shiftless as they are!"

Nicky trailed her onto the porch. She was looking down on the parking lot, at the gap where her car had stood. "You've no right to say that, Florence. I just meant—"

"Don't talk to me about rights. You had no right to ask for my car and give it to that lowlifer."

"Why, I wouldn't call Alfredo that."

"I would. He keeps mistresses. I've heard of his affairs right inside the hotel, and I've heard about his women in Mexico City, too. And now he's probably given my *car* to one of them!" She bent forward and ran with her hands over her face into the bedroom. She cried for several minutes on the bed. Then, when Nicky came out of the bathroom in a clean shirt, freshly shaven, his thin brown hair slicked down with water, she sat up and wiped the tears out of her eyes. "Would you like some breakfast?"

Nicky looked at his watch. "Lunch is more like it."

"Will scrambled eggs be all right? It'll be a long time before Maria comes with the groceries."

"That's fine, Florence." Nicky ran his thumb under the wrapper of his new *Time,* stretched out on the bed, and began to read.

"I was over to look at the house again," Nicky said when he came home that evening. "There's a fellow from Mexico City in the hotel who knows about plumbing, so we went over. He said it wouldn't cost more than six hundred pesos to make those repairs on the bathroom. That's about half what we'd figured, you know."

Florence gazed at him dully. Her face was shiny and tear-swollen.

Nicky talked on and on, oblivious of her expression. He was not clever in perceiving people's moods. In his business, he was used to sizing people up as easily pleased, irascible, or something in between, and he knew Florence belonged in the first category. If he noticed the despair on her face, he thought to himself, "Oh, she's worried about the car, but I've already told her it'll turn up." So he talked on, until one of her sniffles was so loud it interrupted him.

"I'll not buy that house with *my* good money!" she said so suddenly that he jumped.

He stood up in alarm.

"I don't want to live here! I don't want to own land here! You just want me to sink my hard-earned money in property so I'll be anchored here, that's all. You want the car to get stolen, too, so I can't leave. But I'll show you!" She flung the sentences at him defiantly but a little fearfully, as a child might at an unjust governor.

Nicky turned half-away, undecided. It was as if a gale had blown through him, ruffling his tranquil inner being. He did not for an instant believe her threats. It was only her vehemence that shocked him. He was angrier than he had ever been in his life as he lifted his jacket from the hook, put it on, and went out.

Florence spent the rest of the evening weeping and writing a letter to her mother.

April 24th

Dearest Mama,

 Something terrible has happened. Nicky borrowed my car to go to Mexico City with Mr. Sigismundo and Mr. Sigismundo has just kept it. This was three days ago. Nicky thinks he will bring the car back, but I don't. I think he has stolen it. I don't trust Mexicans one inch and for all his manners and education Mr. Sigismundo is still a Mexican.

 Added to all this, life still isn't very pleasant down here. The drought is still on and will be for six more weeks. They are building a dam in the mountains to ensure a water system (supply) all year, but it will be two more years before it is finished. I can't tell you how it is not to have water in the house. You have to go through it to know. Everything seems to be dirty all the time and finally you just accept it and live like a pig.

 Mama, I am tired tonight and can't say things very well, but I must tell you that I don't think I can stand it down here much longer. Nicky can because he is used to it, but I just can't. If I come home, it means leaving Nicky down here, because he won't come to the States to live. He thinks he cannot make the grade in American hotels and I can't even get him to try. I don't want you to think it is because Nicky and I are not getting along. He is very easy to get along with and is a fine husband. It is just the country I can't stand. I haven't even talked to Nicky yet about it, but I wanted to explain to you if I could. I'll write you soon when I decide something.

Ever your loving daughter,
Florence

P.S. *My love to Clara and Ben and the kids. Most of all to you.*

She put the letter in her top drawer under a stack of handkerchiefs, then fell into bed.

When she awoke, it was bright day. Sunshine fell through the single window onto the bed, onto the heap of dirty stockings, socks, and underwear that was collecting beside the bathroom door, onto her dry, dirty-nailed hands that she spread on the coverlet and looked at miserably. She had a headache and a bad taste in her mouth. She had not washed last night, because there was no water, and of course there was none now. She remembered last night, remembered her letter and her decision. Nicky had not come home. She supposed he had slept at the hotel. Tonight she would get things settled with him in a civilized way, and leave as soon as she could.

She drew on a bathrobe. She felt strangely relaxed and free already. Her feet padded across the tiles until her thighs struck the rail of the porch. Through old habit her eyes strayed to the parking lot.

There she saw—with an astonishment that shocked and thrilled her—her car in its usual place! She leaned far over the rail, not yet believing her eyes, but there was no mistake. It was a miracle that had happened in the night!

She got dressed as fast as she could, hurried without fear or mishap down the hill and up to the parking lot. She touched one of the shining fenders. She wanted to laugh and cry at the same time. Then she trotted up the ramp and entered the Estrella del Sud's lobby before she remembered that after last night's quarrel, she ought not to call Nicky. But she was so happy, she could not control herself. She had to tell someone, and there was no one but Nicky. She went into a booth and dialed the number of Nicky's hotel.

"*Está el Señor Spangli?*" she asked, even taking pleasure in her Spanish.

A spate of Spanish came back at her, then silence, and she assumed they were calling him.

Finally Nicky's voice said, "*Bueno?*"

"Nicky, the car's back! It's in the parking lot!"

"I know," Nicky said with a little laugh. "Alfredo got in early this morning."

"I'm so glad it's back!"

"Yes. So am I. He said he was delayed because one of his relatives died and he had to go to the funeral."

"Oh.—Are you feeling all right, Nicky?"

"I guess so. A little headache." He laughed again, apologetically. "I've got to go now, Florence. Someone's calling me."

She walked home rejoicing in her heart. Even as she climbed the hill, her thighs aching, her breath short, she felt she could endure the drought and make the best of things. How could she have thought of leaving Nicky! There never had been a divorce in her family, and it would have hurt her mother terribly if she had caused the first. The car was back! And she would never, never let Mr. Sigismundo use it again.

At the top of the hill, she remembered there was no water. She got two buckets from the house and went down the hill again.

The very next day, Florence fell down in the lane and bruised one knee severely. It gave her agonizing pain, and the doctor Nicky called in said she would have to spend two weeks or more in bed. The knee swelled to frightening size and turned black, purple, brown, and finally a mottled yellow. Nicky tried to comfort her by telling her that injuries always swelled in tropical countries and were not so bad as they seemed. Then during the second week in bed another accident befell her: something stung her over her left eye. She was sure it was the scorpion that lived in the crack in the wall just over the bed. The doctor corroborated her. It was a scorpion bite. The eye also swelled to great size and finally closed, except for a slit she could manage toward evening. The eye, too, went through a weird color cycle, but remained predominantly purple.

With the pain, her ugliness, and the inability to wash, the last ounce of morale left her. She suffered fever and anguish part of the day, and terrifying apathy the rest. At night she either could not sleep for pain or was too tired of bed to sleep. Nicky brought her bougainvilleas from the hotel garden, candy from the shop near the cathedral, but most of his evenings he spent in the cantinas. Florence did not blame him now. Lying there, thinking, she came to realize that there was not much else to do in San Vicente but drink, which was what almost everybody did. She tried to be thankful that Nicky drank only beer and not tequila. She had seen enough to know that in San Vicente drunkard husbands were crosses that many Mexican women and many American women had to bear.

She did not have the energy now to think of leaving. She lay in the state between sleeping and waking that is astir with fantastic dreams, and that finally makes a dream of reality. She believed herself nearer to death than ever before in her life. When she imagined she might die, she thought of leaving the car, her only legacy, and saw it battered and destroyed under Nicky's ownership. Then she would realize she was not dead yet, that the car was waiting for her, that someday she might get in it and go north. But most of the time she had no desire to do anything or go anywhere. She had not the energy to hold a mirror and comb her hair. Above all, she did not want to see her face.

It was on one of the nights in the second week of her illness that Nicky came in about midnight, his eyes pink with drinking. He announced that he and Alfredo and some friends had decided to go to Mexico City to see a bullfight the next day, and that they would need the car.

Florence had awakened from nightmarish half sleep, and she was propped on one elbow, watching dazedly with her good eye as he packed his valise.

"I know you don't like bullfights," he said. "We'll be back day after tomorrow without fail. Alfredo, prince of drivers, will drive us."

"No," she said, and her voice quavered foolishly.

Nicky straightened and looked at her. "Florence, don't get excited."

Florence had a vision of the cantina Nicky had just left, of Nicky treating the house to beers and tequilas and then expansively inviting everyone to go to Mexico City in the car he would provide. She saw the drunken, unshaven Mexican men greeting his proposal with drooling shouts. "Don't take the car."

"I swear to you we'll be careful," Nicky said patiently. He sat on the edge of her bed and stretched his hands toward her shoulders, but she twisted away and got out on the other side.

She slipped into her shoes and hobbled to the bureau where the keys were. Then she went to the closet and took a tweed coat off a hanger.

Nicky stood up slowly. "Really, Florence, you shouldn't be out of bed."

She did not waste energy in replying. She felt nauseous and weak, and she was afraid if she did not keep moving fast, she might faint. She got up the steps to the door, slammed it behind her and plunged recklessly down the hill.

She held her breath and let herself go, bending the tortured knee, taking fast little steps that kept her just ahead of gravity, feeling the same terror she had felt once when someone pushed her off a high diving board. The night was moonless and pitch-black, and her good eye, wildly stretched open, stared at her feet and saw absolutely nothing. She slipped, went down on one hand and pushed up again, hurling herself onward, because she felt that Nicky would come running down any second behind her. Suddenly she felt the road drop as though she had walked off the edge of something. She fell on her side and rolled over twice before her sprawling arms could stop her. She got to her feet, trembling. The ground was level now, and by the bus station's lamp she could see where she was, all the way at the foot of the hill, near the fountain that was growing clearer to her eye.

She ran for the parking lot. No one was about, and she felt she was enacting one of her dreams. She climbed into the front seat with her coat all bunched under her, zoomed the car back, and shot out the gate. She felt strong in the car. Its power was unlimited, far more than she needed. She heard Nicky calling her name out of the darkness of the hill. Passing the plaza, she had a glimpse of Mr. Sigismundo's tall figure rising from a bench under one of the lampposts. There was a woman on the bench also.

Now she was out of the town. The wind came strong and clean through the open window, and the tar highway hissed under the tires.

Her eyes, one wide, the other a slit in a mound of purple and yellow, watched the road at the farthest reach of the headlights. It was a two-lane road that wound around mountainside after mountainside in a general westward direction toward Mexico City. After Mexico City, she would go north on the road to Juarez. She pressed the pedal to the floor and the car leapt like a fish, took a long hill at a smoothly increasing speed, turned abruptly and began another climb.

Then, at a curve to the left, the car leaned in the opposite direction, going too fast for the turn it had to make. The rubber shrieked at Florence's sharp turning, the wheels on the right side struck gravel, dropped, and then the car shot over the edge and began to fall. It turned over and over, bumping down the mountainside with Florence inside it, and burst into flame before it quite came to a stop in the valley.

THE STILL POINT OF THE
TURNING WORLD

There is a small park, hardly more than a square, far over on the West Side in the lower Twenties, that is almost always deserted. A low iron fence runs around it, setting it off from a used car lot, a big redstone public dispensary of some sort, and the plain gray backs of shabby apartment buildings that share the same block with it. Three or four benches stand in pleasant places along the two curving cement paths that one may enter by, and that meet in the center at a cement drinking fountain forever bubbling an inch or so of cool water.

From quite a distance up or down the avenue the little park shines like an emerald isle, a bright and inviting surprise in a sea of drab grayness. Mrs. Robertson noticed it one day from a corner of the Castle Terrace Apartments three blocks away, where she lived. She took her small son Philip to play there that afternoon. It was a splendid place for him, because the low iron fence kept him within bounds even when her back was turned, and it was quiet and sunny, unlittered and untrodden. For a city park it was unusually pretty, too, as if the gardeners had been inspired by a special and personal pride when they made it. The fine close-cropped grass extended into the very corners of the four vaguely triangular lawns. If the grass was not to be walked on, there was no one about to tell her so. Of course, the neighborhood was an abruptly sordid contrast with nearby Castle Terrace, but so was the neighborhood in every direction around Castle Terrace. Its square block of apartments stood like a feudal castle in the center of vassal land in which even the dingiest shops and restaurants bore sycophantic names like the King George, the Crown Tavern, the Belvedere Bar and Grill, as if to curry patronage from the manor. The only people Mrs. Robertson saw near the park, however, were the busy truck drivers who came and went around a diner a block away, and an occasional old man in a pinned-together overcoat who shuffled by too drunk or too tired even to glance at the park. Mrs. Robertson read her book until she grew tired of it, then picked up some knitting she had brought, and after a while just sat and daydreamed in the tranquillity. She debated the item she always left until last in her dinner, the vegetable she would buy in a frozen package on the way home.

She had just decided on mixed carrots and peas when a young woman with a child about the age of Philip came into the park and sat down on one of the benches. The little boy was dark-haired and had a blue and white beach ball which interested Philip.

The dark-haired little boy climbed over the scalloped wire fence into the lawn where Philip played. "Hello," he said.

"Hello," said Philip.

In a minute they were playing together, Philip with the beach ball and the dark-haired little boy with Philip's tricycle. Mrs. Robertson did not like Philip's playing with just any child, but this had happened so quickly there was nothing to be done about it. She intended to leave in about fifteen minutes anyway. Idly, she studied the other woman, surmising immediately that she was rather poor and that she lived in one of the shabby apartment buildings close by. She had very light blond hair that did not quite look bleached, though, and she was rather pretty. She sat with her hands in the pockets of her black polo coat, her knees close together, almost as if she were cold, and she paid little attention to her child, Mrs. Robertson thought, if it was hers. She stared straight before her with a faint smile on her lips, as if she were miles away in thought.

Soon Mrs. Robertson got up and went to get Philip. He and the dark-haired child had become such good friends, Philip cried a little when she loosened his hands from the beach ball and drew him and his tricycle toward the path. Mrs. Robertson and the blond woman exchanged a smile of understanding, but they did not speak to each other. Mrs. Robertson was not given to speaking to strangers, and the other woman seemed still lost in her trance.

The next afternoon, the blond young woman was in the park when Mrs. Robertson arrived, on the same bench, in the same attitude in the black polo coat.

"Dickie!" Philip shrieked when he saw the little boy, and his baby voice cracked with joy.

It gave Mrs. Robertson a tweak of surprise, somehow of unease, that Philip knew the other little boy's name. She watched Philip run totteringly along the path to meet Dickie, who stood with a wide smile, holding his beach ball toward Philip in two outstretched arms. Philip's rush of greeting knocked the other little boy down, and they both scrambled after the rolling ball. Mrs. Robertson knew suddenly in that instant they were together, bound up as one being in play, what had made her uneasy: she was not sure the other little boy was clean. He might even have things in his hair. Mrs. Robertson had lived until recently in a suburb of Philadelphia, but she had heard about the unsanitary conditions of New York's tenement apartments. The dark-haired little boy *looked* washed enough in his pink-and-white striped play overalls, but one never knew what kind of disease a child who lived in a tenement might carry, and Philip would not have the resistance of a child brought up in such an environment. She would have to watch to see he did not put things in his mouth.

Mrs. Robertson gave the blond woman a nod and a smile as she sat down on the bench where she had been the day before. The other woman responded with a nod that Mrs. Robertson could just detect, and her eyes resumed their vacant gaze, quite above the figures of the two little boys playing on the grass. Her expression was so completely oblivious, it aroused Mrs. Robertson's curiosity. Her smile suggested that she saw into some pleasant and fascinating spectacle in a definite place in space. She was quite young, she decided, probably about twenty-one or -two. What was she thinking of? she wondered. And what would her little boy have to do to make her pay him any notice?

On the bench across the path, nearer the fountain than Mrs. Robertson, the blond young woman was awaiting her lover. She was thinking what a beautiful sunny, quiet day it was, and wishing, almost, that these meetings in the little park in April afternoons were all that he and she would know, could know, or would want to know. She was thinking that a mood came upon her every afternoon as she and Dickie left the house, as she descended the brownstone steps, feeling the warmth of the spring sunlight and its calm clarity upon her before she could take her eyes from Dickie's feet to look around her. The street where she lived was especially free of traffic, and at two or three in the afternoons almost as tranquil as the park itself. It presented two smooth parallel walls of brownstone, and even the gray-blue band of street between them was sharp and clear. Here and there a window was dotted by a white bottle of milk on the sill, or a pair of arms at rest on a flattened pillow. Above the arms, resigned and mildly curious eyes gazed down, athirst for any movement on the street, and there was so little: a woman in a housedress airing a nondescript white dog along the curb, a solitary child bouncing a ball beside a stoop post, maybe a boy with a rattly laundry cart, a passing cat. Everyone except the aged and a few women were off at work. Like her husband, Charles, who drove a bus on Broadway, who was gone by eight in the morning and generally did not return until after five. To her, the street seemed empty even of people, because she did not think the woman with her white dog or the arms on the two or three windowsills were alive in the way she knew she was alive. She did not believe they were aware in the same way of the serenity of the street, an odd kind of serenity that clamored to be noticed, or even of its dazzling cleanliness at that hour of the afternoon in the month of April. The woman with the dog did not feel the same as she, coming down her own steps onto the sidewalk, did not sense that the afternoon there belonged to women, to the wives who were alone now with the chores they were complete mistresses of, whose schedule they could rearrange with the flexibility of a woman's day, to an hour earlier if they chose, an hour later, or perhaps not until tomorrow—a woman's world, the street and its two or three reedy trees in iron cages, their thin heads green once more, the street and its unutterable peace. She did not, however, consider herself an ordinary housewife. And there was not the stillness of the street or of the park inside her on the afternoons when he was to come to meet her, though her perception of its stillness and the park's were dependent upon him. On the afternoons she was to see him, she saw beyond the street and the park. She would look eastward where the street disappeared in a huddled jagged mass of buildings, and imagine noise and seething people. She would look west and something in her would leap at the sight of the pier on the river, at a ship's high short mast rising in a cross like a strong and mystic promise above the sooty front of the dock building, above the squared top where the pier's number was written. From this very pier, so close to where she slept every night, she might leave for any corner of the earth, she supposed. And she would wonder if she and Lance would ever really make voyages to foreign places. If she asked him, of course, he would answer such a firm "Certainly we will. Why not?" she would believe and not wonder any longer. Did the woman with the dog ever lift her eyes to look at the pier? Or the woman who had come to the park again today, with the washed and combed little blond boy, who must live in Castle Terrace, did she ever get chills at the sight and smell and sound of the river? But she had probably been all over the world already, been to Europe so many times she knew how each thing would look, what was going to happen next. She would not care to look at the pier.

The blond young woman looked at her now, sitting reading her book, glancing once in a while to see if her little boy was safe. What could happen to anyone in this park? The sweater she wore over her dress was beautiful in the sunlight, the color of a stick of grape ice held to light. Cashmere. She was young, too, she thought, but her manner was so formal she seemed older. She had not talked with her, she supposed, because she considered her an inferior, but she did not care at all. She was not in a mood for talking. She was not in a mood for reading, either. She could have sat all day happily, dreaming on the bench and gazing into space with the green of the park beneath her eyes and reflecting up into them. She was waiting for Lance. And in this park, wasn't she able to sit like this even on the days when he could not come? After the hours here, she could smile, very quietly, as if it amused her, when Charles came in very drunk and cheerful late at night, having drunk up all his pay. Strangely, she did not even blame him, if she had spent the afternoon in the park. His job had ruined his nerves—the pushing crowds, the making change, stopping and starting, the schedules to be met, the dodging of darting pedestrians that made him start up in his sleep at night—so he drank to deaden his nerves. He drank to find the stillness that she found in the park. Once, months ago, before she had met Lance, she had brought Charles to the park and he had not liked it, because he could not sit still anymore anywhere. Now the park belonged to her and Lance. After the hours in the park, she could not blame Charles or herself for what had happened. They simply had stopped loving each other, first

Charles, then herself. It might have been the lack of quiet that had exhausted them, from the very first when they lived in the ground-floor apartment on the East Side, that had left Charles not enough energy to love her any longer. If he could be bathed in stillness, drink it and hear it, see it and breathe it, sleep for hours in it, she could imagine his forehead smooth again, his eyes opening to look at her again as if he loved her. But she did not even want this now, it was too late. She had found Lance and she loved him. And Lance would love her no matter where he or she were, together or apart, in silence or noise, movement or stillness. Lance had something within him that Charles had not and never had. She knew now. She was not eighteen any longer, as she had been when she married Charles.

"Philip!"

Philip stood up and looked guiltily at his mother, who was waiting for him to say, "Yes, Mama," which he did, with the accent on the last syllable.

"Don't get mud on your playsuit, darling! Be careful, now."

"Yes, Mama." And he turned back and squatted down by his friend and finished pouring the Dixie cup of water from the fountain into the little pit they had dug in the smooth grass. Dickie had found the discarded cup at the end of the path, and Philip had automatically kept it out of sight when he spoke to his mother. They did not know what they were going to do with the little pit that kept drinking the water, but they were happy and they found something to say to each other every second, so that both talked at once almost all the time. Neither of them in his life had ever found anyone he liked so much as the other.

Mrs. Robertson looked up immediately when the man came into the park, so few people ever came into the park. He was bareheaded, in a dark suit, and he stopped and stood for a moment on the cement walk, looking at the woman on the bench. Mrs. Robertson's first reaction was the least sensation of alarm: there was something sinister in his intensity, in his half-smiling observation of the blond woman, in his hands rammed into the pockets of his jacket almost as if he were cold—and as she recognized this single similarity between them, she recognized also that they knew each other, though neither made a sign of greeting. Now he walked with a kind of rigid caution in his shortened step toward the woman and sat down easily beside her, not taking his hands from his pockets or his eyes from her face. And the woman's expression of bemused content that Mrs. Robertson had remarked both yesterday and today did not alter even in the least. The man's lips moved, the woman looked at him and smiled, and Mrs. Robertson again felt subtly disturbed by what she beheld. It was vaguely disturbing that a man had come in and sat down on a bench at all. That he was a stranger making advances had flitted into her mind and out, because of the aura of intimacy that wrapped them both. Both looked before them now, leaned very slightly toward each other, though between them was one of the iron arms that divided the bench into four or five seats, and then the man reached over and took the young woman's hand gently from her pocket, drawing it by the wrist beneath the iron bar until he held it in his own hand, resting it on his crossed leg. And suddenly Mrs. Robertson knew: they were lovers. Of course! Why had it taken her so long to guess? Now she began to watch fascinatedly, covertly. For a few moments she was captured by the obvious and attractive happiness in both of them, by the pride in the lift of their heads as they gazed, he, too, now in the sightless, half-smiling way she had seen first in the woman, straight ahead of them as if at something far beyond the park's iron fence. They were certainly unlike husband and wife, she thought, with a strange rise of excitement, yet neither did they behave quite as intensely as she thought lovers should behave, though she reminded herself she had probably never seen a pair of clandestine lovers, only read about them. And these were certainly clandestine lovers. She saw it all: a husband (with dark hair) who worked during the day and came home at six o'clock, all unsuspecting that his wife had spent the afternoon with another man. Mrs. Robertson felt a pang of compassion for the deceived husband. Yes, the blond woman was clearly rather cheap—her high-heeled pumps, her hair lightened with peroxide probably. Would she take the lover home with her? Mrs. Robertson hoped she would not have to witness that. And in the next moment, she admitted to herself she *would* like to see just that, see them go away together. She turned a page she hadn't read, conscious of the sound of her thin gold bracelet touching her watch. She looked over her reading glasses again. The man was talking, but so low she could hear not even a murmur. His head was back, resting on the back of the bench, and the woman watched his face, more alert now than Mrs. Robertson had yet seen her, though still with her soft unconscious-looking smile. The man spread his fingers and took firmer grip on her hand, and Mrs. Robertson felt a small wave of pleasure break over her. What did he talk to her about? she wondered. Or could she possibly be wrong about the whole thing? Was the woman not the child's mother, only a paid sitter, or a nursemaid? But both the woman and the child did not look well enough dressed for such a relationship to be likely. And as if to asseverate her opinion, the child suddenly came running across the path, she watched the woman gather him in her arms, take a handkerchief from her bag, and wipe his nose with a twist, and she caught a quality, in both of them, beyond a shadow of doubt now, that was like a statement that they were mother and child. The man had brought his other hand from his pocket with a handkerchief, too, and having put the handkerchief back, he held now, as if he had just discovered it, a small blue automobile on his palm. The woman said something, and the little boy threw his arms about the man's neck, kissed his cheek, and darted away, so quickly Mrs. Robertson could hardly believe she had seen it. Yet she had seen it, of course, and there had been in that, too, an unmistakable look of its having been done before. She stared at the two unabashedly as they leaned forward together, smilingly watching the children.

Philip! He was playing with the automobile, too. The little boy was sharing it with him. Mrs. Robertson stood up involuntarily, then sat down again. She did not like his playing with the toy, felt somehow that the automobile was not quite right, not quite clean, either, like the little boy. Again she looked at the two on the bench—she could look at them openly for all they appeared aware of her—and again they were leaning back comfortably, more comfortably than seemed possible on the hard bench, and their arms were interlocked, their hands clasped more closely under the iron bar between them. The man talked, and the woman now and again said something in response. It was unusual that he should be so fond of the child. Or was he only pretending? What were they talking about? How they must hate the bench arm between them! And she felt a taut, righteous satisfaction that the iron bar *was* between them. What would the park be like without the iron arms? Men sleeping along the benches. Couples . . .

"He's half you, isn't he?" Lance was saying.

"One day we'll have a child that's all us."

Then they said nothing for a while. A bird sang a few annunciatory notes in a nearby tree—there were only three or four trees in the whole park—then swooped past so that both saw it. Not far away, on the river, a boat sounded its steam toot, not deep enough to be a big liner, not high enough to be a tug: a middle-sized vessel whose toot still said proudly, however, that it could go everywhere on earth and furthermore had been there.

"We'll make a lot of trips," he remarked.

"I want to go to Scotland," the girl said, even more quietly, but her tone was as if she had bought a ticket from someone.

"Scotland must be terrific. We'll definitely go to Scotland . . . the Hebrides."

"Hebrides?"

"'As we in dreams behold the Hebrides.'"

"What are they? Mountains?"

"Mountains and islands. Mountains." He said the words so slowly, so roundly, it was as if he built the islands and the mountains right there.

"Don't say 'dreams,'" the girl chided. "Or is that another poem?"

"It's a poem. But poems are true."

"Sometimes, I guess."

He did not argue. They were silent a longer while.

"Then will you build me a house—after we've finished traveling?"

"I will build you not one house but three . . . four," he said distinctly. "One for every season of the year. A white house for spring, a red house for winter. For autumn, a brown house—"

"I don't like brown."

"For autumn, a *tan* house."

"Lance, are you watching the time?" she barely whispered, like an aside.

"Yes, I am watching the time. The clock in the steeple says five of four."

The clock in the steeple of the little church was only half a block down the avenue, but she had told him she would never look at it while he was with her in the park. The clock in the steeple was always six minutes slow. At 4:09, therefore, he would have to leave in order to report back at his job in a big bookstore on Nassau Street, far downtown. Tomorrow he would not be able to come, nor the next day. He delivered only on Tuesdays and Fridays, an unpopular duty he had asked for so he might manage, perhaps, half an hour or forty-five minutes with her. It was the only time he could see her. As long as she was married to Charles, she would never let him see her in the evening. He put his other hand over hers and smiled at her with sudden tenderness. Somehow, in her mind, his meeting her in the park partook of the accidental, he knew. The one time he had seen her in the evening was the evening they had met, over by the park in Gramercy Square, a park they could not enter because it was locked. In the darkness he had seen her standing before the tall spears of the fence, and with a sense sharpened by his own solitude and loneliness, he had known that whoever and whatever she was, there was something of himself in her, so he had said good evening. They had both been to the same movie on Twenty-third Street that evening, each alone. The one evening they had seen each other, yet in his mind he liked to call himself her lover. What did she call him? She would not call him that, he thought. He lifted his head higher, lolled it back on the edge of the bench back, and one would have thought he had not a care in the world, that he would stay relaxed there the rest of the afternoon.

"This park is the still point of the turning world," he said, and his low voice was steadied with reverence.

"I feel that, too. Yes. And the street where I live. And these days."

"These days." But suddenly he felt guilty for his idleness, even for these half hours with her, because there was so much he had to do. Not guilty so much because he spent the time with her, but that he allowed himself and her to dream so foolishly. Or were the dreams foolish? One could never really tell. He felt guilty because the little park was so good for dreaming, too good, he knew, too quiet and too like an imaginary heaven. And he began to examine caressingly, as he did every afternoon he sat here, the delicate convexity of the little lawns, the sharp delin-eation of the scalloped fences against their bright green fields. His eyes moved casually over Dickie and the other little boy playing with the new automobile. Dickie was always a part of the park, the cherub of its heaven. Today he looked happier than usual because he had the other little boy to play with. He looked at the woman over on the bench, who was again glancing at them, and he smiled a little at her, but she looked down at once at her knitting.

The knitting had got into a small snarl, and Mrs. Robertson was plucking at it anxiously. There was a sensation of clash and disorder within her, as of a distant battle, for which she blamed the knitting. She was dimly aware of an impulse to take Philip and leave the park, correct the knitting at home, as well as a desire to remain because Philip was having such a good time and because the park—perhaps, she admitted, the sight of the two on the other bench—gave her a pleasure akin to an enchantment. The two forces were not at all clear in her mind, but the sense of struggle was as she plucked at the knitting, and while the crystals of herself suffered disorganization, she sat perfectly still except for her fingers, which worked skillfully to rescue the hitherto flawless mitten for Philip. And when the snarl was smoothed out and her course resumed, when the mysterious armies fell silent within her, the outcome of the struggle was veiled, too, leaving her only a subtle sense of irritation, of impatience and somehow of disappointment. *I shall not come here again,* she thought suddenly, and in that decision alone, which seemed to come out of nowhere, she felt substantiality. She would, however, stay just a few minutes more. There was nothing she need run from.

The sunlight stirred all at once like a living thing, climbed over the scalloped fence and fell lightly, soundlessly, half across the walk. Now it lay over the feet of Lance and the girl beside him. A long point of it strove diagonally across the path toward the woman on the bench. He saw her look at it even as he did, but she did not glance up again.

"The still point of the world," the girl whispered.

"The turning world." And again he felt the guilt: the world turned all around them, here on this green island of asylum, machines turned, clocks turned, but he and she were motionless and there was so much to be done and to be fought for.

"Yes, the turning world is nicer. I can feel it—but I can never say it like you. I felt it this afternoon, leaving the house——" But she would not be able to describe it, she knew. "And now."

"Only I didn't say it. That's Eliot. There's another part of it, '. . . at the still point, there the dance is.'" He stopped, knowing suddenly that beside one's beloved is no fixity, though the stillness surpass all other still-nesses and all other kinds of peace, knowing suddenly as if it had been an eternal truth he had just stumbled over and discovered first, that beside one's beloved the beauty of a daydream is never thin, never motionless and flat like a picture as it is in solitude, because beside her there is move-ment forward and electrical energy in the air and a roundness, a whole-ness to things real or imagined. He turned toward her, and he saw her glance prudently at the woman on the bench. But he had not intended to kiss her now.

Bells tinkled. Distant sheep bells on rolling green hills half hidden in mist, he thought: the Hebrides.

"There's the ice-cream man," she said.

The ice-cream wagon came into the path at the downtown end of the park, pushed by a slender young man in white trousers, shirt, and cap.

"Mother," Dickie said, climbing over the path fence, "can I have some ice cream?"

Lance reached into his pocket.

Mrs. Robertson watched the man give the coin to the little boy, who skipped with it to the ice-cream man. Philip stood where he was, watching, knowing he would not be allowed ice cream so soon before his suppertime.

"Can he have one, too?" The man had stood up and was smiling at her, reaching into his pocket again.

"Oh, thank you very much," Mrs. Robertson replied. "It's a bit too near his suppertime."

Her heart was beating faster, she noticed. It had excited her, in a way neither pleasant nor unpleasant, the exchange of conversation with him. His manner, even his face, she decided, were nicer than she had thought, than his unpressed suit had led her to believe. The dark-haired little boy clambered back over the fence in the act of taking his first bite of the ice-cream stick, then ran straight to Philip. She stood up, impelled to stop Philip before he could put the ice cream into his mouth.

"Philip, I don't think—"

She was too late. Philip had the whole top of the ice cream in his mouth, and the other little boy was holding it for him. She did not mean to snatch Philip away, but her tension made it a snatch, and the ice cream suddenly held by no one fell to the grass between the two children.

"Oh!" said Mrs. Robertson, with genuine regret. "I'm terribly sorry!"

After the first stunned moment, the dark-haired little boy stooped to pick it up. But the ice cream fell off the stick, hopelessly broken now, too far gone even for a three-year-old to rescue. Its chocolate crust cracked again even as he watched, as if it were determined to lose itself in the thick smooth grass. He stood up and looked at her, and wiped his hands shyly behind him.

"Where'd the ice-cream man go?" Mrs. Robertson looked around for him, but he was out of sight. She heard his bell up the avenue.

"Lose your ice cream, Dickie?" called the man sympathetically.

"Oh, that's okay," said the little boy, half to him, half to her. He was not angry, but he did not smile, either.

"It's my fault, I'm afraid," Mrs. Robertson said. Then, feeling suddenly ridiculous, she took Philip's arm in one hand and his tricycle handlebar in the other and urged them toward the scalloped fence.

"You have to go now, Philip?" asked the dark-haired little boy.

"Yes," sighed Philip, with resignation. But at the fence he looked back sadly past the arm his mother lifted straight up, as if he had just realized he was actually going.

"See you tomorrow, Philip," said the other little boy, a precocity of phrase that surprised Mrs. Robertson.

He would not see him tomorrow. She did not want Philip to play with him again. She could not say why precisely, but she did not want it. She had been foolish not to take him away as soon as she realized what sort of person his mother was. There was something, somehow she knew it, impure about the little boy no matter how well he might be scrubbed, because his mother was impure. Yet she found herself going past the woman and the man on the bench, though it was the long way out of the park for her, found herself glancing once more at them, quite involuntarily and much to her own annoyance, a furtive sidewise glance that did not even feel like her own. But the man and the woman seemed lost in themselves again, holding hands. She was relieved they hadn't seen her.

When she reached the end of the path, she knew she had left the man and the woman, the little boy and the park forever.

The blond girl had seen the glance, seen in it for all its fleetness the ancient and imperishable look that one woman gives another she knows is well loved, a look made up of desire, admiration, wistfulness, of envy and vicarious pleasure, unveiled for an instant and then veiled again. Seeing it, she had pressed Lance's hand more tightly in quick reflexive pride. Had Lance seen it, too? But probably only a woman would have seen. She would have liked to tell him, but the words for it would be far more difficult to find even than the words about her inner peace as she came down the brownstone steps every afternoon, so instead she said:

"I don't think she likes me. She was here yesterday, too."

Lance only smiled and tucked her arm closer. He had seven minutes more. He drew her arm close until he could feel it all along his side, not feeling any longer the iron arm cutting tense muscles through his jacket sleeve. "Now there's no one," he said.

There was no one. The long point of the wedge of sunlight had reached the bench the woman had been sitting on, had captured one of the curved metal legs. The bird dipped again, crossing their vision, asserting its absolute freedom and security within the tiny park. Now there was no human being along the avenue, not even a blind and impersonal truck hurrying past beyond the boundary of the low iron fence. Yes, there was a nun coming down the steps of the church half a block away, black-clad and in black bonnet, an erect and archaic figure, black skirts rippling with her pace like the carved robes of a ship's figurehead. They turned to each other and their lips met above their clasped hands and entwined arms, above the iron arm, and the kiss became the center of the stillness. The kiss became the narrowed center of the still point of the turning world, so that even the park was turning in comparison to the still peace at their lips.

Then, because there were only three minutes until he had to go, he began to talk casually, but seriously and quickly, of their plans, his work, their money, as if to fortify himself in these last moments before they parted for two days and nights. In three more months they would have enough money to open the next campaign in their struggle, her divorce. It was impossible to talk to her husband now about a divorce so long as she had to live with him. Only three more months. Twenty-four more meetings like this afternoon, he reckoned for the first time, and knew he could not prevent himself from counting them off from now on. Twenty-four . . .

Mrs. Robertson did not go the next day to the little park down the avenue. She took Philip to a court in the center of Castle Terrace where there was a big sandbox and many small children for him to play with.

Philip stood where his mother had turned him loose and looked up at the building that rose like a great tan hollowed-out mountain around him, and asked, "Aren't we going to the park later?"

"Aren't we going to the park later, Mama?" he asked again, when his mother had settled herself in a comfortable metal chair. "I want to see Dickie."

"No, darling, we're not going to the park today." She tried to make her voice gentle and casual, too, and it was difficult. And perhaps she had failed, she thought as she watched Philip pedal off very slowly on his tricycle, with an air of seeing nothing around him.

There were many other young mothers in the play court, and Mrs. Robertson was soon occupied in conversation. She felt right, here in the court of her own apartment building. Why had she tried to be different and find a nicer place? The park was pretty and Philip would miss it, of course, for a few days, but she did not regret her decision not to go back. Here there was sun, too, things for Philip to play on, and an abundance of children for him to make friends with, children she could be sure were clean and being well brought up. And other women, like herself, with whom she could exchange ideas.

"I want Dickie," said Philip, coming up slowly on his tricycle. He had cruised the playground and found it unsatisfactory.

"Darling, there's some little boys over by the sandbox. Don't you want to go play with them?" She turned back to the women she had been talking with, lest she seem as concerned as she felt to Philip.

"I want Dickie!" said Philip two minutes later. Now he had got off his tricycle and stood away from it, as if he would never mount it again unless it was to go see his friend. He had tears in his eyes. He looked at his mother with resentment, and with determined, uncomprehending accusation.

This was the moment to be firm, Mrs. Robertson knew, to ignore it or to say something that would satisfy or silence forever. She hesitated, at a loss.

"Who's Dickie?" asked one of the women.

"He's a little boy he met down the street," Mrs. Robertson answered.

As if piqued at their mention of his friend, Philip about-faced and wandered off with his head up, and thus his mother was spared making the answer she could not find.

Philip asked for Dickie the next afternoon, and the next and the next. But the fifth afternoon he did not ask.

THE PIANOS OF THE STEINACHS

Like a docile but somewhat bewildered monster of an earlier age, the big shiny black Pierce Arrow crept backward down the driveway, popping gravel under its narrow tires. Sunlight made its highlights twinkle. Languid fingers of the weeping willows, their chartreuse just beginning to turn with autumn, brushed its roof and its closed windows with delicate affection: the Pierce Arrow and the willows had grown old together, though both were still beautiful. Next door the Carstairs children and their friends stopped their sidewalk play and stood agape, held by a mild, private kind of awe that did not quite merit comment or perhaps was not expressible. Only once in three weeks or so did anything happen in the Steinach driveway, and besides, how often did they see anywhere such a peculiar car as this?

"Ooh!" shuddered one of the little girls as the wide-set headlights tipped off the driveway and the car aligned itself with Verona Street. With a burst of laughter, the group came to life again.

"Klett! Isn't that an exciting name, Moth-aw?" Agnes Steinach was saying. She rolled the window all the way down, eagerly but jerkily, like one inept at mechanics. Her hands were the long soft ones commonly called a "dreamer's" and they looked completely useless.

"You should not get so excited, Agnes," remarked Mrs. Steinach.

"Oh, Moth-aw!" Agnes laughed a little wildly, aware that she had not felt such exuberance in months. "Do you suppose Margaret has changed much, Moth-aw?"

"I wouldn't wonder, after three years." Mrs. Steinach inclined her head as the delivery boy of Reed's Grocery rode by on his bicycle, tipping his cap. A gray, very small woman, Mrs. Steinach sat as bolt upright as the car seat itself in order to see through the windshield. She looked straight ahead with her habitually preoccupied and somewhat worried expression.

"I don't think Margaret will think *I've* changed much, do you?" Agnes widened her eyes like a child at her mother, but in fact her eyes most of all gave away her thirty-five years. They were surrounded by a fine mesh of wrinkles that made the eyes themselves look like a pair of strange, semitransparent, blue-violet colored fish, caught up in nets. Wavy tresses of black hair made her pallor striking. The even whiteness of her face suggested the purifying effects of raging fever.

"No, indeed, child," Mrs. Steinach said indulgently.

"You don't sound at all excited, Moth-aw."

"We turn here, don't we?"

The Pierce Arrow rounded the corner onto Washington Avenue and proceeded toward the railroad station. The car moved rigidly and at moderate speed as though it were part of a funeral cortege. They were on their way to meet Agnes's sister Margaret, a music teacher who was bringing a student from a San Francisco conservatory to New York. Her letter two days before had said she would have the weekend free to spend with them in Evanston.

But the train from San Francisco was two hours late. Agnes's smile fell away until her mouth, which she rouged heavily, was nothing but soft curves expressive of a petulant sadness. Her great violet eyes stretched wide at the information clerk as though he had done her a personal wrong out of some personal malice.

Mrs. Steinach, on the other hand, accepted the situation with a little "Oh" and remarked they had best go home and come again at five o'clock. It would give Agnes an opportunity to rest, she said. It would be quite a strain on her, the two drives and company, too.

"But Moth-aw, I've never felt so gloriously well in my life!"

Even outdoors her voice sounded as hollow, as capable of echoes and as much like an echo itself as it did in their quiet old house. It slid around high in the treble register like an affected falsetto, or like the tone of a bent saw struck with a rubber hammer.

Back they went, and the willows welcomed the Pierce Arrow as fondly as if its mission had been successful.

Mowgli, the big white Angora, fled nervously from the corner of the sofa when Agnes and her mother entered the living room. Mowgli had been stone deaf since before his prime, which perhaps aggravated his sense of disturbance at the sight of activity. Halfway up the stairs he waited for Agnes or her mother to come and stroke him so he might return with dignity, but today neither of them noticed him.

"Are you sure she said three o'clock, Moth-aw?"

Agnes ignored her mother's ignoring of her—Mrs. Steinach was on the way back to the kitchen—and ran upstairs to make sure once more that the silver thermos in the guest room, which was to be Klett's, was filled with ice water, that the nosegay of little flowers in her father's shaving mug was still fresh, that the not always reliable thermostat promised hot water in case he wanted to shave. Men always wanted *very* hot water, especially in the mornings. But wouldn't it be funny if Klett were too young to shave after all? Margaret's letter had said he was only eighteen.

The guest room was in perfect order, the writing desk opened, its glass inkpot filled, the counterpane newly ironed so its lace ruffles would look their crispest. With the shades up, the wallpaper of cream and tiny royal blue flowers looked really very bright and attractive. There was firewood and kindling ready, though the temperature was just a bit warm for a fire.

"Mr-row?" Mowgli had followed her to the threshold, curious that the room had been opened. His mouth was soft and sad, one of his blue eyes cast. He stared at his mistress with an air of bewilderment and sullen madness.

Agnes floated to the window like a dancer, holding her arms as though they trailed a diaphanous material. She held back a limp brocade curtain and gazed down onto the row of willows, onto the smooth gravel driveway that was itself beautiful, the corner of the front lawn bordered with a few violets that waved like tattered flags in the breeze. And the willows? They were like a forest of little yellow and green barber poles, twisting up and then untwisting. Or were they more like a cluster of champagne fountains? How sweet it would all look to Margaret! And with a vicarious thrill she imagined Klett's first glimpse of their home. Modestly sized as it was, compared to others in the block, everything about it reflected perfect taste. The living room, in which pale blue velvet predominated, certainly invited one to relax in soft comfort and forget all life's difficulties. She felt everyone of sensibility should detect in an instant the particular personality of her home, as a connoisseur detects a special vintage of wine. And of course Klett would be such a person, perhaps in fact a genius. Their *two* pianos in the living room would delight him, though they were a little out of tune. Possibly he and she would play something together. It had been many years since she had played duets with Margaret, many more since she and her father had played. Would Klett be handsome and fiery like Chopin? she wondered. Or would he be moody and somber like a young Beethoven?

Her eyes strayed through the willows to the moving blotch on the Carstairses' front walk. It was a man in a gray suit leading a small child by the hand. A kind of weight gathered and fell quietly inside her, and the diffused sadness in her eyes was focused by a look of fear. She remembered the day Billy Carstairs had been playing on his front lawn and she had invited him into the house for a glass of lemonade and told him a story about his dead father that had made his eyes grow big and his face white. The story had been absolutely false. She still remembered her thrill when Billy had begun to cry. She had made him promise he would never tell anyone, and she had felt she had control over him. But since that day Billy had avoided her on the street. And when he married and his child was born, Agnes had felt deep inside herself a kind of personal defeat. Now she hated it when she saw him with his silly-looking blond wife or with his child.

"Ag-ness?"

"Yes, Moth-aw!"

"Shouldn't you like a cup of tea?"

Agnes thought at first that her mother was going to bring it up, but of course she was not in bed now! And she did not feel weak or ill at all—just the least bit weak perhaps. She folded her hands behind her and leaned against the window jamb. "I'll be down immediately, Moth-aw!"

The hollow, falsetto voice, strong as a singer's, found its way into the varnished hall, down the short wide staircase, into the living room, where her mother poured tea into two flared white cups. Agnes glided down the steps almost, it seemed, before her voice had ceased to echo.

Then a car door slammed, and Agnes turned startled eyes to the front door. "They're here!—Oh, Moth-aw, *you* go!"

The door opened and Margaret almost toppled her mother with her embrace. "Mummy!—Agnie, you look *splendid,* darling!" she shouted over her mother's shoulder.

"Margaret, my angel!" Agnes held open her arms, curving her long fingers upward. She felt she could have wept.

"This is Klett. Klett Buchanan," Margaret said, smiling at the boy who had crept inside the door with the couple of suitcases. "Klett, my mother and my sister Agnes."

Agnes felt a sensation almost like one of recognition. He was so exactly what she had hoped, handsome, intense, with an air of distinction already, though his face was round as a child's.

"How do you do?" he said with a quick bow and a smile, showing even and rather girlish teeth. He was slight and not very tall and wore a plaid muffler tightly buttoned in by a gray and green Tyrolean-style jacket. He looked from one to another of the three with an air of being eager to please.

"How do you do?" whispered Agnes, last of all.

"Just in time for tea, how nice!" Margaret said, dropping her coat into a chair. "I know Klett's even hungrier than I am. They compromised by not taking on a diner and got us here fairly on time after all."

They discussed the trains, the vain trip to the station, while Margaret buttered and marmaladed triangles of toast for everyone. Klett sat beside her in Mowgli's corner of the powder-blue sofa, holding his teacup stiffly.

"Tell us about yourself, Margaret." Mrs. Steinach's face had grown much happier since Margaret's arrival. "It's so seldom we hear from you."

"Oh, I'm just the same, I guess. My work now is more organizing than teaching. I pick the best for Moore's classes and grade them down. I told you about Moore. Then when I find someone like Klett, I recommend him as a special student. Only this time I mean to do some research work on my own in New York." She looked suddenly at Agnes, who was not listening, then back at her mother. Her face with its strong nose lacked the regularity of Agnes's, but it was attractively frank and open, like a vigorous major chord itself. At thirty-eight she was still beautiful, even when she forgot to apply makeup, as she often did. "Oh, all that's dull. You don't look a day older, you know, Mummy. And the house hasn't changed a bit, has it?"

"But however did you find Klett?" Agnes interrupted gaily, feeling Klett with his musical ear must be noticing her voice, which had wider range, was more feminine than Margaret's. "I do wish you'd play something for us. Only"—she caught her breath—"it's too early, isn't it?"

"Much too early." Margaret gazed affectionately at Klett as he circled the two baby grand pianos set curve to curve in the corner of the room. "I didn't mention those, Klett. I'm sure they're horribly out of tune."

"Oh!" Agnes gasped, shocked at Margaret's bluntness, but no one seemed to hear the gasp.

"Do you play?" Klett asked her.

Agnes smiled up at him. "After a fashion. Oh, but music is the joy of my life!" She wished he would ask her to play something now. She had been practicing a Chopin nocturne until she was sure it was perfect. "How wonderful it must be to be master of an instrument at eighteen!"

"Yes," Mrs. Steinach put in.

Klett lowered his smooth face modestly.

"Klett's not quite a master, though he might get there if he works." Margaret extended another toast and marmalade to him. "Here, Klett."

Agnes laughed nervously. "Why you talk to him like a dog, Margaret!"

"Do I? He bears up," she said with a smile. "Mummy, you're sure it won't be too much trouble to put us up until Monday morning?"

"Why, of course not!" Agnes cried. "What a question!"

Only two or three chords had sounded, but each sent a thrill over her. How strange and personal it felt to know that other hands were on her piano!

"You have the most beautiful touch!" she whispered into the mirror. She drew the very soft ivory-backed brush across her black hair once more, letting some of it lie over her shoulders.

She tiptoed down the hall, down the stairs, bending a little so she might sooner see the lighted corner of the room where the pianos were. Middle C sounded, firmly held down.

"Oh!"

"Come on down, Agnie!" Margaret called from where she stood at Agnes's piano. "Klett's upstairs washing for supper."

"Oh." Suddenly she felt she almost hated Margaret.

"You're looking so much better than I'd expected, Agnes. Really, I'm delighted. Mummy's last letter said you'd had more of those pains in the back and had already been in bed a week."

"I've just spent five days in bed," Agnes explained.

"Did you write that lumbar specialist I told you about in Chicago?"

"Oh, yes," Agnes replied wearily. "I don't know, I just don't know. There've been so many specialists. Sometimes I think all they do is take one's money and go off. And who knows? Who knows? Pain is just my cross, darling!"

"How's your sleeping?"

"I sleep when I can," she said with a cheerful laugh.

Seated on the end of the bench, Margaret ran her fingers again over a few notes, sounded them together, but Agnes took no pleasure in them now. "The trouble is, I suppose, if one's in bed all day one simply isn't tired at night. You have gained weight, though, haven't you?"

"Perhaps. So have *you!*" Agnes made herself smile. Margaret had put on tons. It was really disgusting.

"I suppose I have." Margaret smiled. "Bad as the year I was married. But I must say I feel better for it."

Agnes remembered how she had gained pounds when she married, being so happy, happy like a pig with her Austrian musicologist, Dr. Hermann von Haffner. But then of course the divorce had come only two years later. Agnes pressed her palms together, twisted them. "Do ask Klett to come down and play something before supper, Margaret. I think he's perfectly charming!"

"All right. I did want to warn you, Agnie, not to make too much over Klett. He's a very conceited young man and it goes right to his head."

"Oh—did I?" She found a mischievous amusement in the fact she might have.

"Not seriously." Margaret frowned with a look of humor in her eyes, in an old habit Agnes remembered. "He's from a small school where he's had too much praising already. He could develop into a good or a mediocre musician, but at this stage a swelled head won't help."

"Oh! Well——" Agnes laughed a little. "I'll ask him to come down."

She went upstairs to the door at the end of the hall. She heard the snap of a suitcase closing. How exciting it was to have a guest!

"Come in?" he responded to her knock.

She opened the door slowly, smiling. He wore the same Tyrolean jacket, but with a dark blue and red silk scarf knotted at his throat instead of the muffler. His light brown hair was damp from his washing, and the wavy rise of hair over his forehead was higher and bore fresh marks of his comb. *What a handsome figure he makes in this room that has been silent so long,* she thought. She loved his clothes. They reminded her of a conception she had long entertained of Frédéric Chopin. She loved, too, his air of aloofness and nervous impatience that could alternate so quickly with boyish uncertainty. The only thing he was yet certain of, she supposed, was his genius. He gazed back at her now, however, with perfect composure in his gentle, intense face. His slightly parted lips held the merest beginning of an involuntary smile. Surely he understood that she understood him, she thought, and felt a tingling shock pass over her.

"Won't you come down and play something for us?" she asked finally.

He bowed a little. "It would be a pleasure, Miss Steinach." He moved to the mirror, touched the side of his head with his palm, then followed her out of the room.

To Agnes's annoyance, Margaret was still at the piano, but she got up as they crossed the room.

"This one's the best. The other's way out of tune," Margaret said, for Klett had stopped near her father's darker piano. "Well, I'll leave you two. I'm in need of a quick nap."

The *better* piano, thought Agnes, but Margaret's very utterance had offended her most. How could she talk so callously about the piano their father had cherished?

"Beautiful instruments," Klett remarked, feeling the surface of her father's piano with the backs of his fingers.

Agnes's Baldwin and her father's Steinway, except for their want of tuning due to Agnes's basic unmusicalness and consequent neglect, were monuments of judicious care and handling, like the Pierce Arrow Otto Steinach had bought in 1927. Their wax and polish lusters were unbroken by a single scratch, the almost black one of the father, Agnes's of lighter brown mahogany streaked with dark, much like the coat of a tiger-striped cat. Even from some distance in the closed room they gave off the bouquet that pianos, of all musical instruments, seem to possess so richly, of aromatic polish, of felt and steel and a certain dusky sweetness like the piano's versatile music itself. A taffeta-shaded lamp stood on either piano atop a swirled scarf. The scarf over Agnes's was a gloomily colored Persian print, over her father's a heavy and ancient-looking rep of beige fringed with stiffened gilt that looked rather military. Their tops suggested half-conjoined wheels of chance in motion, the black and white keyboards parts of their numbered rims, or so Agnes had often thought when she and her father seated themselves facing each other to play their duets, their Bach and Haydn double concertos, their Chopin "treble and basses." She had seemed to be caught in the centrifugal force of their repertory even before they touched the keys, she remembered. But now as Klett sat down at her piano, she felt only a simple joy that his young genius was about to be expressed on the piano she knew so well.

She looked down at her hands, which she had arranged carefully in her lap, one with palm up, the other lightly at rest upon it, its smooth knuckleless fingers flowing down to oval pale lavenderish nails. Klett was quickly spanning off keys without pressing them, like a musician before a concert, but a tremulous excitement prompted Agnes to interrupt.

"I'm so fortunate in having long fingers. I suppose I should play much better than I do."

Klett looked at her hands. "It doesn't really matter about the length, you know. Yours might be too flexible."

Agnes's face fell. "I can play two notes beyond an octave."

He shrugged. "I can just reach an octave." He held up his right hand, turned it front and back objectively. "My hands are supposed to be the best type."

Agnes watched his hands come together on the keys, the fingers striking with precision, like arched hammers. He had rather unattractive hands, she thought, not at all what she considered a pianist's hands should be. They were short and squarish and their backs round with muscle. Then, aware that he was playing something, she forced herself to listen. "Bach!" she said.

"First prelude from *The Well-Tempered Clavier.*"

"Yes!" Didn't he think she knew that much? When he had finished she asked, "Do you know any Chopin? I adore him."

"Oh, yes," he said casually, and began a Chopin nocturne—the very one she had been practicing!

"Exquisite!"

"It'd sound better if the piano didn't ring so. The felt's worn down apart from the tuning, you know."

Agnes hardly heard. She had never listened to the nocturne played with such thrilling clarity, such surety of rhythm. She felt herself grow taut from head to foot. "Oh, now you look right!" she whispered.

Klett smiled suddenly at her. It was the first time she had seen him smile like that, his face lighted with his own music, with a half-preoccupied tenderness in his eyes. In the close-fitting jacket his arched back, which bent with his playing, his head, round in back and balanced with the crest of hair in front, made a study in reposeful concentration.

"You belong at a piano! You are like a bird that has left off beating its wings—to glide in air!"

He laughed appreciatively. Smiling, lifting his hands high, he played the Chopin Mazurka in A. The tassels danced on the pink lamp. He held the pedal down until Agnes felt swept away on melodious clouds of ringing, echoing, ear-dazzling sound. She wondered what the neighbors, the Carstairses and the Hollinses on the other side, thought of the burst of music coming suddenly at dusk from the Steinach home.

"Klett!—Excuse me." Margaret's voice was drab and ugly, from another world. She stood halfway down the stairs. "Klett, you know that's the very thing I don't want you to play yet."

"All right," Klett said, looking down at the keys he still lightly touched. But he had stopped the melody abruptly.

"Awfully sorry, Agnes." Margaret gave an apologetic laugh. "You don't know it yet and you're just hammering in those mistakes for all you're worth. Play anything else, Klett." She went back upstairs.

Agnes smiled and wrung her hands. "Isn't that annoying!"

Undaunted, Klett had begun a quiet Bach praeludium. He continued with something Agnes thought was Scarlatti, though it might also have been Bach.

"Lovely!" she said once or twice, but Klett did not look up or smile again. Agnes was content to watch him, absorbed in his own easy continuous playing, though she kept wishing he would pay some attention to her.

"Anyway, last year at the fall concerts I found one Scarlatti on the program gave more headaches than all moderns put together," Margaret was saying, adding another pat of butter to her baked potato. "Mummy, I didn't tell you what happened to Schindler this summer. You know, the assistant professor of violin with the horrible temper?" She burst out laughing.

Agnes laid down her fork and looked at her sister almost tearfully. She might have allowed their guest to talk, but there she was babbling on and on, so busy stuffing herself she would never notice a look. Agnes didn't like her new housecoat so much after all, she decided. It was too tailored, not the least in her style, as certainly a sister should have known. Margaret had brought it from San Francisco and, suddenly remembering it, had insisted that Agnes try it on and wear it to supper. Upstairs the maroon flannel and white piping had looked deceptively trim and attractive. Now, looking down at the broad cuffs above her slender hands, she felt it had been part of a deliberate scheme to make her hideous. Small wonder that Klett had not troubled to talk with her! She wished she were in bed in her old satin dressing gown, even if its lace was torn. Who appreciated anyway what it cost her to come down to supper, when almost every day of the world Alantha served three meals to her in bed?

"Oh!" Agnes gasped in a tone of surprise and outrage.

"Darling!"

"Oh, dear," said Mrs. Steinach.

Agnes had bent her head low over her plate. The searing vertical pain along her spine spread into both hips. It was hot, unreasonably cruel, yet tingling like something not quite there. It made a familiar pattern, like an inverted T with a fuzzy crossbar. "It's—all right."

"Can I do anything, Miss Steinach?" Klett asked, half standing.

She shook her head. And indeed the pain had already gone, so suddenly she could almost doubt it had been. It always departed suddenly, but left her so weak, so stricken. "Upstairs," she whispered.

"I'll help you, Agnie," Margaret said.

Agnes teetered to the right, however, and took the arm Klett proffered. She left the dining room with bowed head, the new housecoat trailing the ground, like one on the way to an executioner. She might almost have been willing to go to an executioner on Klett's arm, she thought, he carried himself so beautifully, with such pride and courtliness.

In answer to Mrs. Steinach's summons, Dr. Reese arrived at eight-thirty. He was the family doctor, had officiated at both Margaret's and Agnes's births, and since Agnes's semi-invalidism seventeen years before had called twice or thrice weekly at the house.

"Caught me right in the middle of dinner, Mrs. Steinach," Agnes heard his voice from her bed upstairs. "*Hello,* Margaret! Saints alive! I haven't seen you—" Now he kissed her, Agnes supposed. "How's my girl?"

Their happy pain-free voices blended to Agnes's ears until she could no longer tell what they said. She closed her eyes and made her body rigid as Dr. Reese entered, with Margaret behind him.

"Well! How's my patient?"

His face was unusually radiant, and suddenly Agnes felt strong dislike for him. Ordinarily he was calm, serious, and rather formal. Now he seemed positively silly. His knees jutted awkwardly above the incongruous little potbelly as he walked. His gray head shook more than ever as though he did some foolish dance. Agnes did not reply to his question.

"I'm afraid she's had too much excitement, Dr. Reese. It's all our fault," Margaret said.

"Well, well," said Dr. Reese, holding Agnes's thin limp wrist.

Agnes turned her eyes miserably to one side, and saw Mowgli on his pillow before the gas stove, his tousled white head lifted a little, eying Margaret the intruder resentfully. She wanted to snap the thermometer between her teeth. Surely her inner fury would send her temperature higher. Why had Klett gone? But then if Dr. Reese was being so silly, and she might have known he would be, seeing Margaret again, Margaret who had never been sick a day in her life—

"*Come* in," Dr. Reese called to the door.

Klett entered with a glass in his hand. "Mrs. Steinach asked me to bring this up," he said solemnly.

Agnes knew what it was, sodium bicarbonate for possible indigestion after the large supper. Only she hadn't eaten it, she really *hadn't*! She stirred her legs impatiently beneath the covers.

"Pains?" Dr. Reese asked.

Agnes nodded.

"Dr. Reese," Margaret began concernedly, "you know there must be something one can do—or find out—"

Dr. Reese squinted his eyes, pursed his mouth. Agnes noticed he dandled his watch, got out the sedative powder more bustlingly than usual. He turned a professional face to Margaret as he poised the powder envelope over the glass. "My dear, we've done everything humanly possible. Our plucky patient here . . ." He looked at her, then back to Margaret, nodding. "Your mother knows our efforts, our failures and our successes."

Agnes relaxed and stretched her feet into the cool corners of the bed. Dr. Reese's presence was reassuring. He was, she knew, on her side. She looked at Klett, who stood with hands folded in front of him, like a young knight resting on his sword, earnest, attentive. He could not have behaved more fittingly, Agnes thought, more like a gentleman.

"Fever?" asked Margaret as the doctor read the thermometer.

Dr. Reese only looked up at her with an ambiguous sour expression. "Just try to sleep, my dear," he said to Agnes. "No reading tonight, eh? Not *Ivanhoe* or anything else."

Agnes nodded. Then, as they all turned to leave her room, "Klett?"

"Yes?"

"Would you . . . play something quietly for me?"

"Of course." He smiled, his face brightening as it had downstairs.

"But not for very long, Agnie," Margaret told her. "You do need rest."

Agnes lay then and waited. How swiftly time would pass, she thought, if there would always be Klett in the house! With a feline movement, she turned herself to brush with her fingertips the two or three books atop her bedtable. Somehow she always wanted to plunge immediately into reading after Dr. Reese's visits, but tonight she did not. Why, with Klett in the house even *Ivanhoe* seemed almost dispensable! What need had she now to read of chivalry and romance, of tournaments and fanfare, gonfalons borne on stirrup-set staffs, the smash of armor, and the kiss the mortally wounded knight blows his mistress in the stands? Nevertheless she took the book and laid it on her bosom, composed her hands gently upon it, and fancied herself Rebecca as she appeared in some of the illustrations, jet of hair and white as snow, her figure pliant even in heroic posture as on the battlements of Torquilstone. *There was, therefore, no hope but in passive fortitude, and in that strong reliance on Heaven natural to great and generous characters,* Agnes thought, memory supplying with perfect accuracy the sentence she felt best suited this moment. But Agnes was, in fact, rather plump. Her long limbs suggested gauntness, yet her body itself was broad and even covered with flabby flesh on the lower ribs. It was as though years of lying in bed had flattened her as some types of fish are flattened one way or the other from intense pressures.

It was an old high school text of *Ivanhoe* that she treasured, its navy blue cloth and pasteboard covers splayed at the corners, the edges of its pages adorned with nicknames and initials, a skull and crossbones. In the back were questions on each chapter, and Agnes had read the book so often she could answer every one. Now, waiting for Klett to begin, the image of herself as the beautiful Rebecca took form in her mind, in long white dress and barefoot. She had been cast as Rebecca in the stage play the graduating class of Central High School was to give, but her breakdown had come only a few days before, had in fact prevented her from taking some of her final examinations. Suddenly, with a pang, Walter Mergental's face, healthily round and tanned, smiling, the face of an idealistic twenty-two-year-old medical student, rose above the white collar of an intern's tunic, and just as suddenly she knew why she had thought of him—Klett had reminded her! The roundness of their jaws was the same, and though their eyes were quite different, Walter's blue and Klett's brown, they both had the same curve at the back of their heads, the same rise of light brown hair above the forehead. For an instant, Agnes did not know whether she felt ecstatic or miserable. She had not thought of Walter in years. She did not want to think of him. They had been engaged, but a few days before her graduation he had come to her and broken it off, giving no reason except, stammeringly, that he did not think he loved her enough. She had wept inconsolably for days. Foolish child that she had been! She had not wanted to see anyone, not even her closest friends. It had been a complete nervous breakdown, even Dr. Reese had admitted that. He had been worried enough then! Foolish, foolish child! No, she would not think of Walter again. He was married now, with four children. Would she want *four*—No, she would not think of Walter.

But what was keeping Klett? She listened but she heard no piano. Someone came up the stairs.

Margaret opened the door slowly. "Agnie? Asleep?"

"No. Good heavens, no."

"Klett's finishing his supper. Wouldn't you go to sleep better without music? He'll play all night with a little encouragement."

"Let him. I love it."

"All right." She laughed softly. "Agnie, haven't you got too much heat with the floor vent and the gas stove, too?"

"I like it."

"How about covering up and letting me change the air? All it needs is a fresh—"

"The warmth is good for my back," Agnes said, but she sounded shorter than she intended. "Dr. Reese said so himself."

Margaret's face flushed, Agnes did not know whether from the heat or irritation. She watched Margaret walk to the dresser, look at the photograph of them with their mother on Lake Michigan beach when both of them wore pinafores. Suddenly Margaret's presence galled her. She wished Margaret might drop in a faint. No one had asked her to come in anyway.

"I think Dr. Reese is leading you on," Margaret said quietly, without looking at her. "Don't you see it?"

"What?—What on earth do you mean?"

"Oh, I know he's the family doctor and a fine old gentleman and so forth. But I think he's very fond of visiting the Steinach house."

"Why, I don't know what you're talking about, Margaret." And indeed, Agnes found her mind quite blank.

Margaret turned away. "Then forget it. Can I get you anything?" she asked at the door.

Klett, Agnes wanted to say. You can send Klett up after he plays. But she knew her sister was trying to keep them apart, was pettily but fiercely jealous that she and Klett had liked each other. "Nothing," she said.

She waited with her eyes tightly closed, waiting, waiting until she thought she could not wait a second longer, when the first notes of Chopin's Minute Waltz, light and lightly played, found its way to her ears. Then she smiled and relaxed. *He is here now, playing for me,* she thought. She saw him in profile as she had seen him downstairs, the light from the pink-shaded lamp falling on his forehead, which bulged between the brows and again in two lobes near his hairline. This was Klett, the Chopinesque young man who would one day win tumultuous applause in Carnegie, in Albert Hall, in the capitals of Europe, who would one day write in his memoirs of the strange and beautiful semi-invalid for whom he had played in the autumn of his nineteenth year. He would describe poetically the poetic mood she inspired in him, perhaps, perhaps, the beginning of a love for her.

Now he played one of Wagner's Wesendonk songs. *Träume . . .* and now *Im Treibhaus*. She must remember to thank him, to let him know she recognized them. How lovely it all was! And on her piano!

Agnes awakened to bright sunlight in her room, and remembering the day before, remembering falling asleep to Klett's playing, she smiled and wriggled deeper into her down pillow. Absently she ran her fingers through her long hair so it would spread about her head, like Botticelli's *Birth of Venus,* she always thought. And she got up and started toward the cheval glass, changed her mind and went first to the basin in the corner, where she washed her face and brushed her teeth. She looked at her teeth in the mirror. They were better-shaped than Margaret's, she thought, and very white, though hardly different from her skin. She put on lipstick and powder at the dresser mirror, then returned to the cheval glass, which she unpinned and set in her bed, propped against one of the pineapple-topped footposts. She amused herself for several moments in taking various poses with her head and hands. Favorite was the partially averted face, eyes drowsily half closed, one hand across the top of her blanket and the other arm out and relaxed at her side.

"Miss Agnes?"

"Just a minute, Alantha!" She took the mirror back to the chest, fastened it, then called, "Come in," and walked slowly back to her bed as though from the dresser.

"How're you feeling this morning, Miss Agnes?" Alantha smiled, mechanically but warmly enough, as she did every morning. She set the breakfast tray on the metal support that pulled from under the bedtable.

"Much better, thank you, Alantha." She found herself, actually, interested in the breakfast tray, and did not mind that Alantha noticed. "You might tell our guest, Mr. Buchanan, that his music last night was delightful!"

"I will when he comes back," Alantha said. "He's taken Miss Margaret and your mother to town in the car."

Agnes thrilled as she had when he played her piano. "Has he really?"

"Oh, and he told me to say he hopes you feel well enough to come downstairs today and play the piano with him," Alantha told her as though repeating his very words.

"Did he!"

An hour later, Klett knocked and came into her room with a bouquet of pansies. He looked happier, Agnes thought, more sure of himself. And once more his wide, boyish smile seemed to change his whole being.

"Good morning! Alantha told me you were awake. Do you like these? They're very late ones."

"How like one of the Barrett brothers you are!" Agnes smiled, holding the bouquet beneath her chin. It was the fulfillment of an old desire, to see striding toward her a clear-faced young man like one of the Barrett brothers who had flowed in such abundance, with such an air of devotion, into Elizabeth's sickroom.

"Do you think so?" Klett smiled back, obviously pleased.

"Why, even your clothes are like theirs! You are like something out of another century!"

In the cheval glass that Agnes so often gazed at herself in, Klett touched his silk cravat quickly, tugged down the rather short Tyrolean jacket, while Agnes smoothed out her hair again upon the pillow. She knew well enough how she looked at that moment, centered in the four-poster bed made more massive by her own slenderness, so that her thin oval face, the focus of the entire composition, was almost hard to find, like the frailest white flower in a dancing field. She saw Klett's eyes linger shyly over the expanse of pale blue counterpane until his eyes met hers and she reassured him with a smile.

Klett practiced the rest of the morning and after lunch fingered out phrases, with long pauses, of something he was evidently composing. Perhaps the "Imaginary Adventures" he had told her about, Agnes thought, his series of tone poems. But though she tried hard, and prepared something to say about them, the phrases and the pauses could not hold her interest. She found it more amusing to dream, while Klett provided the musical background, of how pleasant it would be if he stayed on in their house. If he could only go to school in Chicago and commute from Evanston. She might suggest it to Margaret. Probably Klett did not have much money and such an arrangement might help him. How charming of him not to have money and to be so passionately given to his art! How happy it would make her to have him in the guest room, to cater to his tastes and foibles, to play the piano with him on days when she felt well enough.

Once during the afternoon, when the doorbell rang, she heard Klett strike a final cadence and run upstairs to his room. It was a neighbor calling to see Margaret. She smiled at his show of temperament.

That afternoon Agnes washed her hair and set it in rag curlers while she bathed and manicured her nails with colorless polish. Klett called on her when tea downstairs was half over, bearing a cup for her on one of the broad yellow saucers on which he had arranged marmalade toasts, a petit four and a tiny wedge of fruitcake.

"Goodness, do you really think I could eat all this?" she said with a laugh. And really she couldn't eat a thing. She was so delighted that Klett had brought her tea. She knew that he must have insisted, for Alantha or her mother always carried it up themselves.

"If you like Chopin, you must like Debussy." Klett had pulled the chaise longue close by her bed and sat on the end of it, nibbling at the fruitcake, leaning forward eagerly. "I wrote an essay at the conservatory on his influence in modern music."

"Oh, do tell me about it!"

Agnes did not know how the hours flew. But then it was supper-time and Klett was gone, with her promise that she would join him at the piano after dinner if she possibly felt well enough. She thought she would if she took a quiet bit of supper by herself.

He came to escort her downstairs. Dusk had grown to darkness in the last five minutes. She knew her face seemed purely white on the side lighted by her lamp and, asserted by the thin nose and softly curved lips, faded into pale shadow on the other. It was the most poetic hour, her most poetic pose, the simple one in the center of the great bed.

"Can you really? Will you come down?" he asked, offering his arm. "You make me so happy!"

"Of course!" she whispered.

She saw him look at the *Ivanhoe,* which had slid into the hollow made by her body, its title plainly legible in black letters across the blue cover. Somehow she did not like it that he had seen.

Margaret and her mother had gone out to visit one of Margaret's friends, and the living room was silent, lighted only by the two lamps on the pianos. So quietly had they come down that Mowgli did not look up from his corner of the blue velvet sofa.

"You will play mine," Agnes said, for Klett had led her to her own piano. "I will play my father's."

He nodded, his eyes the least bit wide and troubled, and Agnes wondered if he had noticed her voice in that instant, mellifluent but, she admitted, higher than she meant and with a slide of uncontrol.

Carefully, she began to play the Chopin nocturne, and Klett followed. Their hands, the one pair pinkish, silken-looking in the lamplight, the other pale and far larger, lifted in unison, lilted in waltz tempo like two voices. Smoothly they returned to a phrase in the middle and finished the song with a sweep of treble notes that left Agnes breathless and laughing for happiness. Their last chord lingered throbbingly in the silence. Agnes closed her eyes, her fingers still on the keys. The chord pulsed like a living voice itself. Across from her, she felt so sure that the sensitive young man watched her, she could afford to relinquish the pleasure of witnessing his admiration. She did not mind now that the pianos were out of tune. She felt their tones accorded with the house. She heard in their hollowness, their circumvention of the notes themselves, a kind of majestic expansion, as though each tone or chord created a small world, a mirrored hall with chandeliers.

Klett struck his chord again and laughed, but when she opened her eyes, his head was bent and he began another nocturne she knew less well. She followed in the waltz bass well enough, but she was aware that she made a few errors in the treble. Klett evidently knew it very well, for he interpolated runs between phrases, trilled certain notes far beyond their demand in a brilliant display. Dismayed, Agnes left off her right hand, feeling shy all at once and almost like crying. Klett played in his own dramatic tempo, slurring or rushing, leaning with the keyboard's needs. She felt somehow that he had seized a whip from her hands (and yet she had not really imagined herself with a whip against Klett, so how could it be?) and had begun to use it upon her more vigorously and skillfully than she could have hoped to use it. His skillfully young fingers, she thought. His brilliant young fingers!

"Bravo!" she cried when he had finished. "You could not have played more superbly at a concert!"

The crashing chord with which he had concluded teetered like a tightrope walker maintaining balance after a final spectacular sault upon the wire. Klett was standing, daubing his moist brow with his handkerchief, smiling. But, Agnes thought, he smiled straight through her now, as though he smiled at a wildly applauding audience.

"I know you will be great, Klett!" she whispered, feeling the start of tears.

Klett nodded and sat down. He seemed too elated even for speech.

Agnes heard footsteps on the front porch, and the door opened with an unpleasant cracking sound.

"Hello, Agnie! I'm so glad to see you up!" Margaret came across the room to embrace her. "Can you beat it, Molly wasn't even at home. If they'd had a telephone we could have saved ourselves the trip." She waved a hello to Klett, then said to Agnes in a quieter voice, "I think it's just as well. Mummy's sort of done in tonight."

Agnes nodded, hating them all, hating everything. Even "Molly" had reminded her of an old high school friend of Margaret's she had never been able to bear.

"Klett, my mother's rather tired tonight. Do you mind winding up?" Margaret said as she took her coat to the front closet.

Klett looked at her blankly as his fingers continued to play. It was an intricate passage of a Bach fugue and his face seemed rapt, as though he had not heard what she said.

Like a fawn alarmed at some subtle though possibly not really significant disturbance in the forest, Agnes arose and fled lightly up the stairs. When she was near the top there came a clangorous discord, and the piano stopped. As she closed her door, she heard Klett in the hall, heard his own door slam. We are like two outcasts, she thought, our quiet heaven torn down around us.

She thought surely it was Klett when a moment later a knock came at her door. But it was Margaret with a flushed and angry face that put her immediately on guard.

"Well, what's happened to Klett?"

Agnes stretched her eyes at her. "What? What do you mean what's happened to him?"

Margaret gave an exasperated laugh. "I'm not used to rudeness, I suppose, not from students. I certainly won't have my mother subjected to it under her own roof."

"Why, what on earth did he do?" Agnes posed one hand against her bosom, but she could not keep herself from smiling a little, from feeling somehow triumphant that Klett had insulted her mother.

"It's just what I thought would happen. You've inflated his ego till the earth's not fit for him to walk on."

Of course the earth is not fit for him to walk on, Agnes thought. She smiled. "But what influence have *I* over him?"

Margaret looked at her, then went to the window and raised it a couple of inches. "If you don't mind," she said, and stood there.

Without a word, Agnes went to her bed, slipped off her shoes, undid her dressing gown and with the grace of old habit got beneath the covers. She felt better in bed. It was like a fortress.

"I'm taking Klett on tomorrow morning. Frankly I don't think I could stand it until Monday."

"Why are you taking him?" And with the question she felt her anger gathering. "You're taking him away from me, aren't you?"

"Don't be absurd."

"You want to deprive me of everything that can possibly give me a little pleasure, don't you?" she wailed, and she heard it herself now, her voice was an eerie falsetto, not breaking but sliding around in the upper register like something gone askew on slippery ice. Her voice sounded more perturbed than she felt.

"Agnie," Margaret said calmly, "you know that's ridiculous."

"You don't care how I might feel about Klett!" Now all that mattered was that Klett stay another day. She could not bear the thought of his leaving in the morning.

"People care too much how you feel, that's just the trouble," Margaret said slowly. "How you *think* you feel. They've pampered and petted you till you've . . . You're all mixed up inside, Agnie, don't you see that?"

"Nobody cares! They snatch things away from me and here I lie helpless!"

"Helpless!"

"Klett and I love each other and you're determined to separate us!"

"*Love* each other!"

"Just as you separated Walter and me." She knew she had gone astray now, but she had to come out with it, like the pianos ringing around the truth and yet, she felt, somehow true, too.

"Walter?—Don't you remember, Agnie, that I went to Chicago to talk with him—afterwards?"

Agnes remembered. "Love each other!" she gasped into the pillows.

"Agnes, stop it!"

"It's true!" She sat up with the closing of the door. Margaret had gone out. She sat rigidly, listening. Her palm hurt, and looking down, she saw she had twisted up the counterpane in a tight fist. She had almost never seen her hand in that attitude and it fascinated her.

When a moment later Margaret and Klett came into the room, Agnes found herself shaking inside with a feeling of guilt. But she held her head up proudly, smiling a little, looking at neither of them.

"I thought Klett and I might say good night and good-bye, Agnie. We'll be leaving early in the morning before you're awake probably."

"Yes?"

"Do you want to tell Klett what you've just told me?" Margaret asked quietly.

Agnes looked down at the counterpane, at her hand, which was still clenched.

"What is it?" Klett asked finally.

She had never felt so strange. She felt in a way prideless, yet prouder than she had ever been. She knew it would be like a great scalpel slicing through her, worse than the pain along the spine yet like it, too, when she spoke. "That we love each other." She had said it, and the pain came in her back, stiffening her, driving her nails deeper into her palm. But she must not let her head drop to the pillow.

Silence.

I have never cared less for myself, Agnes thought, feeling she soared through heavens, heard wind in her ears. All the banners of *Ivanhoe,* the thunder of battle, the bobbing plumes of Brian de Bois-Guilbert and the Templar a-gallop on the rocking-gaited armored horses, lances ready to tip for combat, all seemed to strike her, naked and vulnerable, with collective impact. *The consequences of the encounter were not instantly seen,* she thought, *for the dust raised by the trampling of so many steeds darkened the air, and it was a minute (a moment?) ere the anxious spectators could see the fate of the encounter. When the fight became visible, half the knights on each side were dismounted . . . some lay stretched on the earth as if never more to rise. . . .* Memory rushed on, and she had not known she remembered so much! . . . *and several on both sides . . . were stopping their blood with their scarfs, and endeavoring to extricate themselves from the tumult. The mounted knights . . . were now closely engaged with their swords, shouting their warcries, and exchanging buffets, as if honour and life depended on the issue of the combat.* In another moment, she thought, her heart must burst inside her and she die!

"Agnes!" It was Klett's voice, gentle, astounded.

She looked at him, so dazed by what she felt she could not see him, but only where his voice had come from. When ever had a love been revealed like this, she wondered, in the presence of a third person, the jealous sister, vanquished by the revelation? "It's true, isn't it, Klett?"

"Yes"—Klett smiled shyly—"it's true."

"Klett!"

Agnes laughed. "Why, you look perfectly horrified, Margaret! You never wanted me to have anything, did you?"

"Klett, are you as out of your mind as she?"

How boldly he faces her, Agnes thought. *Never had he looked more handsome or more courageous.* Then suddenly he turned, seized the hand Agnes extended weakly above the covers and kissed it.

"We're leaving tomorrow, Klett," Margaret said. Her voice was trembling, crawling with defeat, Agnes thought. "Whether you come on to New York or not is your own business now. In fact you can go to blazes!" She seemed about to say something else, but she turned and went out of the room.

Agnes laughed again. "You will stay? You don't have to go with her, Klett. You can go to school in Chicago, can't you?"

He nodded, troubled. Then he released her hand and went toward the door.

"You will stay, Klett?"

"Yes, I'll stay," he said as he went out.

She lay then in a kind of recuperative exhaustion, too exhilarated for the moment even to listen to the brief exchange of voices in the hall. She heard Klett's door close, and she closed her own eyes. She wanted to lie in a half sleep, thinking of the happiness that had come to her, letting herself only half believe it, as though it had been something she had read about or merely hoped for, letting it finally rise into her consciousness as a fact. Then her curiosity to know what Margaret had just said to Klett began to prod her. Suppose after all he had decided to leave with Margaret? He had not seemed quite sure.

She got up and went barefoot, tying the satin belt of her gown, down the hall. She knocked softly on Klett's door, feeling she fled from Margaret's light under the door behind her. She went in and saw him get up from the side of the bed.

"Klett!" She held her arms gently open. Now, really for the first time, she wanted to embrace him. The desire to feel the solidity of his shoulders in her arms, the side of his hair against her cheek, was less a pleasurable thing to anticipate than a relief of a sensation that seemed to rise from the core of her nerves.

But he shook his head. "Give me time to think."

Something had happened, she knew. She felt as though everything trembled on an edge, about to topple to one side or the other. "Klett, my darling, we should be rejoicing! We should sing!—You won't leave me, Klett."

He looked at her, holding himself proudly, though his eyes were miserable. "There is such a thing," he said, "as destiny."

She knew it was the proper answer, the answer to which there was no further question. "I know. Your music," she said quietly. "But you won't leave me, will you? We can be just as close, Klett." He would study in New York, perhaps, but at least he would write her wonderful letters, see her often. Finally he would be free to be with her always.

"Please!" He struck his forehead distractedly. "I must think!"

"I will leave you, my love," she said, proud of her restraint, and went back to her room.

She drew the covers up over her flat waist and pulled the dimmer light until it was almost out. To her surprise she was quite sleepy. She dozed awhile, half asleep, half awake, until a sudden idea, fresh and strong, awakened her completely. She would call Klett and Margaret into her room and all three of them would determine what was to be done. Klett would declare once more his love for her, would state firmly his intention to stay on in the house. Then Margaret would again acknowledge her defeat and prepare to leave them forever. Her mother, too, would be present and would of course side with her and Klett. Beneath her reserve she knew her mother possessed a strong romantic streak. It thrilled Agnes to imagine her mother's joy when she heard of their love.

By the gilt-faced clock always just barely legible in semidarkness from her bed, Agnes saw it was ten past one. Everyone of course was in bed and asleep now. She had a feeling of disappointment, as though she had come too late for some pleasant social event. The silence of sleep in the house first annoyed, then frightened her. She pictured Klett, Margaret, her mother with soft smiles on their reposeful faces. She felt the balance had tipped in her disfavor, that Klett had decided to leave in the morning. He had thought it over after she had left him, then had gone to bed on his decision. Margaret, too, was sleeping on her resolution to depart. Had she and Klett spoken again after she had come to bed? Her hands pulled nervously at the counterpane. Then suddenly she knew what she should do, to tip the balance back, to make sure that Klett would not leave in the morning. Margaret would leave, of course, because she hated her, but not Klett. And after a day or so, she would be surer of their love. It was so young now, how could he, so young himself, be sure? It fell therefore upon her to furnish proof. If she died, she thought, why, love was still stronger than death. Klett would still love her. But she did not believe that she would die, for love itself would preserve her.

She got up from her bed, looked a few seconds at her old pink wrap and finally went in nothing but her pale nightgown out into the hall. Now there was no light at all except that which came from the moon through the window in the door at the end. She opened it and went onto the little terrace of smooth flagstones that sent a chill from her bare feet up to the roots of her hair. She stood tall, lifting her face up.

The night sky looked rich as a painting. A round yellow-white moon floated fast, though not advancing beyond just left of the top of the chinaberry tree, through clouds of electric blue and royal blue shot with white. The sky itself was dark blue streaked with black in which the star groups—Orion, Auriga, Cassiopeia, part of Perseus, Agnes knew them all—could be seen twinkling with the dense blown clouds of the rain that had not come that evening at dusk.

"I have never," she whispered proudly, "cared so little for myself. Klett is all I care for, all that matters."

She stood on the low parapet of bricks that bordered the terrace. The bricks felt crumblike and still somewhat warm from the afternoon sun. From below, the song of the crickets came louder, and she heard the more human whisper of the garden faucet that had always leaked, that was fairly close, she knew exactly where. This was not Rebecca now, nor even Saxon Ulrica on the burning battlements of Torquilstone. This was Agnes, fair Agnes, at the most glorious moment she had ever experienced. Now all was perfect, like Klett, the exhilarating sharpness of the night, the purity of her intention, the slender whiteness of her body beneath the gown, as she poised herself like a diver on the edge of the parapet she gripped with her long toes.

And the air received her like cool water. Though it was much more agreeable than water, before a quick pain gave way to numbness she could not think or move against and did not really care to, before a blankness without moon or stars. Silence. And nothing.

She awakened in a strange room, on a harder bed. Her left arm lay across a stiff thick something over her abdomen. With a prickle of terror that almost immediately subsided, she realized she was in a hospital.

"Agnie?"

She turned toward Margaret's voice. Margaret stood there in hat and coat, with a compassionate expression that even then Agnes could find energy to hate.

"Darling, what happened?" Margaret asked. "Did you . . . fall?"

Agnes debated what to say, and decided the question was beneath reply. She was still exalted by a feeling that she cared nothing for herself, what happened or had happened to her body, so she could still wonder whether to say, "What does it matter?" or as she did:

"Where is Klett?"

"He's here. Shall I ask him to come in?"

Her mother entered with Dr. Reese, both rigid of face, soft of step. Agnes saw them in strange perspective, and realized suddenly she was seeing out of only one eye. Was the other destroyed or merely bandaged?

"Any pain?" Dr. Reese bent over her and she half expected the thermometer to slip into her mouth as it always had.

"Yes," Agnes said.

"Where?"

"All over."

Klett came in then with Margaret. He was in his jacket and plaid muffler and carried a briefcase he had had with him when he came to the house.

"Klett—you *are* staying? You *are* staying, aren't you?" She wanted to get up, and of all times, she thought, when she really could not, when the bed was no longer a coign of vantage.

"Rest yourself, Agnes," said her mother.

Agnes knew that his bent head was a nod as he stood with his hands folded in front of him, as she had seen him stand in her room, the epitome of knightly comportment, behind and to one side of her mother. But now was the time for him to step forward, to make her some declaration, some sign. She tried to sit up, Dr. Reese grasped her arm, but to sit up was impossible anyway. And now Klett's face was round and frightened, plumper and pinker even than she had thought.

"Please!" Dr. Reese exclaimed. "Your back is broken!"

She lay back, looking at Klett with parted lips, getting back her breath. He took a step toward her with a twisted, tragic face. But in the step she saw the urgency of outdoors, of the other world he was about to enter. He looked flat, like something cut from cardboard, and she saw him now backgrounded by the school in New York, the shell shape of an amphitheater above his head, surrounded by strange, earnest musicians' faces.

"I cannot tell you how sorry I am, Miss Steinach," he said, and it did not even sound like his voice.

"The doctors say you'll be quite all right, Agnie," Margaret told her. "And we'll talk to you from New York. They're going to put a phone right here by the bed." Margaret bent to kiss her.

Klett glanced at his wristwatch quickly. "We do have to leave," he said, "unless we catch another train."

"Good-bye, Agnie. Good-bye," Margaret said.

Dr. Reese lowered the shades and told her it would be best if she could sleep. Her mother pressed her toes with tremulous affection beneath the covers, but she knew her mother, too, was quite far from tears. Then she was all alone. She looked toward the shaded window and the tattered *Ivanhoe* on the new bedtable caught her eye. She smiled a little at it. It was like an old friend. And all the friends she had in it! The Templar, Ivanhoe, Rebecca and the Lady Rowena, Front-de-Boeuf and Richard Coeur-de-Lion, king of them all! They were somehow more substantial than Klett, than her sister, or Dr. Reese or her mother. *Ivanhoe* spread balm over her shocked mind and body.

"My back is broken," she whispered, savoring the words. And she knew it was what she had wanted all these years.

A MIGHTY NICE MAN

The child Charlotte sat on the narrow curbstone, her cheek against one knee, drawing idly in the dust with a stick. She sniffed at the flesh of her leg, smelt the dust and the sweat on it. Then she sighed and threw away the stick.

"Em'lie," she said.

Emilie, age nine, was standing behind her, with her back against the sun-warm wooden post, her toes braced on the edge of the sidewalk.

"Huh?" Emilie breathed.

"Play like I've got a store. Play like I've got a grocer store an' you've gotta buy stuff. . . . Huh, Em'lie?"

Emilie was so bored and sleepy she did not reply. Her gray sullen eyes looked out across the road and the whole scene was yellow to her, the dirt of the road, the squatting house just beyond, the dry fields: yellow pulsing heat and silence.

"Em'lie! You crazy? . . . Answer me!" Charlotte turned around on the curb and glowered at her.

"Wha'?" said Emilie, and pushed herself away from the post.

"I've gotta store an' you must buy stuff." She reached for the tiny red truck that was their common property and began filling it with pebbles. "An' then I must deliver it. You gotta go home first an' then you must telephone." She clutched the truck in one dirty hand as she scowled at Emilie.

They heard footsteps in the grit of the road. Charlotte forgot her game and they both looked up the slope. Emilie brushed the mottled blond hair out of her eyes and squinted. Her left eye was cast, and she twisted up that side of her face whenever she looked at anything.

"I betcha it's a boarder from Mrs. Osterman's," Charlotte said. "I betcha he's from New York, too."

He turned onto the sidewalk that began half a block from Charlotte's house. Emilie could see him now, a short figure in unpressed white trousers. He saw them, too, and began whistling a tune.

"Hello," he said, taking in both of them.

"H'lo," they replied in unison.

He stopped a minute, looked about him. "Gonna be here when I get back?" He spoke quietly, smiling. "I'll bring you some candy."

Charlotte and Emilie surveyed him silently.

"I like . . . I like *any* kind of candy," Charlotte told him.

He laughed, winked at them and walked on down the sidewalk. Once he turned and waved, but only Charlotte saw that. They were both motionless a long time, watching.

"Reckon he'll come back, Em'lie?"

"Huh?"

"Reckon he'll come back this way?"

"Huh?"

"I sed . . . reckon he'll come *back?*"

But Emilie moved off without a word toward her house and Charlotte sat on the curb, resting her face against one knee as she traced in the dust. Soon the screen door to Emilie's house screeched, closed with a double slap, and Emilie's bare heels thudded across the porch.

"Huh," said Emilie, and handed Charlotte a small pale peach. Charlotte took it silently, bit into the fruit with darkish baby teeth.

"Betcha that man's got a car."

"Huh?"

"I sed"—she took a deep breath—"I betcha that man's got a *ca-ar.*"

"Wha' man?"

"That *ma-an* . . . what just passed."

Emilie licked her peach-stained fingers. "He ain't comin' back." She sighed, looked across the hot road to the blurry yellowish fields. The bugs in the grass, in the trees, were singing rhythmically. Two clicks and a long buzz. Down the road where it met the street that led into town they heard Mr. Wynecoop's station wagon. They knew it from all the other cars in the neighborhood. Charlotte and Emilie sat on the edge of the curb and looked.

As he passed, Mr. Wynecoop waved a stiff-fingered hand at them, and they chanted, "H'lo, ol' man Wynecoop."

The car pulled up the hill, reached the top, sighed as it hit level ground. Charlotte kept watching for the man in white. She stood up once and looked toward town, but the view was mostly shut out by the trees along the sidewalk.

Emilie smirked and grunted contemptuously.

Charlotte held the empty truck in one hand and stared down the walk. "*You* cou'nt see him if he *was* comin'." Suddenly she drew in her breath. "He's comin', all right," she whispered, and ran stooping over to Emilie by the curb. She began stabbing in the dust, her heart beating fast.

Then Emilie heard his footsteps and twisted around and peered into the yellowness. He was whistling again. The blur of white came closer.

"He's got candy!" Charlotte said.

The man took his cigarette out of his mouth and threw it down.

"Hello," he said quietly, then glanced at the houses and back at the two little girls on the curb. He handed the bag to Charlotte. Two licorice sticks stuck out of the top, and she was disappointed to see that it was all penny candy, unwrapped caramels and sugar hearts that sell five for a cent. Once an old man from Mrs. Osterman's had brought her five-cent candy bars.

Slowly she put one end of a licorice stick into her mouth. The man shuffled uneasily, leaned against a tree and lighted another cigarette. "You didn't tell me your name," he said finally.

She told him, and he said his name was Robbie.

"I've got a car. . . . Want to go riding sometime?" He kept shifting and taking his hands in and out of his pockets. "I bet you like riding, Charlotte."

"I sure do," she said, and a dark stream of licorice juice ran down her chin.

The man leaning against the tree sprang toward her, drew a wadded handkerchief out of his hip pocket. He put one hand back of her head and wiped her face hard. "You're . . . pretty messy." Then he stood up again and put the handkerchief back. Emilie was watching him steadily, curiously. He felt the hostility in her twisted mouth.

He drew viciously on his cigarette. "How'd you like to go riding this evening?" he whispered. "After dinner."

"I'd like that," Charlotte said.

Then he went off quietly, looking back at them, smiling and friendly.

Charlotte was proud of herself. She leaned back on her hands and the thin muscles in her thighs showed under the dirt-streaked skin.

"He didn't ask *you* to go."

Emilie sighed. "He ain't comin'. You wait an' see."

So Charlotte waited. She finished the candy alone, picked at her noon meal, and brooded happily in the shade of the house, humming to herself. Then she lay in the patched-up hammock on her front porch and looked at the pictures in a frayed funny paper book. The afternoon was hot and long and silent.

After supper Charlotte went out to the road and stood by the tree. Her mother had given her a sponge bath, and she had a cotton dress on instead of the thin romper suit she wore all day. She had told her mother nothing about the man from Mrs. Osterman's. The fast-setting sun sent hot horizontal rays into her face. She was sure he would come. She tried to picture the car, like the ones she had seen in the movies. That was the kind of car *he* would have. And she would step into the big front seat and they would drive away with hardly a sound. They would drive fast.

But after a while she got tired and came in to the front porch. The wood was hot to her bare feet. She leaned on one side of the hammock, pushed herself into it. Still she listened and there was no sound of a car. Then the screen door to Emilie's house shrieked, stopped and shrieked again. Emilie appeared, unwashed and tousled, eating the remains of a slice of bread and butter. She came deliberately onto Charlotte's porch, stood chewing reflectively as she stared at her in the hammock. Charlotte disdained to look at her.

"Oh . . . *he* ain't comin'," she said, and turned around and walked to the steps. She heard something down the walk. "That your mother comin'? *She* don't know, I betcha."

Charlotte bounced out of the hammock. "Listen, Em'lie . . ." She frowned furiously. "If you . . . if you say to her . . ." She clenched her fists at her sides and Emilie gazed at her solemnly.

"Huh!"

But Charlotte had won.

There was no more sun, but it was still light. Charlotte's mother came back from the store. None of them said a word. The woman went into the house and Charlotte could hear her drawing water for the baby. Finally Emilie went hop-skipping across the front yard, into her house.

Charlotte lay in the hammock and listened for him. Someone was walking, whistling. She ran down to the sidewalk and saw him coming. He was dressed in white again with his jacket unbuttoned. He stopped when he saw her, smiled and beckoned. And she glanced once at her house, then ran up the warm pavement to where he stood.

"Where's your car?"

He looked about him, grinned and jerked his head. "Up the road. . . . We don't want nobody to know. You didn't tell nobody, did you?"

"No."

They walked together. She could hardly keep up with him, so he took her hand. The fields opened up on either side after the pavement stopped. Charlotte strained up to see the car, and then the road turned suddenly and they came upon it parked by the roadside. It was big, but not so bright as those in the movies. He opened the door and lifted her in, her feet dangling over the edge of the seat. Then he came in from the other side.

"All set?"

"Uh-huh." Charlotte was looking at the car inside.

"Like it?" he asked, and wiped his nose on the back of his hand.

They didn't drive off immediately. Charlotte was examining the gaudily colored dashboard, its clock with green numbers and silver hands. The other circles she did not understand, but they were all beautiful, colored and shining. The man caught her hand suddenly and she felt his fingers warm and moist, felt her mouth twist up as though she were about to cry. Then she wished that she had not come, wished that she were back on the front porch with Emilie. But he was smiling, laughing, even, as he started the car.

"You like to go fast?"

Charlotte tried to answer, but her lips were stiff. He squeezed her hand again.

"I like a lot of speed."

Then through the engine's noise she heard someone calling her name. The man heard it, too, and released her hand. But the car was moving on toward her house.

"Charlotte! Charlo-otte!"

"That's my mother," Charlotte said quietly.

Charlotte noticed that he frowned and that his hands tightened on the steering wheel. She felt the cool breeze in her face and she wanted to go on riding, but they were not going fast and she wanted to go fast. As they came near the house, she pressed herself against the seat, hoping her mother would not see her.

The woman stood with one foot on the curb, her apron hanging almost to the ground. She waved at them and he slowed the car. She came nearer, hiding her hands under her apron.

"Charlotte." She grinned, but she looked at the man almost flirtatiously. "Em'lie said you were out ridin'. I just wanted to make sure where you was . . . an' I need you to help with the baby now." She pushed some strands of hair behind her ear.

The man at the wheel smiled broadly and said, "How d'you do?"

Charlotte's mother nodded to him. "I allus have Charlotte help me with the baby 'bout this time after supper. . . . It's awful nice o' you to take her out ridin', mister, but she didn't say nothin' to me about it." She laughed nervously.

"Sure, I know," he said. He stretched one arm across and opened the door gallantly. "Maybe tomorrow, then. I'll be around for a few days."

The woman looked in awe at the shiny dials and knobs, the upholstered seats. "Why . . . I'd like you to take her ridin' . . . most anytime."

Then Charlotte and her mother walked hand in hand down the sidewalk. Once the woman cast a timid glance back at the car. "He's a mighty nice man for a city fellah, Charlotte. Where'd you meet up with him? . . . An' say, ain't that a pretty car?"

Charlotte watched the ground pass below her bare feet. Her free hand brushed along the coarse grass that grew high.

"Maybe he'll be around tomorrow," her mother said.

One blade of grass Charlotte caught convulsively and the edges jerked through her fingers. As she looked at her thumb, two thin red lines came out of the flesh.

QUIET NIGHT

Hattie pulled the little chain of the reading lamp, drew the covers over her shoulders, and lay tense, listening till Alice's sniffs and coughs should subside.

"Alice," she whispered.

No response. Yes, she was sleeping already, though she insisted she never closed an eye before the clock struck eleven.

Hattie eased herself to the edge of the bed, slowly put out a white stockinged foot. She twisted around to look at Alice, of whom nothing was visible except a thin nose projecting between the ruffle of her nightcap and the sheet pulled over her mouth. She was quite still.

Hattie rose gently from the bed, her breath coming short with excitement. In the semidarkness she could see the two sets of false teeth sitting in their glasses of water on the bed table. She giggled nervously.

Like a white ghost she made her way across the room, past the Victorian upholstered settee. She stopped at the sewing table, lifted the folding top, and groped among the spools and pattern papers till she found the cold metal of the scissors. Then holding them tightly, she crossed the room again. She had left the door of the closet slightly ajar earlier in the evening, and it swung open noiselessly. Hattie reached a trembling hand into the blackness, felt the two stiff woolen coats, a few dresses. Finally she touched a fuzzy thing hanging next to the wall. She was giggling as she lifted the hanger down, and the scissors slipped out of her hand. There was a loud clatter, followed by some half-suppressed laughter. Hattie peeked round the door at Alice, motionless on the bed. Alice was rather hard of hearing.

With her white toes turned up stiffly, Hattie clumped to the easy chair by the window where a bar of moonlight slanted, and sat down with the scissors and the Angora sweater in her lap. In the moonlight her face gleamed, toothless and demoniacal. She examined the sweater in the manner of a person who plays with a piece of steak with a fork before deciding where to put his knife.

It was really a beautiful sweater. Alice had received it the week before from her niece. It was a birthday present, for Alice would never have indulged in such a luxury herself. She was happy as a child with it, and had worn it every day with her dresses.

The scissors cut purringly up the soft wool sleeves, between the wristband and the shoulder. She considered. There should be one more cut. The back, of course. But only about a foot long so it should not be immediately visible.

A few seconds later, she had put the scissors back into the table, hung the sweater in the closet, and was lying between the two feather mattresses. She heaved a tremendous sigh. She thought of the gaping sleeves, of Alice's face the next morning. The sweater was utterly beyond repair and she was immensely pleased with herself.

They were awakened at eight-thirty by the hotel maid. It was a ritual that never failed: three bony raps on the door and a bawling voice, with a hint of insolence: "Eight-thirty. You can get breakfast now." Then Hattie, who always woke first, would poke Alice's shoulder.

Mechanically they sat up on their respective sides of the bed and pulled their nightgowns over their heads, revealing clean white undergarments. They said nothing. Five years of coexistence had dwindled their conversation to rock-bottom efficiency.

This morning, however, Hattie was thinking of the sweater. She felt self-conscious, but she could think of nothing to say or do to relieve the tension. Hattie spent some fifteen minutes doing her hair. She had a braid nearly two feet long when she fixed it at night, and twice a day she would take it down for its hundred strokes. Her hair was her only vanity. Already dressed, she stood shifting uneasily, pretending to be fastening her snaps.

But Alice seemed to take an age at the wash basin, gargling with her solution of salt and tepid water. She held stubbornly to salt and water in the morning, in spite of Hattie's tempting bottle of red mouthwash sitting on the shelf.

"What are you giggling at now?" Alice turned from the basin, her face wet and smiling a little. Hattie could say nothing, looked at the teeth in the glass and snickered again.

"Here's your teeth." She reached the glass awkwardly to Alice. "I thought you were going down to breakfast without them."

"Now when did I ever go off without my teeth, Hattie?"

Alice smiled in spite of herself. It was going to be a good day, she thought. Mrs. Crumm and her sister were back from a weekend, and they could all play rummy together in the afternoon. She walked to the closet in her stocking feet, a smile playing absently about her mouth.

Hattie watched as she took down the powder blue dress, the one that went best with the beige Angora. She fastened all the little buttons in front. She took the sweater off the hanger and put one arm into the sleeve.

"Oh," she breathed painfully. Then like a hurt child her eyes squinted and her face twisted petulantly. Tears came quickly down her cheeks. "H-Hattie . . ." She turned to her and could say nothing else.

Hattie smirked, uncomfortable yet enjoying herself thoroughly. "Well I do know!" she exclaimed. "Who might have done a trick like that!" She went to the bed and sat down, doubled up with laughter.

"Hattie . . . Hattie you did this," Alice declared in unsteady tones. She clutched the sweater to her. "Hattie . . . you're just mean."

Lying across the bed, Hattie was almost hysterical. "You know I didn't now, Alice. . . . Hah-haw! . . . Why do you think I'd . . . ?" Her voice was choked off with uncontrolled laughter.

She lay there several minutes before she was calm enough to go down to breakfast. And when she left the room, Alice was sitting in the big chair by the window, sobbing, her face buried in the Angora sweater.

Alice did not come down until she was called for lunch. She chatted at the table with Mrs. Crumm and her sister and took no notice of Hattie.

She sat opposite Alice, silent and restless, but she was not at all sorry for what she had done. She could have endured days of indifference on Alice's part, without feeling the slightest remorse.

It was a beautiful day. After lunch, they went with Mrs. Crumm, her sister, and the hotel hostess, Mrs. Holland, and sat in Gramercy Park.

Alice pretended to be absorbed in her book. It was a detective story by her favorite author, borrowed from the hotel's circulating library. Mrs. Crumm and her sister did most of the talking. A weekend trip was of sufficient importance to provide a topic of conversation for several afternoons, and Mrs. Crumm was able to remember every item of food she ate on visits for days running.

The monotonous tones of the voices, the warmth of the sunlight lulled Alice into half sleep. The page was blurred to her eyes.

Earlier in the day she had planned to adopt an attitude toward Hattie. She should be cold and aloof, even hostile. It was not the first time Hattie had committed such an outrage. There was the ink spilt on her lace tablecloth four months ago, and her missing morocco volume of Tennyson. She was sure Hattie had it, somewhere. And that evening, she would calmly pack her bag, write Hattie a note, short but carefully worded, and leave the hotel. She could go to another hotel in the neighborhood, let it be known through Mrs. Crumm where she was, and have the satisfaction of Hattie's coming to her and apologizing. But the fact of it was, she was not at all sure that Hattie would come to her, and this embarrassing possibility, plus a characteristic lack of enterprise prevented her taking such a dangerous course. . . . What if she had to spend the rest of her life alone? . . . It was much easier to stay where she was, to have a pleasant game of rummy in the afternoon, with ice cream and cookies, and to take out her revenge in little ways. It was also more ladylike, she consoled herself. She did not think beyond this, of the particular situations when she would say or do things calculated to hurt Hattie. The opportunities would just come of themselves.

Mrs. Holland nudged her. "We're going to get some ice cream now. Then we're going back to play some rummy."

"I was just at the most exciting part of the book." But she rose with the others and was almost cheerful as they walked to the drug store.

She won at rummy, too, and she felt pleased with herself. Hattie, watching her uneasily all day, was much relieved when Alice decreed speaking terms again.

Nevertheless, the thought of the ruined sweater rankled in Alice's mind, prodded her with a sense of injustice. Indeed, she was ashamed of herself for being able to consider it as lightly as she did. It was letting Hattie walk over her. She wished she could muster a really strong hatred.

They were in their room reading at nine o'clock. Every vestige of Hattie's shyness or pretended contrition had vanished.

"Wasn't it a nice day?" she ventured.

"H-m-m." Alice did not raise her head.

"Well," she made the inevitable remark through the inevitable yawn, "I reckon I'll be going off to bed."

And a few minutes later they were both in bed, propped up by four pillows, reading; Hattie with the newspaper and Alice with her detective story. They were silent for a while, then Hattie adjusted her pillows and lay down.

"Good night, Alice."

"Good night."

Soon Alice pulled out the light, and there was absolute silence in the room except for the soft ticking of the clock and the occasional purr of an automobile. The timepiece on the mantel whirred and then began to strike ten.

Alice lay open-eyed. All day her tears had been restrained and now, automatically, she began to cry. She wiped her nose on the top of the sheet. But they were not childish tears.

She raised herself on one elbow. The darkish braid of hair outlined Hattie's neck and shoulder against the white bedclothes. She felt very strong, strong enough to murder Hattie with her own hands. But the idea of murder passed from her mind as swiftly as it had entered. Her revenge had to be something that would last, that would hurt, something that Hattie must endure and that she, Alice, could enjoy.

Then it came to her, and she was out of bed, walking boldly to the sewing table as Hattie had done twenty-four hours before . . . and she was standing by the bed, bending over Hattie, peering at her placid, innocent face through her tears and her short-sighted eyes. Two quick strokes could cut the braid, right near the head.

But suddenly her fingers were limp, hardly strong enough to hold the scissors, much less slice through a rope of hair.

She steadied herself on the bed table . . . Hattie, dear Hattie . . . Hattie meant well. Hattie was just mischievous. She laid the scissors on the table and gave a great sob.

Hattie yawned and squinted her eyes open.

"I . . . I was just getting a drink of water," Alice said. She moved toward the basin.

Hattie yawned and grunted.

"Would you like some?"

"I don't mind if I do," Hattie murmured.

She brought her a tumbler half full, and Hattie took it without a word as a child would. Alice felt her way around the bed and climbed in. She lay there looking at the ceiling with sore tear-pink eyes, and after a moment she heard Hattie set the glass down on the table.

DOORBELL FOR LOUISA

The mere sight of her name spelled "Trott" on the square white envelope whose flap was parsimoniously tucked in was almost enough to make Louisa Trotte throw it away without opening it. It was only an advertisement from the department store where she kept a charge account anyway. But because she seldom got mail of any kind, Louisa, standing by the long table in Mrs. Holpert's dimly lighted hall, slipped the booklet out, slanted it toward the yellowish bulb in a candlelike wall fixture, and gave the fur coats a rather nearsighted, thoughtful, but quite detached attention. Slowly, a strand of copper-tinged brown hair pulled from the bun at the back of her neck, stood out horizontal, then drooped slightly.

"H'lo, Miss Trott."

Louisa Trotte adjusted her glasses a little on the bridge of her long thin nose and peered into the Cimmerian darkness at the hall's rear. "Good morning, Jeannie!" she called as a small pale blur moved closer.

"Did you get a letter?" Jeannie asked, shyly twisting up the tail of her shift till it was above her navel.

Louisa glanced at the big brown stairway, lest one of the male roomers be descending its carpeted steps, then went to Jeannie and pulled her dress down. She gave the child an impulsive hug that brought her soft stomach abruptly against her bony knees, then released her with a pat across the buttocks. "Yes, I've got a letter, Jeannie. Would you like to share it with me?"

"I *wan-nit,*" Mrs. Holpert's little granddaughter replied, and began twisting up her dress again.

"Ju-ust a minute," Louisa said, turning through the last pages as carefully as she had the first. One coat she rather liked, a black Persian lamb with generous, turned-back cuffs. But four hundred and forty-nine dollars!

Closing her mind to the fur coats as abruptly as she closed the booklet, Louisa bent down and presented the latter to the little girl. "Here you are! Pick yourself out a nice warm fur coat and show it to me when I come home. All right?"

"Awright."

From the back of the hall came the sound of a child's coughing, distant and thin.

"How's your little sister?" Louisa asked, jerking straight the jacket of her black suit.

"She's worser," Jeannie replied. "Gramma says."

"*Is* she?" Louisa did not like Eleanor so well as she did Jeannie, though perhaps that was ridiculous to say of a baby hardly three years old. "Well, you be careful you don't catch it. *Sweetie!*" She caught Jeannie again, patted her head with a flat, bony hand, and turned toward the door.

"Got any sugar lumps?"

Louisa stopped and felt in the side pocket of her jacket. "I certainly have. Here!" She laid a wrapped lump in Jeannie's chubby palm and watched the fingers with the incredibly tiny nails close over it. It was one of the lumps she saved from her lunch to give Al, the flower man's horse, who was generally somewhere near on West End Avenue when she came home from work. But tonight there would be more sugar lumps.

"Good-bye, Jeannie!"

She strode across the polished, creaky floor toward the tall double doors with colored glass that opened to a square tile foyer, then through the next pair of doors onto the sunny brownstone steps. She walked briskly toward Riverside Drive and the bus stop one block north.

"Trott indeed!" she murmured as she dropped the empty envelope into a wastepaper receptacle. Bad enough that American pronunciation had won the battle with the final *e* during the fifteen years she had been in the country, people could at least spell the name correctly.

It was not that she was seriously disturbed by her name's misspelling, for she was not vain or small-minded, but that she hated inefficiency and she had nothing else particularly to think of that morning.

Her work was going smoothly at the office, and she had no eye for the changing colors of early autumn that showed in the strip of green park along the drive. Her long upward-sloping nose took no pleasure in the cool new air of eight-thirty in the morning.

And somehow, too, the incompetence of the unknown addresser of her letter prompted her to think, dully and idly as she rode on the top deck of the bus, of other minor irritations in her life, of her liquor-loving brother who was wandering somewhere in Europe, of the increasing difficulties of living in New York on her modest salary, or the fact she had been forced to wait nearly ten minutes for Mr. Noenzi to come out of the bathroom that morning, and of the obliquely slanting handle that projected from the dark ventilator shaft in the ceiling over the tub—a clumsy thick stick of wood that looked violent and made the word *murder* enter her mind every time she saw it. It looked as though someone held the other end of it. But none of these annoyances troubled her gravely. They merely played around in her brain and caused a look of mild distraughtness to be fixed on her face as she scanned the front page of the *Times*. To fret about things gave Louisa, unconsciously, a *raison d'être*.

When the bus turned from Fifty-seventh Street onto Fifth Avenue, she dismounted and began to walk southward. She might have ridden the bus down to Forty-eighth Street, of course, but each morning, if it wasn't raining, she walked the nine blocks for exercise.

Her somewhat tall, somewhat angular figure, the figure of an unmarried, professionally efficient, tolerably content woman of forty-five, had gathered full speed by Fifty-fifth Street. The hem of her black suit's skirt, widened at the bottom by a series of pleats six inches long all the way around, flounced spiritedly about her hustling bony legs, and the wisp of coppery brown hair that had slipped from the big tortoise hairpin undulated behind her with each aggressive step. Atop her head sat a round-brimmed little black hat with straight sides, unobtrusive and meaningless, a dutiful observance of convention. Her shoulders were tense and rather thrust forward beneath the black jacket whose tailoring was relieved by four closely set buttons down the front. Fifteen years of secretarial work had not much broadened her hips, though all her skirts slatted a little across her flat derriere.

Besides classifying her, probably immediately, as a secretary, one thought of Europe when one saw Miss Louisa Trotte hurrying down Fifth Avenue of a morning. There was a more complex emanation from her oxford shoes, her old custom-made suit, and her copper-glinting bun than that of simple practicality. There was the look of an individual about her, and a stamp of romance and adventure that one sees sometimes in a good, well-used suitcase carelessly splotched with faded stickers. She would live, one thought, in a furnished room, for the mobility of a traveler sat lightly upon her, a room whose walls bore photographs of the Black Forest, a canal in Holland, a seaport in Denmark, or a fjord in Norway. Her bathroom would be down the hall in the quiet, irreproachably clean and respectable old house to which her instinct and training would have led her as surely as it leads a homing pigeon back to its base. One might have imagined her cultivating a small window box in spring, on fine Saturday afternoons sitting in a camp chair on the gritty triangle of roof outside her second-story rear window, a roof which overlooks the postage stamp garden of her landlady, drying her hair carefully with a white bath towel. For she would be selfish about her two free days a week, through long habit preferring her own company to that of the best of her few friends. Seeing her en route to work in the morning, one might have imagined her a few minutes earlier standing by an electric plate, dipping a sweet bun into a cup of black coffee and staring into space. And, if one had imagined all this about Louisa Trotte, one would have been almost exactly correct. Except that the pictures on her walls were small oil paintings by her aunt of Copenhagen Harbor and its surroundings, or Gloucester watercolors she had acquired on one of her summer vacations. The fading photographs of the Black Forest and the Spreewald, the strange, haphazard snapshots her brother had made in Holland, treasured just because they were by him, Louisa kept in a leather-bound album that had stayed only half full for the last ten or twelve years.

And anyone with the perspicacity to imagine these things about Louisa would have seen, too, that something in her transcended the frustrated spinster, the eccentric old maid. An air of independence and contentment sheathed her from ridicule. Her patina of an older continent could stop an American's smile and command respect. She looked as though she had a few thoughts and possessions of her own and was not envious of those of other people.

Who knows, maybe he's dead! Louisa thought of her brother as she turned onto Forty-eighth Street. *I'll just put him right out of my mind.* The last a phrase she used very often for matters she was afraid, being alone, and there being so little she could do if she wanted to, to think out.

Then an old image of Europe and her brother rose up before her eyes: a drunken Gert sitting on some tavern bench, and all the chaos of the years of Hitler and the world conflict breaking over him like a great wave that wobbled his head a little, rushed on and left him sitting, sodden, in the same place. No, what could kill Gert? Who would bother killing him?

She had not heard from him in two years, when he had been, of all sober places on earth, at The Hague. It was even a drunken letter he had written last, partly in Dutch, mainly in Danish, not at all about himself or what had happened or what he intended to do, but about sunlight on stone steps somewhere. It had been enough to disgust a decent being who felt some interest and responsibility for what was going on in Europe. Louisa thought herself quite justified in outting him off from her life. Only sometimes, like this morning, when she took inventory of her discomforts, Louisa felt she might be doing something for him, simply because he was one more care her energetic temperament might take on.

"Morning, Miss Trott," said the elevator man.

"Good morning, George," Louisa replied. Her gentle, dark hazel eyes blinked thoughtfully behind her glasses. Her small, tapering and slightly plump face, soft as the limp cotton collar of her blouse that was fastened at the neck with a little bar pin of seed pearls, slowly shed its distraughtness and had taken on a pleasant, alert expression by the time she stepped out of the elevator at the eleventh floor.

Louisa was well into the morning's work before Mr. Bramford entered their office in the Pioneer Engineering and Designing Company. The sight of his slow, substantial figure in the pepper-and-salt suit laid the last ghost of disquietude in Louisa's mind. She could not have imagined a finer, more kindly, yet comfortably impersonal man to work for than Mr. Clarence Bramford, managing editor of publications. In the past ten years, she might have gone elsewhere many times for a higher salary, but Louisa knew something about character and the character of a business organization, and she knew when she was well off.

"It's a fine day, isn't it, Miss Trotte?" Mr. Bramford said as he stuck his hat on top of the clothes tree where Louisa's hat and pocketbook hung.

"It is indeed, Mr. Bramford."

"I imagine the drive looks quite pretty."

"Yes, it does." She thought he seemed a little depressed by something. It was not like him to talk so much.

Louisa was surprised that Jeannie did not come upstairs while she was making her cup of tea. She always drank a cup of tea and relaxed a moment before she went out to supper, and it was Jeannie's habit to stroll in and to eat one of the cookies Louisa kept on hand just for her. With her stockinged feet extended luxuriously before her, Louisa sat a long while in her one easy chair, listening for Jeannie's small knock, low down on the door, but it did not come. She was more disappointed than she admitted to herself, for she remembered the department store booklet, and she had thought that she and Jeannie could choose fur coats for themselves. Then she forced a smile, just to cheer herself up. The child probably had something more amusing to do than to visit her. And the Persian lamb coat, if indeed she had really liked it, would have had to go the way of all her whims, like the ski train she wanted to take north sometime—with skis and full regalia, of course—and the week she wanted to spend at the Plaza Hotel. Funny whims for a woman who got older every year. And poorer! Which was to say, the amount she could save regularly out of her salary grew less every year.

By half past six, washed and in a complete change of clothing to heighten the pleasure of the main meal of her day, Louisa was on her way down Mrs. Holpert's stairs. She heard the front door close, and saw Mrs. Holpert returning to her apartment down the hall.

"Evening, Miss Trott," Mrs. Holpert said.

"Good evening, Mrs. Holpert. Is Eleanor any better this evening?"

Mrs. Holpert's wide form came to a stop. "That was the doctor then. Jeannie's down with the same kind of cough, and the doctor says it looks like scarlet fever."

Scarlet fever! That's quite serious, isn't it?"

"It is." Slouched in her plain housedress and flat-heeled slippers, Mrs. Holpert looked stricken and resigned. "He's coming back for a look tomorrow, and if it's so, why, I've got my hands full, with Helen away."

Louisa had almost forgotten Mrs. Holpert was not the children's mother, but their grandmother. Helen was out of town most of the time with her theater work. It was Louisa's opinion Helen was too interested in men. "I'm very sorry to hear," Louisa said rather formally, for she was not on intimate terms with Mrs. Holpert. "Tell Jeannie Miss Trotte sends her kind regards and for her to get well so we can look at the fur coats together. She'll know what I mean."

The next morning on her way to the bathroom, Louisa encountered Miss Eldstahl, who lived in the next room to hers.

"Did you hear, Miss Trott?" Miss Eldstahl whispered. "Mrs. Holpert's little girls have got scarlet fever!"

"Really? Are they going to the hospital?" Louisa asked casually, determined not to be as emotional as Miss Eldstahl.

"No, they've been quarantined instead. Mrs. Dusenberre said they looked like *two little embers of fever,* and Mrs. Holpert told me last night she thinks she's coming down with it, too. I'm certainly going to give the back hall a wide berth, and you can pass the word on to the others." With a sudden dilation of her eyes, Miss Eldstahl glided up the hall toward her room, her freshly washed face and long bathrobe lending her an air of dramatic tragedy.

When Miss Eldstahl's door had closed, Louisa went and leaned over the thick brown banister. She did not know whether to believe Miss Eldstahl's report entirely. Both she and Mrs. Holpert, Louisa considered, were alarmists. Still, there was a hushed feeling belowstairs. The thought that Jeannie might not stroll out to see her as she looked at the mail, the fact that she had not visited the evening before, sent a twinge of anxiety through Louisa.

Downstairs, as she looked absently through the mail that was not sorted as usual on the long table, Louisa debated whether to go back and call on Mrs. Holpert to see how Jeannie was. She looked at her wrist-watch, saw that she had less time than usual, then strode off toward the darkness at the back of the hall. She was especially pleased that Miss Eld-stahl was descending the stairs at that moment.

"Come in," Mrs. Holpert called weakly in answer to Louisa's knock.

Louisa stepped into a dark foyer, from which she could see, through a half-open door beyond, Mrs. Holpert propped up in her four-poster bed. The single light from the lamp on her bedtable gave an atmosphere of gloom. Mrs. Holpert's apartment was always in twilight, for the windows faced on the side alleys or on the walled-in garden at the rear.

Mrs. Holpert waved her hand above the bedclothes. "Don't come any closer. I thought you was the doctor."

Louisa did not know what to say at first. Mrs. Holpert did not look flushed as she thought the children would. And there was something about the woman's bulk beneath the disheveled sheets that was distaste-ful to Louisa. "Are the children any better, Mrs. Holpert?"

"They'll get worse of course before they're better."

"Well, it's not likely grown people will catch the disease, is it?" Louisa asked, feeling rather foolish backed up against the door where Mrs. Holpert had motioned her.

"It's hit me," Mrs. Holpert averred. "And what it'll do to my heart, Lord only knows. I hear it's death on a weak heart."

"Really!" Louisa almost added, "If there's anything I can do . . ." But Mrs. Holpert, she felt sure, was still able to do for herself. She looked at the closed door off Mrs. Holpert's room, from behind which came Jean-nie's muffled coughing. She would have liked to see Jeannie, but some-how she did not want to ask even this favor of Mrs. Holpert.

"Reach me that water glass, Miss Trott?" Mrs. Holpert requested, extending her arm feebly.

Louisa handed her the glass from the bedtable. Then she glanced at her wristwatch, as though there were things she had to do, too.

Mrs. Holpert, however, did not seem to see the gesture. She was sip-ping slowly from the glass she held with both hands, and her eyes were closed. "Wish you'd see how the children are, Miss Trott. Just look in, if you will."

Louisa started for the door, aware of the contrast of her whiplike fig-

ure with the sluggish obesity on the bed. The room beyond was dark, and
Jeannie sat up and squinted at the light the opening door let in.

"Jeannie, darling? It's Miss Trott."

As though the sight of her friend recalled the pleasures she was
missing, Jeannie screwed her face up and began to wail.

"Jeannie, you mustn't cry!" Louisa felt very inadequate and awkward, with Mrs. Holpert within hearing. She glanced at the smaller
Eleanor, who lay sleeping in her big wooden playpen across the room,
her arms thrown up beside her curly blond head. Louisa thought her face
looked darkly rosy. Scarlet fever! And closed up with her in this room,
Jeannie would certainly have caught it, too. Hadn't Mrs. Holpert the
sense to have kept them separate? Something in Louisa resented the children's suffering with a fighting compassion. It was perhaps her hatred of
inefficiency, her contempt for Mrs. Holpert's carelessness. She wanted to
go and lay her hand on Jeannie's forehead, but she was not sure that
would serve any purpose at all. Moreover, she found herself somewhat
repelled. She felt she could almost see the germs that hung and milled
about in the air. There was a strange smell in the room that put her on
guard, not merely the smell of medicine, but of sickness.

"Why, you'll be feeling fine in no time, Jeannie. Then we can look at
the fur coats together. Remember? Won't that be nice?" How hypocritical
she felt.

"Nope. I'm sick!" Jeannie said, the cry of the betrayed.

Louisa went back into Mrs. Holpert's room and closed the door. She
wanted to haul the woman out of bed. "You're having a nurse, I suppose?"

Mrs. Holpert shook her head. "Not yet. I'll manage somehow. I'll
manage."

Saving her money, but what about the children? Louisa thought, as
she bade good-bye to Mrs. Holpert and walked slowly up the hall. She
stopped at the first doors and stood staring at the multicolored lozenges
of glass. Then suddenly she turned and went to the pay telephone under
the stairs. By the yellow bulb's light she could just see to dial.

"Hello, Miss Freeman? This is Louisa Trotte. Would you tell Mr. Bramford when he comes in that I'll be an hour or so late this morning? . . ."

When Louisa put the receiver down, she felt like a derailed train. For
the first time in five or six years, she was not going to be at work by nine

o'clock. She had decided to wait for the doctor and to ask just how badly off Jeannie was.

"You give the children one of these every two hours, and Mrs. Hoplert two every two hours. It's a mild anti-phlogistine."

Louisa nodded and looked at the bottle of white pills the doctor set on the foyer table. She did not like the doctor. In the first place, he seemed too young and too fast about things. In the second, he could not get Mrs. Holpert's name straight, though she had corrected him twice. And knowing nothing about her except that she was one of the lodgers, he had entrusted her with these pills.

"That clear?" Dr. Marlowe said, throwing on his tweed topcoat.

"Yes." Louisa hesitated. She looked at Mrs. Holpert's door. "But you see I—ordinarily I go to business."

"Oh. But you're taking today off, aren't you?"

"Yes. I suppose so."

"Good. I'll see about getting a nurse or something by tonight. Guess I'll call in about . . . six-thirty."

Louisa listened to his firm tread up the hall. Then the doors slammed and there was silence. She was closed in with the three bedridden, and there was no one in the house on whom she could thrust the pills. The only one who did not go to business was Mr. Noenzi, who was almost too old to move. And Mrs. Dusenberre, of course, but she was too stupid for any use. Mrs. Dusenberre could kill all three of them.

"Louisa?" Mrs. Holpert's voice drifted plaintively.

Well, she thought, Mr. Bramford could do without her for one day. After all these years! She turned and went into Mrs. Holpert's room with the same vigorous step she would have used that morning had she been walking down Fifth Avenue.

The morning had slipped into afternoon before Louisa looked at her watch with an eye to finding out the time for herself. It was quarter past one. Mrs. Holpert was asleep after what Louisa considered a rather hearty meal. Mr. Bramford would be returning from lunch, hanging his brown felt hat on the clothes tree that would be quite bare. Louisa looked about at Mrs. Holpert's bedroom, which she had just dusted and swept, at the articles which had become familiar to her in the past four hours, and she found it strange to think of the interior of Mr. Bramford's office some fifty blocks away. It was strange to think of its being quarter past one of a Thursday afternoon and she not there. Mr. Bramford probably thought she had decided to take the entire morning off, and would come in after lunch. But now that she was *not* there after lunch . . .

She sank down into Mrs. Holpert's armchair, suddenly very tired with the unaccustomed physical activity of the morning, and for a moment yielded to a fancy she had not since childhood, of imagining the movements of a faraway person moment by moment. . . . Mr. Bramford would be standing by the window now, smoothing slowly his graying hair, which had been ruffled by his hat. He would be wondering if she were on her way, or what the matter could be. He would sit down, start to read something, then decide to call her. He would reach for the phone and tell Miss Freeman to dial—

The telephone anticipated Louisa by a few seconds, and she jumped half out of her chair. She hurried into the hall, her heart beating oddly fast as she told herself it could not be he.

But it was Mr. Bramford. The sound of his quiet, hesitant voice reassured her.

"You're not sick, are you?" Mr. Bramford asked worriedly when Louisa had explained.

"No, indeed! It's just that there's no one else here to look after them until the nurse comes tonight. . . . Oh, yes, Mr. Bramford, I'll be in tomorrow. I hope it doesn't inconvenience you too much. . . . Well, thank you, Mr. Bramford. That's very kind of you. And oh, yes, those Phipps Motor letters are in the upper left-hand drawer of my desk. . . ."

Smiling tensely, with an absent look in her eyes, Louisa walked back into Mrs. Holpert's room, through the children's room and down the hall to the kitchen, from whose window she looked out on the little garden she had always seen from her second-story roof. The sunlight fell vertically now on the jungle of pointed leaves of the big tree in the center, and on the scraggly ivy that went partially up the brick wall at one side. She noticed that some of the leaves were turning brown, and realized that it was really autumn now, not merely the vague end of summer. It was nice somehow to have a day in which she did not work as she usually did. She did not feel guilty at all since speaking with Mr. Bramford. She could appreciate the day, even though she had more difficult tasks than usual, just because of its novelty. Funny, she thought, that she should enjoy a break in routine so much, when she knew how devoted she was to routine.

That evening, the young doctor confirmed his belief that Mrs. Holpert had scarlet fever.

"Well," he sighed to Louisa in the outside hall, "she'll fuss about her weak heart, of course, but there's no danger as long as you keep her in bed."

"That'll be easy enough," Louisa said, rather testy after her long day. "Well, shall I try for a nurse?"

Dr. Marlowe shook his head in a way that vexed Louisa. "Miss Trotter, there's not a nurse to be had for a case like this unless you advertise all over the place. I know. I've tried five hospitals."

"But—I've got my work to do, too," Louisa protested.

He nodded. "Try and get someone else in the house to relieve you, that's all. They won't need constant attention. I'll look in tomorrow morning." He screwed his fountain pen cap on and handed Louisa a scrawled note. "Instructions about those new pills. You're doing a fine job so far. See you tomorrow."

Louisa gave a sniff at his retreating figure. Yet his careless phrase about her service had pleased her. She felt needed. She was also needed at the office, but more, she was needed here. Jeannie needed her. There was no one else in the house she could imagine nursing Jeannie properly. She smiled with a look of stern gratification and bent nearer the lamp to read the new instructions she had crumpled in self-generated shyness.

The red spots popped out like suddenly ripening strawberries, borne on pinkish runners that darted here and there like rivulets of water. The red spots covered all her sight, and began to glow and seethe with heat. She could feel their hot radiation all about her, and from somewhere beneath the wild scarlet pattern, Jeannie's hoarse little voice cried bewilderedly. Louisa struggled, opened her eyes, and the red pattern drew back from the sides, revealed the children's room, contracted to Jeannie's shoulders, neck, and face just above the white sheet.

Louisa was across the room in an instant. "There, now, I'll turn your pillow over so it'll be cool again. How's that?"

Jeannie fell back and twisted her head from side to side on the turned pillow, "Miss Trott—Miss Trott, I don't feel good."

Louisa's breast tightened, and its congested pain was repeated throbbingly in her head. She could stand anything, she thought as she salved Jeannie's chest, except the sight of a child suffering, of her Jeannie suffering. How frightful that mothers had to watch their children suffer through so many diseases! Chicken pox, whooping cough, measles—how agonizing it must be! She smoothed the blondish hair back from the child's forehead, which was so hot her fingertips seemed to cling to it. Should she take the temperature again? An hour ago it had been a hundred and two. Dr. Marlowe said this morning that the crisis for the children should come in twenty-four hours. Louisa looked at her wristwatch, saw that it was six-fifteen, and thought that it was just about the time she ordinarily had tea in her room, when Jeannie would come knocking and hold out her hand for the chocolate marshmallow cookie Louisa would give her from a long box. . . . Louisa slid the wristwatch strap nervously up and down on her wrist, which had grown thinner the past two days.

"Water," Jeannie said, at the same time as Eleanor the baby started puling from the bottom of the wooden pen.

Jeannie's water glass was full of little air bubbles, so Louisa hurried to draw a fresh glass from the tap in the bathroom. Over the sound of the running water, she heard Eleanor losing the milk she had got her to drink a few minutes before.

"Miss Trott?" Mrs. Holpert's voice came querulously from the other room.

"Just a minute." Louisa wrung out a washrag, caught up a basin of water and Jeannie's glass and hurried into the children's room.

"My feet hurt," Mrs. Holpert murmured.

The image of Mrs. Holpert's dead-white, varicosed feet and ankles came between her and Jeannie's pink and red face. The disease had bloated Mrs. Holpert's feet as Dr. Marlowe had said it might. In fact, all his dismal prophesies had been fulfilled by one or another of the three patients. All except the ear running, which Louisa dreaded as a last straw from Mrs. Holpert.

There was a knock at the hall door.

"Just a minute, please!" Louisa called, giving Eleanor's face a wipe.

Mrs. Dusenberre stood at the door with an armful of gladiolas. She looked curious but subdued, and made no move to step inside Mrs. Holpert's foyer. "I thought—I mean, I brought these for Mrs. Holpert," she said, staring at Louisa out of a long, sheeplike face.

Louisa took the flowers she extended. "What's the matter?" Louisa asked nervously, for Mrs. Dusenberre had fixed her eyes on her as though one or both of them had lost her mind. Louisa wanted to say, "But you wouldn't come in and help. Oh, no!" But Mrs. Dusenberre did not look bright enough to be of any assistance. "Thank you, Mrs. Dusenberre. I'll give them to her and tell her you sent them."

Mrs. Dusenberre nodded. "Is everybody all right?"

Louisa's three were calling again, and harassedly, in the semidarkness, Louisa closed the door upon Mrs. Dusenberre.

As she turned toward Mrs. Holpert's room, a pain struck her like a hammer in the head. She clutched the corner of a table and looked onto a universe of pulsing spots and ringing space. For an instant, she felt as though she were dying. Could *she* be getting the disease? she wondered. But that was unthinkable. Simply unthinkable. . . . She lifted her head and set her plain face firmly. She stared before her until she stared the spots out of countenance and she could see Mrs. Holpert's doorway and the glow from her light. Whether she was going to get sick or not was one of those things she would just have to put out of her mind, because there was nothing she could do about it one way or the other.

What happened in a crisis? Louisa wondered. What did a crisis look like? She took it for granted one stayed up all night, which she did, reading, dozing, watching at the bedsides of the three whose fevers seemed to be mounting toward a terrific explosion. Night or day did not much matter anymore. Nor did the fact that today was Saturday, her precious Saturday on which she usually washed her hair, took an outing in the park with a book, pottered about the house doing all the odds and ends left over from a busy week. Now it was the middle of Saturday afternoon, and her room upstairs seemed miles away. When once during the afternoon she thought of herself in relation to the room upstairs, she felt quite lost. Once a person has become detached from his possessions, his customary duties, his moments of solitude, where is he? *What* is he? she wondered as she sat in the armchair in Mrs. Holpert's room, half dozing, strangely half alert. She had an odd but not unpleasant sensation of being a mote that floated in space. She felt an unfamiliar freedom and mobility that seemed to increase her vision of things, even her enjoyment of things, like the Vermeer reproduction over Mrs. Holpert's bed, and the cluttered back garden, whose leaves she stared at for longer and longer intervals. She felt closer to Gert for some reason, too. Perhaps, she thought, all her relationships to things had been dislocated. Or perhaps the explanation lay in the mysterious disappearance of time.

She remained in the detached state throughout the afternoon, listened impersonally to Dr. Marlowe as he told her that the turning point had not yet come, that it would probably come tonight. She must have asked him what to expect, for she was aware of his looking at her strangely as he paused in the reading of Jeannie's thermometer.

"The fever will go down suddenly. Then they'll probably want something to eat," he told her.

"Oh." It sounded like a pleasant event, not at all what she had imagined.

"And how are you feeling?" Dr. Marlowe asked. "You don't look too well to me. Maybe I'd better take your temperature."

"Oh, no. I'm fine," Louisa replied.

"Okay." He put away the thermometer without telling Louisa its findings. "Don't know what they'd be doing without you. You're swell."

When he had gone, Louisa sank back into the armchair. She hated herself for feeling tired, but after all, she thought, what else was there to do except rest until she was needed? She pulled an ancient *National Geographic* magazine out of the stand by her chair and tried to fix her attention on an article on phosphorescent animalcules. . . . But she fell into a half sleep in which she had more horrible dreams about rubescent fields, about a large black-winged animal like a bat that went half flying, half scrambling across great snowy mountaintops which became finally rumpled white bedclothes. She awakened squirming in the chair.

The doorbell was ringing impatiently at the front of the house.

Louisa went up the hall, not with her usual elastic step, but rather staggeringly. She was dimly aware that her hair must be a sight, that she could not remember the last time she had combed it, or the last time she had looked into a mirror.

"Flowers for Miss Trott," the boy said.

"I'm Miss Trott," Louisa replied.

The long white box was laid in her arms, and she carried it automatically back to Mrs. Holpert's apartment, where she laid it in the armchair. She straightened up and rubbed her hands slowly, wondering what she should do next.

Then the white of the oblong box, glaring white in the light of the reading lamp beside the chair, caught her eye and demanded attention. The sheen on its white paper awakened her suddenly with a strange excitement. The simple purity of its form was the most beautiful thing in the room. She bent over and read her name, which was printed large on a big card. Flowers. For *her.*

She lifted the top, and wax paper rose a little over the sides, releasing a subtle, nostalgic fragrance. She parted the paper and found white roses, a great white cloud of them at one end of the box. She lifted them out gently, for their long stems bore heavy thorns. Louisa thought she had never seen such roses. They were robust, almost oversized, like something out of one of her own dreams.

A little envelope fell at her feet. She held the roses against her body and opened it. It was in Mr. Bramford's familiar writing.

> *With kindest regards from one who misses you very much.*
>
> Clarence Bramford
>
> (over)

And in smaller, more angular writing:

> *If you are able to leave your charges for a while Sunday evening, perhaps you can have dinner with me. Shall call you Sunday morning.*
>
> C.B.

All at once she was weeping, with her shoulders hunched and the card and envelope caught up against her forehead. It was her nerves, she thought, nothing more. But she suspected she might be pitying herself, so she tried to stop. It *was* self-pity, for no one had sent her flowers since . . . She did not care to remember. Above all, she supposed, she had been surprised that Mr. Bramford had sent her flowers. He was not really the kind of man who sent flowers. Certainly he was very frugal in his habits. Louisa wanted to weep again at this unexpected, undreamed-of token of his concern. Dinner on Sunday. Tomorrow! How nice it would be to have dinner with him, she thought. And how terrifying, too, for she could not really imagine—

A wail from Jeannie brought her back abruptly to where she stood, to the realization that a thorn of the roses she held tightly had gone into one finger. She laid the roses down and went forward. This, she thought, would be the beginning of the crisis.

It was a night of wringing out cold towels, of wiping faces, of holding water glasses, of performing the same duties she had performed for the past three days. Only now, more or less, the woman and the two children seemed to need her all at the same time. Once during the night, Louisa found herself staring at a half-empty bowl of chicken soup and toasted cheese on crackers on the table beside the easy chair, wondering how they got there, and remembering slowly that Mrs. Dusenberre had brought them. She saw the flowers, too, and remembered.

"What a shame, what a shame," she murmured to herself as she took the roses up from the chair. "They'll be all wilted!"

But they were not wilted in the least. They made a handsome group in the big blue vase on the foyer table. Louisa stood back to look at them, reeled a little against a doorjamb and steadied herself. She removed the vase to the children's room where she could see them better. Their vigor made her feel less tired. She noticed now that they were not one dozen but two. How kind Mr. Bramford was, she thought, and wished he were here now to keep her company.

"Nonsense! What could he do?" she said aloud. It was merely that it would have been nice to have a friend to lean on. For she did feel so tired.

"I'm hungry."

Louisa turned around.

"Miss Trott, I'm hungry," Jeannie said, frowning as though this condition were as unreasonable as that of being sick.

"Bless your little heart!" Louisa said. "Bless you, bless you!"

Louisa went into the kitchen and prepared a scrambled egg and buttered toast and poured a glass of milk, so quickly it was all on the tray before she knew it. She felt dazed and elated. Jeannie was well. It was over!

She fed infinitesimal mouthfuls into Jeannie's pink face, while thoughts of Mr. Bramford, of Mrs. Dusenberre, of the morning that was pushing energetically through the back window, and of her brother Gert went swimming around in her head. She turned off the electric light and watched the duller but surer light of day begin to fill the room. She stood in the middle of the floor, tall and smiling and victorious, with her lank coppery hair all askew about her head like arrested flame. She felt very quiet and calm inside, and somehow, contrary to all reason, full of a happy, inexhaustible energy.

"Jeannie. Jeannie?" Louisa said, as though she were about to tell Jeannie something. But she wanted only to hear the child's voice in answer.

"More," Jeannie said quietly.

Louisa returned to the plate of egg and the fork. She was thinking of her brother Gert, thinking that she should write him a letter immediately, today, even though she sent it into a void, that she should even try to send him a package of something. She would also send her sister Aina in Copenhagen another package. A few of her packages had got lost, and she had grown discouraged about transoceanic mails. But there was nothing to do but try. Good lord, her own sister! And brother! And here she was, in America, living off the fat of the earth!

"Miss Trott?"

"Yes, Mrs. Holpert," Louisa called. "Couldn't you take some milk toast and some weak coffee?"

"I was just going to say," Mrs. Holpert sighed.

In the kitchen, preparing Mrs. Holpert's breakfast, Louisa hummed to herself as she generally did only on Saturday afternoons, when she pottered about at her own tasks. She cut one of the roses and put it in a single-stem flower vase on Mrs. Holpert's tray.

She thought of Mrs. Dusenberre, of how she had closed the door upon her stupid face, of Mrs. Dusenberre's kindness in bringing the chicken soup and crackers. And smiling in a way she would have thought rather stupid herself, had she looked into a mirror, Louisa went to the big vase and removed five of the white roses.

I'll take these to Mrs. Dusenberre, she thought, and started with them toward the door.

Then, remembering the early hour, she stopped and looked at her watch. It was only six-twenty. She had better take the flowers up later.

Besides, she must look dreadfully untidy herself. She stumbled into the bathroom, got the washrag and towel she had brought down from her own room, then climbed upstairs to the bathroom at the end of the hall. The house was silent. Neither Mr. Noenzi nor anyone would thwart her this morning.

She closed the door, and felt content with the room's familiarity. Then, as she went to draw her tub, the handle of the ventilator caught her eye. But strangely, it did not chill her with a sense of violence as it always had. It did not look as though a murderer held its other end. It was just a homemade handle. Maybe that was how tired she was, she thought. She wondered when the doctor would come that morning, and imagined how pleased he would be with his three patients. Then she remembered Mr. Bramford. He would call this morning, and ask her where she would like to dine. And she would suggest the Plaza.

The Plaza Hotel!

Louisa dropped the washrag and the towel and leaned back against the door. She could envisage it now, Mr. Bramford and herself opposite each other at a table laid with white linen and silver, with candlelight in a big room filled with soft music. Of course, Mr. Bramford would like the Plaza Hotel, too. . . . The ski train, the black Persian lamb coat, even the week at the Plaza. . . . Suddenly, ever so dimly but surely, like the light of the morning she had just watched enter through Mrs. Holpert's back window, it all seemed possible, and within the realm of truth.

Part II

MIDDLE AND
LATER STORIES
1952–1982

A BIRD IN HAND

As Douglas McKenny neared his door with the new parakeet from the dime store, a neighbor called out, "Hello, Mr. McKenny! Got a new bird?"

His neighbors were under the impression that he bought quite a few birds and gave them away to children, perhaps.

"Nope," said Mr. McKenny. "Lampshade. How're you, Mr. Riley?"

He walked on. Just as he reached his stoop, a small girl skipped up and stopped, breathlessly.

"Oh, Mr. McKenny, can I see it?"

"It's not a parakeet, honey, it's a lampshade," Mr. McKenny said, smiling at her. "How's little Petey?" He had given her the parakeet four years ago, when she was hardly higher than his knee.

"He's swell, Mr. McKenny. He can say the first part of 'The Star-Spangled Banner.' But he always gets stuck on 'what so proudly.'"

"Well, you bring him around to me sometime and we'll see if we can get him over that," he said kindly, patting her on the head.

"Okay, Mr. McKenny!" She darted off like a bird herself, whirling a broken yo-yo around and around on its string.

Mr. McKenny trudged up the stairs. He hadn't wanted to tell a lie. But the less his neighbors knew, the better. He went in and out of the house with parakeets all the time, and always took the trouble to make the bundles and packages he carried them in look different. Sometimes he put a cage into a pillow slip, so that it would look like his laundry. Often he carried a good-sized Schrafft's cake box in a paper bag to the dime store and brought a bird back in it with his fingers under the string, just as if it were a cake from the Schrafft's around the corner.

He put the new parakeet in a cage by itself, talking to it soothingly all the while. "Here, Billy, Billy. . . . Nice Billy. You and I are going to get along fine, aren't we?"

The gray-breasted parakeet eyed him suspiciously and sulked, dumb, on his perch.

Mr. McKenny had seen in the dime store that he was a sullen little fellow, but he had been the only one today with a gray breast. "Bil-ly," Mr. McKenny said slowly and distinctly. "Bil-ly . . . Bil-ly . . ." Very slowly he filled the water cup in the cage from a little pitcher and dropped a few seeds into the feeding trough to show his goodwill. Then he stood behind the closet door, out of sight of the bird and yet only a yard away from him. When teaching a parakeet to say something, it was better to stand out of sight so the bird had the minimum of distraction and could concentrate on imitating the sound it heard. "Bil-ly," Mr. McKenny said slowly. "Bil-ly . . . Bil-ly . . . Bil-ly . . ."

"*Bi-eee!*" chirped Queenie, a mischievous, spoiled green hen in a cage with her mate across the room.

Mr. McKenny began again, patiently. "Bil-ly. . . . Say something, Billy. Kiss me. Kiss me. Kiss me." If he could hit on a phrase a parakeet knew, it sometimes stimulated further talk. But this bird probably did not know a single word.

"*Tin-ng! Rrrrr-rrrr-r!*" the parakeet said finally.

Mr. McKenny sighed. If he was not mistaken, that was the parakeet's attempt to imitate the sound of a cash register.

The telephone rang, and Mr. McKenny left his position behind the closet door to answer it.

"Hello, Mr. McKenny?"

"Yes."

"This is Jack Haley of the *Evening Star.* I understand you returned a lost parakeet named Chou-Chou to a Mrs. Richard Van der Maur yesterday?"

"Yes," said Mr. McKenny, very much on his guard.

"We'd like to get an interview with you. You know, tell us how you captured the bird and all that. Could I—"

"Well, thank you, but there's nothing to tell. The bird flew onto my windowsill, I started talking to it and it hopped in, and that was that."

"Just a little story and maybe a photograph," the reporter begged. "It'll just take a few minutes. I'll be over in about a quarter of an hour."

"Oh, please——"

But the reporter had hung up.

Mr. McKenny spent the quarter of an hour trying to tidy his one-and-one-half-room bachelor apartment, and debating at the same time whether to run out and just not be here when the reporter arrived. Should he hide the eleven parakeets he had? He could put the four cages in the closet with covers over them and the birds would be silent. Or should he display them boldly and say that he had been a parakeet fancier for years? Two minutes before the reporter was due, Mr. McKenny decided on the former course. He set the cages on the floor of his closet atop shoes and a soiled shirt, and closed the door. He wondered if the reporter had heard any parakeets in the background when he telephoned. Well, he'd assume that he hadn't.

The doorbell rang.

After a final glance around and a tug at his vest, Mr. McKenny went bravely to his kitchenette and pushed the release button. He heard quick, youthful footsteps on the two flights of stairs, then a knock. Mr. McKenny opened the door.

"Good morning! Mr. McKenny?" The young man smiled. He had a tablet and pencil in his hand and a camera around his neck.

"Yes," Mr. McKenny said. "Won't you come in?"

"Thank you. Is this the window the bird flew in?"

"No. This one," said Mr. McKenny, pointing.

The questions came fast. How long had it taken him to coax the bird onto his finger? Had he immediately looked in the papers to see if a parakeet had been lost?

Mr. McKenny told his story with an economy of detail and in a disparaging manner. "After all, a thing like this is bound to happen once in a while in a city as big as New York. Where else can a parakeet go except into somebody's window? They're friendly little birds, you know, and they get hungry often. They'd either pick somebody's window or fly straight into a restaurant." Mr. McKenny managed a laugh.

"Still, you made Mrs. Van der Maur very happy, Mr. McKenny. Lots of people would have kept the bird and not bothered to try and return it to the owner. Mrs. Van der Maur called up last night to cancel her ad, and she took the trouble to tell us she was delighted with the fast results. I went over to see her this morning, got a picture of the parakeet and so forth. She sure was happy to have it back. Now, how about a shot of you here sitting by the window where you caught it?" The young man opened his camera.

"I'm rather camera-shy," Mr. McKenny said.

"Aw, come on. Just a little picture for our second section."

Reluctantly, Mr. McKenny sat down in the straight chair the reporter had pulled near the window.

"Now stick your finger out the way you did for the bird and look at me as if you're talking to me. Tell me what happened again."

"I was—the parakeet was right here on the brick part—"

Click!

Mr. McKenny started to get up.

"Just one more, please, in case the first one doesn't turn out."

"—on the brick part, when I—"

Click!

"Thank you, sir. Do you know a lot about parakeets? Have you any pets of your own?"

"No," Mr. McKenny said. "I used to. Not anymore. Parakeets, I mean. I suppose that's why I was able to get this one to come in the room."

"Um-hm. May I ask what business you're in, what you do for a living?"

"I'm retired. I was a civil engineer. I have a small pension."

"I see," the young man said, writing. Then his eye fell on a row of seed boxes on a shelf against the wall. There were also some cuttlebones and a couple of plastic bird toys—a little horse on rockers and a round-bottomed clown that stayed upright however it was pushed. The reporter went closer. "You bought all this for the parakeet?"

"Well—yes," Mr. McKenny said. "I wanted to do the right thing for it. It didn't like the first seed I gave it."

"You're a very kind man, Mr. McKenny. And you only had the bird about three hours, didn't you? From two o'clock when you caught it until you called Mrs. Van der Maur at five?"

"That's correct," Mr. McKenny said.

"Well, it's been a pleasure meeting you, Mr. McKenny. You'll see your story in the afternoon edition. I hope you'll like it. Good-bye." He smiled and opened the door.

"Please don't make too much of it," Mr. McKenny said.

Douglas McKenny was a religious newspaper buyer. He bought the afternoon edition of the paper that had his picture and the parakeet story in it, and read it through with an effort at detachment, as if it weren't really about *him*. Then he checked carefully. There was a notice about Billy, the same one he had seen in the early morning paper, but no new parakeets were lost. Just as well. He could spend the rest of the afternoon and evening on Billy. Billy was not easy to work with, but there was a twenty-dollar reward at stake—not so much as Mrs. Van der Maur's thirty yesterday, but still worth trying for. And the notice about Billy said also that he was a children's pet. Mr. McKenny liked to place birds in homes where there were children.

For over thirty years, Mr. McKenny had been a parakeet lover and a parakeet breeder in a modest way. Up until a few years ago, parakeets had sold for at least five dollars apiece—and were not to be found in dime stores—and Mr. McKenny had been able to supplement his pension income and thus make a small living by breeding and selling them. Two of the birds he had at home, Freddie and Queenie, were the youngest of a couple of dynasties that went back to the time his wife Helen had been alive and even fairly young. In a sense, it was like keeping Helen with him in something more than his memory, having parakeets that were the offspring of offspring back to the many generations that Helen had known and loved. Mr. McKenny had had about forty parakeets in his apartment when the market had taken a slump. He did not mind selling parakeets at a dollar ninety-eight instead of five dollars—he had given enough away to children and grown-ups on his block who couldn't pay five dollars—but a dollar ninety-eight instead of five dollars meant simply that that much less money would come in to pay his rent and buy his food. And really by accident one day, because duplicity of that kind would not have popped into his head out of the blue, he had seen that ten dollars was being offered for the return of a parakeet that had escaped from its home in the Village, a parakeet whose colors were the same as those of a parakeet he happened to have. It had taken some courage for Mr. McKenny to go downtown to the people with his own bird and say that it had flown into his window. But when he had seen the family's face light up at having their pet back, he had felt a little better. After all, parakeets looked very much alike to the average person, and more than likely the bird he had given them was a healthier specimen than the one they had lost. Later, Mr. McKenny had grown able to push his birds a bit. If the people looked doubtful at finding that their bird had forgotten its name or was speechless, Mr. McKenny would say that it had responded at home for him and that it was probably frightened from having just been on the subway. Very seldom were Mr. McKenny's parakeets turned down, and when they were, he could always say, "Well, I guess it's a coincidence that this bird flew in my window." Naturally, he tried to avoid publicity. The reporter who had called on him that morning was the first who had ever crossed his threshold. Most of the time, if the people he brought birds to asked his name, he gave a false one. When he had called on Mrs. Van der Maur with a parakeet, a butler had asked his name, and he had been so surprised that he gave it without thinking.

Mr. McKenny did not answer every lost parakeet notice, only about three out of five, but there was a notice in some paper nearly every day during the summer months. He took in on the average about twenty dollars a week. His pension amounted to another twenty-one dollars a week. On this he could just live.

Billy was accepted the following afternoon by a rather dubious mother and a screaming, wildly happy trio of children. It was Billy, the children insisted, and the parakeet confirmed it by repeating, "*Bu-eee! Bu-eee! Bu-eee!*" though with an air of annoyance at the noise the children were making. The mother said she was almost positive Billy was a little bigger and also had a darker blue tail. Mr. McKenny did not insist.

"Well, it could be that it isn't Billy. I suppose there're quite a few parakeets that take to the outdoors in such nice weather as this. Don't take him if you don't think he's yours."

"He *is* Billy! It's *Billy!*" the children yelled.

"*Tin-ng! Rrrrrr-rrrr-r!*" the parakeet said.

Mr. McKenny left with his ten-dollar reward. He was smiling a little as he walked up York Avenue and it was not because he was ten dollars the richer but because he was thinking of the faces of the three children. Suddenly he realized he was staring into the window of a pet shop. A cage of parakeets hung in an upper corner. One of the parakeets was almost entirely yellow. And there was the standard price fastened to the door of their cage: a dollar ninety-eight each. Mr. McKenny went in and bought the yellow bird with part of his ten dollars. If nobody advertised a missing yellow parakeet—and this yellow one would be hard to pass off as another bird—he would keep her himself.

He lived in a brownstone house, one of about a dozen remaining on either side of the street, crowded in by several colossal apartment buildings. Mr. McKenny had seen all the apartment buildings go up—on the sites of brownstones that had come down—in the seventeen years that he had been living in his present apartment. He knew all his neighbors in the brownstones, that is, the ones who kept window boxes of geraniums and pots of begonias and spent a lot of time sitting at their windows looking out at the street, which was practically everybody. The street was full of elderly people, couples and widows and widowers, many of whom could barely make ends meet, Mr. McKenny knew. He supposed that he fared a little better than most of them. There was a woman in the next house whose husband had died two years ago, to whom Mr. McKenny took a pot of stew or chicken soup now and then when he had the money himself to make a big batch. Another old man, who was confined to a wheelchair, Mr. McKenny often took for outings, wheeling him around and around the block.

Now, as Mr. McKenny walked down his block, three or four thin, veinous hands waved at him from behind morning glory vines and blossoming geraniums. It was June and a fine, bright day.

"Hello, there, Mr. McKenny! Saw your picture in the paper yesterday. Say, you're a celebrity!"

"Not quite!" Mr. McKenny said, chuckling. "Hello, Mrs. Zabriskie," he greeted another woman who was sitting on the cement parapet of her stoop. "How're you?"

"Afternoon, Mr. McKenny. What you got there? Another bird you found?"

Mr. McKenny smiled. "Nope." He lifted the tan paper bag casually. "Just bought myself a summer shirt."

June went by and most of July, bringing such hot, breezeless days that Mr. McKenny put his birdcages out on the fire escape in the early morning before the sun got there and made it too hot. He fixed a cold salmon mold, garnished it with hard-boiled eggs and lettuce, and took it to Mr. Tucker, the man who lived in a wheelchair. He brought ice cream a couple of times a week to the woman whose husband had died.

One morning, as Mr. McKenny leaned out of his window to get his birds in out of the climbing sun, he saw a fine male parakeet of royal blue with touches of green perched on the rail of his fire escape. He knew at once that it was not one of his own, though he had now about twenty-five parakeets in readiness for the increased summer business. The parakeet looked at him brightly, then resumed its chattering and hopping along the rail. It was talking to the other parakeets, all of which were looking with interest at the free bird. Mr. McKenny called to the bird softly, his heart beating fast.

"Fw-w! Fw-w! Here birdie, birdie, birdie," he said gently, not moving from his position, which was bent at the waist, one hand on the top of Freddie and Queenie's cage, the other hand on the windowsill. Then gradually he drew back, taking the cage with him into the room.

The parakeet on the fire escape hopped and chattered as if he were amused.

Mr. McKenny took every cage in. No use trying too hard with a loose parakeet. Either it would join the other birds in the room or it wouldn't. Mr. McKenny crouched on the floor back of the birdcages and began to talk to the parakeet again. "Here, sweetie, sweetie, sweetie. Come on in. Aren't you hungry? Tweetie, tweetie?"

He put on his parakeet record, very low. His other birds cackled and chattered as they ate their breakfast, and the parakeet jumped from the fire escape onto the windowsill to get a better view. He was going to win, Mr. McKenny knew it. After a moment, he crept very slowly toward the window and sprinkled some birdseeds on the carpet. The parakeet looked at them curiously. And then it jumped down. Still moving slowly, Mr. McKenny circled it and closed the window. He had already closed the other front window, which was a little to the left.

He prepared an empty cage with seeds and water and set it on the floor with its door open. Sometimes parakeets liked to go back into cages if they had been on their own and a bit frightened for several hours. Then, having checked to see that there was no possible escape for the parakeet in the apartment, he went out and bought the morning papers.

Mr. McKenny had hardly hoped for a notice this soon, but there it was in the lost and found column of the *Times*: "PARAKEET. Felix. Blue with some green. Lost 48th St. East yesterday. Beloved pet. Reward." And then the phone number.

"Felix?" Mr. McKenny called to the bird.

"*Fee-ix!*" replied the parakeet impatiently, over its shoulder as it were, and continued sidling around the caged parakeets like a cocky sailor.

"Felix!" said Mr. McKenny, extending a finger.

"*Fee-ix! Har! Har! Har!*"

"*Har! Har! Har! Har! Har!*" echoed the parakeets in the cages.

"*Arrrk or-set!*" Queenie suggested.

"Oh, no! No dark closet for Felix! That wouldn't be nice." Mr. McKenny had apologized to Queenie so many times for having put her into a dark closet the day the reporter had come, Queenie had learned the two words. He went to the telephone, held the paper up close to his eyes and carefully dialed the number.

A woman with a foreign accent answered and said it was Miss Somebody's residence, a name Mr. McKenny did not catch.

"I think I have found the parakeet," Mr. McKenny said.

"Ah! Felix? You think so? *Un moment, s'il vous plait!—Mademoiselle!*"

Mr. McKenny held the wire and nearly a minute passed. Then another excited feminine voice said:

"Hello! You've got Felix? Where are you? You really have Felix?"

"Yes, I think so, but I can't be sure," said Mr. McKenny, feeling surer by the minute.

"Where? Where did you find him? Where can I find you?"

"I can bring him to you. I have a cage," Mr. McKenny said out of old habit. "Perhaps you can tell me your address."

Mr. McKenny took down the address and printed the name, Dianne Walker. A simple name, yet when that French maid had said it . . . Mr. McKenny said he could bring Felix over in about forty-five minutes. That would give him time for his cup of tea and piece of toast. Felix would also have to be coaxed into a cage.

In less than fifteen minutes Mr. McKenny had finished his breakfast, but Felix was still at large in the apartment. Mr. McKenny crept up close and, distracting Felix with one hand, set his hat down gently over the bird with the other. He got Felix into the cage with no more damage than a little bleeding V in one forefinger.

"You're going to be very much happier where I'm taking you," Mr. McKenny said soothingly, and with no hard feelings about the bite. "I'm going to take you home."

Automatically, he put the cage into a brown paper shopping bag and laid part of a newspaper over the top so that the cage could not be seen. Then he smiled at himself. This time he needn't hide the parakeet from anyone! But he let the paper stay, anyway. Perhaps the less his neighbors knew, the better.

It was one of those remodeled brownstone houses with the kitchen downstairs in front and a chime doorbell that was answered by a maid—as different from Mr. McKenny's brownstone as a palace is from a third-class rooming house. The maid glanced at the bulky shopping bag.

"Ah! The man with Felix! Yes! Come in!" She swung the door open.

"Thank you." As soon as Mr. McKenny stepped into the hall, he heard a confusion of voices. A couple of men—they looked like reporters—came out of a door into the hall. Then, before he could turn to try to escape, a young woman with blond hair ran past the two men toward him.

"Oh, you dear man! You've got Felix?" she asked excitedly.

Mr. McKenny was surrounded. The shopping bag was taken from

his hand. Somebody pulled the cage out of the bag and a shout went up at the sight of the bird.

"It *is* my Felix!" the young blond woman cried. "Oooooh!" She embraced the cage, sending Felix into a flutter of excitement himself.

A couple of cameras clicked and flashed.

"Tell us how you found the parakeet, sir," a reporter said in Mr. McKenny's face. "Just come in here, sir, will you, please?"

The whole group, including a couple of women reporters, moved into a large living room filled with red roses.

"This story's big. You know who Dianne Walker is, don't you?" the reporter asked.

"I'm afraid—"

"She's number one box office of the year in Hollywood *and* on Broadway," the man whispered in Mr. McKenny's ear.

Mr. McKenny did not understand the sentence. He supposed she was an actress. She was posing for photographers now with Felix sitting on her red-nailed finger, kissing her lips. In fact, a hush came over everybody as all eyes turned to where the camera focused. Once more Mr. McKenny thought of escape. A reward—whatever it was—would not be worth what the publicity would do to him.

"She just told us," the same reporter was saying in his ear, "that she wouldn't go on tonight if she didn't get her parakeet back. She says Felix brings her all her luck."

Click!

"All right, Miss Walker, thank you!"

"Will you tell us how you caught the parakeet?" one of the women reporters asked.

Cameras swung around on Mr. McKenny.

"Well, I—I was getting my own parakeet cages in from my fire escape a little before eight this morning, when I—" At that moment, Mr. McKenny's eye fell on a familiar face: it was the face of the tall young reporter who had come to his house to interview him last month.

"Go on, Mr. *McKenny,*" he said, giving Mr. McKenny a little smile and a wave. It did not somehow look friendly to Mr. McKenny. He plunged on. "I saw this parakeet—Felix—sitting on the rail of my fire escape. I knew it wasn't one of mine because I haven't any just this color."

He had told the young reporter he hadn't any parakeets of his own, he remembered suddenly. "So I called to it—I took my own birds in and set them on the floor—in their cages. I kept calling to Felix to come in."

"Did you know it was Felix then?"

"No, I mean, I kept calling to it the way I'd call to any bird. Finally, he came in and I shut the window. I had bought my papers and saw that a parakeet of this description was lost."

"You mean, you accidentally saw the ad in the paper?"

"*Which* paper?"

"I looked to see if such a parakeet was missing. I immediately called the phone number."

Miss Walker stepped forward—she was wearing a tight black sweater, slacks that seemed to be made of tiger skin, and heelless slippers—holding out several bills in her hand. "I am very happy to give this honest man one hundred dollars as a reward for my beloved Felix Mendelssohn!" she announced to the whole room.

The cameras clicked again as Mr. McKenny looked mutely at the money in his hand. Mr. McKenny was asked to smile. Miss Walker kissed his cheek and held it for what seemed to Mr. McKenny an hour until six cameras clicked. Mr. McKenny murmured that he had to be going.

"Oh-h," said Miss Walker. "Can't I offer you a cup of coffee, at least, before you go?"

"Thank you. I don't drink coffee," said Mr. McKenny. "I think I'd better go. Thank you very much for your generous reward. It's much more than I had expected. I really don't think I—"

"You *will* keep it, too! It's a small thing compared to my Felix!"

Mr. McKenny smiled and made a little bow. "Thank you, Miss Walker." Somebody handed him the empty cage and the shopping bag.

The maid preceded him down the hall to open the door. Mr. McKenny heard a quick pair of feet following him. He knew whose they were.

"Morning," said the young reporter on the pavement. "You remember me, don't you?"

"Yes," said Mr. McKenny. "How are you?"

"Fine. How did you like your write-up the last time?"

"Oh, very nice, I thought."

"You'll get a bigger one this time. You have quite a lot of luck finding parakeets, haven't you, Mr. McKenny?"

"Well—this was luck. I suppose he was attracted to my birds. That's the only way I can explain it."

"I thought you didn't have any birds."

"I've acquired some since. I told you I used to keep them."

"Hm-m. Just how many birds have you found, Mr. McKenny?"

"Oh . . . just these two, I think—that I remember." Mr. McKenny looked up at the young man, half expecting to be struck down, by the young man or by the Lord.

The reporter's mouth was turned down at one corner. "You know, I think you're a big fake. I don't think that's Miss Walker's bird in there at all. I'm going to do a little investigating this morning, and if what I think is true . . . well, I'm going to see that it gets printed, that's all."

Mr. McKenny's knees sagged a little. "All right. That's your privilege," he said softly, and then turned and walked on.

That morning, Mr. McKenny did not greet any of his neighbors. Let them think he had gone deaf or blind overnight, he didn't care. By tomorrow, his neighbors wouldn't want to speak to him, either. Dark, tumultuous thoughts filled his mind. His shame permeated everything, but the thought that he would have to move was almost as horrible, to find another apartment at a rent he could afford and also where he would be allowed to keep his birds. And he would have to find one immediately. He could not bear to think of stepping out his door even once when every person on the block would know of his disgrace.

The greeting from his parakeets when he walked into his apartment shamed him, too. His parakeets were his only friends now, he realized— and that only because they couldn't read a newspaper. In a kind of daze, so that he had to concentrate very hard to understand what the words meant, Mr. McKenny read the advertisements for furnished apartments in the newspapers he had bought that morning. They all sounded extremely bleak and joyless. Or else unbelievably expensive. One place that sounded possible he saw on second reading was a hundred and ten dollars a week, not a month.

He made more tea. He talked with his parakeets, drawing a little cheer from their thoughtless cheerfulness. Finally, he dragged his one trunk out of a closet and began unsystematically to pack. Maybe the evening papers would have an apartment for him, he thought. He knew they wouldn't.

At last, he just stood at his window, staring out with wide eyes and whistling an old song.

The doorbell rang, and Mr. McKenny jumped. More reporters, he thought. Or maybe even the police! For one instant, he thought of escape. There was only one way, out the kitchen window, down into the court. Suicide. But he had never thought suicide honorable. Mr. McKenny straightened up. He would face his punishment or fine or whatever like a man.

The doorbell rang again, and Mr. McKenny went to the kitchenette and pressed the release button.

He recognized the step of the young reporter. He was alone. Perhaps he was the bearer of a summons. Or he wanted a firsthand confession from him for his paper. The young man knocked. Mr. McKenny opened the door.

"Good afternoon, Mr. McKenny," the young man said politely. "May I come in?"

Mr. McKenny opened the door wider.

The young man came in. There was no tablet in his hand. "Mr. McKenny—I was wrong this morning about Miss Walker's parakeet. I went back and talked to her. She's positive the parakeet is hers because he knows some phrases she taught him and she has some color photographs, too. I saw them."

"Well, parakeets do look pretty much alike," Mr. McKenny said. "It's pretty easy to make a mistake, but—"

"But this parakeet really is Miss Walker's." He moistened his lips. "I checked with some back issues of my paper and some other papers, though, and went over to see a couple of the people who'd gotten their parakeets back—from you. One woman over on York Avenue, maybe you remember, had a parakeet named Billy."

"Yes—I remember."

"Well, it's not Billy that she's got now. The kids weren't at home. The woman told me. She said it looked quite a bit like Billy, but it wasn't. They renamed it Ting because that's what it keeps saying. But the kids still think it's their bird, and while they're happy, she can't bring herself to tell them."

Mr. McKenny realized he was smiling. "Good!"

"I told her I thought you'd been doing this all over town, bringing in parakeets and getting rewards. She said she didn't think I ought to report you. In fact, she begged me not to. She said if you were making so many families happy, it didn't really matter. So did a couple of other people say the same thing. Anyway, Mr. McKenny, I feel the same way and I thought I'd drop by and tell you in case you were worried about what I said this morning."

"Oh—not at all," Mr. McKenny said.

"I guess it's kind of like Santa Claus. Santa Claus isn't real, either, but he makes a lot of kids happy." The young man walked toward the door. "Well, so long, Mr. McKenny."

Mr. McKenny turned around, took a deep breath and smiled. There *were* people who understood. The world seemed brighter, full of sunshine and goodwill. He looked at his watch. Three o'clock already! Mr. McKenny went to his closet for his jacket and his hat. Time to go out and get the afternoon papers.

MUSIC TO DIE BY

Aaron Wechsler got home from work at ten past six. He had stayed a few minutes longer than usual helping to sort the mail after the post office closed at five, just to give an impression that today was like any other day, that he was not at all uneasy or anxious to get out of the place, even though Roger Hoolihan's body was crumpled up and bloody in a back storage closet where they kept spare mailbags. Who'd find it? Aaron wondered. Mac, the postmaster? Bobby, Mac's son? One of the carriers? Aaron didn't care who found the body.

He was a middle-sized man with a slight paunch, fifty-five years old, with straight black hair that was graying at the temples. He wore dark-rimmed, thick-lensed glasses that gave a blurry, evasive look to his eyes. Actually, Aaron's eyes were evasive. More and more, he disliked looking straight at people. He was restless and nervous, and he hated his job at the post office, but he was determined to stick it out—to stick it out in some post office, if not this one—until he got his pension, his just reward for a lifetime's work. Aaron went to the kitchen and washed his hands thoroughly with the yellow soap he used for dishes. Then he sat down at the table that served him both as eating table and desk, and opened the gray ledger in which he kept his diary. He wrote:

September 28, 19———

Today I killed Roger Hoolihan. I did it shortly after noon, as I had planned. The others had gone out to lunch and I was supposed to go out at 12 while Roger kept the post office open. Roger was to go out at 1. So about twenty past 12 Roger looked over his shoulder and said with his customary sneer, "Aren't you going out to lunch?" He was standing at the counter going through the money order book. I picked up the stapler and hit him in the back of the head. I probably fractured his skull with the first blow, but I hit him several times. Then I dragged him to the storage closet in back and dumped him on the mailbags. I didn't go home to lunch, but I went out before 1 and came back around 1 when the others did. When Mac asked where Roger was (this was around 2) I said, "I haven't seen him since I went out a little after 12." Mac looked surprised, but didn't say anything. I suppose Mac will call his house tomorrow morning when he doesn't show up or they'll start looking for him tonight when he doesn't come home. But it might be a couple of days before they find the body, as that closet is not opened very often.

Roger Hoolihan. Number One.

Aaron laid his pen down in the groove of the ledger, rubbed his palms gently together, and looked at what he had written. The handwriting was very small and neat, the ink black. Mac was next. Wipe out that self-satisfied expression, stop that scornful head-shaking, the eyes that slurred away, as if whatever or whoever Mac looked at was the lowest of the low, not even worthy of a word of contempt from the great Edward MacAllister, postmaster. Yet whatever bungling Bobby did, that was okay, because Bobby was his son. "Dad, where's the seven-cent airmails? . . . Dad, mind if I shove off? I got an early date with Helen." Bobby might be Number Three. Watch out, Bobby.

Aaron went to the sink again, stooped, and from behind a blue-and-white checked curtain below the sink took a bottle of rye that stood among Clorox and ammonia bottles and other cleaning material. He poured himself a generous drink, dropped in some ice cubes, and sipped it with appreciation. Then he opened a can of corned beef hash, and put it into a frying pan with an egg in the center of it. It crossed his mind, very faintly, that he might have treated himself to something special like a steak or at least lamb chops or pork chops, but the thought did not last long, and brought him no discontent with his simple meal. His wife had used to make fun of him for liking corned beef hash, and said he had the taste of a convict. His memory was confused for a few seconds between

Vera smiling when she had said that and Vera sneering when she said it. Well, maybe she'd done both at different times. She'd ended by walking out on him, and she'd certainly been sneering then. Good riddance, Aaron thought. He hadn't gone to rack and ruin, he hadn't lost his health, or his job, or anything else Vera had predicted. He'd quit the job in the post office in East Orange and moved to Copperville, New Jersey, where he'd had no difficulty at all in getting the same kind of job at the Copperville post office.

"The hell with her," Aaron murmured, and dragged a folded newspaper on the table toward him. His eyes moved over the print, but he did not read. He ate at a steady rate, neither fast nor slow. He got up for a second helping, which finished the hash. The hell with his children, too, Aaron was thinking. Billy was twenty-four now—no, twenty-*seven*—and Edith was twenty-three and already had three kids by that lowlifer she'd married. Yes, there'd been a time when Aaron had had great ambitions for his children, and Billy had gone through college and was a certified public accountant, but Edith had fallen in love in her sophomore year and gotten married, and to a numbskull who was not a college man and who hadn't any money. Aaron had flown into a rage and tried to get the marriage annulled, but alas, Edith was already pregnant, so an annulment was out of the question, but Aaron had fumed—hadn't he reason to, and wasn't he borne out now, with the two of them and their three kids living in some slum in Philadelphia?—and Billy had defended his sister and so had Vera. To Aaron, it had been as if his whole world had suddenly lost its mind, reversed the correct order of things. He had stood alone in his defense of sanity, education, the good life, and his own family had turned traitor, betrayed him and all he had struggled for since the children had been born and before. Aaron had gotten so angry one day, he had wrecked the house. He had torn pictures off the walls and stamped on them, pulled down the curtains and thrown every dish in the house on the floor. Then Vera had burst into tears and said she was leaving him, and she had. And he'd let her.

"Let her," Aaron murmured to himself as he sipped his instant coffee. "Let her!" Let her leave him, with all her talk about psychiatrists for him, a talk with the preacher—"Tschuh," Aaron said with contempt. His blood boiled for an instant, and subsided. He was better off now than he'd ever been in his life. There was a lot to be said for independence. He was saving more money now, too, than he'd ever been able to save since he got married. Last year, he had toyed with the idea of taking a cruise to the West Indies in the summer, but he had postponed it, and postponed it this year, too. Well, one summer it'd be Europe instead, and that was more interesting than the West Indies, which were simply closer and cheaper. Yes, his life was fine now, except for the awful batch of people he had to work with. *They* made him dislike his work, and dislike all the gadgets and rubber stamps and weighing machines and every other mechanical device in the place. He'd been in Copperville three years now. There were times when it didn't seem that long, and times when it seemed much longer. Tonight it didn't seem that long.

Roger Hoolihan had a boy in college and another in high school. Plus a wife. Aaron shrugged. It was no time for pity.

He washed up his dishes, put a couple of shirts and a pair of pajamas in a washtub to soak, and went to bed early. Aaron liked to sleep. He slept ten hours every night.

The next morning was bright and sunny, the temperature a perfect sixty-two, Aaron saw by his thermometer beside his front door. Aaron's house was set behind the larger house of his landlord, at the end and to one side of the driveway which led to a garage where his landlord kept his car, a pale blue Buick. There was a thin lawn between Aaron's house and the landlord's house, and Aaron's feet had worn a faint path from his door diagonally across the lawn to the nearer of the two barren streaks made by the car's wheels in the driveway. Aaron had a five-block walk to the post office, through streets of two-story houses with elm and maple trees growing along the sidewalk.

Mac was in the post office. Mac was always the first to arrive, a few minutes before eight.

"Morning, Aaron," Mac said, not deigning to look up at him.

"Morning," Aaron replied. He hung his jacket on a hook on the back wall.

Mac was slowly putting away sheets of stamps in the broad flat drawers under the counter. He always took a long while putting away stamp sheets, holding them up first and scrutinizing them, especially if they were new stamps. But he apparently enjoyed just staring at the perforations in ordinary stamps, like the four-cent Lincolns and the one-cent Washingtons. The government should know, Aaron thought, just how much time their postmaster, their senior employee at the Copperville, New Jersey, post office, wasted in doing a dozen little jobs that any ordinary office boy could do.

On a large flat desk behind Mac stood a little card that said TENSION, so printed that one's eyes wavered and began to hurt when one looked at it. This small torture was achieved by bands of gray printed alternately above and below the bold black letters, causing a fuzziness in the letters' appearance. Aaron turned the card so that he would not see it while he sorted the morning mail. The office was too hot, already too hot and overheated, but Aaron was afraid this morning to go to the thermostat by the toilet and turn it down. Mac liked it hot and he liked to work in shirtsleeves, so the rest had to sweat it out all day. Aaron watched Mac slide a drawer shut, then walk over to the Muzak box and turn it on. The thing began to play, from the middle of the song "On the Sunny Side of the Street."

He waits till I get here to turn it on, Aaron thought, *just because he knows I don't like it.*

"Aaron—there's mail to be sorted, you know." Mac nodded toward the tied-together bundles of letters on the desk where Aaron had rearranged the TENSION sign.

"I'm getting at it," Aaron said, but not very briskly. He took the first bundle and untied it. There were, Aaron could see at a glance, about eight hundred letters to be sorted for the carriers who took off on their rounds between nine and nine-thirty. He began dropping letters into different piles on the broad desk, according to the zones which Aaron knew from the street names. Copperville was too small to have postal zone numbers. Plop, plop, plop. Some letters, destined for the private boxes at the front of the post office inside the foyer, he put into certain cubbyholes above the desk, which were marked by groups of numbers. Bills, junk mail, junk mail, bills, bulb catalogs, mail-order-house catalogs, junk, junk, junk.

Roger Hoolihan came in. Aaron barely glanced at him, then bent over his work again, frowning. He heard Mac and Roger exchange, "Good morning."

"Feeling any better?" Mac asked.

"Oh, yeah, thanks. Little bicarb did the trick, plus a nap," Roger said.

Mac was leaning on the counter on one elbow, doing nothing. "What was it? Pie à la mode or something?" Mac chuckled.

"No, I had beef stew," Roger said. "Ordinary beef stew and . . ."

Aaron was bored and wished he could stop listening. For a moment, he did stop listening, but then he heard the music: a straining baritone singing "This Almost Was Mine," with a lot of violins playing the tune. Aaron remembered yesterday when Roger came back from lunch at two. He remembered Roger saying with a pained expression to Mac, "Gosh, I'm all doubled up with something I ate. I think I'd better take the afternoon off." Aaron didn't want to remember it. He concentrated on the names, the box numbers on the envelopes he was sorting. Mrs. Lily Foster, Lily Foster, Lily Foster. A divorcée. She had a hat shop in town, and she got more mail than anybody.

"Well, Aaron," Roger said as he came back from hanging his jacket up, "how about oiling the monster this morning, eh?" He jerked his head in the direction of the four-foot-high black machine some six feet away from him in the middle of a clear space in the floor.

Aaron managed a smile at Roger's feeble quip, and also gave him a nod. *Be more polite than he is,* Aaron told himself, *because you're better than he is.* But he did not glance at the monstrous machine. He hated it. He once knew what it was for, but somehow he had obliterated that knowledge from his mind. He simply didn't know what it was for now, he honestly didn't. It looked like a compressed guillotine, as if some giant hand had pressed down on a guillotine and mashed it almost beyond recognition. Yes, what was it? A weighing device? A machine to press letters from a three-foot-square mass into a ten-inch-square? A machine for crushing people's hands? Feet? Heads? *I don't want to have anything to do with that!* Aaron could still hear his own voice shouting at Mac—a month ago? six months ago?—when Mac had asked him to do something on it. Aaron's mind went blank again, and he smiled with satisfaction. No, he didn't know what the black machine did, and he didn't care to know and he never would know. They couldn't fire him for not knowing, either. They couldn't fire him. He was a civil servant who had passed his examinations.

But the music all day long was driving him crazy, and he might quit. *Music to die by,* Aaron often thought. He remembered going up in an elevator somewhere in New York to some appointment he had dreaded—a dentist, a doctor?—and such sick-making music had been coming from the ceiling of the elevator, dulcet strains of violins, calculated to soothe, maybe, but which hadn't soothed, any more than it would have soothed the mind of a man walking to an execution chamber, music that any fool knew was being played to smooth over something, or to conceal something so horrible that the human mind could not face it.

The carriers were coming in. Aaron nodded and grunted in reply to their "Morning, Aaron" or just "Morning." Bobby came over to help him with the sorting. By then it was a quarter past nine. Bobby was quick. Aaron made himself work more quickly, not that he wanted to but because he wouldn't be outdone by the likes of Bobby MacAllister. Bobby was chubby and still had pimples like an adolescent. He'd be heavy to drag anywhere, Aaron realized.

But he began to plan the extinction of Bobby that afternoon. This so absorbed him, that for a few minutes that afternoon, he simply stood at the counter doing nothing, even though several people were waiting with packages to be weighed, and letters for which they had to buy stamps. Roger came up to Aaron and said:

"Snap out of it, Aaron. People're waiting in *line!*"

Aaron looked at him and thought, *You're dead, Roger. You don't bother me. You're dead, and you don't even seem to know it.* After that, Aaron smiled, and went to work quite cheerfully.

That evening, mostly in his diary because he thought better on paper, Aaron planned the murder of Bobby MacAllister. Midway in his plans, Bobby's father Mac seemed a more appropriate victim for his scheme, or rather his scheme more appropriate for Mac. It involved a knife. Mac was thinner than Bobby. It wouldn't take such a deep thrust. Aaron took his carving knife to work one morning and stabbed Mac just after five P.M., when the two of them were the only ones in the post office. He stabbed Mac just as Mac was lifting an arm to get his jacket down from a hook. Mac had time only to turn around with a bewildered expression on his face, and then he slowly slumped to the floor. Aaron left him there, stepped over his body, and walked out.

He described this in detail in his diary. He filled a whole page with closely written words.

The next day, he did not speak to Roger or to Mac. They were both dead. Of course, he had to nod to them once or twice, not in greeting, but just by way of replying to something they said or asked him, but that wasn't the same as communicating with them, speaking to them. Ten days or so went by, and the strange looks that Mac and Roger and Bobby and even some of the carriers gave Aaron did not bother him at all. They couldn't do anything to a man for not speaking, could they? He wrote in his diary:

> *It is strange, the walking dead in the post office. It is strange to think I'll soon be the only one alive in it. I'll walk out one day and leave it empty and lock the door on it myself—after I turn off that Muzak. I'll be the sole survivor. Bobby is next and then the carriers, maybe Vincent first, because I am tired of the smell of his chewing gum and tired of his hand slapping me on the shoulder every morning if I'm near enough to him.*

Aaron wrote some in his diary every evening, and he usually wrote at least half a page every noon when he came home for lunch. Once in a while, he made an entry that was not on the subject of the post office or of his own life, such as:

> *What is the matter with President Kennedy? How can he talk about disarmament and peace out of one side of his mouth and out of the other side talk about how many more billions of dollars we are going to need for armament, for nuclear missiles and so forth? Does this make any sense? Who is crazy?*

Aaron was going to kill Bobby with a hammer. The first blow would knock him out, which was essential considering the size and strength of Bobby, and the blows after that would finish him. Aaron sawed off five inches of the wooden handle of his hammer, so that he could carry it unseen in the pocket of his overcoat. It was November tenth, a Friday, that he took the hammer to work with him. He was going to follow

Bobby when Bobby left the post office, which Aaron knew would be slightly before five, as Bobby always had an early date with Helen on Fridays.

Bobby kept glancing at Aaron all that day. Bobby's heavy black brows looked puzzled. Every time Aaron noticed Bobby, he found Bobby looking at him, or his own glance attracted Bobby's eyes at once. Aaron decided that that day was not the day to do it. By five o'clock, Bobby had not yet left the post office, and Aaron got his coat to leave. To Aaron's great annoyance, Bobby got his own coat and came out with him.

"Say, Aaron——"

"I'm going this way," Aaron interrupted. He lived in a different direction from Bobby and Mac.

"That's okay, I'll walk with you. Say, Aaron, what's the matter? What's the matter lately?" Bobby swung along beside him, though Aaron was walking quickly now.

"Lately?" Aaron said, with a nervous chuckle. "Nothing."

"I don't mean it's any of my business, Aaron, I'm not trying to butt in, but if you've got some . . . kick against any of us, it's better to tell us about it, isn't it?"

The "us" annoyed Aaron, implying that the lot of them were ganged up against him. "I don't care to talk about it," Aaron said.

"Oh." Bobby looked more confused than he had all that day. "You mean, there is something, but you don't want to talk about it."

"That's right," Aaron said emphatically and with finality.

"Oh.——Well, Dad and I were wondering if you'd like to pitch horseshoes with us tomorrow afternoon around two. We don't work tomorrow—tomorrow morning, you know. Veterans Day."

"I know." Did Bobby think he was crazy? Not knowing tomorrow was a holiday? "They haven't the nerve to call it Armistice Day anymore, have they? It's Veterans Day."

Bobby forced a chuckle. He was slowing his pace. "Well, do we see you tomorrow? Vince is coming, too. The weather's supposed to be good, we'll have a couple of beers——"

Aaron stopped and stood up taller. "Sorry. No, thanks. I've got a few letters to write." He saw Bobby's expression change to one of surprise and disbelief. Did Bobby think there were no people in his life to whom he had to write letters? "Thank you, anyway, Bobby. Good night." Aaron walked away quickly before Bobby could say another word.

The evening was hellish for Aaron. He felt he had failed himself, that he had been unforgivably cowardly in not killing Bobby that day—or this evening, walking along the dark sidewalks with him. He could not face his diary, or face writing the disgraceful entry that he had achieved nothing after promising himself and the diary that he would achieve something. He was so angry with himself that he could not sleep. It was a wretched weekend.

On Monday, when Roger called him over to help with a lot of packages that were piling up on the counter, Aaron replied by saying very firmly and clearly, "You're dead."

Roger's mouth opened.

Bobby stared at him.

A couple of people on the other side of the counter who had heard it looked blankly surprised. One of them smiled.

Aaron looked at Roger. *That'll fix Roger,* he thought, and in fact Roger looked quite scared.

"'S matter with *him*?" Roger asked Bobby.

Bobby went over to Aaron. "What's the matter, Aaron? You feeling okay?"

"I'm feeling fine, thank you," Aaron said defiantly, though he knew his eyes were bloodshot from not sleeping.

They persuaded Aaron to go home. They told him he looked very tired. He started to defy them, then quickly gave in. Why not go home? What was pleasant about staying in this overheated musical hellhole? Aaron went home and recorded in his diary that he had informed Roger Hoolihan that he was dead, and that he had upset the entire post office by this fact. *Take a few days off,* Mac had said at the last. What an insult! A few days off. Were they giving him orders?

However, Aaron discovered that he did not at all mind a few days off, so he took them. On the third day, a letter arrived from Mac saying that he (Mac) and also Roger thought it would be a good idea for Aaron to see a doctor. They said they thought he had been working too hard, was under a strain, and that a doctor might prescribe just the right tonic, or a short vacation somewhere. It sounded exactly like Vera. Mac had even tried to make it funny, which Aaron did not appreciate. Mac said he would have called him, if he had had a telephone, and he would have come by to see him, but he did not want to intrude. The letter itself seemed to Aaron an intrusion, and in fact it was the last straw. He gave the two weeks' notice which his landlord had requested (Aaron paid his rent twice a month), and by December Aaron was in a town called Tippstone, Pennsylvania, seventy-five or eighty miles from Copperville, New Jersey. He found another furnished house with a fifty-dollar-a-month rent, more than ten dollars a month cheaper than his Copperville house had been. He intended to do nothing for two or three weeks except think and plan his next move, which he supposed would be to take a similar job in the local post office. Meanwhile, he had sufficient funds, and could afford not to work until after the New Year without going seriously into his savings or precluding a vacation for himself in the following summer.

Four days before Christmas, a bomb exploded in the Copperville post office, killing Mac, Roger, and three people who had been standing on the other side of the counter. Bobby, several feet behind them at the big desk, was wounded in the right arm and in his face. The package that had contained the bomb was hopelessly unidentifiable, as every shred of it went up in bits and pieces, and if Mac or Roger had noticed the return address, they were not alive to tell it. One of the Copperville citizens who had been killed was a teenager named Kenny Hall, who worked as errand boy for a local gift shop, and the newspaper said it was conceivable that someone had handed Kenny the package containing the bomb to mail. Kenny had been the first on the line and Mac had been weighing his packages when the bomb exploded, according to Bobby.

Aaron read the news with some pleasure. He was glad to know that Mac and Roger were no longer. He wished that he had thought of the same means of getting rid of them—even though he admitted to himself he would have been hard-pressed to acquire or create a bomb that would have gone off at just the right moment. Still, he dreamt about it, and they were dreams of glory and success that filled Aaron's mind. The bomber had set his bomb, it had gone off at the right time, and he had gotten away with it. Aaron burnt his diary. The bomb was better. He cut the newspaper stories out of the paper and put them into his billfold.

On December 27, Aaron presented himself at the Copperville police station and admitted having sent the bomb to the Copperville post office. The two rugged policemen to whom he spoke, both blond and young, seemed slightly doubtful.

"Can I see Bobby MacAllister?" Aaron asked.

"He's still in the hospital," said one of the police officers.

But Aaron persuaded them to take him there. Bobby's arm was in a heavy bandage. He had some dark red cuts above his right eyebrow. Aaron told his story to Bobby, about making the bomb at home, setting the time device, coming to Copperville and sending the packaged bomb via Kenny to the post office. When he had finished his confession, he stood erect, justified, not ashamed of what he had done, but quite willing to take any punishment the law chose to mete out to him.

Bobby's dark, empty eyes looked frightened.

"Well, Bobby?" one of the policemen asked. "You know this man, you said. He worked in the post office—three years?"

"About three years. You remember him in the post office, don't you?"

The policemen acknowledged that they did remember Aaron in the post office.

"I'm sure he's telling the truth," Bobby said. "He used to go around saying, 'You're dead,' to Roger and even to Dad, if he—" Bobby choked up.

Aaron watched him patiently.

"I'm sure he's telling the truth," Bobby said. "He's cracked, that's all."

So the police took Aaron away. It was one more case solved on their books. Aaron was not (and neither were the victims) of such importance that a psychiatrist would examine him to make sure he was telling the truth. Aaron was put into the state prison, where he chose to work in the laundry. The prison had one psychiatrist, who held a group therapy session once a week, and Aaron was made to attend it, but Aaron was not inclined to talk. His existence was boring, he admitted to himself, but he felt he had achieved something few men can or do achieve, the annihilation of people they despise. He was therefore a good prisoner.

MAN'S BEST FRIEND

Every morning at seven-thirty, Dr. Edmund Fenton left his apartment in the east sixties and headed for Central Park with his German shepherd, Baldur. After a brisk walk of half an hour or so, they went home to breakfast—Baldur on the warm milk and dry toast prescribed in the dog book, and Dr. Fenton on orange juice, dry toast, and coffee. At nine o'clock, Dr. Fenton arrived at his office on Lexington Avenue with Baldur, who lay all morning in the well under Dr. Fenton's desk, patiently awaiting the break at one o'clock for the walk home and lunch.

At six and again before bedtime, Dr. Fenton took Baldur for walks either in Central Park or down Madison Avenue. He followed to the letter the instructions for rearing in his dog book, and under the fine care, Baldur grew strong and handsome. He had a rich black stripe down his back, blending through brown to a pale buff on belly and legs. His manners were perfect. He never barked and never tugged at his leash. He did his teething on the leather toy that Dr. Fenton provided for the purpose. In elevators, if he was standing at the rear, Baldur always waited until everybody else was off before he moved. He behaved, indeed, in a more civilized fashion than most people. Once, when Dr. Fenton had given a party and some of the guests had stayed until the small hours, delaying Baldur's nightly outing as well as preventing his sleeping, Baldur accompanied the guests to the door finally with a more genuine friendliness than had Dr. Fenton, whose hospitality was wearing thin by that time. One of the guests, Bill Kirstein, even said something about it.

"Awright, Ed, we're leaving," he had said. "You don't have to throw us out. Why don't you learn some manners from that dog of yours?"

The remark had hurt Dr. Fenton, falling as it did on a part of him already wounded—his pride. It had hit all the more directly because, in the previous week or so, the same idea had crossed Dr. Fenton's mind: that Baldur's general comportment put his own to shame. Baldur could wait in a butcher's shop, for instance, with better grace than Dr. Fenton could, especially if there were a couple of garrulous housewives ahead of him. Dr. Fenton had once tried to sneak his order in out of turn, a woman had said something to him about it, and he had slunk from the butcher's shop feeling like a criminal.

Looking back on it, Dr. Fenton felt that his unhappiness dated from the time of Bill Kirstein's remark. From then on, he took no pleasure in Baldur and no real pleasure in anything. He began to feel inferior to the dog. He tried to improve his own manners, made himself also wait at elevators, and removed his hat more often, but he never felt that his courtesy matched Baldur's, which was apparently inborn, since Dr. Fenton had devoted no time at all to training Baldur in etiquette. Baldur's face, too, had a dignity and intelligence that made him look as if he regarded the man in the street—and even his master—with a profound and uncompromising judgment from behind a cordial exterior. Dr. Fenton began to feel the dog knew why he had been given him and knew Dr. Fenton's particular faiblesse, a sense of failure. After all, the dog had been a present from a woman who had rejected Dr. Fenton's proposal of marriage six months ago.

It had happened like this: for five years, Dr. Fenton had been mutely in love with the wife of his friend Alex Wilkes. Theodora Wilkes was a tall, good-looking woman of about thirty-five, with sleek black hair drawn into a roll at the back of her neck, and long beautiful hands which, though they did nothing, looked as if they could cope with any situation. Theodora liked people around her, and it was seldom that Dr. Fenton had been able to speak with her alone, except in the corner of a room at a cocktail party. When he was in a corner with her and free to utter a few shy banalities, he felt in the presence of a goddess of love, happiness, and savoir vivre—in short, a goddess of all that Dr. Fenton was not. Dr. Fenton had never been married. A son of poor parents, he had worked his way through dental school, and being modest and unaggressive, he had not capitalized on his abilities as he might have done, so that even with an office at a good address, he was earning no more than twelve thousand a year at the end of his first ten years of practice, and much of this had to go for overhead. And after five years, his abject love of Theodora had made no progress, either. But his dreams had grown bolder and bolder. If he could marry her, he dreamt, his income would quadruple, his skill would increase, and even his voice would change for the better.

Then something happened that Dr. Fenton had never dared dream: Alex Wilkes died suddenly of a heart attack. Tactfully, Dr. Fenton had begun his courtship of Theodora. After three months, he had asked her to marry him. The moment when Theodora had looked at him tenderly, and said she must take some time to consider, had been the happiest of Dr. Fenton's life. Then, at their next meeting, she had told him she could not marry him. No, it did not mean that she would never marry, she said, and the inference was clear: she would never marry *him*. Dr. Fenton had dragged through several weeks on the brink of suicide from depression. Then one day Theodora had called him and they made an appointment to see each other. Dr. Fenton, who had hoped for a change of heart in Theodora, had gone home after the interview with nothing but a four-month-old German shepherd puppy, Baldur von Hohenfeld-Neuheim. She had wanted to give him something alive, she said. The puppy would be a companion to him and would get him out-of-doors more often.

Dr. Fenton did not want to see Theodora again, even the memory of her long hands was painful to him, yet he had been inspired to take especially good care of Baldur, because he had been a present from her. And being a man of some mental discipline, he had managed to combine his nurture of the puppy with an exclusion of brooding, negative thoughts about Theodora. Still, she had rejected him, and the wound remained.

A knowledge of this was what Dr. Fenton felt he could see in Baldur's brown eyes as the dog lay watching him sometimes, particularly at dinner, which Dr. Fenton ate at the end of a white enamel table in his kitchen. He felt the dog was saying as he stared down his long nose: "You failure, you poor excuse for a man! Now I see you in your proper setting, eating your miserable dinner in shirtsleeves at the end of a kitchen table." There would swim before Dr. Fenton's eyes Baldur von Hohenfeld-Neuheim's pedigree, with all the Grosseltern and Urgrosseltern, all the Odins and Waldos and Ulks von this and that and their respective prizes. Dr. Fenton had finally rolled his sleeves down and put on his jacket, and then set up the bridge table in the living room to eat on. Now he set the bridge table every evening with a tablecloth. Baldur moved into the living room and lay nearby on the rug, regarding him calmly, not ever begging, not commenting in any way except with those eloquent and majestic eyes, which for all Dr. Fenton's efforts still seemed to scorn and condemn without pity. When Dr. Fenton offered him the bone from his steak or chop, Baldur accepted it with the formal, distant air of royalty accepting a purely symbolic tithe.

Yet Dr. Fenton could not have said that the dog was not loyal, reasonably affectionate, and all that a good dog should have been. On Thursdays, when Dr. Fenton worked at a clinic and could not take him along, Baldur greeted him at the door at six o'clock and seemed to shrug off Dr. Fenton's apologies for not having been able to take him out since morning. But Dr. Fenton saw in the dog's unfailing courtesy, which he felt cloaked an inner contempt, the same attitude he had seen or imagined so often in Theodora. For instance, Theodora had often pressed him to stay on when the hour was late, which he knew now she had done for politeness' sake and not because she wanted his company. Dr. Fenton was no longer at ease in his own house, for the same reason he would not have been at ease had Theodora been living in the apartment with him on some incredible platonic basis.

Dr. Fenton never sat around his apartment in shirtsleeves now, much less in pajamas, even on Sundays. He almost never saw any friends, but he talked sometimes with Baldur. He would ask Baldur if he were ready to go out—Baldur would signal with a wag or droop of his tail—and asked him what he preferred for his dinner. Baldur knew the names of several kinds of meat, liked liver once a week, and signaled for hamburger most of the time. Truthfully, Dr. Fenton would have loved to be free of him, but the dog's keen intelligence, which Dr. Fenton believed amounted almost to clairvoyance, kept him from even thinking of this. His depression deepened, and he brooded on suicide.

He was brooding on it very late one night as he walked the Queensboro Bridge with Baldur. He released the dog with a command to run ahead of him. With a leap, Dr. Fenton cleared the iron balustrade. Another step or two and he was at the edge of the girders that hung above the river. Then he felt himself yanked backward and he fell, grasping instinctively at the girders under his hands. Baldur was standing over him, looking at him bewilderedly but with wagging tail. Dr. Fenton's mood had passed, and he proceeded on his way home.

The following weekend, he read in the Sunday *Times* of the marriage of Mrs. Theodora Wilkes to Robert Frazier II of Pennsylvania. Dr. Fenton had never heard of him, but his very name evoked a picture of a handsome, cultured Main Liner, a man of leisure and means. He imagined Theodora and her new spouse on a long honeymoon, perhaps a 'round-the-world cruise, their friends the cream of society. He took Baldur out for a long walk to try to change his thoughts. A man stopped him in Central Park, said he was a dog dealer, and asked if Dr. Fenton possibly wanted to sell Baldur. Dr. Fenton flinched at the words. If he didn't want to sell, then he certainly wanted to enter him in a few shows, didn't he? The man told Dr. Fenton of a dog show in New Jersey in three weeks, in which Baldur could take first prize in the German shepherd class hands down.

"Of course. It really wouldn't be fair to the others to enter him," Dr. Fenton murmured nervously, and walked on.

His practice was declining. He made two bad blunders—in both cases forgetting to remove some medicated cotton in the bottom of a cavity before filling it—and he slept wretchedly, expecting at any hour the ringing of the telephone and the voice of some agonized client. His drooping posture reflected his spirits and contrasted with Baldur's fine bearing. When they walked on the street together, Dr. Fenton felt he could read in the eyes of passersby what they thought of the two of them. He no longer had the pride to care. His one objective was to care for the dog to the best of his ability. On Baldur's first birthday, he gave him a new chain collar and leash and Baldur had a steak at a fine restaurant. Then they went to an open-air concert of Viennese music.

Dr. Fenton had come to dread his weekends, because he could never escape the dog's disapproving eyes. And with delayed reaction, he had begun to brood over Theodora and to imagine her life with Robert Frazier II. On long Sunday afternoons, his imagination expanded in wild arabesques. He saw Theodora wrapped in clouds of happiness and tobacco smoke, covered with jewelry he would never have been able to buy her, smiling contemptuously down on him. He had the form of a small skunk or a vermin-ridden rat, cringing at her feet, while Baldur cavorted mockingly around him, nipping him and laughing.

It was on a dismal Sunday afternoon that Dr. Fenton made his second suicide attempt. He sealed his kitchen window with adhesive tape, then persuaded Baldur into the bedroom and closed the door. He sealed the door of the kitchen, and turned on all the gas jets of the stove. Then he sat down in front of the oven with his head resting on the open oven door and inhaled deep, delicious drafts of the sweet, dizzy-making gas. For the first time in many months, he felt happy.

Dr. Fenton awakened slowly and found himself surrounded by blurry human forms. His head felt as if it were being crushed in a vise.

"You'll be all right," one figure said. "We heard your dog barking. He nearly broke the door down. Good dog . . ."

Dr. Fenton saw Baldur's handsome face peering down at him, and realized he was back in the old world again.

Later, he learned that Baldur had opened the bedroom door, which had no key for its lock, then had yanked the kitchen door open, despite its adhesive tape sealing, dragged him into the air, then barked and barked until some neighbors had called the superintendent and gotten in. Baldur was photographed by every newspaper in New York, and Dr. Fenton was interviewed thoroughly about him, his personality, what he ate, what tricks he could do, and so on. No one asked Dr. Fenton a single question about himself. The next day, Baldur's face smiled out from the front pages of two tabloids, while inside there was a reenactment of the rescue in six consecutive pictures, which Baldur must have obliged with while Dr. Fenton had been shunted off to bed by the doctors. Even the more conservative papers gave two columns to the story with a photograph of Baldur. "A Man's Best Friend," they called the dog. Dr. Fenton was called "Dr. Benton" in one newspaper, "Mr. Fenton" in another, and "an obstetrician" in another.

For days afterward, people stopped and petted Baldur on the street, and Dr. Fenton was asked if he were really Baldur. Baldur acknowledged the pats and praise with tail wags, but as time passed he acted impatient with the acclaim, as if he knew when the excitement should be wearing off. Dr. Fenton felt that Baldur kept a sharper eye than ever on him, and he decided to give up the idea of suicide as long as Baldur was with him. He felt trapped, but from the time of his decision not to attempt suicide again, he felt also reconciled. His feeble instinct of self-preservation began to stir again, and showed first in his holding his head up when he and Baldur walked on the street together. He also squared his shoulders and walked with a quicker step. Now, at least, Dr. Fenton thought, passersby could not say that he *looked* so much worse than his dog.

Dr. Fenton tried hard to take pride in his work, too. He did not know if his work improved, but three weeks passed without his making a mistake. Evenings after his dinner, he plunged into books of philosophy and history. He bought Berlitz School records and studied French. His mind, trained in dental school to attack facts and retain them, assailed his French grammar the same way. To improve his fluency, he chatted with himself in French under the shower and while he shaved. Studying and reading until midnight or later made it difficult for him to fall asleep once he went to bed, so he kept his radio on softly all night, tuned to an FM station that played only classical music, which he knew Baldur preferred to dance music. Mozart and Richard Strauss Dr. Fenton found he liked, too, and he bought some long-playing records of their music for the phonograph that he had not touched for two or three years.

When the Kirsteins called him up to invite him to a Saturday night poker game, Dr. Fenton politely begged out on the grounds of having another engagement. Actually, he preferred to stay home with his books, he realized, and the prospect of Bill Kirstein's loud laughter, of losing twenty or thirty dollars, which he always did, and of having a hangover Sunday besides was not attractive to him. He had used to see the Kirsteins out of loneliness, but he no longer felt so lonely. After all, there was Baldur, and he felt that the dog regarded him less critically since he had taken up French and classical music, but perhaps it was only that Baldur was glad himself of quiet company every evening. It had been weeks now since Dr. Fenton had even gone to a movie.

His practice slowly began to pick up. There were no more empty hours and half hours in the day. His old clients had always sent a few new ones to his office, but now they arrived at the rate of half a dozen a week. Dr. Fenton raised his prices very slightly. He was still below the price level of the majority of dentists of his ability—two or three of his clients told him so themselves—and he knew that people would respect him more if his prices were not rock bottom. That was human nature. With the extra money, he bought new carpets for his office, some attractive Cézanne and Matisse reproductions for his walls, and finally even had his office repainted a dark, pleasant green.

All this put him on a different footing with Baldur. At first, he had thought he only imagined it, but now he was sure. Baldur really smiled at him when Dr. Fenton proposed a walk in the park. When he ate his dinner, with a book propped in front of him, the dog lay quite close to his feet and no longer stared at him with a covert disgust. And in fact Dr. Fenton did not see how the dog could view him with disgust at dinner now, since the table was always impeccably set, lit with candles, and the food was no longer out of a can, either. In the last months, Dr. Fenton had been reading a French cookbook by way of familiarizing himself with the phrases found on French menus, and was experimenting with many of the recipes. There were evenings when his cooking was so good, he wished he had invited a friend to dinner. This wish lasted only while he was eating. He was glad enough to have the rest of his evening to himself.

One morning he received a telephone call in his office from Theodora. For an instant, his blood ran cold and a kind of panic made him tongue-tied. The Robert Fraziers II stood for a Medusa-like monster that he had been trying to keep at the very back of his mind, since to think of them even briefly was to paralyze himself, to demolish the ego that he had been so painfully rebuilding. Fortunately, during the minute he felt tongue-tied, Theodora kept talking. She said in a very kind tone that she hoped he had been well the last year, and that she was calling to ask if he would come to a cocktail party that she and her husband were giving the following Friday.

"I—well, I think I am free, yes. That's very—"

"Good! Bring Baldur, too, Ed. We've got a Briard and they can keep each other company." She laughed her gay, easy laugh, and gave him the address.

When he hung up, he was trembling. He had accepted before he realized what he was doing. If he'd only had some warning, so that he could have prepared a courteous, convincing statement as to why he could *not* come! He thought of calling back that evening and declining, but it seemed cowardly. *No, face it,* he told himself. *Keep your head up the way Baldur does, face it for half an hour and take your leave.*

Friday at six, as he rang the bell marked R. FRAZIER in the East Eighty-eighth Street apartment building, he felt that his self-confidence was only a thin shell around him, no deeper than his freshly pressed suit. The first sight of Theodora, he thought, radiantly happy in her marriage to Robert Frazier II, would crumple him to that wretched image of the skunk which he still vividly remembered. Theodora answered the bell. Dr. Fenton had rather expected a maid.

"Welcome, Ed!" she said with an abandoned swing of her arm. "And Baldur! *My,* hasn't he grown! Come in!"

The room was quite small and crowded with people, all noisily talking. Theodora took him directly to a gateleg table covered with bottles and glasses and soup bowls of ice cubes, and mixed a strong scotch and soda for him, saying that he probably didn't know anybody here and could face it better with a glass of something. He realized then that she was a little high.

Suddenly a huge, shaggy Briard bounded out of nowhere and crashed against Dr. Fenton's thighs, nearly knocking him down. His grip on Baldur's short leash tightened, but there was no need, because Baldur stood quite still in the face of the Briard's barking, which sounded like claps of thunder in the small room.

"Susie!—Susie, *quiet!*" Theodora was yelling, tugging at the dog's collar, but Susie would not be silenced and her splayed legs made it impossible for Theodora to budge her. Susie crouched, barking, wagging her tail, inviting Baldur to romp, but Baldur only gazed at the dog with the smiling indulgence that an adult might show toward an unruly child.

"I suppose Susie's just a pup!" Dr. Fenton shouted over the barking, smiling.

"A *what?*—*Susie!*" Theodora's head snapped back alarmingly as Susie bolted free, and she caught herself against Dr. Fenton's shoulder.

Susie had begun to run in a circle around Baldur. People shrank against the walls to get out of her way, jostling each other, spilling drinks. A small end table was knocked over.

"I shouldn't have brought *Baldur!*" Dr. Fenton yelled apologetically. "I'm sorry! Shall I take him out?"

"Susie, *stop!*—*Bob,* lock her up in the bathroom!"

"Somebody'll only let her out again!" shouted a plump, pink-faced man.

One of the male guests made a dive for Susie's collar, hung on and stopped her, then tugged her into an adjacent hall.

"I suppose she's just a pup," Dr. Fenton said to Theodora, smiling.

"She's four. She's Bob's dog. I can't do anything with her and he *won't*. Just look what she's done to the sofa end."

Dr. Fenton realized with a shock that was almost horror that the plump, pink-faced man in the armchair, whom Theodora had called Bob, must be Robert Frazier II. "He's—your husband?" Dr. Fenton asked, still incredulous.

"Yes. Come and meet him. Bob? Want you to meet Ed Fenton, one of my former husband's old friends," Theodora said carelessly.

Robert Frazier II did not get up, only waved his glass and said, "Hi, Ed, make yourself at home. This is a housewarming, y'know, and we want it *warm*."

"I didn't know," Dr. Fenton said, not knowing what to say. The man's appearance still held him rigid with surprise. He looked about thirty-five, though his face was so soft and weak, he might have been older. And he was certainly drunk. "Where have you been living?"

"With his parents in Pennsylvania," supplied the blond girl seated on an arm of Robert Frazier's chair. "But they've thrown the honeymooners out now, and he's going to make his own way in the world, isn't he, Bobsie?" She kissed him on the cheek.

"She's my cousin, y'know," Robert Frazier said with a wink to nobody in particular.

"Kissing cousins! Ha! Ha! Ha!" somebody yelled.

Speechless with shock and embarrassment, Dr. Fenton moved away, looking for Theodora. She was standing by a window, gazing dreamily out. Once beside her, he did not know what to say. He had prepared himself to ask if she had gone to Europe since he had seen her, prepared even a congratulatory statement about her husband. The statement was quite impossible to make now. Dr. Fenton glanced around the room and his eye fell on a wide silver bowl that he recalled from the days when Theodora had been married to Alex Wilkes. It was a beautiful bowl, Grecian in spirit, and it had always held grapes or floating flowers of some kind at

Alex and Theodora's house. Someone had set a half-finished highball in it. The beauty of the silver bowl made him realize the ugliness and mediocrity of the rest of the furnishings—the varnished bookshelf, the busily patterned drapes, the clumsy armchair in which Robert Frazier II slumped. Dr. Fenton suddenly recalled the smell of lamb stew that had greeted him when he stepped out of the elevator a few minutes ago. And the people here—Dr. Fenton had expected the upper crust of international society, or at least of American society. It was almost funny. The people were about the caliber of the Kirsteins. He had no sooner thought that than the Kirsteins came in the door. One of the guests had opened the door for them.

Bill Kirstein greeted Robert Frazier noisily, then saw Dr. Fenton and charged toward him. "Ed, you old jerk, where've you been hiding? I didn't expect to see *you* here!" His hearty slam of Dr. Fenton's shoulder brought a very low growl of warning from Baldur, which Dr. Fenton felt as a slight vibration of the leash. "Business still the same old grind? Still got that hound, I see."

"Oh, I've been staying home quite a bit lately," Dr. Fenton said with a smile. "How've you people been?"

Bill Kirstein looked at him suspiciously. "Say, what're you getting so high-hat about? Snubbing all your old friends?"

"Not at all!" Dr. Fenton felt himself blushing a little. On the other hand, why should he feel apologetic? What had he done? He stood up still straighter and looked Bill right in the eye, pleasantly.

"Be seeing you." Smiling in a slightly rattled way, Bill drifted off to Theodora. Dr. Fenton watched her come awake and kiss Bill on the cheek, and Bill circled her waist with his arm, familiarly. He never would have done that with Alex around, Dr. Fenton thought, and Theodora would not have permitted it, either. Alex and Theodora had known the Kirsteins slightly for several years, Dr. Fenton knew, but they had never been close friends and the Wilkeses had not invited them, he distinctly remembered, after one party at their house at which Bill had gotten obstreperously drunk.

Baldur stood by his side, gazing straight before him with a rather puzzled expression, Dr. Fenton thought, at a woman who was sitting on a man's lap.

"*Tell* me about Baldur," Theodora said suddenly, reaching down to pet the dog's head. "Has he been a good companion for you?"

She evidently hadn't read about Baldur saving his life, or was too drunk to remember it now, Dr. Fenton thought. "He's been a wonderful companion," he said, smiling. "Haven't you, Baldur? Don't you recognize Theodora?" he asked the dog, and the look in Baldur's eyes as he glanced up at him made Dr. Fenton wish he hadn't asked that question.

"Have you taught him any tricks?" Theodora asked, pushing back some straying hair with one of the long, limp hands that Dr. Fenton had once thought so exquisite.

"He doesn't need to learn tricks. He understands everything that goes on, just like a human being," Dr. Fenton replied.

Theodora's face changed slowly. She tried to stand taller, swaying a bit. "You're different, Ed.—You've changed a *lot,*" she said almost hostilely. Drunken tears suddenly poured into her eyes, making them glassier. "If you don't like me anymore, why'd you come here?"

"But Theodora, I do like—"

"I may be living a lot more simply, but it's my life, isn't it? Who're you to look down your nose?" Her voice rose and the hubbub in the room came to an abrupt halt.

"Siddown, hon, you've had enough!" yelled Robert Frazier II from the depths of his armchair.

Somebody laughed. Conversation started again.

"My apologies, Theodora, but I still don't know what I've done," Dr. Fenton said with a smile. "It's a charming party and I'm very happy to see you."

"I don't *believe* you!" Theodora said with a persistent stare, and though her voice was loud, nobody paid any attention now.

"I think I should be going, Theodora. Thank you *very* much for asking me, and thanks from Baldur, too." He turned and walked to Robert Frazier II. "Good-bye, Mr. Frazier. It's been a pleasure meeting you."

"Glad you came. Don't mind Theo, she gets like that." Robert Frazier waved casually.

"And good riddance! Stuffed shirt!" Theodora's voice yelled behind him as he opened the door.

The door closed behind him, but did not quite shut out a horse-laugh from Bill Kirstein. Dr. Fenton caught the elevator down and started walking the twenty-odd blocks to his apartment, conjugating French subjunctives to relax his taut nerves. After several blocks he began to feel better, and he remarked to Baldur that it was only two more weeks until summer vacation. Dr. Fenton was taking a month off and going to a hotel in the Adirondacks where Baldur, he had learned, would be welcome.

Baldur looked up at him with a smiling adoration and with understanding. Dr. Fenton winked at him. Never again would he see Theodora Frazier on an unapproachable pedestal, never again envy the man whose wife she was, never again see a golden aura around Robert Frazier II. Dr. Fenton began to whistle like a schoolboy. Life, his very own life, which he had thought so humdrum and hopeless, seemed a blessed and happy thing, full of promise and full of joy. His eyes lingered on a pretty woman who approached him and went by.

"I've walked up an appetite, Baldur. What do you say we find a restaurant and share a nice steak right now?"

Baldur looked up at the word "steak," and pulled a trifle more eagerly on his leash, turning at the next corner toward the restaurant between Madison and Park which he knew his master favored when it came to steaks.

BORN FAILURE

Some men are born to success as the sparks fly upward. Some men start making a profit on penny lemonades at the age of five, gather a little backlog swapping old cars at fifteen, and by fifty the thousands are gushing in from oil, cotton, babies' didy services, frozen cheese blintzes, or whatever else they have applied, however casually, their golden-touched brains to.

Such was not Winthrop Hazlewood. Winnie was a born failure. He looked like a failure even at the age of five, sitting with his big brother (who looked like a success at the age of ten) in a goat-cart photograph that still stands on the piano in Winnie's house in Bingley, Vermont. There is another picture on the piano showing Winnie at twenty-one with his college mates on graduation day, Winnie fifth from the left in the back row, hangdog and unobtrusive, as if he were actually ashamed of the occasion that caused him to be photographed that day.

But Winnie had an aspiration, even at twenty-one. He wanted to open a general store. It was characteristic of Winnie that he never spoke of it as a "department store" but as a "general store." Winnie wanted to live in a small town. His idea was to learn the business by clerking in a department store in Bennington, his hometown, and then open a store for himself. In his seventh year of clerking, his fiancée, Rose Adams, got tired of waiting for him to learn the business and yanked him from the job and from Bennington to Bingley-on-the-Dardle, where Winnie had always said he wanted to live. Winnie had a little money saved up, and Rose's father gave her a thousand dollars as a dowry, plus another thousand exclusively for the new store. It took Winnie over five years to pay the thousand dollars back to Mr. Adams with interest. By that time, Winnie's first and last child, Mary, had been born and had died in the second month of its life. The doctor said that Rose should never try to have another. Winnie was deeply disappointed, because he loved children, but he never showed his disappointment to Rose. Winnie was a man of resignation.

Winnie had wanted a store that specialized in men's clothing, especially workingmen's clothing, because Bingley was a farm community, and in such things as ribbons, buttons, nails, and hammers—the kind of things people needed every day, Winnie said. It didn't take Rose a minute to see that two other stores took care of Bingley's needs in these lines, but that what the town lacked was a good dry goods store. So Winnie took her advice and concentrated on dry goods, from cottons up to heavy woolens. He also sold some haberdashery, soaps, stationery, toys, overshoes, percolators, and floor wax. These last stocks varied, because Winnie was a great one for buying a bargain in any line of goods when a salesman offered it to him. And the stocks moved very slowly for the reason, as Rose always pointed out, that people never knew what he had at any certain time. If they came back to buy a second box of soap, for instance, there wouldn't be any more in stock, no soap at all, which didn't make for steady customers. The women of Bingley all sewed, but there just weren't enough of them to make Winnie rich. Winnie was fifty-two, and a tired, skinny old man, before he paid off his two-story house on Independence Street.

And even that was at the expense of not getting his store painted, or reroofed, or the cellar waterproofed, or anything else that a respectable emporium needs. Like Winnie, the old middle-sized cracker box of a store on the river side of Main Street looked a lot older than it was. The reddish paint had weathered to a mottled brown, and nearly all the gilt letters on the sign in front that said HAZLEWOOD'S GENERAL MERCHANDISE had chipped off so that you couldn't read them unless you knew what they were supposed to say. Yet the store had become a fixture in the town, and most Bingley women wouldn't buy their materials anywhere else, even in Bennington. As low as Winnie's cash reserves got sometimes, they never quite went down to zero, and he and Rose managed to eat, though not much by the looks of Winnie. He was about the size of a skinny fourteen-year-old boy, not very tall and inclined to stoop. He had a clean-shaven, completely forgettable face—a nose that was just a nose, a mouth as gentle as a sheep's, and steady but tired gray eyes that looked out from under very ordinary brown eyebrows. His father had grown bald early, but Winnie's straight brown-and-gray hair grew tenaciously, as thick as it had ever been, parted on the left and hanging over his forehead a little, as it had since he was a small boy. In a bigger town, few people would ever have noticed Winnie, but in Bingley everybody knew him and spoke to him on the street, as if in a town of Bingley's smallness Winnie had become distinctive just for ordinariness. His bookkeeping kept him at the store until nine o'clock and after in the evenings, about the time when Bingley's young men were walking their girls home from the seven o'clock movie at the Orpheus. All of them said hello to Winnie if they passed him, or if the light was still on in the back room of the store they would say, "I guess Winnie's still at it, poor old guy." And if they didn't see him, and saw no light, they would remark that Winnie must be home early for a change. In short, Winnie was not really a forgotten man in Bingley, not a cog in a machine the way a lot of big-city dwellers are. But Winnie was very much aware that he hadn't gotten half as far as most men in Bingley, though he worked twice as hard as most.

Besides having a streak of middling to bad luck for years and years, Winnie had a few misfortunes that were plain unusual. Like the time his older brother turned up in Bingley, fifty years old and flat broke. The last Winnie had heard of Richard, he had made a quarter of a million dollars on the stock market playing Mexican mines. Richard had written him a triumphant letter about that, and had said he was off to Mexico to buy himself a village to retire in. But the Richard that turned up in Bingley was a shadow of his old self. He had put all his money into a silver mine that never produced, had sold at a loss, and then lost that money at a gambling casino in Mexico City. Richard asked Winnie for a job in his store. Winnie said he could put him up at the house all right, but he couldn't possibly take him on at the store. There wasn't enough work, and there wasn't enough money coming in to pay a salary with. But Richard pled with him.

"Can you do bookkeeping?" Winnie asked.

"Anything! Sure I can do bookkeeping, Winnie. Figures were always my specialty, don't you remember?" Richard made wavy gestures with his hands, and a ghost of his jaunty smile came back.

"I sure do need a bookkeeper," Winnie said. "But I couldn't pay you more than . . . say, twenty-five dollars a week."

Richard said that was fine. "I'll help you out with the clerking, too," Richard said.

Rose was furious with Winnie. "Richard, who's never given you a cent!" Rose said.

"Well, I never asked him for any," Winnie replied.

"I bet he can't add six and four! He never could do anything but sport around and blow his own horn!" And Rose would have said a lot more, if she hadn't been glad, in a way, that Winnie was taking on a bookkeeper, even a bad one. It hurt Rose that everybody in Bingley talked about Winnie's not having a single clerk in the store, and coming home late at night summer and winter because he had to stay late totaling up his own accounts. Rose had had high aspirations when they first came to Bingley. Gradually she had turned loose of most of them, but she still longed for a refrigerator and a new sewing machine that worked by electricity. Now, what with paying Richard twenty-five dollars in cash every week, it was hopeless to dream of a refrigerator and a sewing machine anyways soon.

Richard had no knack at all for bookkeeping, or even arithmetic. He would sit bent over his desk in the back corner of the store all day, apparently working with his pen, but actually just doodling in the margins, and scheming up ways to make another pot of easy money and move on to a gayer place than Bingley. Far from helping Winnie with the clerking, on the rare occasions when there was more than one person in the store, Richard would choose these times to disappear entirely, sometimes into the bathroom, sometimes out the back door for a walk. He was trying to build up some social contacts in Bingley, and he did not want everybody in town to know that he was working for his brother. If Richard ever approached a counter, it was to pick out a new tie for himself, or to get himself a clean pair of socks.

So it was not long before Winnie was doing his own bookkeeping again, and trudging home through knee-deep snow at ten o'clock at night, so bent over with fatigue that he looked smaller and more insignificant than ever. But Winnie never told Rose that Richard was not doing well, and he continued to pay Richard twenty-five dollars a week for practically nothing. And Rose asked only ten dollars a week for his room and board, though Richard ate more than she and Winnie put together. Richard gained weight and the color came back to his face.

"I don't expect he'll be with us much longer," Winnie said.

"Did he say when he was leaving?" Rose asked hopefully.

"Nope, but I can tell."

"You'd just better search him the day he takes off," Rose warned Winnie.

But that would not have done any good, because Richard departed one day—and Winnie and Rose saw him off at the station and gave him a box lunch of fried chicken and angel food cake—in possession of valuables that could not have been detected on him: seven hundred fifty dollars transferred from Winnie's store accounts to a bank in New York City. Winnie did not discover this loss for nearly a month. And he kept it a secret from Rose.

That was near Christmas, and every year Winnie had been in Bingley he had managed to set aside a hundred dollars or so for a Christmas party and presents for the children at the county orphanage a few miles out of town. These parties always cleaned out his stock of toys at the store, too. That year, even with the loss of Richard's seven hundred fifty dollars to be covered, Winnie managed to scrape up a hundred in cash to buy candy and cookies and to hire the sleigh and horses in which he gave all the orphans rides in groups of six and eight. Rose did not begrudge the money Winnie spent on the children's Christmas. She loved to see Winnie's skinny, tired face light up when he sat with the reins in his hands surrounded by children, with the breeze flattening the fur of his raccoon cap as he clucked up the horses to a good lively trot. Rose knew how much he missed having children of his own.

There was a heavy fall of snow the winter that Richard came and went, and an early thaw that caught everybody unawares, and Winnie more than anybody. About three thousand dollars' worth of woolens, cottons, denim shirts, nails, and whatever else happened to be stored around the walls of the cellar got ruined by mildew and rust. It wasn't only the thaw, of course. Winnie's cellar had always been damp. Winnie had been going to have it recemented, but he had never seen his way clear to spending that amount of money. Now it was too late. Winnie expected Rose to fly off the handle about the cellar, because she had been after him to have it repaired for years. But she didn't. She just put her arm around him and patted his shoulder, without saying a word. Rose's patience with him that day affected Winnie so much that tears came to his eyes.

"Don't you worry, Rose. I'll make up for it this year," Winnie promised.

A few months later, when a salesman from New Haven told him about a cotton shipment from India that he could have for less than a third of its actual value, Winnie thought that his opportunity to recoup his losses had come. The salesmen had a sample of the material.

"Only one thousand dollars," the salesman said. "The only trouble is that the cargo isn't insured. The company in India has just gone bankrupt and they haven't a cent."

Winnie thought about this. He decided to be on the safe side. "I'll insure it from here," he said. "How soon will they be able to send it?"

"It's already on the way. It's due in another three weeks, via Suez and Gibraltar. You'd be buying moving cargo."

Winnie could see no advantage in buying moving cargo, but the salesman seemed to think he should. The only advantage was the low price, and even Winnie was enough of a businessman to know why it was low.

"Are you game to take a gamble? Cash on the line now?"

"Yes," Winnie said. He paid the salesman seventy-five in cash, and the rest in a check on his bank in Bingley, which granted him a loan.

Three weeks to the day after the transaction, Winnie received a letter from the salesman saying that the freighter *Bena-Li* out of Calcutta, bound for Gibraltar, had caught fire in the Mediterranean and sunk. Rose made him take steps to investigate the fire. The salesman never replied to Winnie's letter, but the Port Authority of New York confirmed the fact that a ship of that name had sunk in the Mediterranean on the date the salesman said. Its cargo, said the letter, was raw cotton, bamboo, and some tea. No cloth was mentioned.

"It's my opinion there never was any cloth anywhere," Rose said. "Why would the salesman have had one little piece of it in Vermont to show you?"

Winnie knew she was probably right. He stood in the middle of the living room, too ashamed of himself to say anything.

"Do you know what I think you should do? Take a good long vacation," Rose said. "Go up to Maine and do some fishing. Remember how you used to talk about going to Maine for some fishing?"

Winnie barely remembered. He had not dreamt of taking a vacation in years. He could not remember the last vacation he'd had. "I don't deserve it, Rose."

"But it'd do you so much good. Just close up the store and go, Winnie. This very month!"

Winnie said he might in the latter part of July. Then in August, and then in September. And then he never did. He was worried about the loan he had to pay back to the bank. Winnie went on working from seven in the morning till ten at night, sorting stocks, making change, renewing orders in cautious quantities, and totaling up at the end of the day his intakes of $6.25, $11.19, and sometimes only $3.10.

One evening he picked up the antimacassar that lay on the back of his armchair, and it fell apart in his fingers. Rather, it *dissolved* in his fingers, like so much smoke. He dropped the weightless fragments into the wastebasket. They were so fine, he doubted that Rose would even notice them when she emptied the basket.

Five more years passed, and in spite of many little ups and downs, Winnie's bank account stayed around a hundred and seventy-five dollars, just about what it had been after Richard absconded with the seven hundred fifty. The only thing that changed was Rose's hair, which got grayer and grayer, and the sensations in Winnie's legs as he trudged home in the winter evenings, lifting his feet high to get through the snow. Winnie felt tireder every winter.

Then one day in April, when Winnie was sixty-one, a letter came from a lawyers' firm in New York. It said that Oliver Hazlewood, an old uncle of Winnie's, had died and left him a hundred thousand dollars in his will. It would take a year to probate the will, but after taxes and legal fees, Winthrop Hazlewood would receive eighty thousand.

Winnie and Rose took this news very calmly, because neither of them could quite realize it was true. They didn't even talk about the money for days. Finally Rose broke the silence by speaking of old Oliver

Hazlewood, whom she had met only once, at her wedding. Rose said it was very nice of him to have remembered Winnie so well, since as far as she knew Winnie had never been close to him, had he? Winnie said he hadn't been at all close to him, and that he was very touched at Uncle Oliver's giving him all that.

A little later, they began to talk of what they would do when the money came. They would go to Florida for a vacation. Or perhaps to California. They might even buy a *house* in Florida or California.

"That'd mean selling the store," Winnie said.

Both of them sat kind of stunned for a minute, trying to imagine a life without the store.

"We're getting on, Rose. We'd best enjoy to the full what's left of our lives," Winnie said courageously.

Rose tried to imagine enjoying the rest of her life to the full. Lemonade in a hammock somewhere. All the new dresses she wanted. Bridge parties with tea and candy like she read about. But Rose didn't know how to play bridge. Sea voyages. . . . There were so many things she could do, Rose got dizzy as soon as she started to think about them.

They decided that when the money came next May, they would sell the store and the house, take a slow trip by train along the border of Canada, which they had always wanted to see, and then go to California. They didn't know exactly where, but they had heard of beautiful little towns along the coast south of Los Angeles. By the time next summer rolled around, they would have a better idea as to which town would most likely suit them.

Christmas found Winnie as pinched as ever, but he rented the sleigh, loaded it with presents for the orphans, and drove out to the orphanage for a Christmas Eve afternoon like all the thirty-odd others he had spent in Bingley. But this time there was a surprise for Winnie.

Above the gates of the orphanage fluttered a red streamer with gold letters, saying, MERRY CHRISTMAS, WINNIE!

All the children were waiting for him on the orphanage steps, and Sister Josephine, the superintendent, was there, too. Sister Josephine came forward as soon as Winnie drew rein and handed him a little box.

"The children made up a collection to buy you this for Christmas,

Winnie," Sister Josephine said. "They asked me to give it to you, but it's their present, every bit of it."

Winnie opened the box. Inside was a gold watch, engraved with flowery scrolls on the cover that flipped open to show the watch face. On the back, it was engraved with his interwined initials.

"Merry Christmas, Winnie!" the children yelled.

Winnie was blushing. All he could think of was that the children had donated thousands of precious pennies to buy the expensive watch, and that he was soon going to be so rich, he could easily buy himself a watch like this and not even feel it. He decided he must talk to Sister Josephine in private, tell her about the money he was going to get, and ask her to sell the watch and return the money to the children. But that could wait a few days, until after Christmas, of course.

Winnie showed the watch to Rose. Rose told him he ought to keep it, no matter what. It was the sentiment attached to it, not so much the money, she said.

"Besides, you wouldn't want everybody in town to know we're going to get all that money—yet—would you?"

Winnie certainly didn't. The eighty thousand dollars put him into an agony of shyness every time he thought about it. They would have to tell everybody eventually, of course, but Winnie wanted it to be at the last moment, and as quietly as possible.

"Sister Josephine can keep a secret, though," Winnie said. "I ought to give the watch back soon, so they can get the same price they paid for it."

Rose saw there was no arguing with him, either about keeping the watch or talking to Sister Josephine right away.

Winnie went to Sister Josephine on the second of January, and asked her to take the watch back. Sister Josephine wanted him to keep the watch and give its value back in money, when he got his money. But Winnie couldn't bring himself to wait till May.

"It's going to make the children very disappointed," she told him.

"I hope not for long," Winnie said. Then he crept out of her office, bent and small and more humble in his heart than any child who had ever crept out of Sister Josephine's office after being scolded.

May came around finally, and Winnie got a letter from Mr. Hughes of the law firm, asking him to come to New York to sign some papers and to receive the money.

"Well, I suppose it's time we told Ed we want to put the house and the store up for sale," Winnie said. Ed Stevens was the real estate agent in Bingley.

"I suppose it is," Rose said.

Winnie spoke to Ed that afternoon, and told him the reason: he was going to get eighty thousand dollars, and he and Rose were going to live in California. Within an hour, the news was all over town. That afternoon, Winnie's store was jammed with people coming in to congratulate him and shake his hand. Winnie thought from their smiles that they meant it, too. He had been worried that some people might be envious.

The next day, Winnie went to New York. It was only the second time in his life he had been to the big town. The first time he had been so small he couldn't remember much, so it was a brand-new experience to him, and just riding by taxi—Winnie would have walked but he was afraid of getting lost and being late for the appointment with Mr. Hughes—from Grand Central Station to East Fifty-second Street made Winnie feel like a piece of pine he had watched once being shot through a sawmill in Bennington, barked, dressed, and cut up for kitchen matches in less time than it takes to tell. Winnie felt about as insignificant as a kitchen match when he walked into Mr. Hughes's plush-carpeted office. But Mr. Hughes was awfully friendly and nice to him, and explained what all the papers were before he signed them, as if Winnie were quite familiar with such matters.

"What bank would you like the eighty thousand deposited in, Mr. Hazlewood?" the lawyer asked. "Or do you want the whole thing in trust?"

Winnie gulped, thinking of eighty thousand dollars landing in the Bingley Bank. "My wife and I are going right off to Canada," Winnie said. "Then we're going to California to stay, so we'll be giving up our present bank. I don't suppose you could give me the money in cash, could you?"

Mr. Hughes looked surprised for a minute, then he smiled and said, "Why, yes, we could by this afternoon. But are you sure you want to risk carrying all that with you to Vermont, just in your pocket?"

Winnie had with him an old briefcase in which he had intended to carry the money away. "I never lost a dime in my life just by leaving it somewheres. Or even by getting robbed," Winnie added with a smile.

So Winnie arranged to come back to Mr. Hughes's office at four, which would still give him time to catch the sleeper at five-thirty for Vermont. Winnie passed the time by walking slowly up Fifth Avenue, which he knew was the most famous street, looking wonderingly at the big buses, the taxis that raced by painted every color in the rainbow, and at the shop windows full of expensive articles. Winnie was attracted by a pair of binoculars priced at eighty-five dollars. He looked at them with a vague longing, and from the great distance of the unattainable, just as he had looked all his life at every costly object that he would have liked to possess. Then suddenly he realized that he could buy them by this afternoon at four. Why, eighty-five dollars was only about one *thousandth* of the money he would have! The idea made Winnie feel light in the head, and he walked on up the avenue, trying to get his bearings by thinking of something else. He sat for a while in Central Park. The trees looked pretty puny, but he felt better surrounded by the green things than by all the concrete buildings.

At a little after four, Mr. Hughes handed Winnie eight packets of banknotes, each one containing ten one-thousand dollar bills. The bills didn't even look like money with those little 1000 figures in the corners, but Winnie's hands were trembling as he put the packets into the briefcase. Mr. Hughes shook his hand warmly, and wished him a glorious time in Canada and California. Winnie thanked him very kindly, both for himself and for Rose.

Winnie tried not to think about the money on the train. He just put the briefcase in the net over his head in the upper berth, and fell asleep about as quickly as he usually did.

It was only the next morning, on the ferry across the Dardle to Bingley, that Winnie began to think about the money in the briefcase. He thought about how hard he had worked all his life, and how little he had ever made. Not even enough to buy Rose a refrigerator yet. He thought about all the mistakes he had made, and the bad luck that had followed him like a hound dog on a sure trail, ever since he had come to Bingley— his brother's going off with all that money, and the mildew in the cellar, and all the times he couldn't even count when he had bought goods that wouldn't sell, when he had given the wrong people credit, and all the times he had *not* bought certain goods that would have sold and made some money if he had bought them. It was just as if he had *looked* for failure all his life, he thought, and as if *finding* failure was the only thing he had ever done successfully. And now he'd been handed a fortune on a silver platter, eighty thousand dollars for doing absolutely nothing. He didn't deserve it. It didn't seem fated, this piece of luck that was going to change his life completely. Winnie reached for a handkerchief in his hip pocket. He was thinking about leaving Bingley, and there were tears in his eyes. Just as he brought the handkerchief up, his hand hit the briefcase, which was lying on the rail of the ferry.

Winnie grabbed for it, but he was too late. The briefcase dropped down and down and fell with a quiet plop into the water. Winnie leaned over the rail. It was gone without a trace.

"Hey!" Winnie yelled up at the bridge. "Say, stop the boat! I just lost eighty thousand dollars!"

"Lost what?" asked one of the passengers on the deck, a man Winnie didn't know.

Winnie headed for the steps that went up to the bridge. Then he stopped, shaking from head to foot. It was silly to think of stopping the boat. The way the river was rushing by—high water, too, swirly and full of mud from the spring rains—he'd never get that briefcase back in a thousand years, not even if he hired a crew of divers to go down and look for it!

"*What* did you say you lost?" asked the man beside him.

"Nothing," Winnie said.

The boat was drawing near the Bingley slip. There seemed to be a lot of people down at the dock. Winnie had hoped he could get home unseen by anybody, because he knew the first person who saw him coming back from New York was going to rush up and congratulate him on having the money. Now he knew he couldn't. Just as he stepped on the gangplank, a roar went up from the crowd.

"*Welcome home, Winnie!*"

"*How's the millionaire?*"

"*Where's your Rolls-Royce, Winnie?*"

The firemen's band by the boathouse started playing "There'll Be a

Hot Time in the Old Town Tonight," loud enough to drown out all the yelling and cheering, and Winnie saw Rose, all dressed up in her Sunday best, with flowers pinned on her shoulder. Now everybody was yelling, "*Speech! Speech!*" Winnie walked down the gangplank toward Rose. He felt like a whipped dog, and he supposed he looked like one, but nobody seemed to gather anything from that fact.

Cal Whiting, president of the Bingley Bank, held up his hand for silence.

Winnie braced himself. Now was as good a time as any, Winnie told himself. They'd all know in a few hours, anyway. "Ladies and gentlemen—my old friends of Bingley," Winnie began, and loud applause followed those words. "I am deeply ashamed to tell you all that I just dropped the money over the rail of that boat there. By accident."

There was a groaning "Oh-h."

And several incredulous "Huh?"s.

"Oh, Winnie!" Rose's face had twisted up. She put out her hand as if she were going to collapse, and Winnie caught her in his arm.

"What you mean, Winnie?" a voice asked.

"I mean, I don't have the money anymore. I lost it all. In cash. It fell in the river. So I guess I'm just the same old failure you folks know, anyway—and I don't guess Rose and I'll be leaving Bingley."

It took the big crowd about a full minute to realize what Winnie had told them. Winnie had never felt so low, so worse than worthless, so unworthy of living. There they stood, he and Rose, clinging to each other, defeated again, and before the whole town for every eye to see.

Suddenly Cal Whiting said in a loud voice, "Well, folks, I think it's a cause for celebration that Winnie *isn't* leaving Bingley. What's gone is gone, so let's go on up to my house and have the party like we planned!"

Everybody agreed to that. Winnie was whisked like a straw up on the shoulders of the two or three men nearest him, and carried up Main Street and then over on Walnut toward Cal Whiting's house. Winnie lost sight of Rose, and in all the jostling and singing he couldn't call out for her. On the big Whiting lawn stood four or five long tables loaded with punch bowls, sandwiches, cakes, cookies, doughnuts, and candy, enough to feed the whole town, Winnie thought. All the kids from the orphanage were there, too, and Sister Josephine, smiling at him in a way that made Winnie sure she hadn't heard the bad news yet. Sister Josephine came right up to him as soon as the men put him down from their shoulders.

"Winnie—"

"Sister Josephine, I lost the money. I just told everybody about it," Winnie said in a small voice.

"I heard about it already from a little boy." Sister Josephine took his hand and pressed something into it. "I hope you'll keep the watch now, Winnie. I never gave it back. It's been waiting for you."

Winnie closed his hand around the watch. "Thank you, Sister Josephine."

Then they began to ply Winnie with strawberry punch and chicken sandwiches and devil's food cake, until Winnie had to retreat to a corner of the lawn for self-preservation. Rose came after him. She didn't say anything to him, just stood beside him. She was smiling, though not in the same way she had on the dock before she found out about the money.

"Are you very disappointed, Rose?" he asked her.

"I don't think I'm disappointed at all. I think today is the happiest day of my life, Winnie."

Winnie looked at her patient face. He had the feeling he'd suddenly been reprieved from death. But he felt he didn't deserve that, either. "You know, Rose, on the ferry this morning, just before I lost the money, I sort of *saw* myself—I mean, saw that I've been looking for failure in one way and another all my—Rose, listen for a minute."

"Come on and join the party, Winnie. We can talk later." Rose pulled at his hand.

"But I have to finish this. I want to say—"

She turned loose of his hand, and he watched her go over to one of the tables, graceful and happy-looking, almost like the day he married her. Winnie stayed where he was in the corner of the lawn. He felt strange and wonderful suddenly, as if he were twenty or thirty years younger himself.

He was having another revelation: he saw all his life leading up to this moment, all the years of doubt, of hopelessness, of hard, unrewarded effort, leading up to this moment when all the people who he hadn't known were really his friends were showing him that he had everything that he could possibly want in abundance. And that warmth around his heart now, the certainty that Rose loved him and that everybody in town loved him, what else had he been seeking all his life? What more could anybody want? Winnie wasn't worried about anything anymore. Winnie felt—he was almost ashamed even to think it about himself—successful.

A DANGEROUS HOBBY

Andrew Forster, thirty-seven, married, the father of a fourteen-year-old girl and a topnotch salesman of the Marvel Vacuum Company, had developed a curious hobby. He would call up women, give them a long, slow, subtly flattering line, make a date with them (sometimes it took two dates, if the woman did not permit him on the first date to call for her at her house), and then he would rob them of some possession small enough to be put in his pocket.

Sometimes it was no more than a silver cigarette lighter or a ring of middling value that he picked up from a dressing table; but it satisfied him, and after his petty thievery, he dropped the women. He was never, so far as he knew, suspected. His courteous, serious, intelligent manner put him above reproach. After all, his job was selling, and the first thing a salesman had to do in order to get into a living room to demonstrate a vacuum was to sell himself. This Andy Forster could do superbly well.

And of course he picked his victims with care. They were all women with careers or professions, and all were single, though this last did not matter too much. One had been an actress, one a fairly well-known journalist, another a dress designer. He had boned up on their careers and current activities so that he could sing their praises in his very first telephone conversation.

To the dress designer he had spoken about his fourteen-year-old daughter who, he said, was determined to be a dress designer herself, and though he realized it was an unusual request from a total stranger, could he possibly meet her and talk with her for fifteen minutes or so somewhere? He had made sure he had seen the actress's last play and could therefore talk about it with conviction. He had especially admired the journalist's piece on such and such, and had some flattering questions to ask her. He had never been refused an appointment.

His appearance, when he arrived at their doors or when he stood up with a quizzical expression, not quite sure they were the right women, to greet them in a tearoom or a cocktail lounge, was even more reassuring than his voice on the telephone. He was about five-ten, a trifle over-weight though not soft, conservatively dressed, and his cheeks were pink and firm, suggestive of clean living. His manner was quiet and soft-spoken, but not unpleasantly so. He gave an impression of being some-what in awe of the particular woman he was with, or at least of being extremely respectful of her. His conversation was always intelligent, since Andy kept himself well informed on many subjects.

He always had his car with him, a big impressive company car but with no insignia of the company on it, and at the end of the tea or the two-drink-apiece cocktail date (that was all women dared to have with a strange man, it seemed) he had so won the women's confidence that they invariably accepted his offer to drive them back to their apartments or to wherever they were going. His robberies were usually committed during the second meeting. In two instances he had made third dates, after the robberies, as a kind of challenge to fate. But the missing articles had not even been mentioned.

"How do you know so much?" they would ask him, fascinated by his explanation of the failure of the Gallipoli campaign in the First World War.

Then Andy would tell them that he had been going to be a profes-sor of history, or of physics, or of geography, or of oceanography, but had his mind changed for him by his wife, who had said (when he was twenty-two and just about to get his degree) that she would never be happy as the wife of a college professor, because their salaries were so low.

This pitiful story, told with manly understatement and absence of resentment, made women feel extremely sympathetic, and they loudly decried the selfishness and pettiness of their own sex. They were different, of course. Just see how they could talk on an equal footing with a man, how this man listened when they spoke, and seemed to value them as a person, not just a female to jump into bed with. The furthest Andy went in familiarity was to touch their elbows as they crossed a street or got into or out of his car.

As a matter of fact, an injury Andy had received in the Korean War had made him impotent, and psychologically also he had given women up now, beginning with his wife, who had in a sense given Andy up a decade ago. His wife, Juliette, was home to cook his dinner every evening, but as likely as not she went out after dinner to work at some hospital—volunteer work or paid work, it didn't matter to Juliette. She was a registered nurse, slender, quietly efficient, with the energy of two men in her short, compact body. Juliette never talked about her work. It was simply her whole world and she could not wait to get back to it after her minimal attentions to her husband and daughter.

Andy was bright enough to realize that he hated women, though he had not realized it until after the Korean injury. That incident had made him realize that he had hated Juliette and very likely all other women for nearly the past ten years. He had once loved Juliette, but she had let him down—stupidly and without mercy let him down. And yet she was the mother of his daughter Martha, whom he adored.

In the evenings, every evening, Andy read, and he read until nearly three A.M. He was a poor sleeper. Sometimes even between three and seven A.M. when he got up, it seemed he did not sleep at all, merely rested his eyes beneath closed lids. Twelve years ago he had bought an *Encyclopedia Britannica*, and he was eighty percent through it now. Usually he read this in the evenings, propping the heavy volumes against the wall as he lay on his stomach in bed. When Juliette finally crawled into the bed on the opposite side, he simply tried to ignore her.

The loot from his encounters with women he put into a leather briefcase stamped with the Marvel Vacuum Company's trademark, which he kept at the back of his bottom drawer. Nothing was more certain than that Juliette would never look into that drawer: his bottom drawers for as long as he could remember had amassed, as if by their own power of attraction, unmended socks, shirts with missing buttons, shorts too worn out to wear but not worn out enough to be discarded, pajama tops with no pants, and vice versa. Andy did his own button-sewing and sock-mending, when he troubled to do it.

The briefcase now contained the actress's wristwatch, a sculptress's ring, the dress designer's silver twelve-inch ruler, the journalist's Javanese cigarette box studded with garnets, a thin gold necklace from a violinist of the New York Philharmonic, a pretty little silver pencil whose owner he had forgotten, a perfume bottle of blue glass enclosed in filigreed silver, a topaz ring he had picked up from the top of a toilet tank in the bathroom of a slightly tipsy nightclub singer who hadn't minded drinking a good deal in her own apartment, a Tanagra figurine that he kept wrapped in a handkerchief, and an antique silver flask of pocket size.

Andy had in mind giving many of these things to Martha when she would be twenty-one or so and out of college, and perhaps even out of the house, if she were married by then. He would bestow the presents slowly over the years, in a way that would excite no suspicion in Juliette, he hoped. She paid so little attention to what he did that it was hard to imagine her being suspicious of anything.

After six weeks of selling vacuums all day and coming home to a more or less silent wife, Andy would begin to feel restless and start planning a new adventure. One afternoon in mid-May he entered a telephone booth in the Bronx to call a woman anthropologist named Rebecca Wooster, whom he had seen one Sunday afternoon on a television program. She had just returned from the West Indies and Central America, where she had been making studies. Andy had found her number in the telephone book, but the number had been changed, the operator said, and she gave him the new one, which he made a note of, and dialed. A woman's voice answered, and when Andy ascertained that she was Miss Wooster, he continued in his usual style.

"My name is Robert Garrett." (He never gave his real name.) "I hope you'll forgive me for calling you out of the blue like this, but I saw you on television a few Sundays ago, and I've been—well, I've been thinking ever since about some of the things you said. I'm something of an amateur anthropologist myself, and I'm working on a theory just now using psychological rather than racial grouping. I'd like very much to ask you a few questions, that is, if you've got half an hour to spare—and I'd be very grateful to you if you could possibly spare the time to look over the outline I've made. It's just a matter of three pages."

He went on for another few minutes in a slow, earnest way, giving her time to respond now and then with a word or two that showed she was following him, in fact listening with interest. He had seen in the television show that she was a warm and friendly woman, patient with the questions that had been asked her at the end of the program, some of which had not been very pertinent. Finally, he apologized for taking so much of her time with the telephone call, and put in a modest plea that she would grant him a personal interview, however brief.

"Why, I think I can manage that," she said in her slow, pleasant voice. "How would tomorrow be? Say around five-thirty?"

"That would be fine," Andy replied. "Really I'm very honored, Miss Wooster." He asked for her address, she gave it to him, and they said good-bye cordially.

Andy was punctual the following afternoon, bringing with him a folded map of the world on which he had drawn various circles, some overlapping, to indicate his "psychologically similar groups." Most of it had no validity at all, he knew, but he had made the circles as best he could after consulting a few sociology books. He also had an "outline" of three typed pages.

Miss Wooster lived on the fourteenth floor—actually the thirteenth of a rather formal building on Park Avenue. She received him in a foyer as soon as he stepped out of the elevator. Andy introduced himself with a little bow, and they went into a large room that looked like a living room except for a massive desk near the window.

"You say you're not an anthropologist by profession," Miss Wooster began after they had seated themselves on the sofa.

"No. I work for a company that compiles reference books for the public library, not a very interesting job, I'm afraid, but it gives me a chance to read a lot." He got up with a murmured apology and walked in an awestruck way toward her bookshelves, on which stood, among the books, a dozen or more small sculptures and jeweled pieces of primitive art. "I hope you don't mind," he apologized. "These fascinate me, and I've never seen anything like these except in a glass case in a museum."

She got up, smiling with pleasure at his interest, and they talked and examined the pieces for fifteen minutes. What interested Andy most was a Mayan ornament of hammered gold, all a-tinkle with small gold pendants, each weighted with a tiny green stone. It was small enough to fit into his jacket pocket, and he had only to wait for the proper time to whisk it there, perhaps when Miss Wooster would turn to answer the telephone on the desk. Andy hated to resort to asking for a glass of water, though sometimes he had done so. At any rate, if he did have to ask for water, there did not seem to be any servant about who might get it for him.

"Well, let me see the outline you were talking about," Miss Wooster said, seating herself in a chair near the bookshelves. "I have an appointment at six, I'm sorry to say, but I couldn't arrange it any later."

Andy glanced at his watch, saw that it was 5:47, and said, "I'll make it as brief as I can." He crossed the room for his briefcase, and from among pamphlets concerning Marvel vacuums removed his map of the world and his three-page outline. Then he took a deep breath and began, slowly, but in a way that did not permit Miss Wooster to interrupt him.

A smile of incredulity, perhaps of amusement, was growing on her lips.

"You may think—I suppose I am incompetent to make such a study," he finished.

"No. It's quite interesting. I admire your enthusiasm." She had looked over his outline. "But I think you're wrong about the Adonis and the Chinese. I mean, the similarity you spoke of . . ."

Andy listened carefully as she talked and as the minutes ticked away. He wondered if he could get the Mayan piece on his first visit and if not, could he persuade her to let him see her again. Immediately, he forced the doubt from his mind. To doubt was fatal. At any rate, she was not telling him that his idea was *absolutely* off the beam, or unworthy of being written about.

A bell rang in the hall.

"Oh, dear, that must be my appointment," Miss Wooster said, getting up. "It's a bit early. Excuse me, Mr. Garrett."

Andy stood up, smiling. He couldn't have planned it better. Miss Wooster went into the foyer to speak over the telephone to the caller downstairs, and Andy quickly pocketed the Mayan piece, making sure that the gap it left would not be noticed until he was out of the house.

When Miss Wooster came in again, he was slowly putting his papers back into his briefcase.

"I've overstayed," he said sadly.

"Oh, no. But I do have to see this person now, because she's coming to interview me." She smiled and held out her hand. "It's been such a pleasure meeting you. I hope you'll go on with your book. You say you've written a hundred pages?"

"Yes." Andy was now moving toward the foyer.

"If you hit any snags, don't hesitate to call me. I'm always glad to talk about my favorite subject."

"Thank you—"

The elevator door had slid open. A tall woman of about thirty-five came slowly out and looked at Andy in a puzzled way. He looked at her in the same way, and then realized with horror that she was the journalist from whom he had stolen—what was it?

"Well! Mr.—O'Neill, isn't it?" she asked.

"No," said Miss Wooster. "This is Mr. Garrett. Mr. Garrett, Miss Holquist. Or—have you met before?"

"*Yes,*" said Miss Holquist.

Andy knew he couldn't get away with it. Even though his face was more or less ordinary, Myra Holquist had seen him on two occasions not more than six months ago. "Sorry," he said. "My name is Garrett. I don't know why I told you it was O'Neill. Just to be adventurous, I guess. Or I think I was trying out my pen name. There are enough writers named Garrett."

Myra Holquist nodded, as if she were thinking of something else. "How's the journalism going? Weren't you interested in writing something about the passing of the vacant lot in the lives of New York children? Something like that?

Now Miss Wooster was looking at him oddly.

"Something like that," Andy admitted weakly. "Well, I must be going."

He felt utterly defeated, shamed, humiliated. All his style was gone. He rang for the elevator, which unfortunately had closed and disappeared.

"Just a minute—Mr. Garrett. Excuse me, Miss Wooster. I wondered why you disappeared so suddenly," Miss Holquist continued to Andy. "It didn't by any chance have anything to do with a Javanese cigarette box?"

"I don't know what you mean," Andy said, frowning with feigned perplexity.

She gave him a bitter smile. "But you look as if you do. Miss Wooster, have you known this man very long?"

"Why, no," Miss Wooster replied. "Just this afternoon. He—"

"Then before he leaves, I think you'd be wise to look around your house and see if anything's missing."

Miss Wooster gasped, and Andy gritted his teeth and prayed for the elevator door to slide open. But he couldn't even hear the thing coming.

"I mean it, Miss Wooster," said Miss Holquist in a tone of command.

Some remnant of pride, perhaps even the beginning of a plan, inspired Andy to motion the elevator away as its door slid open. "Thanks, not just yet," he said to the elevator man, and turned like one about to be executed and followed Miss Wooster back into the living room.

Myra Holquist also came in from the foyer.

"Why—my gold Mayan piece!" Miss Wooster exclaimed. "It's gone!" And she looked at Andy with wide, frightened eyes. "D-did you see it?" she stammered.

"Give it to her, Mr. O'Neill, or Mr. Garrett," said Miss Holquist coolly.

Then Andy struck her in the side of the head with all the force of his muscular right arm, and she fell to the floor. He knelt and throttled her, bumping her head again and again on the floor, oblivious of Miss Wooster's screams, of her ineffectual efforts to pull him away. Nothing that could be described as a thought was in Andy's mind during those few violent seconds, only a feeling, a consciousness that the woman he was attacking had betrayed him, stripped him of decency, had filled him with an intolerable shame. Her overly made-up face symbolized to him all that he despised in the female sex—its coldness, mercilessness, indifference.

"Shut up!" Andy blazed at Miss Wooster as he got to his feet. But when he saw her retreating from him, he became frightened himself. She had become silent now, but he was afraid someone might appear at any moment in response to her screams. She kept retreating and he kept walking toward her. He wanted a rope, a gag—anything to tie her up until he could get away.

"Where's the bedroom? Go in the bedroom," he ordered. He saw the bedroom behind her and there was a key in its ornate door. "Get in there."

She went in obediently.

"And here. You can have this," he said, pulling the Mayan piece from his jacket pocket. He laid it on the top of a chest just inside the bedroom door. "I'm sorry, really sorry." Inarticulate, he jerked his head to one side in shamed apology, pulled the door to, and locked it, leaving the key in it.

Then he dashed back to the living room for his briefcase—Miss Holquist was motionless—and not daring to leave by the elevator he looked for the kitchen. Just as he had hoped, it had a delivery entrance, and outside this door he found a service elevator and some stairs.

He took the stairs. Down and down, thirteen unlucky floors. It put him out in a cellar, unlighted except for a little daylight that showed through an open door. He went out this door, up some iron steps, and he was on Seventy-eighth Street, between Park and Lexington, only fifteen feet from his car. Slowly he walked to the car, feeling in his pocket for his keys.

He lived on one of those peculiarly gloomy streets of apartment houses near the Manhattan approach of the George Washington Bridge. The bars of that neighborhood were gloomy, too, but Andy went into one and had two quick shots of rye to steady himself before he went home. For once he was grateful that Juliette scarcely spoke to him and never looked him fully in the face. And Martha, he remembered, was having supper with a school friend tonight, and was going to spend the evening with the friend doing homework.

That night Andy did not sleep at all. He was haunted by Miss Wooster's muffled cries through her bedroom door. Had there been a telephone in the room? How soon had she been able to get out? *Mr. Garrett, Mr. O'Neill,* she had called and called.

Andy turned in his bed with shame and thought of the cache of treasures in his bottom drawer. It was as if he had never seen his revolting pastime objectively before—he who had always considered himself a fairly intelligent man!

The next morning Andy bought a paper at the newsstand near his office, where he checked in every morning at eight forty-five. He found nothing in it about the nightmare of the last evening, but he was not sure if the morning papers could have picked up the story in time. He sold one vacuum cleaner to an elderly lady who had an apartment full of singing canaries.

Then he bought an afternoon paper, which said that Myra Holquist, the well-known journalist, had been throttled to death in the apartment of Rebecca Wooster, the eminent anthropologist, whom she had come to interview. Like the encounter itself yesterday, it seemed fantastic and unreal, until he went on to read the doctor's statement and also the description of "Robert Garrett or O'Neill" given by Miss Wooster. It was him to a T, a portrait of himself in words.

But a *murderer!* Murder was something Andy had not bargained for.

He knew what the police would do first: look for a Robert Garrett or an O'Neill answering his description, not find any (Andy hoped they would not find any), then a man of his description connected with any company that compiled reference books for the public library. Then they would start looking for a man of his description in the streets, anywhere. And maybe one day—

It crossed Andy's mind to turn himself in, and yet the murder, to him, seemed such an accident, such a piece of bad luck, that he felt he deserved better than to give himself into the merciless custody of the law. So he steeled himself to live with the awful fact that another person, a woman, had witnessed his crime and could, if she ever spotted him, put an end to his present way of life. The briefcase of stolen articles in the bottom of his drawer he could not even touch now. Merely the thought of it was enough to paralyze any action he might have taken to get rid of it.

Six months went by. Andy lost a little weight, but it was so gradual that neither Juliette nor anyone at his office made a remark about it. He could not look a policeman in the face on the street and he could not get over the habit of glancing quickly at all the faces that came flooding out from any opened elevator. The one time he and Juliette had gone to the theater (Juliette's request on her birthday), the intermissions in the lobby had been hell for him.

And then Andy read in the newspaper that Rebecca Wooster, forty-nine, had succumbed to a heart attack while at work in Ceylon. His reaction to this was very slow, covering a period of three days, at the end of which he took the briefcase from his bottom drawer and dropped it from the George Washington Bridge.

After this he felt better, and he expected that he would feel better and better as time went on. He did sleep better for a while, and then his sleep began to grow worse again. He developed circles under his eyes, permanent circles of purple.

Tossing in his bed one night, sleepless, he knew what was the matter. He had no specific enemy now, no one who shared the knowledge of his guilt. He had only himself.

For weeks now he had fought against a compulsion to confess, realizing what it would mean to his daughter and even to Juliette. But he could not convince himself that he was not behaving more heinously by keeping his secret, his unpunished crime, to himself. After all, he was a member of society, and so were his daughter and his wife.

So one cold afternoon in February, Andy went into a police station in the east fifties and gave himself up. He said that he was the Robert Garrett, alias O'Neill, who last May had throttled Myra Holquist to death in the apartment of the late Rebecca Wooster.

His eyelids twitched, as they did habitually now, and he realized that he did not sound very convincing. But he was not prepared for the stone wall of disbelief that confronted him in that police staton. A high-ranking officer questioned him in detail for several minutes, called another station for a check on the description of Garrett-O'Neill, and even then expressed his doubt.

"Have you ever been in a mental institution?" the officer asked.

"No," Andy answered.

Another officer of rank arrived and Andy repeated his story, adding now the details of his petty larcenies. But somehow his memory had deserted him. He could not remember more than one name of all the women he had pilfered from—Irene Cassidy, the dress designer. But what had be taken from her? He could describe several of the articles he had stolen, but he could not produce them, he explained, because he had dropped them off the George Washington Bridge two weeks ago.

"Call Irene Cassidy," the new officer said.

Miss Cassidy worked in her own studio, and she was in. The officer explained the situation laboriously—as if he were trying deliberately to muddle the woman, Andy thought. He could tell from the officer's words that he was getting negative replies to everything, so Andy asked if he could speak with her. The telephone was passed over to him.

"Hello, Miss Cassidy," Andy said. "I can't remember the name I used when I saw you, but I asked to talk to you because I had a fourteen-year-old daughter who wanted to be a dress designer. Remember that? It must have been—I suppose over a year ago." Maybe it had been two years ago.

"Well—I might remember if I saw you," Miss Cassidy replied, "but I see a lot of people who want to talk to me because they or somebody they know wanted to be dress designers."

"You didn't notice that something was missing—after I saw you that time?"

"Missing? What?"

"Some small thing from your studio—or your desk—I don't remember exactly."

"The guy's nuts," murmured a voice behind him.

"Can you come down to this station? Please?" Andy pleaded.

Miss Cassidy did not want to be bothered. Andy asked her to wait a moment, then passed the telephone to an officer and told him to do what he could to persuade her to come to the station. The officer was more successful.

There was a painful wait of forty-five minutes, during which time they let Andy sit on a bench from which he could easily have slipped out the door and into the street. At last Miss Cassidy arrived, small and chic, in a short fur wrap, a hat of bird feathers. The police led her to Andy and asked her if she had ever seen him before. Miss Cassidy looked blank.

"I've lost a little weight," Andy said to her. "Not much, but it might make a difference. We talked about Yves St. Laurent, remember? The talent of youth and all that?"

It was hopeless. There was a run-down, somewhat shabby look about him now. He was no longer the robust, self-confident man she had talked with a year ago, or perhaps two years ago.

Miss Cassidy shook her head, and looked at the officers. "I hope I'm not standing in the way of justice or anything like that, but to the best of my recollection I never saw this man before. Is he trying to save himself from something?"

"No, he's trying to confess to a murder," the officer said with a smile. "A sensation seeker. We get a lot of 'em like this. He's throwing in a lot of other things about robberies all over town."

Now Miss Cassidy looked positively frightened of him. Women,

Andy thought. Why should she have forgotten? It was not even deliberate, he thought, only an unconscious blow she had struck in the eternal battle of the sexes.

"We checked with the company he works for," the officer continued. "He hasn't missed a day's work in the nine years he's been there. Hey, is there a psychiatrist or something your company uses?" he asked Andy. "I think you better have a checkup, Forster. Maybe you've been working too hard lately."

A few minutes later Andy was released and out on the street again.

He went into a subway and threw himself on the tracks in front of an onrushing train.

THE RETURNEES

The return of Esther and Richard Friedmann to Germany in 1952 was a kind of triumphant reinstatement for both of them. It was as if a miracle had been visited upon them, as miraculous turns of fortune are visited upon banished but worthy kings in fairy tales, causing them to be returned to their domains, except that in the Friedmanns' case, their fortunes had risen even beyond what they had been before. Richard now had his old job back with his publishing house in Munich, at a salary higher than he had earned before the war. And Esther and he, after fourteen years of cohabitation, more or less furtive and awkward for the first several years, were now man and wife.

Richard had wanted to get settled immediately in a permanent home in Munich, and Esther, who was energetic and practical, had found in a very short time a two-story stone house in Bogenhausen, an old residential quarter of the city. Richard had told Esther that they would have to do a lot of entertaining, and on a much more formal scale than they had in England. Richard was very satisfied with the new house. He remarked that it was only three blocks from the big square house where Thomas Mann had lived and worked for twenty-five years.

During the first week, Esther busied herself with getting the linens and silverware in order—all hers, the things she had salvaged from her last and rather disastrous marriage, and sentimentally kept through thick and thin for just such a time as this—hiring two full-time maids, and laying down a routine for the household. She called up two friends in Munich, Greta Schwarzenfeld and Hermione Pieterich, and they both shrieked their surprise and delight at finding her once more in Germany. And married! Esther thought she noticed the least cooling off when she told them she had married Richard Friedmann, perhaps because of his

Jewish name, Esther thought. Greta said she remembered him from a meeting ages ago. Hermione didn't know him. "He's back with his old firm, Beckhof Verlag," Esther said. "You must come to see us as soon as we get straightened out." They both said they would. Esther forgot that hint of coolness. She was very busy those first days. Richard had buried himself at once in his new job, and in the evenings he buried himself in his study, so Esther had to do everything herself, even get the tickets for the opera and ballet they went to.

For Esther, it was a delicious pleasure to have a house again after the rather cramped flat in London. Esther reckoned up: sixteen whole years since she had had a house of her own. Sixteen years since she had left Germany so casually to spend a month with Vincente dalla Palma and his dull wife at Cap d'Antibes. Then she had been Baroness Esther von Dorhn-Neven. Hitler had been in power about three years, and the talk of purges, armament, and more horrible things to come was already dampening the conversation at dinner parties in Berlin. At her husband's table it had been worse, especially when any of their guests were Jewish. Her husband had been an outspoken anti-Nazi, and even before she left Germany, Esther remembered, the government had been making it difficult for him to get chemicals, because he had refused to convert his two plastics factories for military purposes. Her husband's letters during that summer of 1936 had become grimmer and grimmer, and Esther had chosen to stay on the Cap. She remembered that her husband had never made the least reference to Vincente, though the whole Côte had known that they were having an affair. All the international set knew that Esther von Dorhn-Neven had had a reputation for being a flirt as well as a beauty since she was seventeen. The baron was her third husband. The baron could see, perhaps, but he did not want to believe. Then, sometime in the winter of 1936–37, a mutual friend brought the baron positive proof in the form of several French newspapers full of photographs. The baron at once filed for divorce. Esther was even more shocked than all her friends, who marveled that anyone would divorce for such a trivial reason. Esther felt he had acted completely out of character. Actually, he behaved absolutely true to character. Esther had simply misjudged him. So had she misjudged also the character and generosity of her lover, Vincente. The baron cut her off without a cent, and Count Vincente dalla Palma, furious at all the publicity, made it very clear he did not want to see her again.

It spoiled all the fun on the Côte, so Esther went to England and recuperated from her shock in a comfortable London hotel for several weeks. She met some attractive people, but none she very much cared for. She knew she was not the type that Englishmen generally liked—dark-haired, lively, with an earthy wit that seemed to keep them off balance. Moreover, she could not easily return hospitality, and she was that awkward quantity, a single woman. She went for a while to Paris, but no one she knew was there except the Rosenfelds, who were actually refugees, they said. Things were going from bad to worse in Germany. The people seemed to be paralyzed, and the Jews, those who had any intelligence, the Rosenfelds said, were getting out. Esther thought the Rosenfelds were exaggerating. She went back to England, intending to wait a few more months until the talk about her divorce, and the Hitler craze in Germany, had quieted down before she went back and resumed her place—after all quite outside her husband's stodgy circle—in Berlin society.

Then, quite by accident, she met Richard Friedmann at a cocktail party in Chelsea. She had met him three or four years before in Berlin. He remembered her, too, from an evening at her husband's house.

He seemed terribly happy to see her, his ugly, lean, chinless face lighted with sudden warmth, and he showed his rather bad teeth in a boyish grin. He had come to England about a year ago, he said, and was now working for a publishing house in Chelsea, and also for a Fleet Street political magazine. In a corner of the room, they began to talk in German. He told her he had left Germany because, being half Jewish, he had been liable at any minute to be called up to work in the coal mines or at some other equally dangerous job where he would have been killed sooner or later. Either that or a concentration camp. He babbled it all out to her in his naive way, and the fact that he spoke in German made it all more real to Esther than ever it had been when she read it in the newspapers. He asked Esther to have dinner with him that evening.

She was not particularly taken with him; he certainly wasn't handsome, and obviously could hardly keep himself on what he made, but she was attracted to his frankness, his pleasure in being with her, and she found it wonderfully comfortable to be with someone who, if he did not come exactly from her own social set in Berlin, at least had an idea of it. Esther saw him several times a week, and on Sunday mornings he invited her to breakfast with him in his two-room flat, because in the furnished room that Esther lived in, she could not cook. Esther, who spoke English more correctly than he, helped him polish up his articles for the political magazine, and typed them over for him, as his typing was very bad. Inevitably came a Saturday night when Esther did not go home, and after that, they spent every weekend together in Richard's flat. He was not the best lover she had ever known in her life, and neither was he very gallant. Esther thought he treated her with an amazing indifference, in fact, considering her background and the men she had been used to—only one of lesser rank than a baron—which certainly Richard might have guessed. He asked her very few questions about herself, and when she did start to answer, to reminisce about some summer in Ravello or Capri, Richard would interrupt her with something that had happened that day in the office or in the newspaper.

Esther took a job as typist and letter writer for an auditing firm near Shaftesbury Avenue. It paid little and was a crashing bore, but she faced the fact that nearly every piece of jewelry she owned was gone now, and that Richard couldn't possibly support her. She still went to fashionable parties now and then, but Esther knew that at forty-five she couldn't expect to have the same success with men that she had had at thirty-five, or even at forty, when she had come to England. She had lived hard and fast since eighteen, and the last four years in London, on little money, had been even harder for all their boredom. She had put on weight around the hips, her chin had begun to sag with a look of middle-aged plumpness, and no amount of alcohol daubing could make the pouches under her eyes entirely disappear. Her beautiful nose stayed the same, but it was unobtrusive, too, and did not compensate for the rest. Only one man seemed to care for her, and he was Richard. But he had told her at the start of their relationship that he would never want to marry. He'd been born a bachelor, he said, and he would die one. That rather selfish bachelor attitude accounted, Esther thought, for his cautiousness about money, and the fact he'd never bought her a single present, except at

Christmas. But neither was Esther in a hurry to marry. Besides, she was not quite sure she loved Richard enough to marry him.

Richard, and Esther, too, were among the few people who were thrown into a panic on the day in September 1938 when Czechoslovakia was abandoned by the Allied powers. Only a month before, Esther had learned through a letter from a friend in Germany that her former husband had disappeared from Berlin, and that all his properties had been confiscated. Esther had heard of five or six of her friends who had disappeared during the previous year. Esther told Richard she would like to move into his flat with him, and he agreed. Esther was frightened, and she felt less frightened living with Richard. As to what the neighbors said about their having two different names, Richard didn't give a hang, and neither did she. But Esther was not too frightened to join firefighting and plane-spotting squads, and to stand side by side with the Londoners during the air battles of Britain. Both she and Richard stayed in London during the whole war, and neither of them ever suggested leaving for a safer place inland. With Richard it was a fatalistic indifference; with Esther, perhaps, that she never quite had time to realize how frightened she was. At the end of the war, when Germany was defeated, and she had been cited for personal bravery in saving an old man from a burning building near St. Paul's, Esther realized that she had accepted the facts of the war with a numbness that, five years before, would have been completely unlike her. She realized, too, that she accepted Richard now in the same way. She no longer considered him in her secret heart a faute de mieux. She had grown to love his ugliness, his indifference, his dependability, which was nothing really but a bachelor's rigid routine. The war years had welded their existences together, and it was no longer thinkable to Esther that she, or even he, could live alone again.

The friends they had in London were mostly artists, writers, and editors, not the sort of people to care whether she and Richard were married or not, but it had begun to bother Esther vaguely—like a tooth that doesn't yet hurt but ought to be taken care of before it does—that she and Richard were not married. But whenever Esther hinted that they should marry, Richard escaped behind the wall of economic fact: he didn't have the money to support a wife, he said.

"I don't see that we'd be spending any more than now. I'd keep on working, you know," Esther said.

Richard pondered this a moment. "This doesn't embarrass you, this kind of life, does it, Esther?"

Esther assured him that it didn't, but it did, a little. And as people got to be fifty and over, it seemed the logical thing to her to consolidate oneself somehow. Esther said this, and Richard simply looked blank.

"You said you're making twelve or thirteen pounds a week?" Esther asked. It varied because of Richard's freelance writing.

"Yes," Richard answered solemnly.

"Well, I make seven a week. That's at least nineteen or twenty pounds a week. We could live on that. We're living on it now."

"Esther, I——" he said between puffs as he got his pipe going. "If I do a thing like getting married, I want to do it right, not on a shoestring."

The conversation more or less ended there. They had said the same things before. Esther did not want to remind him again that she would be just as happy living the way they were now, that she didn't want any fancy apartment with new linens and expensive dishes. She was not twenty years old anymore. But the fact was, she did not really know the state of his finances. Was he in debt? Was he already getting some of his frozen accounts out of Germany and banking them here? Did he really make about twelve pounds a week, or less? She felt most of his answers were only half-truths, and so long as she was not his wife, she felt she could not insist on exact answers.

So their life went on in the same way, and Esther adjusted herself to the prospect of an eternal loose relationship with Richard, as she adjusted herself to the prospect of eternal rationing in England. Things were far worse in Germany, she knew. But her cousin, Lotte Kiefer, who had just come from Munich, had told her that a great many German firms were on their feet again. Esther told Richard that Lotte had said Leopold Beck-hof, the son of the founder of Beckhof Verlag, had bought back half his presses. Richard surprised her by saying that he knew it already. He had exchanged a few letters with Leopold's secretary, he said, because he thought it was a good idea to keep Beckhof Verlag informed where he was.

Lotte and her husband stayed for several weeks with some English friends in Kent. Esther saw them a few times in London during the first of their stay, but when they left, Lotte merely called her to say good-bye. Lotte Kiefer, like most of Esther's family, was on the stuffy side and considered Esther rather bohemian. Esther had no doubt that Lotte had heard, while she was in England, of her liaison with Richard Friedmann. Lotte must have remembered him from Munich, because Richard said he remembered her. It crossed Esther's mind that Lotte had been cool to her because Richard was half Jewish, though she could not really believe that her family, proud of its blood though it was, could have been taken in by the vulgar Nazi propaganda. Nevertheless, Esther felt she had been slighted, but she accepted the slight as she had accepted her poverty, the war, Richard, and her graying hair and coarsening figure, with a shrug and a smile.

Then came the morning when Richard received the letter asking him to resume his old position with Beckhof Verlag in Munich. And at a salary Esther knew would go far in Germany now, four thousand marks per month. "Oh, Richard! *Wie wunderschön!* You'll go, of course, won't you?" Esther asked. Richard's small hazel eyes had suddenly brightened. "Yes. I suppose I will." They both had had to start off for their respective jobs a few moments later, and there had been no time to talk or to ask questions, except Esther's "When do you want to go?" and Richard's answer, "Oh, as soon as possible."

Esther wondered if Richard would happily go off without her. She could not very well go to Munich with him, or just turn up as if by accident in a few weeks, not with all the people they both knew in Munich. The question was settled that night almost as soon as Richard came in the door. He said, "Esther, will you marry me now?" Esther said, "Of course." She reached up and put her arms around his thin neck, and kissed him tenderly. There were tears of pleasure and surprise in her eyes, and for a few minutes she could say nothing. Richard said, "I told you, Esther, it was the money that prevented. Now that's not a problem anymore."

Esther and Richard were married quietly, and they gave a wedding supper for about ten of their friends at a restaurant in the King's Road.

Esther almost broke down at the thought of leaving all the people who had been such loyal friends to her and Richard—the Campbells, Tom Bradley and his girl Edna, and the Jordans. Esther got promises from Tom Bradley and Edna and from the Campbells that they would try to come to Munich before Christmas. "You can stay with us, so don't worry about the travel allowance. I know we'll have a place big enough," Esther said.

As they were leaving the restaurant, John Campbell patted Richard on the back and said, "I've been wanting to do this for a long time."

"What?" asked Richard.

"Look behind you!" Esther said, laughing.

Pinned to his back was a cardboard sign saying: "We finally tied it!"

They had very little baggage, so they flew. Esther sat up close to the window during the short low hops over France and western Germany, but Richard read material that Beckhof's had forwarded to him, and showed a total disinterest in what the face of Europe looked like. It rather exasperated Esther, though she said nothing. She had the feeling he was putting on an act for somebody, pretending to have made the trip dozens of times, and to know all there was to know. He behaved the same way in Munich. All he wanted to do was to get settled and to begin work as soon as he could.

Twice during the first week, Esther went with Richard to dinner parties where she met the Beckhof editors and their representatives from Düsseldorf, Frankfurt, and Berlin. It thrilled Esther to see Richard treated as a man of importance now. Esther got on well with everyone at the parties. She had always gotten on well with writers and intellectuals. Adjusting to life in Germany would be very easy after all, she thought, here in Munich where people either didn't know or didn't care that she and Richard had just been married, and if there were any anti-Jewish sentiment anywhere, it would not exist among the kind of people she and Richard came in contact with.

They had hardly moved into the Bogenhausen house when Richard said he wanted to have some people over. "Not just business people. Some of our own old friends, too," he said gaily.

"All right," Esther agreed. But she didn't know who their old friends could be, because she and Richard had known almost no one in common in Munich. It turned out that Richard meant he would invite some of his old friends, and she some of hers.

The day before the party, Lotte Kiefer called up. She had heard the good news, she said, through Leopold Beckhof himself, whom she knew. She congratulated them on their marriage, and sounded so warm and friendly that Esther invited her and her husband to come to the party. "It's just some old friends of Richard's and mine whom we haven't seen in ages—a little reunion." Esther felt suddenly happy and optimistic about the party. She might have been mistaken about Lotte's coolness in London, she thought. She hoped so.

Everyone they had invited came. The big living room was completely filled, and she and Richard took turns showing people over the house. Lotte Kiefer asked all about Richard's work, and said she and Richard must come for dinner at their apartment in Schwabing. "It's a little on the arty side, compared to this," Lotte said apologetically, "but it overlooks the Englischer Garten and I think it has charm." Esther beamed with gratitude and said she and Richard would be delighted to come. It was not until after the buffet supper had been served, when people were sitting about with coffee and cigarettes—English cigarettes that Richard had thoughtfully brought over with him, because German cigarettes were still so bad—that Esther realized how shabbily Lotte was dressed. There was a worn streak in the brown fox piece around her neck, and cracks in her black alligator shoes, the kind of cracks that only slow time can put in good leather, for the shoes had obviously been expensive. And the poverty showed not only in her clothes but in her pinched face as well. Esther stared at her like a person who cannot believe his eyes, because Esther had been brought up to believe that Lotte's branch of the family had much more money than her own. They had simply lost it, of course, since the war. Lotte was really just as shabby now as old Professor Haggenbach in his shiny black suit, or the dowdy woman called Frieda whom Richard had been talking to most of the evening.

Lotte said, "It's just like slipping back into an old glove for Richard, I suppose, isn't it? He has his old secretary back, too."

"Who?" Esther asked.

"Why, Frieda Meyer. Didn't he ever—" She stopped, and Esther looked at her. Lotte was smiling a little. "That's Frieda he's talking to now," she said. Her name had not registered with Esther, she had met so many new people tonight. She did not think Richard had ever mentioned her.

Later that evening, when she and Richard were alone in their bedroom, Esther told Richard her surprise about Lotte Kiefer's apparent lack of money. "It doesn't surprise me," Richard said. "Now it's the commercial upstarts who've got the money. The old aristocracy and even most of the old solid merchants like the Kiefers are down and out." He said it in such a loud, matter-of-fact voice, Esther was a little shocked. Moreover, the Kiefers were not merely old solid merchants, but a very good family.

"Why didn't you tell me that Fräulein Meyer was your old secretary? I didn't have any idea who she was," Esther said.

"Oh. Yes, Frieda worked for me before the war. I understand she's worked for Leopold off and on all during the war years."

In the next weeks, Esther thought a great deal about the financial reversals of people like Lotte Kiefer, not so much because it interested her as an economic phenomenon but because she began to see that the people who had had money before and had little now were making an effort to cultivate her and Richard for what they could get out of them. Lotte Esther minded least; she was merely hungry for invitations and for the aesthetic pleasure of a well-served dinner, because she had evidently been more or less dropped by her wealthier friends. Professor Haggenbach, retired and living on an inadequate pension, was interested in getting Beckhof to support him while he finished a book on philosophy. As to the Krügers, who were exactly the commercial upstart type Richard had spoken of, Esther could not bear them. Hermann Krüger had recently made his money from a new weaving method which he had sold to an Augsburg stocking factory. She and Richard had nothing in common with the Krügers, and it was obvious that the Krügers were interested in them for purely social-climbing purposes, because other people in comparable income brackets had not yet admitted the Krügers into their circle.

"It's not that I particularly dislike them," Esther said to Richard, "but what can we ever talk to them about except soccer and *Strümpfen*? There're so many nice people in Munich, I don't see why we have to get mixed up with these."

Richard said with a little smile, "I don't see what's the matter with them. You aren't getting snobbish, are you, Esther?"

So they accepted the Krügers' invitation to tea on Saturday. It was a dreary, almost terrifying imitation of the old Munich Konzert afternoons that Esther remembered from her early twenties, when she had at least been able to amuse herself by flirting with handsome young men during the arias of the hired female singer. The other guests, without exception, were people like the Krügers, who could talk of nothing but textile manufacture and sport. But Richard chatted with everyone, and he told Esther he had had a very good time. Perhaps it was inevitable, Esther thought, that Richard did not judge such gatherings in the same way she did. He had a curiously impersonal attitude to people, and even, she admitted, to herself. And he was working so hard that any kind of social life was probably an agreeable relief. He had worked in his office all day that Saturday until time for the tea party, and that same evening he had to go out again to dinner with Leopold Beckhof and a man from Paris.

That evening, Leopold Beckhof telephoned and asked to talk to Richard. Esther said Richard had gone to meet him. Herr Beckhof said they had no appointment that he knew of, but he wanted to give Richard some instructions about a manuscript he was reading that weekend. He asked her to tell Richard to call him tomorrow morning. Esther felt curiously shaken when she hung up. She had suddenly remembered Lotte telling her several days ago that she had seen Richard and Frieda Meyer one evening about ten o'clock, having coffee together at the Rathskeller Restaurant. Esther had thought very little of it, had thought perhaps Richard had invited her for coffee after one of the late sessions with Leopold at the office. But she remembered Lotte's amused smile when she had told her. Now Esther had a vision of Richard sitting opposite Frieda Meyer in some restaurant, having dinner. Could it be possible? That dowdy, colorless woman? She even wore horn-rimmed glasses. And hardly any lipstick. Esther evoked in her memory Frieda Meyer's thick body sitting on the hassock in front of the fireplace, and tried to divine what Richard might possibly be attracted to. She lifted the telephone again, with the idea of calling Lotte and asking her outright if she suspected that anything was going on between Richard and Frieda, then put it down, thinking that the next time she saw Lotte would be more fitting, more dignified. Then this struck her as absurd, and she picked up the telephone and dialed Lotte's number. "I called to ask you . . . a rather personal question, Lotte. You don't have to answer it if you don't want to." But she heard Lotte's sudden curiosity, and she was sure Lotte would be delighted to answer.

"Well, Esther—I thought you knew," Lotte replied. "You must be the only person in Munich who doesn't. Richard and Frieda had an affair that lasted for years before the war. Of course, when I told you I saw her with Richard in the Rathskeller, I didn't mean to imply that I thought anything *now*. I mean, naturally I don't think Richard would do a thing like that now that he's married."

Esther waited up till eleven in the living room, nervously smoking and trying to read. Richard came in at eleven-thirty. Esther asked him how the evening had gone, and Richard said fine, they had gotten a lot accomplished. "Leopold called here for you around eight o'clock. Did you see him?"

Richard's lips parted stupidly for an instant, and Esther could fairly see the tremor that went through him. Then he said, "No, Leopold couldn't join us. I saw the man alone."

"With Frieda Meyer?"

Richard looked at her again the same way. "What's this, Esther?"

Esther had decided on a direct approach. "Are you in love with Frieda Meyer? Is she in love with you?"

Richard laughed incredulously. "*Mein Gott,* Esther! How absurd!"

"Well, I know you were once," Esther said.

Richard came toward her and put a hand under her chin. "I love you and I am married to you. To *you,*" he repeated.

"You swear that?" Esther asked.

"Yes!" Richard said, laughing.

Esther hesitated for a moment, then decided to believe him. But she could not keep from saying, "The reason I asked—I heard you were in the Rathskeller with Frieda one evening last week. You didn't mention it to me. So I wondered."

Richard frowned. "Who told you that?"

"But it is true, isn't it?"

"Yes," Richard admitted readily. "I just wondered who took the trouble to tell you."

"I'd rather not say," Esther said. She took pleasure in keeping her source of information from Richard.

They went to bed that evening with hardly another word to each other.

Esther had another talk with Lotte. She hated Lotte for the pleasure she derived from the situation, but Esther found her a mine of information. Lotte had been to Frieda's apartment once, and she knew that the woman with whom Frieda shared it was a hotel receptionist who worked from four till midnight, so Frieda's apartment would be empty practically every evening. And she learned from Lotte that Frieda Meyer had a Prussian determination beneath her rather docile exterior, and that she had never made any bones about Richard's being the only man she had ever cared for. The logical surmise was that she would try to get him back one day. Esther found she was not alarmed so much by Frieda as by what she knew of Richard's own character. Richard was a creature of habit. He fretted a little under the obligations of marriage, and Frieda, especially in her present position, was the kind of woman who would probably make no demands on him. Esther could imagine him slipping back into a routine he had known with Frieda before the war—living apart from her but seeing her a few times a week, sleeping with her perhaps once a week. He could easily arrange that in his present schedule, and he might already have done so. One fact that led Esther to think this was that Richard seldom came home anymore before seven-thirty, for one reason or another, though Esther knew that his office closed before six. There would be no way of actually finding out, of course, without watching Frieda's apartment house, and this Esther shrank from doing. Leopold Beckhof might know it, a half dozen other people might know it, but they would never betray Richard. People didn't. Except people like Lotte, whom Esther despised for it.

Esther found herself with more and more time on her hands. The two maids had taken over every smallest chore of the household and, being gluttons for work, resisted Esther's attempts to take back some of her old duties, like darning Richard's socks, which she actually enjoyed. When Esther had an errand, she stretched it out as long as possible, strolling down Theatinerstrasse where the smartest shops were, stopping at a certain *Konditorei* where she drank a cup of good coffee with cream and ate one of the delicious pastries that filled the front windows. Then she would take a taxi home, and there would be an hour or more in which to write letters before Richard came home. Esther was a faithful correspondent with her friends in England. She had invited Tom Bradley and Edna to come over during the last two weeks in November, but Tom wrote that he had just taken a job, and couldn't. Esther was now awaiting a letter from the Campbells, in answer to her invitation, though without much hope, because John had a job he couldn't very well leave. And as to her other English friends, they had either too little money or too little time, she knew. Esther missed them sorely.

She might have overcome her boredom by taking a job, but she couldn't in Munich because she was a British subject. All her women friends had jobs during the daytime, so there was no one she could call up to join her on a shopping tour, or to meet her for lunch somewhere. She might have called up Frau Krüger, or others like her of that group who were trying to get on friendlier terms with her and Richard, but as a point of pride, Esther forbade herself to seek them out. Esther felt actually hostile to these leechlike acquaintances now. She sensed that they took liberties, had a kind of arrogance of their own with her and Richard, because Richard after all was Jewish and therefore inferior to them. A certain woman with dyed red hair, a friend of Frau Krüger's, had asked her point-blank last week if Richard was entirely Jewish or only part. No, anti-Semitism was far from dead in Germany. There had been the incident in Koebler's Bakery, too. Esther had asked the bakery to deliver a large order for a tea, and she had spelled out her name and address for the salesgirl. Then Esther had become aware that the other women in the bakery were staring at her in a strange way, because she had a Jewish name, and that could mean only one thing: that she or her husband had crept back into Germany after once having been thrown out. Esther had never gone back to that particular bakery. And overshadowing all of her existence was her doubt of Richard, the fact that she had been brought to a point of doubting him, whether she had reason to or not.

Just before Christmas, Esther and Richard invited some fifteen people to a dinner party. Esther figured that the total cost would be over five hundred marks, which, plus the bills for two new rugs and the upstairs stove, would wipe out Richard's salary for the month. She found a few ways to economize on the menu, and suggested them to Richard, but he told her not to bother, because he wanted the dinner to be perfect. Still, it bothered Esther, because at the rate they had been spending, she did not think they had been able to lay anything by in the three months they had been in Munich.

"Have we any reserve money, Richard?" she asked suddenly.

"Oh, we have a little," he said.

"But don't you think we should know exactly how much money we have to fall back on—and how much money I should and shouldn't spend, now that we're married?" The last word hung in the air, and she felt it had never meant so little to Richard as now, that in fact he hated the word and was ashamed that it applied to him.

"Have I ever said you were spending too much?" Richard asked with a smile.

Esther sighed, and gave it up. Richard had never shown her his bankbooks, even on the one or two occasions she had expressly asked to see them. She said, "Would you mind giving me some pocket money for the rest of the week? I went around town today with only two marks fifty in my purse. I couldn't even have lunch with Greta when I ran into her, because I thought it might have cost more than I had."

Richard at once pulled out his wallet and gave her thirty marks. Esther had an impulse to ask him again why she couldn't have a regular allowance, but she knew what Richard would have said, that he didn't have much on him just now, but that she could always come to him and he would give her what she needed.

Frieda Meyer came to the party. Richard had not told Esther he had invited her, though when Esther said this, Richard insisted that he had told her. But Esther knew that because Raimund von Hagen had been unable to come at the last minute, Richard had asked Frieda.

"I wish you'd go and talk with her," Richard said to Esther. "She's not nearly so standoffish as you think."

"I tried a few minutes ago. She doesn't want to talk to *me*," Esther said. Esther left Richard and went over to the sofa, where Lotte and the Countess von Bernsdorf were sitting. Everyone was drinking an aperitif, and there was a lively, cheerful atmosphere in the room generated by the anticipation of a good dinner. All the editors of Beckhof and their wives were present, and some of the more attractive and intelligent people she and Richard knew, but it depressed Esther suddenly when she realized that none of them was anyone she could actually call a friend. Not even Lotte, who was her cousin.

Esther sat down beside Lotte. The Countess von Bernsdorf turned away for a moment, and Lotte remarked quickly to Esther, "I must say, Frieda looks a little out of place in this crowd. Do you suppose Leopold brought her along to take shorthand notes on the conversation?" Lotte said it in English, so it would not likely be overheard and understood. It was exactly what Esther had been vaguely thinking herself, and she felt her face grow warm. A half dozen questions she might have asked Lotte passed through her mind, but she could not utter any of them, surrounded as she was by other people. And one question she asked of herself: *What are we doing here, Richard and I? What are we trying to prove by having these people here tonight? Whom are we trying to prove it to?* For an instant, an irrational terror seized her, and she felt she was enduring some kind of punishment, an unending disgrace, in being here in Germany, and married to a half Jew who did not really love her. It was the same panicky feeling she had had that moment in Koebler's Bakery.

All during the evening, Esther observed Richard's and Frieda's careful avoidance of each other. Frieda chatted with Leopold Beckhof at the table, and lingered around him after dinner, too, as if she were afraid of talking with the other guests. "If you invited Frieda, I should think you'd talk to her," Esther said to Richard. "I don't think she's having a very good time."

"Oh, all right," Richard said. Then Esther watched Frieda's dull, plump face come to life as Richard spoke to her and handed her a glass of brandy. Esther did not want anything more to drink. When her guests were busy with coffee and brandy in the living room, Esther slipped away to her room upstairs.

She sat down in front of her mirror and looked at herself critically. She saw that her hair and her face still looked exactly the same as at the beginning of the evening, only now she seemed much less attractive. The pouches under her eyes looked heavier. The interstices of her large teeth had become stained during the last year, and they looked worse when her face was pale as it was tonight. Lipstick made her even coarser and uglier, she thought, like a clown. Frieda Meyer, for all her lack of chic, was younger than she. Esther started at the light knock on her door.

It was Lotte. "We missed you," Lotte said. "Are you all right, darling?" Esther tried to smile, too, tried to think of something casual to say, but she could not. "I'd like to know if you have heard anything else," Esther said.

"About Richard?—N-not precisely, I suppose. But I talked with Leopold, and from what he implied, I assumed . . ." Lotte was completely in command of her words. She deliberately left the sentence dangling, and smiled at Esther again, tenderly. "I suppose one can only face it, darling. If you really want my opinion as a friend. I don't think Richard's the kind of man who can be told what he should and shouldn't do. I suppose he thinks of Frieda as a rightful piece of property."

(Oh, yes, Esther could see it, his making love to her without gallantry, without flowers, as if Frieda were an old chair he had come back to in Germany. Esther had come this far in her thoughts week ago. The only thing she was still uncertain of was whether she could take it, what she would do, how she would react in the horrible crisis that she imagined looming ahead, that would descend on her at some unpredictable moment.)

Lotte put her hand on her shoulder. "If there's anything I can do, Esther—I hope you'll feel free to come and talk to me at any time. Not that I've had any personal experience with this kind of thing, but I've known plenty of women who have."

Esther could not look into Lotte's face, because it was not the face of a friend at all. "Let's go downstairs," Esther said.

Esther did her duties as hostess faithfully the rest of the evening. Richard was generous with his French brandy. He seemed to be having a wonderful time. He was happier here than he had ever been in London, Esther knew. Richard was probably not the only man in the room tonight who was unfaithful to his wife, but in an English gathering, even among the artists and writers they had known in Chelsea, infidelity was the exception. And perhaps she had absorbed more of that English morality than she had realized, Esther thought, for she didn't think she would have had these reactions had her first three husbands, in Germany, been unfaithful to her. Then there was the added disgrace that Frieda was a secretary, by no means Richard's equal. And at Richard's age, fifty-six, it seemed doubly absurd. She would not dream of being unfaithful to Richard. But hadn't she been unfaithful to her first two husbands, too? And to her last husband? And wasn't this perhaps only justice wreaked on her at last? Esther had been staring at Richard, and suddenly he turned and looked at her, and she saw the gay, triumphant little smile that he directed to her, as if to say: "Well, what're you going to do about it all, my dear?" And even as she watched him, he put an arm familiarly about Frieda's shoulder, and they both laughed heartily. Esther watched for an opportunity to speak with Richard alone, just to tell him that she wanted to talk with him upstairs as soon as the guests went home. It was a message that did not need to be delivered, but Esther felt it pressing urgently inside her to be uttered, and she knew it was because she resented Richard's high spirits.

But Richard slipped out the door when the last group of people were leaving, and Esther heard him say to her over his shoulder, "I'm going to drive a few people home, Esther. See you in a little while."

Frieda was among the people, Esther saw. Over an hour later, Richard had still not come home, and Esther knew he would say to her, "Oh, I stopped in the Schwarzwälder for a final drink with the Bernsdorfs," which would be most unlikely considering the way he had dispensed the brandy tonight. With satisfaction, Esther saw that it was a quarter to one. The woman Frieda shared her apartment with should be getting home now, and Esther hoped grimly that she might catch Frieda and Richard in an embarrassing position. But on the other hand, the woman might know of it already, Esther thought, and, being the same kind of woman as Frieda, might even condone it. That was much more likely.

Richard came in just after one and closed the front door stealthily, as if he thought she might be already asleep upstairs. When he saw her in the living room, he looked surprised.

"Why are you so late?" Esther asked. It was not at all how she had planned to begin.

"Oh, the Bernsdorfs suggested we have another drink. We stopped in a funny little bar called Die Spinne."

"I don't believe you. I think you were with Frieda at her house." Richard's face looked as blank and astonished as if he had just realized she had clairvoyant powers. "You don't have to lie, Richard. I know it now. I would like it much better if you just admitted it, and also that you see her nearly every afternoon after work. Do you think I'm so stupid I can't find out when your office really closes?"

Richard had a small guilty smile on his thin lips. He rubbed his mustache self-consciously. "Well . . . yes, Esther. It's true. If you insist on my telling you." He smiled wider.

"And what do you expect me to do?" Esther asked. She was shaking, though somewhere inside herself, she felt firm and hard as stone.

"Why . . ."—he opened his bony hands—"do whatever you like, of course, my dear," he said almost tenderly, but in those words Esther heard his unconcern whether she suffered now or not, whether she stayed with him or not, and she hated him. He was like a strange machine rather than a human being, a machine that had gone back to its old movements and was blind and deaf to her, as if their years in London had never been. Esther knew suddenly she would not want to talk with him, would not want to touch him or even see him ever again. He started to say something to her, and she said she did not want to talk anymore. Then Richard went upstairs.

Esther called the maid, and had her make up a bed for her on the sofa. She did not even want to sleep in one of the guest beds upstairs. She lay without sleeping for several hours, thinking of London and of her friends there. She imagined the Campbells and Tom Bradley and Edna welcoming her back, and all of them having dinner together in the restaurant in the King's Road again. She imagined getting her old job back, and the routine of her London life, marketing for the little she needed on the way home from work, buying tea biscuits at the shop off the Strand. No matter how poor she would be in England, she would be happy there. It seemed to Esther that the greatest happiness in the world would be to have her own little job back, and her own money in her pocket, and to be able to do what *she* wanted to do in the evenings. Esther could hear English voices around her, the clipped shouts of Cockneys in Shaftesbury Avenue near her office. She saw a man step courteously aside to let her go first into the big red bus at Hyde Park Corner, where she always changed, and then she fell asleep.

Esther left for England two days later. She had wired to Tom Bradley she was coming, and he had wired back he would meet her at the air terminus. Richard maintained a shrugging attitude to the last, mitigated somewhat by a pretense of believing that she would surely change her mind and come back soon. Esther did not even reply to this suggestion. But she was smiling as she said good-bye to him at the airport. She was so happy to be free!

"Good-bye," Richard said, trying to make his tone and his look say everything he was too lazy or too selfish to say to her.

Esther shook his hand and said, "Good-bye, Richard," but she looked right through him, and his bony hand might have been so much dust.

NOTHING THAT MEETS THE EYE

There was nothing unusual about Helene that met the eye. She was a little taller than most women, five feet seven and a half, and perhaps more attractive, but not remarkably so. She had eyes that looked sometimes blue, sometimes gray. Her hair was a dark reddish brown, parted in the middle and drawn back in a small knot that was tidy only for five minutes after she did it in the morning and after her predinner bath. Her lips were somewhat thin, and when she smiled, the smile seemed brighter because of the sharp upward corners of her mouth. Her nose was slim and straight until the tip, which turned suddenly up. Helene thought her nose comical, and her worst feature. She was neither thin nor plump, and she walked a little stiffly, as she was inclined to be knock-kneed. She was forty-five.

There was nothing unusual about her appearance as she came into the Hotel Waldhaus in Alpenbach on a Wednesday afternoon in January, wearing stretch ski pants and black boots lined with white fur, a green Tyrolean jacket, and stood at the hotel desk to register, yet—after her first brief, approving glance around the simple green and white lobby, her head back, a smile of satisfaction and recognition on her face—everyone's eyes seemed drawn to her. The hair bun was untidy, and her lipstick had worn off during the sleigh ride from the station. There were little wrinkles under her eyes, and two horizontal ones across her forehead. She looked not nearly so glamorous as most women who entered the Waldhaus, yet the bellboys—two lads in Austrian green hovering expectantly at the end of the desk—the tall porter in long green overcoat with double row of silver buttons down the front, the manager in wing-collar and cutaway, and two men guests and the wife of one who were then crossing the lobby, all turned their heads to look at Helene, and their eyes inexplicably lingered.

"Sorry! I made a mistake," Helene said in English with a Viennese accent, laughing.

"Your hands are cold. It's a cold day." The manager was practicing his English, though he knew she came from Munich. The hotel and most of its guests spoke German by preference, but French, Italian, and English or a mixture of all was frequently heard and was the rule rather than the exception.

Helene corrected her blotch of the date, and followed the small boy who was carrying her worn antelope suitcase. The boy kept glancing up at her as they rose to the third floor in the lift. "Lots of people here now?" asked Helene. The boy was hardly older than her son Klaus.

"Oh—enough," replied the boy. Then, gulping, "Will you stay long?" He asked it like a question he should not have asked.

"A few days," said Helene, smiling at him as she stepped out of the lift.

Her room was large, square, and white-walled, decorated with a green carpet and green curtains embroidered in red. The windows looked out on a snowy slope on which a few distant skiers glided. She tipped the boy with a ten-schilling note, which he glanced at before his eyes returned to Helene, and he backed out of the room, murmuring his thanks.

Helene hung up a few of her clothes, and rang for a half bottle of champagne. She sipped a glass as she gazed out the window. The world looked wonderfully pure. She opened the window and leaned on the sill, and wriggled her toes inside her heavy socks. Her toes were warm now. She was pleased with the place she had chosen—Alpenbach. Once she had been here with her husband and another couple from Vienna, but so many years ago, her memory of the town was vague. She remembered only that it was rather pretty. That was what she wanted, something rather pretty and with no strong memories attached.

She put on her boots again, and the loden Walkjanke, a ski hood, and went out for a walk. The road led down to the village half a mile away. Helene hesitated, then turned and took the path on the other side of the hotel, which climbed.

"*Guten Tag . . . Bon jour,*" she replied to the greetings of returning skiers whom she passed.

She did not realize that they turned to look at her, and then asked each other, "Who is she?"

The wind had blown the sandlike snow from the larger rocks of the mountain, exposing tiny flowers that grew in the rocks' shelter. Many had intricate blossoms of blue petals, some were pink, some yellow, some white. Together, they looked like the patterns of a kaleidoscope. Others, isolated, suggested miniatures of blossoms under the glass of Victorian paperweights. Helene bent low over a few of them, wondering at their delicate color against the frozen whiteness of the snow around them. The little flowers were prepared for the snow by long experience and by old adaptation, she thought. At the proper time, they opened their minuscule blossoms with a gentle and cheerful defiance, as easily as a magician creates a miracle with a turn of the wrist. Helene heard a soft crunch of footfalls behind her, and saw a blond young man in a fur-lined jacket trudging toward her.

"Good afternoon! You're walking all the way up?" he asked in German.

Helene looked up at the mountain in front of her, then back at the young man. "I don't know. I doubt it." She was annoyed at being joined, but only briefly annoyed. What did it matter?

They fell into step together, as the path was just wide enough for two.

"My name is Gert von Boechlein," the young man said. "You've just arrived today, haven't you?"

His face was open and smiling, he was no more than twenty, and he did not look the kind of boy who would speak to a middle-aged woman without being introduced, Helene thought.

"I arrived about an hour ago," Helene said, brushing some strands of hair back from her face. "Whew! I'm not sure I care to go all the way up there."

"I shouldn't think so! Do you know it's eight kilometers to the top?" He laughed. "However . . ."

"However?"

"We might go a little farther. There's a very pretty view from that rock." He pointed to a great black rock a quarter of a mile up.

They climbed on, he glancing at her every few steps. "You're from Vienna?"

"Yes. But I've lived in Munich for years."

"But you have the Viennese style." He waved airily a hand encased in a thick sheepskin mitten. "My mother and sister are here at the hotel. You must meet them. I mean, they must meet you, if you'd like." A blush made his cheeks pinker. "Would you think me impolite if I asked your name?"

"Helene Sacher-Hartmann," she replied. She bent to look at another tiny patchwork of flowers, plucked a pink one and pulled its stem through a buttonhole of her jacket. "It's so small, it's lost on me," she said.

"Oh, no. No, it isn't at all."

They looked at the town from the height of the rock. The boy pointed out where the best *Konditorei* was, just around a curve past the church spire, where a sleigh with two horses was then turning. He said his mother and sister Hedwig, who was fourteen, had hot chocolate and cake there every afternoon at four.

"Don't you go with them?" Helene asked.

Gert blushed again. "Not—not today."

As they were descending the hill, Helene slipped and Gert caught her hand swiftly and just as swiftly released it, as if he had burnt himself. "Pardon!" he said. Then, a few seconds later, "I didn't go today with my mother and sister because I saw you come into the hotel and I—I wanted to meet you."

"That's very nice," said Helene, smiling, but she spoke absently, because she was not listening. She was conscious of the pure cold air in her lungs, delicious as cool water when one is thirsty.

The boy chattered on about his school now. He was studying in Graz to be a hydraulic engineer. At the hotel, he spoke with a frantic undertone in his voice. Could she possibly, would she possibly join him and his mother and sister in the bar of the hotel at seven-thirty for an aperitif?

Helene looked at her wristwatch and saw without thought of any

kind that it was thirty-five minutes past five. "Yes, why not? Thank you."
Then she left him to go to her room.

Helene was early for her appointment in the bar, and in fact she had half
forgotten it. At seven, after a hot bath and a change into a dark green
woolen suit with a wide fringed scarf of the same material draped around
her neck, she entered the bar, which was already full of people. A leaping
fire crackled in a white fireplace. Ordinarily, Helene would have been
uncomfortable entering a room like this, for she was somewhat shy, and
it gave her pleasure to realize that she did not feel shy or unsure now, not
for an instant. She glanced around quickly, remembering Gert, and, not
seeing him, continued toward the bar's counter, where as it happened
every stool was taken. But a man slid off his stool and offered it to her.

"*Permettez-moi, madame.*"

"Oh, thank you. I only want to order something," Helene said in
French, smiling at him.

"But do sit down. You see there isn't a free table."

"Thank you." Helene ordered a *Kirschwasser*.

The Frenchman insisted on paying for it with some money he had
on the counter. He was about forty-five with dark hair, a small mustache,
and heavy black eyebrows. He asked her if she had been to Alpenbach
before, how long she was staying, and other usual questions, and the man
seated on the other side of the Frenchman, who was now standing, listened and watched as if he knew the Frenchman, though the Frenchman
did not introduce him.

"Do you know Paris?" asked the Frenchman with a sudden tenderness in his voice.

A few moments later, he asked if she would join him at his table at
dinner. Helene had suddenly realized that one of his gray eyes was of
glass. He had slender, restless hands. He had said he was a cellist in an
orchestra in Paris. Helene accepted his invitation, but said she was to meet
some people in the bar at seven-thirty.

"I don't know why I wear this watch anymore," she said, glancing at her wristwatch. "I never pay attention to it. I'm early."

"If you had come at seven-thirty, I might not have been able to meet you," said the Frenchman. "My name is André Lemaitre.—But yes," he added with a frown, smiling. "I would have met you somehow."

When Gert and his party of two arrived, she left the Frenchman and her empty glass, and sat at a small table which Gert had reserved. His mother, fine-featured and blond, seemed a bit cool at first, which did not bother Helene in the least, but after five minutes the mother warmed up, and they were all laughing and talking as if they had known each other a long while. The subject was the cross-eyed and possibly half-witted stationmaster at Alpenbach who had today misdirected a mountain of Alpenbach luggage which had barely escaped being sent on to Vienna. Gert's sister Hedwig wore a touch of rouge on her lips and was beginning to bloom with adolescence. She stared at Helene with a pleasant, dreamy expression, but said little. Gert was the man of the table, making sure the drinks were attended to, and behaving with an air of pride and possession toward Helene, as if she were a captured prize, which amused her. When they got up to go to dinner, it seemed understood that Helene would join them, and Helene had forgotten the Frenchman until he pursued her down the hall to the dining room.

"Madame!—Pardon, madame, you have not forgotten that you—"

"Oh!" Helene touched her forehead like one gone mad, but she laughed at herself. "Will you forgive me, Frau von Boechlein—and Gert—but I did promise this gentleman I would dine with him."

"You what?" Gert burst out, then controlled himself. "Yes. Well—if you did, I am certainly very sorry. Very." He looked absolutely grief-stricken.

"There is tomorrow, Gert."

"Tomorrow," Gert said firmly. "For lunch? If you are not out skiing."

His mother gave him a glance which he did not notice.

"Yes, tomorrow luncheon if you like," said Helene, including all the three in her look. "Thank you for the aperitif. It was a pleasure to meet you."

"A pleasure," Frau von Boechlein said kindly.

At their table, which was a table at which four could sit, they were joined by the man who had been on the other side of André in the bar. André did not seem pleased about this, but he introduced him to Helene as his "skiing friend," and within a few minutes André seemed to have forgotten his annoyance. Each of the two men talked with Helene as if the other man did not exist.

By eleven o'clock, they had become nine, including an Italian couple from Milan. They were to have played a card game in the bar, but they only talked, and Helene quite to her surprise found herself the center of interest, though—as usual—she felt she had nothing of importance to say, and in truth said nothing of importance, yet everyone seemed to hang on her words. They asked her about her life in Munich, and she told them about the book and stationery shop which she owned with two other women, and how they took turns clerking in it, so that each of them could have considerable vacation during the year, while still being partners in a successful business. Helene did not say she was not going to see the shop again. She thought of this, but it did not trouble her. Esther and Henriette could and would carry on quite well without her. Everything that was her responsibility was in order. Esther, who had no furniture of her own and a rather expensive rented room just now, would be happy to move into Helene's apartment, and Helene had left a note in her closed apartment saying she could. But of this Helene did not speak, nor of her son. When they asked, Helene said she had no children. All seemed to think what little she said was quite fascinating, even when she spoke of the little snow flowers which she loved.

It's as if I have on some bewitching perfume, Helene thought, *something even the women are charmed by. It's very strange.*

And in the next days, it was impossible for Helene to have any moment alone outside her room. Resentment showed in the men when they were joined by others, then disappeared when they all decided to go on a walk, to take a trip in the ski lift to the lodge (Helene did not ski and did not wish to) or to have tea in the village. Only Gert showed a resentment that did not die down, and one morning he darted from a chair in the lobby to join her before anyone else could, and as soon as they were outside the door, he told her that he was in love with her.

"Why, Gert, I'm old enough to be your mother," Helene blurted out. "And then some!"

"Oh, don't laugh, Helene, please," he said desperately. For the last couple of days, he called her Helene with her permission. "I can't stand seeing you with all these men around you, these men who don't care half as much as I do. *Ich kann es nicht mehr ertragen!*" He pressed his bare fist to his temple as if his fist were a pistol.

"But—" Helene gestured, then didn't know what to say. She was amused, yet she knew she should not be amused, because the young man was deadly serious. She had never had appropriate comments ready for emotional situations, and now she regretted that she hadn't.

"How can I live without you, Helene? I can't!"

"Gert, what nonsense! Really, in a week—"

"Not in a year, not ever, I swear it. This is forever. *Für immer und ewig!*"

"Let's go for a walk."

They walked up the path on which he had first spoken to her.

"You see, I'm going away soon, and I won't be able to see you," Helene said.

"Where are you going?—And why can't I see you again?"

Back to Munich, Helene thought automatically, but since she wasn't, she couldn't say it. "You'll be in Graz soon."

"But I would go anywhere to see you," he declared. "Australia, China, anywhere!"

But not where she was going, she thought with a faint and impatient smile. "I told you I was married, Gert."

"Yes, but—I noticed you didn't mention your husband when you spoke about Munich. Where is he?"

"He's in Vienna. But I'm not divorced."

"Ah, what do I care about marriage and divorce? I love you quite apart from all that. Above and beyond and apart." His mittened hand waved toward the mountain in front of them. His other hand, bare, held Helene's gloved hand.

"I'll be here perhaps four more days, and then we'll see how you feel." She said it gently and casually as she could, but with some misgiving as to how he would take it.

He took it with grim calm, and said, "I'll feel the same forever, and if I can't see you again, my life is not worth living. I know."

"Hallo!" cried a voice, and the mountain echoed it twice.

Below them on the path stood the two Frenchmen, André waving an arm.

Gert groaned.

There were flowers in Helene's room when she returned that morning, but no card with them. The maid had put them into a vase for her. They were large red roses, a few small white roses, and a single bird of paradise that must have been flown from Nice, she thought. A knock came at the door. She went to answer it and found not the donor of the flowers, not a messenger with the forgotten card, but the small boy who had brought her luggage up. He was holding a red candy box.

"For you, *gnädige Frau*," said the boy.

"Thank you," she said, taking it. Again there was no card. "From whom?"

The boy smiled shyly and backed away. "I am not to say, *gnädige Frau.*"

Gert, Helene supposed. There was a wild, romantic youth. Goethe would have appreciated him. But Helene did not think Gert's passion would last as long as Werther's. She lunched with Gert and his mother and sister, but Gert made no reference to the flowers or the candy, and as Helene looked around the dining room, her eye attracted by the Italian couple who saluted her with smiles and a nod, by the two Frenchmen who smiled at her also, by four or five other men and women who seemed to be looking at her every time she looked at them—Helene found she really could not guess who might have sent her the flowers and the candy, but now she did not think it was Gert. Gert would think of something more expensive and important.

Later that afternoon, when Helene had changed into skirt and sweater to lounge on her bed with a book, Gert rang up and asked if he could see her for a moment. Helene hadn't the heart to refuse him. He came up and promptly presented her with a large ruby brooch which he said had belonged to his grandmother, and which he wanted her to have.

"Oh, Gert, I'm sure you're supposed to give this to your bride!" Helene said, smiling with surprise at him.

"You are my bride," Gert said solemnly.

"Your mother would be very displeased, dear boy, if she knew you wanted to give this to me."

"The pin is mine, to do what I like with. I always have it with me, even at school.—Don't you want it, Helene? Won't you accept it?"

Helene thought of a way she could accept it, and return it to him, too. And to refuse it now would hurt him, she could see. "Very well, I will accept it with pleasure. I am honored," Helene said, and took the brooch in its crumpled white tissue from his palm.

Gert smiled broadly. "Thank you, my love."

He stepped forward, and she lifted her face to be kissed. It was a chaste kiss on the lips, brief, strange—because it was neither a kiss of passion nor could it be symbolic, Helene felt, of anything, and yet it seemed appropriate for now.

"I will leave you for a while," Gert said, backing toward the door. His face was aglow with happiness. He closed the door softly.

She was rather glad she had not promised to dine with the von Boechleins that evening, as she felt Gert's glow might be noticed by his mother. What an absurd boy, so confident of the permanence of his emotions! Helene was to meet André in the bar at seven. André wanted to take a sleigh to a restaurant in the village for a change.

When Helene and André arrived at the restaurant down in the village, they were greeted like royalty by the headwaiter. The place was small, but André had reserved an entire room for him and her, and the room was decorated with red roses and fleurettes of the tiny mountain flowers which Helene adored.

"Well, here we are. I hope they haven't overdone it," murmured André a little embarrassedly after they had sat down.

A waiter appeared at once with champagne cocktails.

André talked slowly about Paris, about his experiences in the war, of being held prisoner in Germany, of losing an eye later in France in the Résistance. Of his two-year marriage which had been a failure, ten years ago, of his struggles as a musician, and of his successes which had come only recently. There were long pauses between the stories to give Helene a chance to speak or to change the subject, but she did not. She was rather interested in his stories, and touched that he liked her enough to tell her them.

"You perhaps think it strange that I tell you all this," he said as they were nearly through their dinner, "but the fact is, I would like to ask you to marry me, and if I do that—you see—it is a good idea if you know something about me. Will you marry me, Helene?"

It was a total surprise to Helene. "But you know absolutely nothing about me."

"That doesn't matter. Of course, I would like to know more about you," he added with a smile, "but essentially it doesn't matter, because I know you are pure and good—beautiful is the word, beautiful within. The details can come later. I also realize you are probably married. That doesn't matter, either, because I will wait. I will wait the rest of my life, if necessary, but I hope it won't be necessary. You are married, aren't you?"

"Yes."

"Your husband is in Munich?"

"No, Vienna. We are separated and I haven't seen him in three years. I have a child," she said softly, "but . . ."

"But?"

"He is twelve. And . . . well, he is very much like his father, and I think he prefers his father. Anyway, Klaus decided he preferred to live with his father. This was a year ago. His father has a great deal of money, you see, and the boy always spent his summers with his father. That is, since he was eight. My husband makes a great fuss over him, has bought him a horse, and a boat, lots of clothes—teaches him to shoot now. I don't care for shooting."

"I understand," said André.

"My son likes all these things. I can't help that, that's the way he is, like his father, really." And Helene smiled, put her fork down, and pressed her palms together as if she were saying something that pleased her, or that she were praying for—and actually weeks, months ago, she had stopped grieving over the situation and reconciled herself to it, and saying all this now had no longer an emotional effect upon her. She felt André could understand that. "I like you very much, André, really," Helene said, "but I am not contemplating another marriage. It's nothing to do with you or with anybody else. Perhaps we've met at the wrong time."

André pondered this a moment, then said, "No. No, but I will wait. I will wait happily," he said with a sudden smile that reminded her of Gert's smile, "because no other woman could attract me after you. So it will be a happy wait."

Several minutes later, when they were having a brandy, André said, "I suppose at some time you will get a divorce from your husband?"

"I suppose." Helene left it at that.

"Would you consider coming to Paris with me? My apartment is very large. It's behind les Invalidea. A lovely view of——"

Helene shook her head and smiled. "No, thank you. I can't see that just now, either." *Really,* she thought, *the people in the Hotel Waldhaus are mad. It must be the altitude.*

"You may think this is absurd of me—at my age," André said. "I mean, that I propose these things to you rather out of the blue. But on the other hand, I am old enough to know what is right when I see it."

The following morning, Gert accompanied Helene on her morning walk, having jumped up from a lobby chair as he had the previous morning. But now he was unsmiling and a little stiff. When they had walked several yards from the hotel, he said:

"I know that last night you had dinner with the Frenchman in the village. A very gay affair, from what the porter told me."

Busybody porters, Helene thought with a vague irritation. "Well? And what's wrong with dinner in the village for a change?"

"On the evening of the day I gave you my grandmother's brooch? And with a man who everyone knows is in love with you?" Gert's voice shook with indignation.

"He means nothing to me," Helene said quickly and apologetically.

"And perhaps I don't, either! Say it, if it's true."

What was true? One thing she was sure was true was that she did not want to hurt Gert's feelings. But she sensed also that his blustering was his self-defense, and no doubt all for his good. "That is not true. But I made you no promises, Gert. You may have your brooch back.—I am not playing games with you."

"If you don't want me—if you prefer that Frenchman—I prefer to kill myself, and I will!"

She did not believe him at all, but did not want him to see that she didn't. She continued to walk up the snowy path, Gert beside her, his eyes fixed avidly on her face. They were draining her somehow, Helene thought, and since she felt there was not much of her to drain, she did not wonder that she felt exhausted, at a loss. And she sought in vain for some conventional manner in which to handle the situation with Gert. She found none, she supposed, because she had abandoned such things before she came to Alpenbach, in fact days before she had left Munich. She remembered suddenly with a nostalgic pang the good-byes at the station, her surprise that Frau Müller, her charwoman, had come on her bicycle to the station to see her off. It had been as if everyone had known it was the last time they would see Helene, and yet everyone had been especially merry and affectionate, too.

"You see that rock?" Gert said, pointing up to the rocks at the top of the small mountain which they had never climbed. "That's where I'll jump from—unless . . ."

"Unless?" Helene said, as casually as she might have said "Pardon?" to something she had not quite heard and was not very interested in. She had thought of that mountain peak herself. She felt a possessiveness about it which was strange and a little ludicrous. Gert would never make use of those rocks, and it was simply a funny coincidence that he had spoken of them this way now.

"Unless you'll let me see you again. Unless we can make some kind of . . . arrangement."

She knew what he meant: for him to be her only lover, yet a lover in a very romantic sense, probably with no physical contact whatever. He wanted to be able to come and have coffee or dinner with her in her Munich apartment once in a while, and to know that she permitted no other man to do that. Helene shook her head impatiently, involuntarily.

"What do you mean?" Gert asked. He was still watching her every expression.

Crunch, crunch—crunch-crunch went their boots in the snow, and Helene could suddenly stand no more of it. She stopped, lifted her head briefly to look up the gently sloping mountain to its top—which was certainly not eight kilometers high, as Gert had said—then turned around.

But they stood still.

"May I see you again?" Gert asked in his firm way.

"Yes. Here. But not in Munich," she said flatly. She was tired of explanations, or of the impossibility of them. She began to walk back toward the hotel.

"Then I shall do what I said," Gert said. Now his arms hung, like his head, as he walked. "But I shall write a poem to you first."

That's a good thing to do, Helene thought, *before dying.* Then she realized that writing the poem would probably so ease his mind, all thought of suicide would leave him. At any rate, she felt absolutely sure he wouldn't kill himself, but she could not have said why. It was just a feeling of certainty, like the instant of realizing that one has fallen in love.

"May I offer you a cup of tea?" Gert asked when they were standing in front of the hotel door again.

Helene had not wanted to come back so soon, but now she wanted only to be alone, and the only place for that was in her room. "No, thank you, Gert. If you'll excuse me, I'll go up to my room for a while."

"If I'll excuse you!" Gert said, smiling a little. "Of course."

"Bye-bye," Helene said in English, patting his arm quickly, then she went into the hotel.

In her room, she took off her hood, slipped out of her boots, and automatically carried them into the tiled bathroom so the few flecks of snow that remained on them would not melt on the carpet. Then she took off her jacket, and walked to the window. In the distance, the black, irregular top of the mountain showed against a pale, bright blue sky. All the ground was white except for three or four huge green firs. No skiers were in sight now, and when she realized this, the scene took on a melancholy, a look of loneliness.

All these people want me only because I don't need them any longer, Helene thought suddenly. *It's ironic, but perfectly human, after all. They think I won't take anything from them, and they're right.*

And it was quite funny. If she, for instance, had come here and fallen in love with the Frenchman, or with Gert if she had been younger, and had consequently tried to win them, she would probably have failed. She was not beautiful, and there had been a few times in her life—maybe two or three—when she had been attracted to certain men, and had failed utterly to make them notice her. Helene smiled on the view outside. It was beautiful again, very beautiful. She felt strangely beautiful herself, and strangely pure and guiltless. No one looks more beautifully on the world than someone who is going to leave it, Helene thought. And of course, the world never looks more beautiful than then, either, probably, but not like something beautiful that one desires to possess, or regrets leaving. She was filled with a happy knowledge that the world would remain, slowly changing, but remain—as beautiful as it was now.

Consequently, having had these thoughts at eleven in the morning, she was somewhat prepared for Signora Cacciaguerra's strange words at twelve-thirty. Helene had come down for a *Kirschwasser* before lunch, but before she reached the bar, Signora Cacciaguerra, a smallish, brunette woman of about forty, well dressed and well groomed, in a black and red ski outfit, accosted Helene in the hall. She asked if she could speak with Helene alone for a moment, and Helene suggested they go into the bar.

Signora Cacciaguerra looked quite distrait, and her forehead had puckered with an anxious frown. "Would you mind, please, if we had a conversation in your room?"

"Has something happened to your husband?" Helene asked, thinking at once of a skiing accident.

"No, nothing like that," she replied, making a gesture toward the lift. "May we——"

"Oh, of course." Helene followed her into the elevator. When they reached her room, Helene said, "We can have something sent up here, if you like." But Signora Cacciaguerra didn't answer, so Helene ordered a *Kirschwasser* and an *americano* by telephone. "Do sit down, signora," Helene said for the second time.

At last, Signora Cacciaguerra sat, on the edge of the armchair. "You may think it very strange—you will think it strange that a wife comes to you with . . . But my husband . . ." She groped for words, smiled, and struggled on. "He acts very strange. Not—I mean, he doesn't say anything definite, but he is always looking at you, and he daydreams about you. You must have noticed."

Helene hadn't particularly, because Signor Cacciaguerra looked at her no more often than three or four other men and women did—including Signora Cacciaguerra herself.

"He is also moody now—alternately happy and moody. Staring out the window. But he doesn't want to go outdoors. I am not jealous of you, that's the funny part," the woman said with a little laugh. "Strangely enough, I came to ask for your advice. Even, for instance . . ."

"For instance?"

"Shall we all have dinner tonight together? Perhaps it would help if my husband would be with you. He does speak of you, now and then, it's just the way he speaks of you that's so strange. I have seen him a little interested in other women now and then, believe me, but not like this. He puts you on a pedestal."

The boy with the drinks knocked just then, and Helene was glad of the interruption. She took a ten-schilling note from her bag, and handed it to the boy with her thanks.

"*Danke vielmal, gnädige Frau,*" he said, and departed, leaving the tray on her dressing table.

Helene handed Signora Cacciaguerra the *americano.* "I hope you like this."

"I do, it's my favorite. I drink it always in Milano. Cheers."

Helene echoed the English word, "Cheers." Signora Cacciaguerra had been speaking in Italian, Helene in French, which she spoke better. They had all spoken French the evening they sat at a table together after dinner. "It's too beautiful here to be worried by small things. Besides, I'm leaving in a day or so, if that's any comfort to you," Helene said cheerfully.

"Oh, but it is not, you know? And I am not sorry to have met you." Signora Cacciaguerra returned Helene's smile with a smile of equal sincerity. "Yes, I feel better already. But what about dinner tonight?"

"I've promised to have dinner with Monsieur Lemaitre tonight. But why can't we all sit at the same table?"

"No. I am sure Monsieur Lemaitre wouldn't like that," said Signora Cacciaguerra graciously, "thank you. And neither will my husband like it that Monsieur Lemaitre is dining with you." She laughed heartily at her own remark.

Helene was smiling also, and still standing. There would be no dinner for her tonight. She suddenly felt that tonight was her night.

Signora Cacciaguerra stayed a few minutes more, drinking her *americano* and telling Helene about her two sons in Milano. They were eleven and thirteen, and very different. One wanted to be a painter, the younger was going to be an engineer and build skyscrapers. They were so different, they had to have separate rooms now. "I would like you to meet my children," she said with enthusiasm. "Do you ever come to Milano?"

"Only once every five years or so, I'm afraid."

Signora Cacciaguerra gave Helene her address, then left by herself, saying she did not want her husband to see them together downstairs for fear he might guess she had spoken to her.

Helene went down a few minutes later. André met her near the door of the dining room, and asked if she would join him and a friend who had just come from Paris for lunch.

"That is, if you don't think you'll be bored if you see me at dinner tonight as well," André added.

Helene accepted.

That afternoon, Helene packed her suitcase for tidiness' sake, and asked for her bill to be prepared. The manager was surprised that she was leaving so soon, but Helene said that it was probable she would leave the following day, and she wanted to settle. She paid for the extra day, and left a good sum under the lamp on her bedtable. In an envelope of the hotel's stationery, she left a hundred and fifty schillings for the maid Kaethe. She put Gert's brooch into an envelope, thought of writing a note, and decided not to. She addressed the envelope to Gert von Boechlein. There was no need to write to her husband or her son, she felt, even though she was capable of writing a friendly good-bye to both: notes would only stir up sentiment, would be kept perhaps for years, and might wound her son's heart years from now, if his heart should ever become capable of being wounded. She had said the only kind of good-byes she wanted to say to her cheerful friends at the Munich Hauptbahnhof before she came to Alpenbach.

At six o'clock, she went out in her ski pants, with hood and mittens. It was the hour when most people bathed and changed their clothes, and she was glad not to run into anyone in the lobby. Then she began to climb the snowy path, estimating that by the time she reached the top, it would be dark. She was sorry to inconvenience the hotel with a death, but death, she supposed, was always a nuisance: if one dove into a river, for instance, many people would spend days looking for the body, or there would be inconvenience if the body were found unexpectedly on the riverbank days or weeks later. At least she was not going to die in the hotel. She supposed she would land in a pile of snow yards deep and be frozen or suffocate. The words had no terror and almost no meaning now. And what if she met Gert at the top of the mountain about to do the same thing? Helene thought, and laughed a little, because she was so sure he wouldn't.

By the time she neared the top, she could not see her footing. She pulled herself up by her hands on the bare, irregular rocks. And when she reached the top, she did not hesitate for more than ten seconds, paused only to take two or three deep breaths of air, then she walked forward, tumbled over headlong, and fell into emptiness. The wind whistled through her hood into her ears. Though she hurtled downward, she had a sensation of weightlessness, of bodilessness also. She saw her whole life, from her yellow-haired childhood to her university days, her marriage, its slow decline, to the last sections of her life in Munich—but all so quickly, it might have been one panoramic snapshot—*click!* And all in all, life was not bad, she thought. It was her last thought, before a dark and final click.

TWO DISAGREEABLE PIGEONS

They lived in Trafalgar Square, two pigeons which for convenience shall be called Maud and Claud, though they didn't give each other names. They were simply mates, for two or three years now, loyal in a way, though at the bottom of their little pigeon hearts they detested each other. Their days were spent pecking grain and peanuts strewn by endless tourists and Londoners who bought the stuff from peddlers. *Peck-peck,* all day amid hundreds of other pigeons who like Maud and Claud had nearly lost the ability to fly, because it was hardly necessary any longer. Often Maud was separated from Claud in a bobbing field of pigeons, but by nightfall they somehow found each other and made their way to a cranny in the back of a stone parapet near the National Gallery. *Uff!* and they'd heave their bulging breasts up the two or three feet to their domicile.

Maud would make disagreeable noises in her throat, signifying both pique and scorn. She was the same age as Claud, which wasn't young. Her first mate had been hit in the prime of life by a bus while trying to capture part of a sandwich.

Maud's standoffish sounds could have been interpreted as "At it again today, eh?" or various other taunts at Claud's virility and his groundless self-esteem. Perhaps Claud hadn't been at it again today, but his was a roving eye. Often Maud had the satisfaction of seeing Claud bested by a younger male who swooped down at the wrong moment for Claud and his newly found female. Claud would put up a blustering show, pretend he was willing to fight, but the younger male would go for his eyes and Claud would retreat.

"Shut up," Claud would reply finally, and settle himself for sleep.

Once in a while, for a change of scene, Claud and Maud took the tube to Hampstead Heath. Rather, once they had taken the tube and found themselves at Hampstead Heath, much to their delight. Space! Plenty of things to peck at! No people! Or almost no people. Sometimes they took the tube for amusement, not caring where they might be when they got off. They could always find their way back to Trafalgar Square, even if they had to make a bit of an effort and fly a few yards here and there. Buses were safer as to direction, though there wasn't much to hang on to on the top of a bus. They certainly remembered the direction of Hampstead Heath, and by hopping a bus starting in that direction there was a fair chance they'd get there, and if the bus veered, they simply flew to another bus that looked more promising. They'd made it twice by bus.

However, tubes were more fun, because Maud and Claud enjoyed making people step out of their way. People laughed and pointed when Maud and Claud rode the escalators up and down. Sometimes people whipped out cameras, as in the Square, and they'd be photographed by flash.

"Look out! Don't step on the pigeons! Ha-ha!" That was a familiar cry by now.

Maud was haunted by a vague memory of a daughter who had been clubbed before her eyes on a pavement near the Square. That had been an offspring by her first mate. Or had she imagined it? Maud was shy to this day of people carrying sticks, even umbrellas, of which she saw plenty. Maud would flinch and sidle away a few inches. Maud fancied that she could acquire another mate if she wished, but something—she couldn't say what—kept her with boring Claud.

With mutual consent, they decided to head for Hampstead Heath one Saturday morning. Something awful was going on in Trafalgar Square. There were hordes of people, and bleachers and loudspeakers were being set up. Not a day for peanuts and popcorn. Maud and Claud descended to the underground in Whitehall.

"Ooh, lookie, Mummy!" cried a little girl. "Pigeons!"

Maud and Claud ignored it and kept hopping down. They went under the turnstile, unnoticed but kicked by someone, then took the escalator down. Claud led, though he didn't know where he was going. He hopped onto the first train.

"Look at that! Pigeons!" someone said.

A couple of people laughed.

Maud and Claud were among the few passengers not jostled. They had a clear circle around them. Again it was Claud who led when they got off, his head bobbing authoritatively. He didn't know where he was, but liked giving the impression that he did.

"They're getting on the lift! Ha-haa-aa!"

A way was cleared for them as if they were VIPs.

In the rush of people up the stairs to pavement level, Maud and Claud had to take to their wings. This left them exhausted when they stood finally in the sunlight near a news vendor. Maud started out, leading. The pavement sloped upward, and this direction she took. The pavements near Hampstead Heath usually sloped upward, she remembered. Claud followed.

"Ah, romance," a male voice said.

The voice was wrong. Often Claud led, when he wanted to appear superior to Maud, knowing Maud would follow no matter what. Sometimes it was just the reverse, and it had nothing to do with the mating urge. After three streets, hopping down and up curbs, Maud was becoming tired. Claud had made a wrong decision, detraining when he did, and Maud got beside him and indicated this with a glance and a derogatory rattle. She didn't know where she was, either, though she knew that Trafalgar Square was somewhere behind and to her right. No problem getting home, at least. But this wasn't the Heath.

Then Maud sensed or spotted a patch of green ahead on the left, and with a toss of her head, which made her breast glisten blue and green in the sunlight, she steered Claud to the left. They paused to let a taxi turn, then continued. Up the curb. Now Maud could see the greenery, and she put on some speed, fluttering her wings as her feet moved in double time on the pavement. She mustered the energy to fly over the three-foot-high rail of a little park.

There were benches on which people sat peacefully, and a fair-sized expanse of green grass, untrammeled. A pond in the center. Maud began to peck.

Claud noticed three other pigeons, a female and two males, not far away on the grass. They wouldn't take kindly to him and Maud. But the males were otherwise absorbed at the moment. Maud said something to the effect that Claud might try his luck there, and Claud replied promptly that she might try hers. Maud walked off, turning her back on the lot of them, including Claud. Claud was pecking at a worm, and thinking that he preferred dried corn, when one of the males swooped on him.

The attacking bird was in better physical shape. Claud only rose a few inches in the air, and slammed himself down, not to much effect. Claud beat a retreat, walking, flapping his wings and making noises to indicate that he was annoyed but by no means vanquished and that he simply wasn't going to bother to fight.

Maud affected amusement and indifference.

It began to rain, quite suddenly. Claud and Maud walked toward the nearest tree. The rain had the look of lasting. Should they take the tube for home? It was only midafternoon. Rain would bring the worms out, maybe a snail or two. Suddenly Maud flew at Claud and attacked him in the neck.

Claud was already in a bad mood, and he stalked off toward a path. When he reached the pavement, he turned smartly left. This was the way back to the tube, he thought, and it was even the direction of home.

Maud followed, hating herself for following, but consoled by the fact that she had Claud under her eye and that it was the general direction of Trafalgar Square. Claud's day would come, Maud thought. If she made sufficient effort, a younger male might actually invade their home and rout Claud from his own premises. That would pay him back for—

Clomp!

What was that?

A blackness had descended. Claud was in it with her, squawking and flapping.

Maud heard children's laughter. A box! Maud had had it once before, and she'd escaped, she reminded herself. The cardboard box scraped along the pavement, catching one of her legs painfully. She and Claud were tumbled suddenly upside down, they saw a brief patch of sky, then a nasty coat or something was thrown over the box. They were jiggled and jostled as the children ran. They went down steps. Maud and Claud were tossed onto the floor of a brightly lighted room. They were inside a house.

A woman shouted something.

The children, two boys, laughed.

Maud flew onto a table. It was a kitchen in one of those edifices she and Claud had often looked into through a semi-basement window.

"What're you going to do with them?—A-aak!"

Claud had taken off, up to the sink rim. A boy came for him, and Claud hopped down into a corner by a door that was open only a crack.

One boy strewed bread on the floor, which Claud ignored. Claud was interested in the door, Maud saw, but the rest of the house might not be open anywhere, so what good was the door? Maud defecated.

This produced a yelp from the woman. Good! Maud knew that a dropping could go a long way: it meant contempt, for one thing. Maud had been kicked a few times—deliberately—when she'd done it on her own land, Trafalgar Square, not even meaning it as an insult. But then people weren't normal, they were insane, most of them. You could never tell what people were going to do. Peanuts one minute and a club the next.

The woman was still jabbering, and there was a whoop from the boys, and they lunged at Claud with open arms, trying to grab him. Claud flew up and loosed a dropping, hitting one boy in the face. Laughter. Claud teetered on a clothes dryer near the ceiling, oscillating.

A big man with a loud voice came in. Maud detested him on sight. He made a long, bellowing speech, then bent close to Maud and spoke more softly. Maud took two steps backward, knocking a china lid off something, keeping an eye on the man, ready to join Claud if he came any closer. The man left the kitchen.

The woman was making popcorn at the stove. Maud and Claud recognized the smell. Meanwhile the children tittered stupidly by the sink. The man came back with a tall tripod affair. Bright lights came on. Then Maud and Claud understood. They'd seen the same thing in Trafalgar Square on a larger scale—tripods, moving platforms, awful lights everywhere that turned night into day. Now the light was right in Maud's eyes, and she turned in a circle. The camera buzzed. Maud would have defecated again, but at the moment was not able.

"Popcorn!" the man cried.

"Coming!" The woman swung around with the pan just in time to collide with Claud, who had been going to try the window. He had hoped that the top part might be open, but before he had time to see, he was on his side on the floor. He got to his feet. The woman spilled some popcorn on the floor near him, and Claud backed away as if it were poison.

"Ha-ha!" the man laughed. "Scare 'em up again, Simon!"

The smaller of the odious two flailed his arms at Maud, while the other boy stomped toward Claud.

Maud and Claud rose, wings flapping wildly. Claud dropped like a fat eagle onto the forehead and hair of the bigger boy, all claws out.

"Ow!" the boy cried.

Maud contented herself with two hard pecks at the smaller boy's cheeks and as much clawing as she could get in, before she pushed herself off just in time to avoid a swat of the man's fist. It was going to be a fight for life, Maud realized, and she and Claud were trapped.

The woman took a broom to Claud, missing at every swing. "Open the window! Get them *out*!"

"I'll wring their necks! They're insane!" yelled the red-faced man, striding toward the window.

Maud could see that the man was *angry*, but who had brought them here but his own nauseating children? Maud attacked the man just as he was pulling the window down from the top. He fended Maud off with an elbow and ducked.

Claud flew out the window.

"Use the broom!" said the woman, handing it to the man.

Maud evaded the broom, flew to the dish rack over the sink, seized a saucer to brace herself, and as she took off toward the window, the saucer fell in the sink and shattered.

Another cry from the woman, a roar from the man, both of which faded as Maud flew, flew several yards with the energy of her wrath, and then she sank to the civilized pavement, where she could walk normally again and recover her breath. What a relief to get out of that madhouse! Good Lord! Such people should be reported! Maud held her head high and thrust her beak forward with every step. There were groups—*people, in fact*—who fought for pigeons. She'd seen people in Trafalgar Square stopping boys from using guns or even from throwing things at pigeons. If they ever got hold of this family, there'd be hell to pay.

Where was Claud?

Maud stopped and turned. Not that she cared much where Claud was. If she went straight home, as she intended to do, Claud would turn up this evening, she had no doubt. What help had he been to her just now? None.

She heard his voice. Then he appeared behind her, rushing toward her on legs and wings, looking exhausted. Maud shook her feathers and walked on. Claud walked beside her, grumbling a little, as did Maud, but gradually their sounds became calmer. They were, after all, free again, and they were walking in the direction of home. Suddenly Maud made for a bus. Claud followed, getting himself with some difficulty up to the roof. They crouched for better grip. Some buses lurched horribly. They had to switch to another bus, hoping for the best, but their instinct was right and they soon found themselves jolting down the Haymarket. Home! And it wasn't yet dark. The sky was a smoky blue where the sun was setting.

Still time to find a few pickings in the Square before retiring, Maud thought. Claud was thinking the same thing, so they left the bus in Whitehall, and glided down to the familiar ground.

There were not many pigeons still about. Lights were coming on in shop windows. The pickings were poor and trampled. And Maud felt tired and out of sorts.

Claud thrust his head in her way and seized a peanut fragment that Maud had been about to peck.

Maud flew at him, flapping her wings. Why did she put up with him? Selfish, greedy—she couldn't count on him for anything, not even to guard the nest when there was an egg!

Claud retaliated with an ill-meant peck at Maud's eye, which missed her and got her in the head.

Then suddenly—it was impossible to tell whether Maud or Claud moved first—they attacked a passing perambulator. They went for the baby, pecking its cheeks, its eyes. The young woman pushing the pram let out a scream and hit at the pigeons, knocking the breath out of Maud, but she rejoined Claud in the pram in a matter of seconds. A couple of people ran toward the pram, and the pigeons took off. They flew over the heads of their would-be attackers and settled in a group of twenty-odd pigeons who were pecking around a litter basket.

When the two people, plus the woman with the pram, came close to the pigeons, Maud and Claud were not in the least afraid, though some of the other pigeons looked up, startled by the angry voices.

One of the people, a man, rushed among the pigeons, kicking, waving his arms and yelling. Most of the pigeons took lazy flight. Maud headed for home, the nook behind the low stone wall, and when she got there, Claud had already arrived. They settled themselves for sleep, too tired even to grumble to each other. But Maud was not too tired to recall the half peanut that Claud had snatched. Why did she live with him? Why did she, or they, live *here,* running the risk daily of being captured, as they'd been today, or kicked by people who objected even to their droppings? Why? Maud fell asleep, exhausted by her discontent.

The incident of the pecked baby, blinded in one eye, in Trafalgar Square, inspired a couple of letters to the *Times*. But nothing was done about it.

VARIATIONS ON A GAME

It was an impossible situation. Penn Knowlton had realized that as soon as he realized he was in love with Ginnie Ostrander—Mrs. David Ostrander. Penn couldn't see himself in the role of a marriage-breaker, even though Ginnie said she had wanted to divorce David long before she met him. David wouldn't give her a divorce, that was the point. The only decent thing to do, Penn had decided, was to clear out, leave before David suspected anything. Not that he considered himself noble, but there were some situations . . .

Penn went to Ginnie's room on the second floor of the house and knocked.

Her rather high, cheerful voice called, "You, Penn? Come in!"

She was lying on the sunlit chaise longue, wearing black, close-fitting slacks and a yellow blouse, and she was sewing a button on one of David's shirts.

"Don't I look domestic?" she asked, pushing her yellow hair back from her forehead. "Need any buttons sewed on, darling?" Sometimes she called him darling when David was around, too.

"No," he said, smiling, and sat down on a hassock.

She glanced at the door as if to make sure no one was about, then pursed her lips and kissed the empty air between them. "I'll miss you this weekend. What time are you leaving tomorrow?"

"David wants to leave just after lunch. It's my last assignment, Ginnie. David's last book with me. I'm quitting."

"Quitting?" She let her sewing fall into her lap. "You've told David, too?"

"No. I'll tell him tomorrow. I don't know why you're surprised. You're the reason, Ginnie. I don't think I have to make any speeches."

"I understand, Penn. You know I've asked for a divorce. But I'll keep on asking. I'll work something out and then—" She was on her knees suddenly in front of him, crying, her head down on her hands that gripped his hands.

He turned his eyes away and slowly stood up, drawing her up with him. "I'll be around another two weeks, probably; long enough for David to finish this book, if he wants me around that long. And you needn't worry. I won't tell him why I'm quitting." His voice had sunk to a whisper, though David was downstairs in his soundproofed study, and the maid, Penn thought, was in the basement.

"I wouldn't care if you told him," she said with quiet defiance.

"It's a wonder he doesn't know."

"Will you be around, say in three months, if I can get a divorce?" she asked.

He nodded; then, feeling his own eyes start to burn, he smiled. "I'll be around an awful long time. I'm just not so sure you want a divorce."

Her eyebrows drew down, stubborn and serious. "You'll see. I don't want to make David angry. I'm afraid of his temper, I've told you that. But maybe I'll have to stop being afraid." Her blue eyes looked straight into his. "Remember that dream you told us, about the man you were walking with on the country road, who disappeared? And you kept calling him and you couldn't find him?"

"Yes," he said, smiling.

"I wish it would happen to you—with David. I wish David would just disappear suddenly, this weekend, and be out of my life forever, so I could be with you."

Her words did strange and terrible things to him. He released her arm. "People don't just disappear. There're other ways." He was going to add, "Such as divorce," but he didn't.

"Such as?"

"I'd better get back to my typewriter. I've got another half-hour tape to do."

David and Penn left in the black convertible the next afternoon with a small suitcase apiece, one typewriter, the tape recorder, and an iced carton of steaks and beer and a few other items of food. David was in a good mood, talking about an idea that had come to him during the night for a new book. David Ostrander wrote science fiction so prolifically that he used half a dozen pen names. He seldom took longer than a month to write a book, and he worked every month of the year. More ideas came to him than he could use, and he was in the habit of passing them on to other writers at his Wednesday night Guild meetings.

David Ostrander was forty-three, lean and wiry, with a thin, dry-skinned face thatched with fine, intersecting wrinkles—the only part of him that showed his age at all and exaggerated it at that—wrinkles that looked as if he had spent all his forty-three years in the dry, sterile winds of the fantastic planets about which he wrote.

Ginnie was only twenty-four, Penn remembered, two years younger than himself. Her skin was pliant and smooth, her lips like a poppy's petals. He stopped thinking about her. It irked him to think of David's lips kissing hers. How could she have married him? Or why? Or was there something about David's intellect, his bitter humor, his energy, that a woman would find attractive? Of course David had money, a comfortable income plus the profits of his writing, but what did Ginnie do with it? Nice clothes, yes, but did David ever take her out? They hardly ever entertained. As far as Penn had been able to learn, they had never traveled anywhere.

"Eh? What do you think of that, Penn? The poison gas emanating from the blue vegetation and conquering the green until the whole earth perishes! Say, where are you today?"

"I got it," Penn said without taking his eyes from the road. "Shall I put it down in the notebook?"

"Yes. No. I'll think about it a little more today." David lit another cigarette. "Something's on your mind, Penn, my boy. What is it?"

Penn's hands tightened on the wheel. Well, no other moment was going to be any better, was it? A couple of scotches this evening wouldn't help, just be a little more cowardly, Penn decided. "David, I think after this book is over, I'll be leaving you."

"Oh," said David, not manifesting any surprise. He puffed on his cigarette. "Any particular reason?"

"Well, as I've told you, I have a book of my own to write. The Coast Guard thing." Penn had spent the last four years in the Coast Guard, which was the main reason David had hired him as a secretary. David had advertised for a secretary "preferably with a firsthand knowledge of Navy life." The first book he had worked on with David had a Navy background—Navy life in 2800 A.D., when the whole globe had been made radioactive. Penn's book would have to do with real life, and it had an orthodox plot, ending on a note of hope. It seemed at that moment a frail and hopeless thing compared to a book by the great David Ostrander.

"I'll miss you," David said finally. "So'll Ginnie. She's very fond of you, you know."

From any other man it might have been a snide comment, but not from David, who positively encouraged him to spend time with Ginnie, to take walks in the woods around the estate with her, to play tennis on the clay court behind the summer house. "I'll miss you both, too," Penn said. "And who wouldn't prefer the environment to an apartment in New York?"

"Don't make any speeches, Penn. We know each other too well." David rubbed the side of his nose with a nicotine-stained forefinger. "What if I put you on a part-time basis and gave you most of the day for your own work? You could have a whole wing of the house to yourself."

Penn declined it politely. He wanted to get away by himself for a while.

"Ginnie's going to sulk," David said, as if to himself.

They reached the lodge at sundown. It was a substantial one-story affair made of unhewn logs, with a stone chimney at one end. White birches and huge pine trees swayed in the autumn breeze. By the time they unpacked and got a fire going for the steak, it was seven o'clock. David said little, but he seemed cheerful, as if their conversation about Penn's quitting had never taken place. They had two drinks each before dinner, two being David's limit for himself on the nights he worked and also those on which he did not work, which were rare.

David looked at him across the wooden table. "Did you tell Ginnie you were leaving?"

Penn nodded, and swallowed with an effort. "I told her yesterday." Then he wished he hadn't admitted it. Wasn't it more logical to tell one's employer first?

David's eyes seemed to be asking the same question. "And how did she take it?"

"Said she'd be sorry to see me go," Penn said casually, and cut another bite of steak.

"Oh. Like that. I'm sure she'll be devastated."

Penn jumped as if a knife had been stuck into him.

"I'm not blind, you know, Penn. I know you two think you're in love with each other."

"Now listen, David, just a minute. If you possibly imagine—"

"I know what I know, that's all. I know what's going on behind my back when I'm in my study or when I'm in town Wednesday nights at the Guild meeting!" David's eyes shone with blue fire, like the cold lights of his lunar landscapes.

"David, there's nothing going on behind your back," Penn said evenly. "If you doubt me, ask Ginnie."

"Hah!"

"But I think you'll understand why it's better that I leave. I should think you'd approve of it, in fact."

"I do." David lit a cigarette.

"I'm sorry this happened," Penn added. "Ginnie's very young. I also think she's bored—with her life, not necessarily with you."

"Thanks!" David said like a pistol shot.

Penn lit a cigarette, too. They were both on their feet now. The half-eaten meal was over. Penn watched David moving about as he might have watched an armed man who at any minute might pull a gun or a knife. He didn't trust David, couldn't predict him. The last thing he would have predicted was David's burst of temper tonight, the first Penn had seen. "Okay, David. I'll say again that I'm sorry. But you've no reason to hold a grudge against me."

"That's enough of your words! I know a heel when I see one!"

"If you were my weight, I'd break your jaw for that!" Penn yelled, advancing on him with his fists clenched. "I've had enough of your words tonight, too. I suppose you'll go home and throw your bilge at Ginnie. Well, where do *you* get off, shoving a bored, good-looking girl at your male secretary, telling us to go off on picnic lunches together? Can you blame either of us?"

David muttered something unintelligible in the direction of the fireplace. Then he turned and said, "I'm going for a walk." He went out and slammed the thick door so hard that the floor shook.

Automatically, Penn began clearing the dishes away, the untouched salad. They had started the refrigerator, and Penn carefully put the butter away on a shelf. The thought of spending the night here with David was ghastly, yet where else could he go? They were six miles from the nearest town, and there was only one car.

The door suddenly opened, and Penn nearly dropped the coffeepot.

"Come out for a walk with me," David said. "Maybe it'll do us both good." He was not smiling.

Penn set the coffeepot back on the stove. A walk with David was the last thing he wanted, but he was afraid to refuse. "Have you got the flashlight?"

"No, but we don't need it. There's moonlight."

They walked from the lodge door to the car, then turned left onto the dirt road that went on for two miles through the woods to the highway.

"This is a half moon," David said. "Mind if I try a little experiment? Walk on ahead of me, here where it's pretty clear, and let me see how much of you I can make out at thirty yards. Take big strides and count off thirty. You know, it's for that business about Faro."

Penn nodded. He knew. They were back on the book again, and they'd probably work a couple of hours tonight when they went back to the lodge. Penn started counting, taking big strides.

"Fine, keep going!" David called.

Twenty-eight . . . twenty-nine . . . thirty. Penn stopped and stood still. He turned around. He couldn't see David. "Hey! Where are you?"

No answer.

Penn smiled wryly, and stuffed his hands into his pockets. "Can you see me, David?"

Silence. Penn started slowly back to where he had left David. A little joke, he supposed, a mildly insulting joke, but he resolved to take no offense.

He walked on toward the lodge, where he was sure he would find David thoughtfully pacing the floor as he pondered his work, perhaps dictating already into the tape recorder; but the main room was empty. There was no sound from the corner room where they worked, nor from the closed room where David slept. Penn lit a cigarette, picked up the newspaper and sat down in the single armchair. He read with deliberate concentration, finished his cigarette and lit another. The second cigarette was gone when he got up, and he felt angry and a little scared at the same time.

He went to the lodge door and called, "David!" a couple of times, loudly. He walked toward the car, got close enough to see that there was no one sitting in it. Then he returned to the lodge and methodically searched it, looking even under the bunks.

What was David going to do, come back in the middle of the night and kill him in his sleep? No, that was crazy, as crazy as one of David's story ideas. Penn suddenly thought of his dream, remembered David's brief but intense interest in it the night he had told it at the dinner table. "Who was the man with you?" David had asked. But in the dream, Penn hadn't been able to identify him. He was just a shadowy companion on a walk. "Maybe it was me," David had said, his blue eyes shining. "Maybe you'd like *me* to disappear, Penn." Neither Ginnie nor he had made a comment, Penn recalled, nor had they discussed David's remark when they were alone. It had been so long ago, over two months ago.

Penn put that out of his mind. David had probably wandered down to the lake to be alone for a while, and hadn't been courteous enough to tell him. Penn did the dishes, took a shower and crawled into his bunk. It was twelve-ten. He had thought he wouldn't be able to sleep, but he was asleep in less than two minutes.

The raucous cries of ducks on the wing awakened him at six-thirty. He put on his robe and went into the bathroom, noting that David's towel, which he had stuck hastily over the rack last night, had not been touched. Penn went to David's room and knocked. Then he opened the door a crack. The two bunks, one above the other, were still made up. Penn washed hurriedly, dressed, and went out.

He looked over the ground on both sides of the road where he had last seen David, looking for shoe prints in the moist pine needles. He walked to the lake and looked around its marshy edge; not a footprint, not a cigarette butt.

He yelled David's name, three times, and gave it up.

By seven-thirty A.M. Penn was in the town of Croydon. He saw a small rectangular sign between a barber's shop and a paint store that said POLICE. He parked the car, went into the station, and told his story. As Penn had thought, the police wanted to look over the lodge. Penn led them back in David's car.

The two policemen had heard of David Ostrander, not as a writer, apparently, but as one of the few people who had a lodge in the area. Penn showed them where he had last seen David, and told them that Mr. Ostrander had been experimenting to see how well he could see him at thirty yards.

"How long have you been working for Mr. Ostrander?"

"Four months. Three months and three weeks to be exact."

"Had he been drinking?"

"Two scotches. His usual amount. I had the same."

Then they walked to the lake and looked around.

"Mr. Ostrander have a wife?" one of the men asked.

"Yes. She's at the house in Stonebridge, New York."

"We'd better notify her."

There was no telephone at the lodge. Penn wanted to stay on in case David turned up, but the police asked him to come with them back to the station, and Penn did not argue. At least he would be there when they talked with Ginnie, and he'd be able to speak with her himself. Maybe David had decided to go back to Stonebridge and was already home. The highway was only two miles from the lodge, and David could have flagged a bus or picked up a ride from someone, but Penn couldn't really imagine David Ostrander doing anything that simple or obvious.

"Listen," Penn said to the policemen before he got into David's convertible, "I think I ought to tell you that Mr. Ostrander is kind of an odd one. He writes science fiction. I don't know what his objective is, but I think he deliberately disappeared last night. I don't think he was kidnapped or attacked by a bear or anything like that."

The policemen looked at him thoughtfully.

"Okay, Mr. Knowlton," one of them said. "Now you drive on ahead of us, will you?"

Back at the station in Croydon, they called the number Penn gave them. Hanna, the maid, answered. Penn, six feet from the telephone, could hear her shrill, German-accented voice; then Ginnie came on. The officer reported that David Ostrander was missing since ten o'clock last night, and asked her if she'd had any word from him. Ginnie's voice, after the first exclamation which Penn had heard, sounded alarmed. The officer watched Penn as he listened to her.

"Yes . . . What's that again? . . . No, no blood or anything. Not a clue so far. That's why we're calling you." A long pause. The officer's pencil tapped but did not write. "I see . . . I see . . . We'll call you, Mrs. Ostrander."

"May I speak to her?" Penn reached for the telephone.

The captain hesitated, then said, "Good-bye, Mrs. Ostrander," and put the telephone down. "Well, Mr. Knowlton, are you prepared to swear that the story you told us is true?"

"Absolutely."

"Because I've just heard a motive if I ever heard one. A motive for getting Mr. Ostrander out of the way. Now, just what did you do to him—or maybe *say* to him?" The officer leaned forward, palms on his desk.

"What did she just tell you?"

"That you're in love with her and you might have wanted her husband out of the picture."

Penn tried to keep calm. "I was quitting my job to get *away* from the situation! I told Mr. Ostrander yesterday that I was going to quit, and I told his wife the day before."

"So you admit there was a situation."

The police, four of them now, looked at him with frank disbelief.

"Mrs. Ostrander's upset," Penn said. "She doesn't know what she's saying. Can I talk to her, please? Now?"

"You'll see her when she gets here." The officer sat down and picked up a pen. "Knowlton, we're booking you on suspicion. Sorry."

They questioned him until one P.M., then gave him a hamburger and a paper container of weak coffee. They kept asking him if there hadn't been a gun at the lodge—there hadn't been—and if he hadn't weighted David's body and thrown it in the lake along with the gun.

"We walked half around the lake this morning," Penn said. "Did you notice any footprints anywhere?"

By that time, he had told them about his dream and suggested that David Ostrander was trying to enact it, an idea that brought incredulous smiles, and he had laid bare his heart in regard to Ginnie, and also his intentions with her, which were nil. Penn didn't say that Ginnie had said she was in love with him, too. He couldn't bear to tell them that, in view of what she had said about him.

They went into his past. No police record. Born in Raleigh, Virginia, graduated from the state university, a major in journalism, worked on a Baltimore paper for a year, then four years in the Coast Guard. A clean slate everywhere, and this the police seemed to believe. It was, specifically, the cleanliness of his slate with the Ostranders that they doubted. He was in love with Mrs. Ostrander and yet he was really going to quit his job and leave? Hadn't he any plans about her?

"Ask her," Penn said tiredly.

"We'll do that," replied the officer who was called Mac.

"She knows about the dream I had, too, and the questions her husband asked me about it," Penn said. "Ask her in privacy, if you doubt me."

"Get this, Knowlton," Mac said. "We don't fool around with dreams. We want facts."

Ginnie arrived a little after three P.M. Catching a glimpse of her through the bars of the cell they had put him in, Penn sighed with relief. She looked calm, perfectly in command of herself. The police took her to another room for ten minutes or so, and then they came and unlocked Penn's cell door. As he approached Ginnie, she looked at him with a hostility or fear that was like a kick in the pit of his stomach. It checked the "Hello, Ginnie" that he wanted to say.

"Will you repeat to him what he said to you day before yesterday, Mrs. Ostrander?" asked Mac.

"Yes. He said, 'I wish David would disappear the way he did in my dream. I wish he were out of your life so I could be alone with you.'"

Penn stared at her. "Ginnie, *you* said that!"

"I think what we want to know from you, Knowlton, is what you did with her husband," said Mac.

"Ginnie," Penn said desperately, "I don't know why you're saying that. I can repeat every word of the conversation we had that afternoon, beginning with me saying I wanted to quit. That much you'll agree with, won't you?"

"Why, my husband had *fired* him—because of his attentions to *me*!" Ginnie glared at Penn and at the man around her.

Penn felt a panic, a nausea rising. Ginnie looked insane—or like a woman who was positive she was looking at her husband's murderer. There flashed to his mind her amazing coolness the moment after the one time he had kissed her, when David, by an unhappy stroke of luck, had tapped on her door and walked in. Ginnie hadn't turned a hair. She was an actress by nature, apparently, and she was acting now. "That's a lie and you know it," Penn said.

"And it's a lie what you said to her about wanting to get rid of her husband?" Mac asked.

"Mrs. Ostrander said that, I didn't," Penn replied, feeling suddenly weak in the knees. "That's why I was quitting. I didn't want to interfere with a marriage that—"

The listening policeman smiled.

"My husband and I were devoted."

Then Ginnie bent her head and gave in, it appeared, to the most genuine tears in the world.

Penn turned to the desk. "All right, lock me up. I'll be glad to stay here till David Ostrander turns up—because I'll bet my life he's not dead."

Penn pressed his palms against the cool wall of the cell. He was aware that Ginnie had left the station, but that was the only external circumstance of which he was aware.

A funny girl, Ginnie. She was mad about David, after all. She must worship David for his talent, for his discipline, and for his liking her. What was she, after all? A good-looking girl who hadn't succeeded as an actress (until now), who hadn't enough inner resources to amuse herself while her husband worked twelve hours a day, so she had started flirting with her husband's secretary. Penn remembered that Ginnie had said their chauffeur had quit five months ago. They hadn't hired another. Penn wondered if the chauffeur had quit for the same reason he had been going to leave. Or had David fired him? Penn didn't dare believe anything, now, that Ginnie had ever said to him.

A more nightmarish thought crossed his mind: suppose Ginnie really didn't love David, and had stopped on her way to Croydon and found David in the lodge and had shot him? Or if she had found him on the grounds, in the woods, had she shot him and left him to be discovered later, so that he would get the blame? So that she would be free of David and free of him, too? Or was there even a gun in Stonebridge that Ginnie could have taken?

Did Ginnie hate David or love him? On that incredible question his own future might hang, because if Ginnie had killed him herself . . . But how did it explain David's voluntarily disappearing last night?

Penn heard footsteps and stood up.

Mac stopped in front of his cell. "You're telling the truth, Knowlton?" he asked a little dubiously.

"Yes."

"So, the worst that can happen is, you'll sit a couple of days till Ostrander turns up."

"I hope you're looking for him."

"That we are, all over the state and farther if we have to." He started to go, then turned back.

"Thought I'd bring you a stronger light bulb and something to read, if you're in any mood for reading."

There was no news the next morning.

Then, around four P.M., a policeman came and unlocked Penn's cell.

"What's up?" Penn asked.

"Ostrander turned up at his house in Stonebridge," the man said with a trace of a smile.

Penn smiled, too, slightly. He followed him out to the front desk.

Mac gave Penn a nod of greeting. "We just called Mr. Ostrander's house. He came home half an hour ago. Said he'd taken a walk to do some thinking, and he can't understand what all the fuss is about."

Penn's hand shook as he signed his own release paper. He was dreading the return to the lodge to get his possessions, the inevitable few minutes at the Stonebridge house while he packed up the rest of his things.

David's convertible was at the curb where Penn had left it yesterday. He got in and headed for the lodge. There, he packed first his own things and closed his suitcase, then started to carry it and the tape recorder to the car, but on second thought decided to leave the tape recorder. How was he supposed to know what David wanted done with his stuff?

As he drove south toward Stonebridge, Penn realized that he didn't know what he felt or how he ought to behave. Ginnie: it wasn't worthwhile to say anything to her, either in anger or by way of asking her why. David: it was going to be hard to resist saying, "I hope you enjoyed your little joke. Are you trying to get a plot out of it?" Penn's foot pressed the accelerator, but he checked his speed abruptly. *Don't lose your temper,* he told himself. *Just get your stuff quietly and get out.*

Lights were on in the living room, and also in Ginnie's room upstairs. It was around nine o'clock. They'd have dined, and sometimes they sat awhile in the living room over coffee, but usually David went into his study to work. Penn couldn't see David's study window. He rang the bell.

Hanna opened the door. "Mister Knowlton!" she exclaimed. "They told me you'd gone away for good!"

"I have," Penn said. "Just came by to pick up my things."

"Come right in, sir! Mister and Missus are in the living room. I'll tell them you're here." She went trotting off before he could stop her.

Penn followed her across the broad foyer. He wanted a look at David, just a look. Penn stopped a little short of the door. David and Ginnie were sitting close together on the sofa, facing him, David's arm on the back of the sofa, and as Hanna told them he was here, David dropped his arm so that it circled Ginnie's waist. Ginnie did not show any reaction, only took a puff on her cigarette.

"Come on in, Penn!" David called, smiling. "What're you so shy about?"

"Nothing at all." Penn stopped at the threshold now. "I came to get my things, if I may."

"If you may!" David mocked. "Why, of course, Penn!" He stood up, holding Ginnie's hand now, as if he wanted to flaunt before Penn how affectionate they had become.

"Tell him to get his things and go," Ginnie said, smashing her cigarette in the ashtray. Her tone wasn't angry, in fact it was gentle, but she'd had a few drinks.

David came toward Penn, his lean, wrinkled face smiling. "I'll come with you. Maybe I can help."

Penn turned stiffly and walked to his room, which was down the hall. He went in, dragged a large suitcase out of the bottom of a closet, and began with a bureau drawer, lifting out socks and pajamas. He was conscious of David watching him with an amused smile. The smile was like an animal's claws in Penn's back. "Where'd you hide that night, David?"

"Hide? Nowhere!" David chuckled. "Just took a little walk and didn't answer you. I was interested to see what would happen. Rather, I *knew* what would happen. Everything was just as I'd predicted."

"What do you mean?" Penn's hands trembled as he slid open his top drawer.

"With Ginnie," David said. "I knew she'd turn against you and turn to me. It's happened before, you see. You were a fool to think if you waited for her she'd divorce me and come to you. An absolute fool!"

Penn whirled around, his hands full of folded shirts. "Listen, David, I wasn't waiting for Ginnie. I was clearing out of this—"

"Don't give me that, you sneak! Carrying on behind your employer's back!"

Penn flung the shirts into his suitcase. "What do you mean, it's happened before?"

"With our last chauffeur. And my last secretary, too. I'd get a girl secretary, you see, but Ginnie likes these little dramas. They serve to draw us together and they keep her from getting bored. Your dream gave me a splendid idea for this one. You see how affectionate Ginnie is with me now? And she thinks you're a prizewinning sucker." David laughed and lifted his cigarette to his lips.

A second later, Penn landed the hardest blow he had ever struck, on David's jaw. David's feet flew up in the wake of his body, and his head hit a wall six feet away.

Penn threw the rest of his things into his suitcase and crushed the lid down as furiously as if he were still fighting David. He pulled the suitcase off the bed and turned to the door.

Ginnie blocked his way. "What've you *done* to him?"

"Not as much as I'd like to do."

Ginnie rushed past him to David, and Penn went out the door.

Hanna was hurrying down the hall. "Something the matter, Mr. Knowlton?"

"Nothing serious. Good-bye, Hanna," Penn said, trying to control his hoarse voice. "And thanks," he added, and went on toward the front door.

"He's *dead*!" Ginnie cried wailingly.

Hanna was running to the room. Penn hesitated, then went on toward the door. The little liar! Anything for a dramatic kick!

"*Stop him!*" Ginnie yelled. "Hanna, he's trying to get away!"

Penn set his suitcase down and went back. He'd yank David up and douse his head in water. "He's not dead," Penn said as he strode into the room.

Hanna was standing beside David with a twisted face, ready for tears. "Yes—he is, Mr. Knowlton."

Penn bent to pull David up, but his hand stopped before it touched him. Something shiny was sticking out of David's throat, and Penn recognized it—the haft of his own paper knife that he'd neglected to pack.

A long, crazy laugh—or maybe it was a wailing sob—came from Ginnie behind him. "You *monster*! I suppose you wiped your fingerprints off it! But it won't do you any good, Penn! Hanna, call the police at once. Tell them we've got a murderer here!"

Hanna looked at her with horror. "I'll call them, ma'am. But it was you that wiped the handle. You were wiping it with your skirt when I came in the door."

Penn stared at Ginnie. He and she were not finished with each other yet.

A GIRL LIKE PHYL

Jeff Cormack stood looking through a thick glass window onto a field of Kennedy Airport, drawing on a cigarette that he hoped would be his last before he boarded. Twice they had announced delays that had caused the passengers to disperse, humping hand luggage back to the departure lounge or to one of the bars for a drink. It was a foggy day in November.

Here it came again, the droning female voice, "Passengers on TWA Flight eight-oh-seven to Paris are kindly requested . . ."

A collective groan, mumbles of impatience drowned out the voice, so that people asked others, "Did she say half an hour?" The answer was yes.

Jeff picked up his attaché case, and was turning toward the doorway when he saw a face some five yards away that made him stop and stay motionless for a few seconds. *Phyl.* No, it *couldn't* be. This girl looked hardly twenty. But the resemblance! The light brown eyes with the sharp upward slant at the outer corners, the fresh pink at the cheekbones, the soft abundant hair of the same dark brown as Phyl's. And the lips! The girl was like Phyl at the time Jeff had met her. Jeff tore his eyes away and reached for his black case, which was somehow on the floor again.

He felt shattered, and noticed that his hands trembled a little.

He mustn't look at the girl again, he thought, not try to find her again. She was evidently on the same flight. He walked slowly toward the bar, not caring where he walked, because he had no purpose in doing anything except to kill the next half hour. He'd be quite late getting to Paris at this rate, after midnight certainly before he got to his hotel. He would still try to reach Kyrogin by telephone tonight, and he envisaged staying up all night, because he didn't know and his office scouts hadn't been able to find out exactly when Kyrogin was arriving in Paris and where he was staying. At least it wouldn't be at the Russian Embassy, Jeff thought. Kyrogin was an engineer, an important man but not a Communist deputy. Jeff knew that Kyrogin's mission was semi-secret, that he was in search of a bargain, and Jeff wanted to get to him first, meaning before any other American firm, or maybe an English firm, got to him. Jeff had to convince Kyrogin that his company, Ander-Mack, was the best possible one for setting up oil rigs.

Thinking of the job he had to do in the next twenty-four hours gave Jeff a sense of solidity, of definite time and place.

The girl's face had whisked him back eighteen—no, twenty—years, to the year he had met Phyl. Not that he had stopped thinking about Phyl during all that time. They had been together for a little over a year. Then, after they had parted, he had thought about her a lot for the next two years, the Awful Years, as he called them. Then had come a three- or four-year break, in a manner of speaking, when he had not thought about her (not with the same intensity), when he had worked even harder at his own work in order to keep Phyl out of his mind, not to mention that during that period he had met someone else and got married. His son Bernard was now fifteen, going to Groton and not doing too well. Bernard had no idea of what he wanted to be as yet. Maybe an actor. And Betty, his wife, lived in Manhattan. He'd said good-bye to her this morning, and said he would be back in three days, maybe sooner. Just three hours ago. Was it possible?

Jeff found himself stirring his usual one lump of sugar into his coffee. He didn't remember ordering coffee. He stood with one leg over the seat of a stool, his topcoat folded over his arm. And his black case was at his feet, he saw. In it was the informal contract that he wanted Kyrogin to sign, or agree to. He'd make it. Jeff downed the last of his coffee and, feeling more sure of himself, surveyed the people at the little tables along the glass wall. He was looking deliberately now for the girl who resembled Phyl.

There she was, seated at a table with a young man in blue jeans and denim jacket, and Jeff judged from their attitudes that they were not together. The girl was neatly dressed (as Phyl would have been) in a well-cut navy blue coat, an expensive-looking scarf at her neck. Suddenly it crossed Jeff's mind that she could be Phyl's daughter. How else could there be such a resemblance? Phyl had married—nineteen years ago, Jeff remembered with painful accuracy—a man called Guy. Guy what? Fraser or Frazier, something like that. Jeff had deliberately tried to forget how to spell it, and had succeeded.

The girl looked at him, happened to lift her eyes straight toward him, and Jeff felt as if he had been shot.

Jeff dropped his own eyes, closed them, heard his heart catching up, and he slowly reached for his wallet and put a dollar bill on the counter. That had been like the first time he had seen Phyl, in that room full of other people. *Worse* now, because he knew Phyl. He knew also that he still loved her. He had come to terms with that years ago, he reminded himself. A man didn't commit suicide, didn't ruin his career, just because he was in love with a girl he couldn't have. There was such a thing as trying to forget, which really meant trying not to dwell upon it, or let it become an obsession. His love for Phyl was now something he had to live with, he had decided. But he had to admit that not a month, not a week went by, even now, when he didn't think of Phyl, didn't imagine being with her— in bed, out of bed, just existing, with her. And now he was married, the outer trappings were there, solid, tangible as his son Bernard, real as the ugly brown formica bar under his fingers now, or as a bullet that might penetrate his forehead and kill him.

He hoped he would not be seated next to the girl on the seven-hour flight to Paris. If that happened, he'd ask for his seat to be changed on some pretext. But with two hundred or so passengers, it wasn't likely.

Twenty minutes later, Jeff was being borne at increasing speed across the airfield, and then came the lift, the wonderful lightness as the air took over and the ground dropped below and the roar of the motors became fainter. On Jeff's left was a window looking out on a gray wing, and on his right a plump woman with a midwestern accent, and next to her a man who was probably her husband. From where he sat, Jeff couldn't see the girl, and he had avoided looking for her when the scores of passengers had been boarding.

Jeff unfastened his seat belt and lit a cigarette. A stewardess made slow progress up the aisle, and when she arrived, Jeff ordered a scotch on the rocks. Then came lunch. Then the sky began to darken as they raced in the same direction as the earth turned. A film made its appearance at the end of the plane's aisle. Jeff had declined the use of earphones. He wanted to snooze if he could. He lowered the back of his seat, closed his eyes and loosened his tie.

Kyrogin, Jeff was thinking, might not be difficult. Kyrogin had showed a sense of humor on the telephone last week. "Our seas are not made of vodka," Kyrogin had said, his accent heavy in a baritone voice. Meaning it was not pleasant to fall into the White Sea in winter or any other time. That was a crack against Ander-Mack's safety laws. Jeff's company avoided unions. They hired roustabouts for dangerous work at high wages. The Russians were not famous for unions or for respect for life and limb, so Jeff wasn't worried. If he could only show Kyrogin the contract, then the deal was clinched, Jeff thought. Jeff envisaged Russian labor plus some Scots and English dropouts from the British North Sea oil operations. The boys were tough, they got injured, or killed, they became bored, a lot quit. But no one could deny that the pay was good. That was what counted for them, and what counted for the Russians was speed.

As a matter of fact, Jeff thought as he looked down the dimly lit aisle of the plane, there might be a representative of a rival firm on this flight. If so, Jeff didn't know what man, even what type of man to look for. Young or old, conservative or—the opposite, he'd be carrying the same kind of papers as Jeff, carrying the same kind of hope. Jeff slumped in his seat, and tried to relax and doze off.

You haven't any time for me *anymore. . . .*

Jeff sat up again. Through the gentle hum of the jets, Phyl's voice had come, straight into his ears. Jeff rubbed his eyes, deliberately yawned, and lay back again. He locked his fingers across his waist, and was about to close his eyes when the girl who looked like Phyl, coatless now and in a light-colored blouse, dark skirt, walked toward him in the aisle. She was going to stop and say something to him, he thought. Absurd! He was half asleep. But he sat up just as the girl passed his seat row, as if to brace himself, as if there weren't two people between him and the girl.

Down the aisle, a pair of horses galloped noiselessly, in color, straight toward the audience. Wide awake now, Jeff suffered a long minute of depression, as if his mind, somewhere unknown even to him, had taken a toboggan ride into a dark valley. He knew why he had gone over his current assignment, why he had reaffirmed his confidence in himself: his work was all he had. And yet he knew that because of his work he had lost Phyl. Phyl had been engaged to Guy. And Guy—or rather his family—had money. Jeff had wanted to compete, to prove himself, in the way he thought would count with Phyl, by making money, solid, big money. Oddly and ironically, Jeff thought, Phyl might have stayed with him if he hadn't made a lot of money, just a bit, and if he'd spent more time with her. Ironically, Phyl had drifted away, because she had thought he was drifting away. They'd had just thirteen months together, composed of a week snatched here and there, a few days in hotels in Chicago, San Francisco, Dallas, happy moments when Jeff had clasped Phyl in his arms (in motels, hotels, in a certain apartment in Evanston rented in Phyl's name), when he had said to her, "Everything went great today! We're ten thousand dollars richer. Maybe more, I haven't figured it out yet." But what had counted, it seemed, and against him, was the time he had spent away from Phyl, too many days, perhaps just three days at a time, but too many. That was how Jeff saw it, anyway. But the loss! When he had thought he had "succeeded" to find it a "failure"! For Phyl, he had summoned all his drive. He didn't regret that.

Wasn't the girl going to return down the aisle? Jeff slumped again and put his hand over his eyes, so he couldn't possibly know when she passed again.

At Roissy Airport, the passengers from Flight 807 trickled toward the passport control desks and became three solid lines. The girl, Jeff saw, was the second person in front of him. Then the man between them hailed someone behind Jeff and quit the line, and Jeff was right behind the girl. She had a white plastic carryall at her feet, and out of the top of it, beside an open carton of Camels from which one pack had been removed, poked the furry head of a toy panda. Jeff let the distance between him and the girl widen by a few inches. The passport stamps thumped, the lines crept. When the girl reached for the carryall, the panda fell out, and the girl didn't notice.

Jeff retrieved the panda. "Excuse me," he said. "You dropped this."

Phyl's eyes glanced at him, then the panda. "Oh, thank you! My good luck piece!" She smiled.

Even her teeth were like Phyl's, the eyeteeth slightly pointed. Jeff acknowledged her thanks with a slight nod. The line moved.

"I'd've missed that. If I'd lost it, I mean. Thanks very much," the girl said over her shoulder.

"Not at all." Was her voice like Phyl's? Not really, Jeff thought.

The girl, then Jeff, passed the control desk and walked into the freedom of Paris. Jeff's pulse slowed to normal. He did not look to see if the girl was being met by any of the people waiting, some of them waving to faces that they recognized.

Jeff was able to claim his suitcase quickly, and then he headed for the taxi rank. He asked the driver to go to the Hôtel Lutetia. It was just after one A.M. and raining slightly.

"*Bon soir,*" Jeff said to the clerk at the hotel desk, and continued in French, "I have a reservation since yesterday. Cormack."

The clerk smiled as he greeted Jeff. Jeff didn't know this clerk, but the clerk evidently knew Jeff's name. "Monsieur Cormack! Yes, sir. You have an *appartement,* as your cable requested. That is number twenty-four, sir."

The bar was still functioning, Jeff saw. He intended to send for a bottle of cold mineral water, maybe coffee also. In his room—a nice, spacious room adjoining a salon—Jeff hung up a dark blue suit and tossed folded white silk pajamas on the turned-down bed, washed his face and hands at the bathroom basin, then picked up the telephone. He had a sudden hunch, for no reason at all, that Kyrogin was at the George V, and he was going to try it.

There was a soft knock at the door. Jeff put the telephone down.

A bellhop stood outside the door with a message on a tray. "A cable for you, sir. We regret we forgot to give it to you downstairs."

"Thank you," Jeff said, and took the cable. He closed the door and tore the envelope open. The cable said:

EITHER INTER-CONTINENTALE OR GEORGE V.

Jeff smiled a little. He'd been right about the George V. That was a good omen. The cable was unsigned. Jeff knew it was from Ed Simmons. Ed had been pulling every string in New York and Moscow to find out where Kyrogin would be staying in Paris, in order to save Jeff some time.

Jeff picked up the telephone again. "I would like to ring the George

V, please." After a few seconds, he had the George V switchboard. "May I speak with Monsieur Kyrogin, please? That's K-y-r-o-g-i-n."

"One moment, sir."

If the clerk demurred about ringing Kyrogin, Jeff was prepared to say that Monsieur Kyrogin was expecting his call, regardless of the hour.

"I am sorry, sir, there is no Monsieur Kyrogin here."

"May I ask what time you are expecting him?" Jeff asked in a tone of confidence.

"We are not expecting him, sir. I have the reservations here before me. No one by the name of Kyrogin is expected."

"I see. Thank you." Jeff put the telephone down. That was a disappointment. Was the operator correct?

There was still the Inter-Continentale, and Jeff took up the phone again, and glanced at his watch. Exactly two A.M. Jeff asked the Lutetia operator to ring the Inter-Continentale for him and, when Jeff's telephone rang, went through the same procedure.

"One moment, sir," said the Inter-Continentale operator. And then, after a moment, "He has not yet arrived, sir."

Jeff smiled, relieved. "But you are expecting him—when?"

"Any moment, sir. The note here says he will be arriving tonight but possibly quite late."

"May I leave a message? I would like him to ring Monsieur Cormack"—Jeff spelled this—"at the Hôtel Lutetia." He gave his hotel's number, which was on a card by the telephone. "It is most important, tell him, and he may ring me when he comes in, at any hour tonight. Is this understood?"

"Yes, sir. Very good, sir."

Jeff was not at all sure Kyrogin would ring at any hour, not if he came in tired at three A.M., not if he was in Paris this very minute, still with his suitcase, talking to the representative of some other firm, and maybe concluding a deal. Kyrogin would know what Jeff's message meant, and he would know the name Cormack from Ander-Mack. So what Jeff had to do tonight was ring every fifteen minutes or so, and hope to catch Kyrogin at the Inter-Continentale when he arrived and before he went to bed and refused to take any calls.

Jeff unpacked the rest of his things, put his attaché case on the writing table in his bedroom and his memo book on the oval table in the salon by the telephone. There was also a telephone by his bedside. Then he lifted the telephone again and ordered a large bottle of Vichy. "Just put it in my room, would you? I'm going down to the bar for a coffee." Jeff suddenly wanted to get out of his room, to move around a little.

He took the stairs down. The first thing he saw, the first thing his eyes focused on, when he reached the lobby, was the girl. The *girl* again. Yes. With the long brown hair, and in the navy blue coat. She stood talking to the man behind the desk. Jeff wanted to speak with the clerk before he went into the bar, and he walked toward the desk with a deliberate casualness.

The clerk looked at him, and Jeff said:

"I'm expecting a telephone call at any moment. I'll be in the bar—at least for the next fifteen minutes."

"*Oui, monsieur,*" said the clerk.

The girl recognized Jeff. "Well—hello again!" She looked a little tired, and worried.

Jeff smiled. "Hello again." He went into the nearly empty bar, and took a stool at the counter. When the barman had finished polishing a glass, Jeff ordered a coffee.

"We are closing soon, sir, but there is just time for a coffee."

The girl—Jeff could see half her figure, the back of her head and coat—stood with an indefinite air in front of the desk. Then she walked slowly with her suitcase and the carryall into the bar. She gave him barely a glance, and took one of the stools three distant from Jeff, occupied it by putting her handbag on it.

"Have you any fresh orange juice?" she asked the barman in English.

"I am sorry, mademoiselle, the bar is close," said the barman in English also. He was again polishing glasses.

"A glass of water?" the girl asked.

"Certainly, miss." The barman poured it and set it in front of her.

She was waiting for someone, Jeff supposed. Maybe the room reserved wasn't in her name. If so, the hotel perhaps couldn't let her take the room. Jeff concentrated on finishing his coffee, which was very hot.

Suddenly—Jeff felt it—the girl turned her eyes toward him.

"Can you imagine, I've had a room reserved here for at least two weeks, and because I'm a day early, maybe a typographical error on some-body's part, not mine—" She gave a sigh. "Well, I'm supposed to wait till noon tomorrow and take a seat in the lobby, unless some other hotel comes up with a room tonight, and it doesn't look like it, because they've already called three."

This burst made Jeff dismount from his stool. His mind was dazzled by the memory of Phyl losing her temper in the same manner, talking in the same way. Jeff was also trying to think of a solution. Some fleabag hotel would have a room at this hour, but he didn't think the girl would want such a hotel. "That's tough.—There's not even a small room free here?"

"No! I've really asked." She sipped her water with an air of disgust.

Jeff put a five-franc piece on the counter. "I'll speak with the desk, see what I can do," he said to the girl, and went into the lobby.

The desk clerk, courteous as ever, said, "I know, Monsieur Cor-mack, it is a mistake with the date. By one day. But we simply have no room, not even a little one. There is only a cot in a servants' corridor—absurd! And the less good hotels—they are not even answering the tele-phone at this hour!" He shrugged.

"I see." Jeff went back into the bar.

The girl looked at him with a faint hope in her face.

"No luck there. If it's just a matter of waiting . . ." He struggled with his words, reassured himself that his objective was to be helpful, and plunged ahead. "You could sit down more comfortably in my suite. I've got two rooms. In what's left of the night . . ."

The girl was hesitating, too tired to decide at once.

"We can speak to the desk, tell them you're in my suite, if you're expecting someone."

"Yes, but I'm expecting someone tomorrow.—Frankly, I'd give any-thing just to wash my face," the girl said in a whisper. She looked near tears.

Jeff smiled. "Come on, we'll tell the desk," he said, and picked up her suitcase. He noticed that the panda was still in the carryall. At the desk, he said, "Mademoiselle has decided to wait in my apartment."

The clerk looked a little surprised, then relieved that the problem had been solved. "*Très bien, monsieur.*" He nodded a good night to them.

They went up in the elevator, which was self-operating, and Jeff pulled out his key and opened the door.

He had left the lights on. He followed the girl into the salon with her suitcase, and closed the door. "Please make yourself at home." He put her suitcase by the sofa. "The bathroom's beyond the bedroom. I think I've got to stay up all night for a business call, so it won't bother me at all if you walk through."

"Thanks *very* much," the girl said.

Then she was in the bathroom, her coat lay on the sofa, her suitcase was opened on the floor, and Jeff stood listening to the water running. He felt curiously stunned. Frightened, even. He didn't want to know if the girl was Phyl's daughter, he realized. He wasn't going to ask her anything that might lead to information about her mother.

Jeff picked up the telephone and asked for the Inter-Continentale again. Now it was 2:37 A.M.

"No, Monsieur Kyrogin has not arrived, sir," said the male voice at the other end.

"Thank you." Jeff felt suddenly discouraged. He imagined Kyrogin having been met at the airport by some enterprising fellow who had found out his arrival time, imagined them talking now in a bar or in the hotel room of the other man, and Kyrogin agreeing to the other man's proposal. They'd maybe toast it in vodka.

The girl came back. Jeff was still standing by the telephone.

She smiled, fresh-faced. "That was wonderful!"

Jeff nodded absently. He had been calculating flying time from Moscow. And could Kyrogin be at another hotel, not the Inter-Continentale, even though he'd made a reservation there? Of course he could be. "I'll go into the bedroom. So make yourself comfortable here. You probably want to sleep. I think that sofa's just about long enough."

She had sat down on the sofa, slipped off her shoes. "Why do you have to stay up all night?" she asked with a childlike curiosity.

"Because—I'm trying to reach a man who's due in from Moscow. And he hasn't arrived at his hotel yet."

"Moscow—you're a government official?"

"No, just an engineer." Jeff smiled. "Would you like some mineral water? It's all I have to offer." The Vichy stood in an ice bucket on the oval table.

The girl said she would, and Jeff poured it. He went to get a glass for himself from the bathroom. The girl had left her wash cloth spread on the basin rim, out of habit, probably. He took off his tie, opened his shirt collar, then took off his jacket. He went back to the anteroom and poured himself a glass of Vichy. He was thirsty.

"I'm going to have a shower," he said. "If the telephone rings, give me a shout, would you? I'm not sure I'll be able to hear it."

"Sure."

Jeff showered, put on pajamas and because of the girl's presence put on also a seersucker dressing gown. He had closed the door to the salon, and now he knocked gently, in case she was asleep.

"Yes?"

He opened the door. The girl was half reclined on the sofa, still dressed, reading a magazine.

"It just occurred to me you might want a shower or a bath. Why not? Anyway you're not going to sit up all night, I hope."

"I don't know. I suddenly don't feel sleepy. Second wind, maybe. It's so strange being here."

Jeff gave a laugh. "It's a strange night. Or morning. I've got to try my quarry again in a minute and after that I'll be reading, too, so it won't bother me in the least if you walk through to the bathroom."

"Thanks. Maybe I will."

Jeff went into his room, this time did not quite close his door, and tried the Inter-Continentale again. The answer was the same. Now it was after three. What other hotel should he try? The Hilton? Should he ring Roissy and ask about incoming flights from Moscow? Abruptly Jeff remembered that he had a bottle of scotch in a plastic bag by his suitcase. He opened the bottle, and poured some into his glass.

Then he tapped on the half-open door again. "Hey . . ." The girl was still reading. "I don't even know your name."

"Eileen."

Eileen what? he wondered, then remembered that he didn't want to know. "Eileen—would you possibly like a nightcap? Scotch."

"Yes! I think that would be nice."

He added scotch to her Vichy water, then brought the bucket and offered it to her. "Ice down there."

"Any luck with your phone calls?" She fished ice cubes out.

"No. No." Jeff took a cigarette.

"What's it all about?—Or is it a secret?"

"Not unless you're a competitor. It's about setting up oil rigs in the White Sea. My firm does that—that kind of thing. We want the job.—And I have a good offer to make," he added, as if thinking out loud or justifying himself, and he began walking slowly around the room. He remembered talking to Phyl about his work, just like this, but in those days he would have been smiling, would have gone to Phyl and kissed her, and then—

"You're a very serious man, aren't you?"

You haven't any time for me anymore, Jeff heard in his ears again. The girl's voice was like Phyl's, or her accent was, and there was a ringing quality in the higher tones, a resonance like that of a stringed instrument, that was also like Phyl's.

"I hope you make it," the girl said. "The White Sea—I only know where the Baltic is."

Jeff smiled. "The White Sea's north of that. The big port there's Archangel." The girl was looking at him in awe, Jeff could see.

She took a swallow of her drink. "I wish I were here for something as sensible as that—as important as that."

Jeff looked at his watch, wishing the time would pass faster, that it would be eight or nine A.M., hours when people could do business. Maybe. "You're here on vacation?"

"I'm here to get married."

"Really?"

"Yeah. It's funny, isn't it? I mean, since I'm alone now. But my mother's due tomorrow and my—my fiancé's coming in a couple of days. We're going to Venice—for the wedding. Well, I'm not sure Mom's coming to Venice. She's funny." The girl looked suddenly uncomfortable and glanced at Jeff with a nervous smile.

Mom was coming to this hotel, Jeff was thinking. He put out his cigarette, started to sit down and didn't. "She's funny?"

"Oh, she thinks *I'm* funny. Maybe it's true. But I'm not sure I want to get married. You see?"

Jeff supposed the young man was a "nice" young man, approved by her family. Jeff wasn't interested in asking anything about him. "If you're not sure, then why do you even consider marrying?"

"That's just it! That's the way *I* feel.—Do you think I could have just a little more scotch?"

"All you want," Jeff said, and set the bottle on the table in front of the sofa. "You pour it."

She poured an inch, the bottle slipped and more went in. Jeff brought the Vichy bottle.

"I wish I were someone else. I wish I weren't *here*. He's—" She stopped, frowning into space. "It's not so much him as the fact I don't want to get tied down. After all, I'm only eighteen."

"Well . . . can't you postpone it?"

"Yes-s. Indefinitely. That's what I'd like to do." She drank off all her glass. "You really wouldn't mind if I took a shower? That's what I need." She stood up.

"All yours," Jeff said, nodding toward the bathroom. "You can even borrow my dressing gown."

In the doorway the girl hesitated, as if it were a big decision, then said, "I'd like to borrow it, if I may, even though I've got one." She held out her hand.

Smiling, Jeff untied his belt, and handed the dressing gown to her. Ah, youth! Troubles! Rebellion! Eileen didn't know yet what troubles were! Apparently she wasn't even in love with the young man. Or was she? Jeff looked into the long mirror between the windows, reassured himself that he was presentable in his pajamas, then something occurred to him that had to do with the word *rebellion*. Phyl had rebelled against her fiancé Guy. Almost for the sake of rebelling, it seemed to Jeff in retrospect—and it was a horrible thought for him. She'd fairly jilted Guy and run off with him, Jeff, for more than a year. Then convention or "sanity" had returned to Phyl, according to her lights. And at what pain to him! He still had the pain, and it was still sharp—after nineteen years. The girl Eileen needed a lecture, Jeff thought, from someone. He wasn't going to give it to her.

He looked at his watch again, as if to drag himself back to his job, his search for the elusive Kyrogin. Before long, they'd be serving breakfast in the hotel. That was what he and the girl needed, a seven A.M. breakfast with strong coffee.

Jeff laughed out loud. Here he was, a forty-four-year-old man in a Paris hotel suite with a good-looking girl he hadn't made the slightest pass at, longing for breakfast at seven A.M., or even earlier if possible. Jeff stared into his own smiling eyes in the long mirror, then the smile left his eyes as it had left his lips. He thought his dark hair had a bit more gray in it than the last time he had taken a look. He touched his cheek. He could use a shave.

The girl was coming in, barefoot, carrying her clothes over her arm. Now she looked even lovelier with her hair slightly dampened. "What were you laughing at?"

Jeff shook his head. "Can't tell you."

"You were laughing at me," she said.

"No!—What does your father say about your marriage?"

"Oh—Dad." She collapsed on the sofa again, dumped her clothes beside her, then took a cigarette and lit it. "Well, basically he takes an 'I'll keep out' attitude, but he definitely wants me to get married. Now, I mean. After all, I quit college because I fell in love, I thought—and because I thought I preferred to get married rather than spend another nearly three years in college. You see?"

Jeff was sitting in an upholstered chair. "I suppose I see. In other words, your mother and father are in agreement—that you ought to get married."

"Yes. But Phyl—that's my mother, and half the time I call her Phyl—she's more insistent about it. I mean, she tries to exert more control over me than Dad.—What's the matter?"

Jeff felt weak, a little dizzy. He sat up and leaned forward, like a man trying to pull out of a faint. "Nothing. Suddenly tired. I think I'll have another snort. I need it." He got up and poured some scotch, straight, into his empty glass. He sipped it, letting it burn his tongue and his throat back to life.

"You look pale. I bet you've been working like mad lately. . . ."

Now she was just like Phyl, comforting in a crisis, ready to minister—providing it was a minor crisis like this one. Jeff slowly felt stronger. The sips of scotch did him good, and quickly.

". . . tell you how much I admire you. You're doing something important. You're a man of the world. You've achieved something."

Jeff exploded in a laugh.

"Don't laugh," the girl said, frowning. "How many men—and you're not even old. My Dad's important, maybe, but he just inherited his job and I bet *you* didn't. And I frankly can't imagine Malc getting very far in life. He's had it too easy."

Malc, Malcolm was doubtless the fiancé. Had Phyl ever mentioned his own name? Jeff wondered. Maybe once or twice? But if only once or twice, the girl wouldn't remember, probably. He hoped she didn't know, or hadn't heard his name. Suddenly the girl stood close in front of him, her hands on his shoulders. She put her arms around his neck.

"Do you mind," she whispered, "if I put my arms around you?"

Jeff's hands lifted also, he pulled the girl toward him, for seconds closed his eyes and felt her hair against his forehead. She was the same height as Phyl. How well he remembered! Then he released her and stepped back.

"You're annoyed?" she asked. "I'll tell you something—straight—if I may. I'd like to go to bed with you." The last words were so soft, he barely heard them.

But he had heard them.

"Are you afraid of me? I'm not going to tell anybody. And I'm not feeling my drinks, if I may say so. I'm quite sober." Her eyes, Phyl's eyes, looked straight at him, steady, and with a smile in them.

"It's not that."

"Not what?"

Why not? Jeff was thinking then. As the girl said, who would know? And what would it matter even if Phyl found out? If Jeff wanted to be vindictive—it would serve Phyl right if she found out. But Jeff really didn't feel vindictive.

"And another thing," the girl continued in the same soft voice, "I'd like to see you again. Maybe again and again. Do you travel a lot? So could I. I'm in the mood for traveling a lot." She still held to Jeff's right hand, and her fingers tightened on his.

His desire was there, and so was a thought, and the thought was that he'd be taking advantage of the girl when she was in an upset state (as nearly every man would, he realized, too), and he was also thinking that he didn't want to lose his memory of Phyl, Phyl as she had been with him, not as this girl would be, a nearly identical copy of Phyl, but not quite identical. Even her face wasn't *quite* identical. Jeff smiled, and tugged his hand from hers. "Take it easy. You're upset."

She wasn't hurt. She looked at him mischievously. "You're an odd one."

He didn't rise to the bait. He lit another cigarette. "You know you're going to marry your Mister Right, so why do you fool around with other people?"

"Do you think I'm in the habit of——"

"Oh, stop the crap!"

This time it sank in. "Now you sound like an American."

"I said I was an American." He was angry, and now he knew why, exactly why. This girl would lead him on, might lead other younger men on, exactly as Phyl had, lead them into misery if they were dumb enough to fall in love. The very harshness of his thoughts made him feel a sudden pity for the girl, as if he had said out loud what he was thinking, and had wounded her. "It doesn't mean . . . I'm your enemy," he said. But of course it did. "Why not leave things the way they are? Simple."

Now she looked puzzled.

The telephone rang, and Jeff for a second relaxed, as if he had been a boxer, saved, and in the next second thought, who could it be except Kyrogin, then thought that was too good to be true. He lifted the telephone.

"Allo?" said a deep voice.

"Hello. Cormack here."

"Ha-ha. Kyrogin here. What time is it?"

Kyrogin sounded a bit drunk. "I dunno. Four, maybe. Mr. Kyrogin, I'd like very much to see you. And thank you for ringing me. You're at the Inter-Continentale?"

"Yes, and I am very sleepy. But I know—I know—you are an American engineer."

"Yes. Look, can I see you early tomorrow morning? I mean this morning? After you've had some sleep?"

Silence. Deep breathing. Was Kyrogin lighting a cigarette or passing out?

"Mr. Kyrogin—Semyon," Jeff said.

"Semyon here," said Kyrogin.

"It's about the White Sea thing, you know," Jeff persisted, thinking if anyone were listening at this hour, they deserved a medal. "Have you—have you done anything about the deal, or can we still discuss it?" Long pause. "Have you spoken with anybody else about it tonight?"

"I was with my French girlfriend tonight," said Kyrogin.

Jeff smiled. "I see." He sat down in the chair behind him. "In that case, after you've slept—can I phone you around ten? I'll phone you around ten. Your first appointment is with *me*, understand, Mr. Kyrogin? Jeff Cormack."

"Right you are," said Kyrogin, as if remembering some of his English lessons. "I have done no work at all tonight," he added sadly.

It was the sweetest confession Jeff had ever heard. "That's all right, Semyon. Sleep well. Good night." Jeff hung up and turned to the girl, beaming.

Eileen smiled back at him, with a look of triumph, as if the victory was hers, too. "You're going to be the first to see him."

"Yes, so it seems." Jeff slapped his hands together, then stood up. "And I'm going to have another scotch."

"Good. May I join you?"

Jeff made them both fresh drinks. The Vichy bottle was empty. He filled the third glass in the bathroom and brought it, in case they wanted more water. He could feel the girl's zest and pleasure in his success (the first step to success, anyway) as he had felt Phyl's in the old days. It was the same. The girl had brought him luck, as Phyl had done. It was Phyl who had given Jeff the courage to break away from his boss, and start a company on his own. Phyl who had launched him like a rocket, Phyl who had given him all the confidence in the world and all the happiness. And Jeff knew he could go to bed with the girl now, as he had so often with Phyl, under the same circumstances, in the same mood. Jeff felt the same desire, and he looked at the girl differently now, as if seeing her for the first time.

She understood. She put her glass down and embraced him, pressed herself against him. "Yes?" she said.

It was still no. And this time Jeff couldn't explain, didn't want to try to find words to explain to himself or to her. "No," he said, and extricated himself.

He went into the bedroom, got his battery razor and went to work on his beard. He brushed his teeth. Then he went in to see the girl.

"I'm going to get some sleep till nine-thirty. Don't you want to do the same?—Maybe you'd prefer my bed and I'll take the sofa?"

"No," she said sleepily, tired at last.

Jeff wasn't going to argue. He was also tired. "Can I ask you one favor?"

"Sure."

"Don't mention my name to your mother—ever. All right?"

"Why should I? You haven't done anything."

He smiled. Maybe she wouldn't remember his name, anyway. "Okay, Eileen. Good night." He closed his door, then rang the desk downstairs and asked to be called at nine-thirty A.M. He got into bed, and after one long sigh fell sound asleep.

When the telephone rang the next morning and awakened him, he found the girl already up and dressed, putting on makeup in the salon mirror. Jeff had ordered breakfast for two.

"What time is your mother due?" he asked.

"Oh—her plane comes in at ten, I think."

Jeff was relieved. He would pack his suitcase, check out this morning and spend—he hoped—most of the morning with Kyrogin. Anyway, Phyl was not due now, or even in the next hour, at the hotel. With his first cup of coffee, Jeff rang up Kyrogin. To Jeff's surprise, Kyrogin answered promptly and sounded wide awake.

"Fine, Mr. Cormack! Come over anytime!"

Jeff packed his suitcase quickly, and when he had closed it, he said to the girl, "You're welcome to stay here till noon, if you like. I'm checking out now, because——"

"Good luck with the Russian," she interrupted him. She was having her breakfast at the oval table in the salon.

Jeff grinned. "Thanks, Eileen. I've got an optimistic feeling. You brought me luck, I think. I'm due there now, so I'll say good-bye."

She had lit a cigarette, and now she stood up. "Bye-bye. Thank you—thank you for putting me up."

"No thanks necessary. Be happy! Bye-bye, Eileen." Jeff went out with his suitcase and attaché case.

He left his suitcase downstairs with the desk clerk, asked for his bill, and said he would settle it later when he came to pick up the suitcase. He was in a hurry to get to Kyrogin. He took a taxi. The ride was not long.

Kyrogin asked Jeff to come up to his room. Kyrogin was in a silk dressing gown, and there was a demolished breakfast tray and a bottle of vodka, half empty, on his table. They ordered more coffee. Kyrogin added vodka to his. The telephone rang, and Kyrogin spoke in English, telling someone he was sorry, he was busy just now. In less than half an hour, Jeff had Kyrogin's verbal agreement. Jeff used his usual method of persuasion, talking first about the difficulties and expense, then estimating the expense and time that another company might take in comparison with Ander-Mack, leaving Kyrogin to make the decision—a verbal one at that, so Kyrogin would not feel bound. Jeff had six copies of his estimate with him, and he gave Kyrogin what he wanted, four, to show his colleagues.

"Now you'll have a vodka maybe," said Kyrogin.

"Now maybe I will. With pleasure! I've got good news to take back to New York."

"Phone them now. Tell them!" said Kyrogin with a wave of his hand toward the telephone.

"I'd like to. You really don't mind?" Jeff was moving toward the telephone. Plainly Kyrogin wouldn't mind. Jeff asked the operator to dial a New York number which was Ed Simmons's home number. It would be around five A.M. in New York, but Ed wouldn't mind being awakened with the news Jeff had. The operator said she would ring Jeff back, and then said the call was going through at once, and Jeff could hear Ed's telephone ringing.

Ed answered sleepily, and came awake at the sound of Jeff's voice.

"It's okay at this end!" Jeff said.

"We've got the deal?"

"We've got it. See you soon as pos, old pal." Jeff hung up.

Kyrogin gave Jeff an excellent cigar. It was like the old days, Jeff thought, when he'd been twenty-three and had concluded a fabulous deal (or so he'd thought then) and would be going home to—to Phyl, Phyl somewhere. It was because of the girl Eileen that Phyl seemed so close now, Phyl with the twinkle in her eyes, her pride in his victory that was like a whole football stadium cheering. And each victory had meant he was closer to her. . . .

"What are you thinking about?" Kyrogin asked through a cloud of cigar smoke, smiling.

"I was daydreaming. It's your good vodka," Jeff said, and stood up and took his leave. They shook hands warmly. The Russian had a powerful grip.

It was already two minutes to noon. Jeff took a taxi at the door of Kyrogin's hotel and rode to the Lutetia.

When he walked into the lobby, he saw the girl again. And with her was Phyl. Now he really stopped dead, a couple of paces within the lobby. Phyl wore a hat. She was standing at a little distance from the desk, and she was plainly angry, furious even. Her cheeks were a bright pink as she delivered a tirade, apparently, to her daughter. Phyl looked shorter than the girl, than he remembered her, but it was because she had gained weight, Jeff realized. Phyl raised a fist and brandished it. The girl barely turned her head, didn't retreat. What was Phyl scolding her about? Phyl might have heard that the girl had spent the night in a man's suite, either from the girl herself or from the desk, Jeff supposed.

Suddenly his dream fell away. Something fell away, something died. Everything died. Phyl turned toward him, but in her anger didn't see him, and Jeff saw that her face had grown pudgy, that her shorter hair under the hat was some odd reddish color. But it wasn't that that upset him, it was the wrath in her face, the ugliness of spirit—her scolding of the girl. And he was positive Phyl was scolding her because she'd spent the night in a hotel room with a man, even if she "hadn't done anything." It was the goddamn prudishness, the conventionality, the phoniness, the holier-than-thou or than-the-girl part of it, the hypocrisy—because for Christ's sake, hadn't Phyl done the same thing when she was the girl's age? Had an affair with a man if she damned pleased—the man being Jeff? And then, of course, back to Mister Right, back to the respectably-married-woman act, which she so ponderously embodied now.

Was *this* what he'd been in love with all this time?

Suppose he was married to Phyl now?

Jeff felt about to die. He wasn't weak, wasn't swaying on his feet. In fact he stood like a statue, where he was. Then Phyl and Eileen moved, toward the elevators, Phyl's figure still stiff with rage, the girl's flexible and rebellious. And Jeff was reminded of what he'd thought upstairs in his hotel room: the girl, like Phyl, would go on from him, find another fellow (maybe before she married) and lead him on, and abandon him, and get married, and maybe have a daughter—very pretty, of course—who'd do the same thing, in endless progression or procession.

And there was a second terrible thought, which Jeff had now and not for the first time, that if Phyl had betrayed Guy, who'd been not yet her husband but almost, then he, Jeff, might have been betrayed also in due time, even if he had married Phyl. If promises to lovers didn't mean much, then neither would marital vows. In fact, which came first and which second? Yet it all hung together, and there was nothing lasting, for girls like Phyl, about any of it. What counted finally was "the way things looked." And what girls like Phyl had in common was a certain coldness at the heart.

The elevator door mercifully closed the two of them from Jeff's sight.

Jeff went and claimed his suitcase. He pulled his bill from a pocket, and paid in cash. Then he walked out of the hotel with his suitcase and attaché case, and said, "No" to the doorman who offered to hail a taxi for him. Jeff walked on, and for no particular reason turned the first corner to the right. He was lucid enough to know that he was in a daze, that somehow nothing mattered any longer, where he went, what he did, where he was, even who he was. Or what time it was, or what country it was. For several minutes Jeff walked with his suitcase that did not weigh much.

The holier-than-thou, do-the-right-thing attitude, Jeff was thinking. It was disgusting. Not like Phyl at all! And yet it was Phyl, now. He'd been living on a dream, some crazy dream. A dream of what? Not even a dream of marrying her one day, but still a dream. If he only hadn't seen her this morning!

Well, then what?

He'd be able to live, that was what. That was clear. That was the only thing that was clear. It was something, to have something clear. And he'd succeeded with Kyrogin, and he'd be going back today to New York, to his office. And all this suddenly didn't matter a damn. All of it mattered as little as the phony home he had with Betty, the phony outward appearance of a decent marriage, a teenage son going to the right school. Money. It didn't mean anything. His life simply didn't mean anything.

Somebody jolted Jeff in the shoulders. Jeff realized he was standing at the crossing of a big four- or six-lane avenue, and he hadn't moved when the lights permitted the pedestrians to cross. But Jeff knew what he wanted to do, or rather half his mind knew, or realized. The other half didn't matter. He wasn't thinking. He knew he was past the point of thinking. Hadn't he thought enough? All this went through his head in seconds, and when a big truck came thundering toward him, going to pass him at full speed right in front of him, Jeff dropped his suitcase and attaché case and flung himself in front of it, flat down, like a football tackler tackling nothing. He felt only the impact of the cobbly street, really.

IT'S A DEAL

After Joel had done it, he collapsed in a chair in the bedroom, out of breath, depleted. He looked at his dead wife lying aslant on the bed, the toes of her bare left foot touching the white rug, shuddered and closed his eyes—not out of genuine horror or remorse, he thought, but because confronted by a bruised corpse, no matter whose it was, one probably involuntarily shuddered and closed one's eyes.

He had come home and found Lucy beaten up—by Robbie, of course, who had just left the house—and Joel had simply finished the job. In a fury of pent-up hatred, he had lashed out at Lucy with his fists, the backs of his hands, maybe even his feet, and finished what Robbie Vanderholt had started. They'd hardly said a word, he and Lucy, and if they had, he couldn't remember it now. Maybe he'd said, "That's a fine black eye Robbie gave you," or maybe he hadn't.

A sound of splattering water in the bathroom made him jump up. The tub was running over. Joel plunged a hand into the hot water and turned it off, then pulled the stopper that drained the tub.

He had to get rid of the body. A classical problem. He took off his jacket and stood tensely in the bedroom, looking at Lucy. There was no blood. Two not-quite-finished glasses of scotch and soda, with the little soda bottle, stood on the low chest of drawers against the wall. Robbie's fingerprints would be everywhere. Robbie's cork-tipped cigarettes had been left behind, and one of the butts was in an ashtray. Robbie was the man.

Joel looked at his watch: 5:35 P.M. Friday afternoon. He went out and stood on the lawn between the house and his car, which was halfway up the driveway. The next house was thirty yards away, Betty Newman's house, where her eleven-year-old son was throwing a balsa wood air-plane around on the lawn. A light was on in the kitchen. If Betty looked out and saw him now, fine, Joel thought. He'd look a little puzzled, as if he'd come out to see if Lucy was anywhere around, and found that she wasn't. Joel walked around the garage until he could see the low, smoke-blue skyline of Pennerlake, the town where he worked. Beyond Penner-lake, where the land rose paler blue yet, were some mountains and a forest. Last Sunday, driving about aimlessly after a quarrel with Lucy, he had seen that they had planted hundreds of little pines on the side of one mountain there. The ground was dug up and loose. It would be a fine spot for burying a body.

A few minutes before eight o'clock, Joel telephoned the Richard-sons in Pennerlake. Jamie Richardson answered.

"Hi," Joel said. "This is Joel Lucas. I don't suppose my other half—my better half—is still playing bridge or something?"

"Ha-a!" Jamie shrieked like a squeezed chicken. "Bridge day's Tues-day, dear. She's not here."

"Oh. Any idea where she is?"

"No, not the slightest." (And Joel heard a note of satisfaction in that.) "She didn't leave you a note? When were you expecting her?"

Joel smiled a little, detecting satisfaction in Jamie's question, too. Everyone knew about Lucy's afternoon pastimes. "Usually she's home when I come home," Joel said with husbandly loyalty. "She could have gone to the supermarket, but I've been home since about five-thirty."

"Well—sorry I can't help you, Joel."

The telephone did not ring that evening. Joel and Lucy had planned to go to a drive-in movie. They had no engagements until tomorrow evening, when they were supposed to go to Manhattan to join Gert and Stan Merrill for an early dinner and the theater, for which Stan had the tickets.

Around ten P.M., Joel force himself into the bedroom, got the army blanket, which they never used except in emergency, from the closet, and bent Lucy's legs, folded her arms, until she took up as small a space as pos-sible, and threw the blanket over her. He closed the bedroom door and slept on the living room sofa.

He did not sleep well, but he used his waking moments to think about Robbie Vanderholt. Robbie was around thirty, dark-haired, a well-paid accountant with a Philadelphia firm. Lucy had met him at a party given by the Merrills. Or had it been a party in Philadelphia? No matter. Robbie had a way of twitching his mouth and rubbing his forefinger vigorously against the side of his nose, and sometimes he shifted on his feet at the same time. This seemed to give him a boyish appeal to women, but it had as much charm to Joel as an epileptic attack. Under the surface, Robbie was arrogant and belligerent. Robbie dressed carelessly, and affected corduroys and caps on weekends. Joel had no cap, but he did have a pair of old brown corduroys.

His plan was bold and brazen, right in the open air, really, but Joel thought boldness the wisest course.

Joel risked one more telephone call the next morning. He called the Zabriskies. The Zabriskies had three children. Sometimes Lucy baby-sat for them at odd hours of the day. Mrs. Zabriskie always picked Lucy up, as Joel used the one car to get to work. Lucy wasn't at the Zabriskies', either.

"I thought she might have spent the night or something," Joel said gloomily. "I haven't seen her since yesterday morning."

"My *goodness*," said Hazel Zabriskie. "Maybe she . . ."

Joel imagined her face smiling with amusement but frowning also for the benefit of the telephone, which could not convey her image. *Maybe she's with a boyfriend,* Hazel wanted to say. "Well—I'll make a couple more phone calls," Joel said.

Then he put on the corduroys, and suddenly remembered a cap someone had given him years ago for Christmas. He had to look in three suitcases full of clothes in the attic, but at last he found it—a black and white houndstooth pattern, spuriously new, but a little grubbing with it on the garage floor would fix that, and it was safer to wear this one than to buy one somewhere. Joel went down with it to the garage. He drove his car into the garage, and carried Lucy's body in the blanket out the door that opened from one side of the living room. With a fine disdain, he wedged her between the back of the front seat and the backseat, on the floor. Then he put the spade into the car, and threw onto the backseat a roll of twine and three or four old burlap bags from the stack in a corner of the garage. He drove off for the mountain where he had seen the pines being planted.

The road became unpaved, and gravel crackled against the back fenders. It was the ideal country for Boy Scout expeditions, but Joel didn't see any. He saw absolutely no one. Here the forest was wild, and among the giant oaks and pines grew an occasional little pine. Joel stopped the car and got out with his spade. He knew that a pine, even a baby one, had formidable roots. It took him nearly ten minutes to dig up a little pine tree. He put the pine in the backseat, got in himself and stuck the tree's roots as far down as he could in an opening of the blanket. Then he put the burlap bags around Lucy and the roots, and tied it up. This was a long operation, as he had to get the twine under Lucy's weight a couple of times. A fitting memorial, he thought, a little pine tree, and better than she deserved. Long may its roots be nourished by her—by her what? Her rich experiences, perhaps.

He drove on to the newly forested section of the mountain, which now resembled the side of a ham stuck with green cloves—other little pine trees. He noted with a faint dismay that a picnicking unit, table, benches, and rubbish basket, had sprung up in a clearing just to the side of the planted area. But it was only a bit after ten A.M., and he doubted if any picnickers would arrive before noon. The worst moment was now, when he had to carry Lucy's hundred-and-ten-pound weight, topped by the tree, from the car up the slope of the mountain. Joel had imagined parking the car out of sight of the place of interment, but he remembered the weight from the bedroom to the garage. He decided to chance it, and stopped the car at the side of the road, took the big bundle out, and tottered up the hill with it. He forced himself onward and upward, and at last dumped his load, gasping. Joel trotted down the hill, got into his car, and drove it about sixty yards farther along the dirt road, where he saw a lane that went steeply up to the right. He went a little way up this, got his spade out, and returned to his baby pine.

The sun was clear and strong, and soon he was perspiring. He struck thin, leathery roots from the big trees nearby. He rested, panting, when the hole was two feet deep, not nearly deep enough.

And here came three people, two young men and a girl, with picnic baskets. They were all laughing. Joel braced himself for the possibility that they were going to plunk themselves down at the picnic table, forty feet away. They seemed to be having a little discussion, a little variance of opinion about this, so Joel looked away and poked with his spade at the hole he had dug. *Face up to it, if it happens,* he told himself. *You're planting a tree.*

"Mister!—Sir!" called the girl, and began to laugh so much, she couldn't talk, as the boys behind her guffawed. She came on toward him. "My friends have just made a bet with me that I'd ask you—I mean, *wouldn't* ask you"—more laughter—"if you're burying your wife."

Joel's face spread in a shy grin, but he kept his head down. He twisted his face around and rubbed his nose. "Yep." He shifted on his feet and gestured toward the hump of what was supposed to be the pine tree's roots. "You tell them that's just what I'm doing, burying my wife."

The girl turned around and called, "Yes!" to her two waiting friends.

The boys roared again, and doubled up.

"'Bye now. Thank you. I've won!" said the girl, and ran down the hill in her tight dungarees and sneakers.

Joel leaned on his spade and watched them. It was over. He rubbed his nose again as the girl looked back and gave him a friendly wave. Then the trio moved out of sight.

Perfect, Joel thought. Lucy's body might never be found, but if it was, the trail would lead straight to Robbie Vanderholt.

In the twenty minutes more that it took him, nobody passed by. He walked away with his spade without a backward look.

Joel went home and changed into the old gray slacks he usually wore on weekends. Then he took the cap and corduroys out with the collection of paper trash that he always burned on Saturdays, and lit a fire in the wire basket behind the house. When all the cloth of the cap and trousers had become ashes, he went into the house and called the Merrills.

"Hi, Stan, this is Joel. Listen, about our date tonight—I don't know where *Lucy* is."

"What do you mean?"

"I mean, she wasn't here when I got home yesterday. I've called a couple of people, but no luck."

"Hm-m," said Stan Merrill, knowing full well. "You mean you really don't know where to call her?"

"Well—I could try a couple of other places, I suppose. But I didn't want to hold you people up about tonight. I better call you again after I find her. She might—you know—not feel like going tonight."

"Yeah," Stan said in a disappointed tone. "Well, let me know, Joel, and good luck."

Then Joel looked up Robert Vanderholt's number in the Philadelphia directory and called him.

"I hope I'm not disturbing you," Joel said, "but do you happen to know where my wife is?"

Robbie gave a laugh. "No, I don't."

"You don't? Didn't you see her yesterday afternoon? Say around five?"

"Yes, I did see her yesterday," Robbie said. "Maybe she went out afterwards for a long walk."

"If so, she hasn't come back. You evidently had a little argument with her. The room was sort of a mess."

"Oh? Sorry."

Joel set his feet firmly on the floor. "I'm not kidding, Robbie, where is she? I don't want any more games."

"I'm not playing games, either. I left her in the house. Why don't you keep a better watch on her?" Robbie put the telephone down.

Joel was furious for an instant, then he smiled.

It was now time for the police. Joel looked up the number in the front of his Pennerlake and vicinity directory, called, and told them his trouble. Yes, he had asked everyone he knew to ask. "Twenty-six years old, five feet two, dark blond hair, blue eyes, a hundred and ten pounds," Joel said in answer to their questions.

The police said they would send out a missing persons alarm, and would also come to his house.

Two policemen arrived thirty minutes later. Joel was smoking a cigarette and walking the floor. In the course of their inquiry, they looked in the bedroom, which Joel had left just as it was. No, he had not been having a drink with her, he said, her guest had been Robert Vanderholt, whom of course Joel had already telephoned. Lucy wasn't with him.

"Still—it seems he was the last person who saw her," Joel added. "The last I know of, that is. He said she was here when he left."

"The bedspread was like this, too?" asked one of the policemen.

"Yes. Sort of twisted. I . . . just left the room the way it was. Didn't even sleep in here last night."

This remark led them into the relationship between Lucy and Robbie, which Joel disclosed with appropriate reluctance. "I suppose they're having an affair—yes."

Then the police went off to visit Robert Vanderholt. In about an hour, they brought Robbie back with them. Robbie was in a go-to-hell, what-do-I-know-about-it mood, but nervousness made him grimace and rub his nose, and Joel thought it made a bad impression on the police.

"What did you do after you left her yesterday at five o'clock?" asked one of the policemen.

"I went home—played some records—stayed in," Robbie said.

"Did you have a quarrel with Mrs. Lucas yesterday?"

They were all standing in the bedroom, and now Robbie looked around him uneasily at the twisted bedspread, the glasses in which some pale scotch and water remained.

"We had a little quarrel, yes," Robbie said.

"What about?"

Robbie shrugged, then rubbed his nose again. "It's embarrassing to say, but we quarreled because Lucy wanted to see me more often." He threw a cocky glance at Joel.

"Did you strike her?" asked the policeman.

"I did, I'm sorry to say. I slapped her face. She hit me back, then I pushed her and she fell on the bed."

"Anything after that?"

"No, I walked out after that."

"Did she make any threats? Say where she might go?"

"No. If you want my opinion, she called for a taxi, took it to Philly or New York and spent last night in a hotel—under another name. She wants to get everybody worried over her. Or maybe she's hiding a black eye, I don't know." Robbie shifted and started toward the door, as if he considered the interview over.

The two policemen seemed to think it was over, too. One said to Joel, "We'll keep you posted, Mr. Lucas."

Betty Newman was looking out her window as the police went off. She came over with Chuckie, her son, trailing behind.

"Something the matter, Joel?" she asked.

"Joel looked worried. "I don't know. I can't find Lucy. I haven't seen her since yesterday morning at breakfast."

"*What?*"

Joel explained the situation and why he had called the police. "When did you see her last, Betty?"

"I don't think I saw her all yesterday.—No, I didn't. I go off at eight-thirty, you know, and I'm not back till four-thirty." Betty was a cashier at a roadside diner near Pennerlake. Her husband had run off with another woman years ago, Joel had heard. Betty was rather blowsy and getting on to forty. She and Lucy had never been chummy.

"One of our friends—uh—visited Lucy yesterday afternoon," Joel said.

"I do remember seeing a blue convertible in your driveway, yes," Betty said with an air of innocence, though Joel was sure she knew, just as the whole neighborhood knew, about Lucy.

"And do you know if Lucy went off with him? Around five?"

"I don't know. I really don't."

That was just the answer Joel wanted.

"You think she was maybe kidnapped and murdered?" asked Chuckie Newman, who had been listening intently.

"Chuckie!" said his mother in horror.

Joel felt his face go fittingly white. "Let's hope not."

Then Joel went into his house and called the Merrills. He said they had better not count on him and Lucy making it that evening, and to find another couple who could use the tickets. The Merrills didn't sound too upset, but asked him to call them as soon as he found out anything.

Sunday morning at eight, Joel was awakened by a telephone call from the Pennerlake police.

"Last night," said the police officer, "a girl named Elinor Farrington called up after she heard the missing persons report on the radio. She said she and a couple of fellows had a conversation with a man planting a tree on Scrubby Mountain, kidding him, y'know, about maybe he was burying his wife. He said he was. Well, we couldn't investigate last night in the dark, but we did early this morning. Mr. Lucas, there was a body under that new tree, and the description certainly fits your wife's, so we'd like you to come over to the station and have a look, if you don't mind."

Joel said he would be right over. He put on a fresh shirt and his best suit, thinking he might see the Farrington girl at the station.

They had Lucy on a table in a back room. Joel identified her.

"You recognize this blanket, Mr. Lucas?" asked the policeman, holding up the army blanket.

Joel nodded. "It's from our house."

"The Farrington girl described the man she saw planting the tree. About five-ten, around thirty, wearing corduroy pants and a cap. She can't remember what color hair he had. I'd like you to talk to her." He led Joel toward another room.

The Farrington girl, very sober-faced now and in a skirt, was sitting on a straight chair in a kind of waiting room. She repeated her description of the man she saw planting the tree, while Joel, looking very straightforward and neat in his dark blue suit and white shirt, listened attentively.

"She doesn't remember seeing any car nearby," the officer said to Joel. Then, to the girl, "Is this the man you saw?"

Elinor Farrington looked at Joel, looked him up and down. "I don't think so, because the man was a different type. Very different. He was sort of squirmy. He rubbed his nose and wouldn't look me in the eye."

The police officer looked at Joel. "Any ideas who the killer might be, Mr. Lucas?"

"I'm bound to have an idea," Joel said carefully, "and I think it was the last person she was with. Robbie Vanderholt. Look at the way she was dressed—or rather not dressed." He cleared his throat. "I think Vanderholt killed her and took her body out in the army blanket, kept it in his car over Friday night, and buried her yesterday morning. What else can I think?"

"We'll go back to Vanderholt," said the police officer.

Joel went home again.

Before noon, the telephone rang, and the police had made great progress. They had found several caps and four pairs of corduroys, one old and mud-stained, in Vanderholt's closet. They had brought Vanderholt to the Pennerlake station and the Farrington girl had identified him.

"Vanderholt says he didn't do it," said the officer, "but he may break down in a few hours."

Joel called up the Merrills and solemnly reported the news: Robbie Vanderholt had killed Lucy. The Merrills had seen Robbie a couple of times, had noticed Lucy's interest in him, Joel knew, and so undoubtedly guessed that he was her latest.

"You poor darling!" Gert Merrill said. "Would you like to come and stay with us for a few days? You shouldn't be in that house all alone."

Joel protested bravely that he was bearing up all right. And so he did to the Zabriskies and the Richardsons and a few other people who called up after the news appeared in Monday morning's newspapers. Three months later, the trial was over, and Robbie Vanderholt was sentenced to twenty-five years in a Trenton prison. He protested his innocence to the last, and accused Joel of having killed her in anger, but Robbie's words didn't stand up against fact: Robbie had a lot of corduroys and caps, Robbie twisted his face and rubbed his nose (he had on the stand also), and the Farrington girl had positively identified him.

Lucy's income from a trust fund left her by her family reverted to Joel: a hundred and fifty dollars per month, a sum that Lucy had managed to spend entirely on herself. Joel had certainly not killed her for that, but it was a nice addition to his salary. He bought a few things that he had wanted for a long time, a stereo, a new set of golf clubs, and a new dinner suit. He especially needed the last, as his friends were constantly inviting him to dinners to meet this or that pretty and eligible girl. Joel enjoyed his role as widower, after six months still too stunned by his wife's murder to contemplate marrying again, though his friends had reached the point of saying he deserved a better life than Lucy had been leading him.

One evening around nine, when Joel had just got settled with a beer in front of a promising television play, his doorbell rang. It was Betty Newman from next door.

"Oh, hello," Joel said, surprised. "Come in."

"Thanks." Betty came in. She was in high heels, and Joel got a whiff of perfume as she walked past him.

"I was just starting to watch some TV," Joel said. "Want to——"

"I'm not much in the mood," Betty interrupted.

After a couple of minutes, it was obvious what she was in the mood for, and Joel was flabbergasted. Betty had had him over to dinner a couple of times since Lucy's death, but there hadn't been a hint of anything romantic or sexy in her attitude. Joel parried her as politely as he could.

"Oh, come on, Betty. I'm very flattered, but—I guess I'm the old-fashioned type. I still believe marital bliss is the only real thing, and I'd rather—"

"As a matter of fact, I'm talking about marriage," Betty said. She was leaning back on his sofa now, with a glass of beer. Her pudgy face looked even less attractive than usual with the extra lipstick and the splotches of rouge on her cheeks.

"Well—I certainly can't think of marriage yet."

"Can't you? I think you'd better. I know a little secret about you, Joel. And I think I've waited a decent length of time, don't you?"

Then Joel knew, and ice went down his veins. He sat up stiffly in his armchair. "What're you talking about?" he asked with an effort at a smile, and at the same time he was thinking: Betty might suspect, but she can't *prove* anything. Maybe she saw him drive out of the garage that Saturday morning, but she hadn't seen the body on the floor in the back of the car.

"I know what you're thinking," Betty said. "But I saw Robbie Van-derholt go off by himself at five-fifteen that afternoon. He wasn't carrying any corpse with him. Then you came home." She waited.

"You're making that up, Betty."

"I am not. And furthermore, I'll spill it to the police—if you're not more cooperative. I've been very cooperative with the police so far—from your point of view."

Joel chewed the inside of his cheek, suddenly seeing a vista, a long one, of his life ahead with Betty. Saggy breasts and blowsy cheeks and that awful freckle-faced goon of a son that went with the deal. A situation that would inspire a second murder, if any situation would. But he could never dare risk a second murder. Or could he?

Betty recrossed her plump legs. She looked absolutely confident. "I'll make you as happy as I can, Joel. How about it? Don't you think we could have a pretty good life together?" She smiled as winningly as she was able.

His heart heaved, like a sick stomach. "Yeah, sure, Betty. Sure we could."

"So, it's a deal?"

It's a deal," Joel said.

THINGS HAD GONE BADLY

This was the story in the newspapers, in the local paper and in the *New York Times,* and it merited about five lines in both:

> *Robert Lottman, 25, a sculptor, confessed having killed his wife, Lee, 23, by blows about the head with a rolling pin in the kitchen of their home near Bloomington, Indiana. Their two-year-old daughter, Melinda, in the kitchen at the time, was unhurt in her crib when police arrived, after having been summoned by Lottman.*

Robert Lottman went quietly into the hands of the police, then into a jail cell, his manner described by one journalist as "cool" and by another as "cold and indifferent."

The two-year-old Melinda was at once sent to her grandmother, Evelyn Watts, of Evanston, Illinois. Mrs. Watts expressed disbelief of her son-in-law's act. She had liked Robert Lottman, until now. She had been sure that he loved her daughter. She couldn't understand why the murder had happened. She had never seen Robert lose his temper. Robert didn't drink or take drugs. What had happened?

The psychiatrists—two—were asking the same questions in the Bloomington jail. They were not keenly interested, but a psychiatric questionnaire was a necessary formality.

"I don't know," Robert Lottman replied. "I loved her, yes. I loved her." He detested saying that to the officially engaged psychiatrists, but it seemed little to reveal, since why should he have married Lee if he hadn't loved her?

"You had quarrels?" said one psychiatrist. It was more a statement than a question. "Fights before?" That was a question.

"No, never," said Robert. He looked his interrogator in the eyes.

"Then why did you do this?" Long pause. "Sudden fit of temper?"

Robert remained silent, uncomfortable. He was thinking that he didn't have to answer, anyway. Since he had admitted striking the fatal blows, what did it matter if they had had a quarrel, if he had had a fit of temper, or not? "I was not angry," Robert said finally, hoping this would satisfy the two and that they would go away. He had been sitting on the hard chair for twenty minutes.

Now the dark-haired psychiatrist said to Robert, "You know, if you and your wife had been having a quarrel—about anything—it could be a manslaughter charge. Lighter than premeditated murder."

"Come on, Stanley, no one's bringing up premeditated in this—as yet. It's a household affair."

Robert wanted to switch them both off. He wagged his head, tired and bored. The psychiatrists might think that movement "evasive," he thought. Robert did not feel in the least evasive. He felt contemptuous of the two men before him, questioning him. Robert had pride. He was not going to tell them why he killed Lee. These two might never understand. They didn't look the types to take the time. Maybe he would write out why he had killed Lee. But write it for whom? Not the court, certainly. Maybe for himself only. Robert was a sculptor, not a writer, but he could make himself clear in words if he wanted to.

"We're trying to do the best for you before the—the—uh—trial," said one of the men.

"Sentence. Before the sentence," said the other.

The best for him? What did it matter? Robert said nothing.

"You don't care what kind of sentence they give you?" asked the dark-haired one.

"That's correct. I don't care."

"There wasn't another man in the picture?" asked the plump, bald-ish one, in a tone of hoping that there had been.

"No. I've said that." How he had hoped for another man! "Isn't this enough? I don't know how I can tell you any more."

A minute later he was free, at least of those two. A prison guard came in and accompanied him back to his cell. Robert paid no attention to the guard. He had no intention of trying to escape out one of the doors, two of which gave onto a parking lot. The jail did not look grim or well guarded, it was just a jail.

Robert's mind was on *another man*. There had not been another man. Funny, in a way, since Lee had been so fantastically popular when Robert had met her.

Back in his cell he was still thinking of that, Lee's popularity. She had been twenty going to art school in Chicago, when Robert met her. He had visited the Reinecker Art Institute in quest of a part-time job, two or three mornings a week, teaching sculpture. He had his own credentials from the Art Students League in New York and from a Brooklyn academy, less well known, but he had a prize from that school, attested to by a certificate and a photograph of his work which had taken first prize. The Reinecker, however, had wanted a teacher for five mornings a week, and Robert had hesitated, said he would think it over. Nine to noon, five days a week. They would have taken Robert on, yes, and they hadn't thought it unusual that Robert wished to consider it for a few days. Robert had walked out of the superintendent's office and into the hall, down a short flight of stairs, and met Lee coming up the stairs.

He had not met her in the usual sense, and she had been with two young men, one on either side of her, all three talking, as Robert remembered it, but his eyes had met Lee's eyes for an instant. Robert could still see it as clearly as if it had been a color photograph that he carried with him. Lee was blond, not very tall, and had blue eyes. She had been wearing beige trousers, like chino pants, a pale blue shirt or blouse.

Robert had turned and followed her. She had a smooth, oval face, a high forehead, round and rather bulging. The important thing was her eyes—intelligent, appraising, cool. Who wouldn't have followed those eyes? Robert wondered. As he had walked behind the trio in the corridor, Lee had looked back once at him, aware that he was following her. The two boys with her had eyes only for Lee, Robert remembered. Robert was to see plenty of this later. But Lee had stopped and turned, looking at him.

Robert had said, "Hello," like one stunned. Hadn't the other two fallen back a step, stunned also in the presence of love at first sight? Robert was not sure. He had managed to get out something, because he wanted her as a model, quite apart from the fact that he had fallen suddenly in love with her. "You're a student here?" Maybe he had said something like that. Anyway, Lee had said that she was not studying painting any longer and was intending to go to a photography school, somewhere else. Robert had whipped his little sketchbook from a back pocket, a pencil, had got Lee's name and address, and had given her his own. She had a telephone number. She lived with her mother in Evanston.

She had liked him, that was the important thing, enough to give him her name and address. And suddenly, too, she had been walking with him, back down the long cream-colored corridor with its closed doors on either side, bulletins and posters everywhere on the walls—and the other two young men had vanished, or were maybe standing in the corridor behind them, puzzled.

And then things had gone badly.

Robert was now sitting on his bed, thinking: *things had gone badly.* But he was thinking of two periods of time—just after he had met Lee and the past weeks. Between times about three years had passed.

In the first bad or uncertain period, just after he met Lee, it had seemed to Robert that she was afraid of him. She refused to make dates with him, she wrote him an ambiguous note: did she want to see him again, or not? Robert lived just thirty miles or so from Evanston. One of the young men in whose company Robert had first seen Lee was still present and in full force. This Robert had discovered when he had his first date with Lee. She had had to ease the young man politely from her mother's house, and he had gone off with a smirk at Robert, as if to say, "You're wasting your time, fellow."

Robert and Lee had gone back to her mother's house after dinner (her mother was divorced), and Lee had shown him her drawings, some paintings that were not as good as her drawings, and her new photographic efforts. Robert was impressed. Many were portraits of people she knew, young and old. She had imagination and energy. The energy showed in Lee herself—a strong body neither slender nor sturdy but something in between, with a grace of movement. Above all, her energy showed in her enthusiasm for her work.

Robert had blurted out around midnight, "I *love* you—you know?" Then Lee had been silent, as if surprised (how could she be, when half a dozen men must be in love with her? Robert had thought), and then she had gone on putting away her photographs in their labeled folders and portfolios. He had not tried to take her hand or to kiss her.

And then silence—for two weeks, for a month. She was too busy to make dates, she said when he telephoned. And Robert recalled his friends' advice, with mingled gratefulness and annoyance: "Play it cool, Bob, and she'll come around to you." He was not the type to play it cool, but he had done his best, and Lee had come around, made dates with him, even said yes when he asked her to marry him. By then they had been to bed together several times in his studio. Robert was head over heels. He felt he had met a goddess. He did not care for the word *goddess,* but he didn't know what else to liken her to, because there was no other girl in the world like her.

The advice. Robert lit one of his remaining five cigarettes. *Advice* reminded him of his parents in New York. They had telephoned him yesterday, and he had been allowed to speak with both of them.

"Is it true, Bobby?" his mother had asked in a voice that pained Robert to remember.

"We just can't believe it," his father had said in a heavy, hopeless tone. "We thought it was a mistake—of names, identity—"

It wasn't a mistake, Robert had told him. Yes, he had done it. How could he explain on the telephone? Did it really matter if he explained it, much as he liked and loved his parents? Could they ever understand even if he wrote it out for them? "My life is finished," Robert had said at the end. The guard had beckoned to him then (even though his parents had been paying for the call), and Robert had told his father that he had to hang up.

If he were writing it—Robert was walking around his cell, whose confinement and barred door did not bother him in the least now—he would say that Lee had become a different person. That was it, and Robert had realized that long ago, nearly two years ago. If he ever wrote anything about Lee and himself, he would have to say this from the start and emphatically. That was the essence, and that was what he had been unable to take, or accept, whatever you wanted to call it. *His fault.* Sure. Lee had the right to change, or maybe just to become herself.

When the baby was less than a year old, Robert had asked her if she wanted to divorce him.

"But why?" Lee had asked back. "What's wrong, Bob? Are you so unhappy?"

They hadn't made love for a month or more. Robert couldn't, and maybe Lee hadn't even noticed, absorbed as she was in Melinda. It wasn't the act or the pleasure of making love that was so important, meaning not even the absence of it was so important, but the fact that Lee had become another person with motherhood—formidable word—and with all the fussing around the house, which had begun early in their marriage. Gradually she had dropped her photography. The equipment in her darkroom had begun to gather dust before Melinda's birth, Robert remembered. They had got a mortgage on a pretty house, not too big or too small, outside the town where Robert had had his rented studio. There had been a period of shopping for furniture, curtains, buying a fridge and a stove, but Lee hadn't stopped. Then it had been slipcovers for the sofa and living room armchairs, and Lee was good at the sewing machine. Then she had become pregnant. Nothing wrong with that, of course, and Robert had been as happy as she. Sunday afternoon dinners at her mother's, a bit boring but bearable, sometimes even cozy and reassuring.

Robert paused in front of the not very big mirror fastened to the wall above his basin. He saw that he was frowning. He rubbed his chin brusquely, barely met his own eyes. He was not interested in looking at himself. Rotten shave he had given himself that morning. What had he been thinking of then?

The magic just fell away, Robert thought. Would he write a sentence like that, if he were writing about himself and Lee?

Robert felt suddenly puzzled. How could anyone write something about anything, until it was clear in his own head? How could anyone put into words or phrases how much he had loved Lee? The clumsiness, the bluntness of certain pop-song lyrics came now to Robert . . . *the catch in my throat when we meet . . . when I look in your eyes, I want to die . . . the places we yee-eewst to go together . . .* Lee had liked pop music as background sometimes when she sewed, changed the baby, or gave her a bath. If only Lee had stopped doing little things, let him change the baby (he could), just dropped everything and got back to her own work!

Robert was working himself into a torment again. Absurd. Lee was dead and forever dead. What good did tension, even analysis, do now, really?

In the next seconds he was back to the present. His parents were coming to see him tomorrow. Lee's mother evidently did not wish to see him, and she had gone with Melinda to a sister's house somewhere in Illinois. Rather, she was going, after the funeral. The funeral was *today*. Robert realized that with only a mild shock; he had an impulse to look at his wristwatch, and didn't. He knew it was still before noon, because the guard had not brought his lunch tray. Funerals were always in the morning, weren't they?

Then for another few seconds Robert felt that he couldn't realize what he had done. That was almost comforting, like a pill he might have taken. He did realize that his life and his work, whatever he had wanted to do in life, was over, finished. He might as well be dead now, like Lee. But they weren't going to kill him, just sentence him and imprison him. That was worse. Think about that later. He was pushing his tongue against his left eyetooth, which was nicked from a football game, way back, when Robert had been fourteen or fifteen. A vision of little white houses, blue sea behind them, came into his eyes. Greece. Robert had been to Greece when he was twenty, pack on his back, sleeping on beaches and in pine woods, getting to know the land and the people. He had hoped to have enough money one day to buy a house on a Greek island, and to live there with Lee at least half of the year, the other half in America. He had never forgotten Greece or his dream of a house there. He and Lee had used to talk about it, now and then. Greek music.

Lee's music. Lee hadn't always played pop, either on the radio or on the record player. She had liked Mahler, oddly. Depressing sometimes to Robert, fear-making, unfathomable sometimes to him. Yet now the memory of the Mahler Sixth steadied him. He had come to a big decision about Lee while Mahler's Sixth Symphony played one afternoon. He had been working on a clay model of what he called *A Dreaming Woman*, the woman not reclining but on her knees with arms raised as if half ambulant in her dream. He had gone to speak with Lee about his idea.

And what had she been doing? Putting adhesive paper down on some kitchen shelves, standing on a low formica stool. Robert proposed that she divorce him and marry Tony, the bachelor architect-carpenter who lived about eight miles away, the same fellow who had hung the shelf Lee was now busy with.

"Tony?"

Robert could still hear her voice and the astonishment in it. "He's in love with you," Robert had said. "Just too polite to do anything about it. You must know it yourself."

"Are you out of your mind, Bob?"

Robert remembered her eyes then, the same straight clear gaze at him, but what a different mind or brain behind those eyes!

The difference in her was affecting his work, at least affecting his sketches of Lee. He could not see her the same way as before, because she wasn't the same. His nearly life-size nudes of her, a couple of years old by then, thumbtacked to the walls of his workroom, had seemed to mock him: you can't do it again, they seemed to say. The drawings had spirit, enthusiasm, even genius. Whose genius, his or Lee's? Robert wasn't vain, it could be his or hers, and he preferred to think it both his and hers.

So Robert had turned himself to other themes, other women's figures, if he needed them, abstracts, nature forms. Lee had become "any woman," ordinary, pretty, but uninspired and uninspiring. Robert had managed a teaching job for three mornings a week in Chicago. They could have afforded a baby-sitter, a woman to do the housecleaning once or twice a week, but Lee seemed to enjoy these chores, and she said she didn't want anyone else in the house.

If Lee began to be the cliché, the woman-next-door, Tony Wagener was the archetype of the man-next-door (formerly the nice-boy-next-door) whom the average girl would be lucky to marry. He was healthy, attractive, good-natured, age twenty-five, and he couldn't take his eyes off Lee. Was it any wonder that a happy idea had crossed Robert's mind? Robert had thought it might work. He still loved Lee, even in a physical way, in fact, but the letdown—of his dream? No, because Lee *had* been the way he remembered her when he met her and when they had married, for a while. Witness his drawings! Witness his three statues of her, two small and one life-size! They were good, really good!

Therefore, Tony.

"Don't you like Tony?" Robert had asked on another occasion.

"Like him? I never think about him. Why should I? He brings us wood for the fireplace—because he doesn't need it." She had shrugged.

"It might be better. You might be happier. Tony would." Robert remembered he had laughed here.

Lee had still been puzzled. "*I* don't want Tony!" And what else had she said? Had she asked him if he was miserable with her, if he didn't love her any longer?

What would he have answered in that case?

It had crossed Robert's mind to run away, simply abandon Lee and the baby. He loved the baby, was rather in awe of it as his and Lee's creation, but he had still been able to envisage disappearing rather than—something worse. The something worse hadn't been definite in Robert's mind then, he had merely feared it.

If he disappeared, Robert remembered thinking, mightn't things be better? Lee would land on her feet, if she fell at all. Tony would dance attendance and step in as soon as Lee let him, and why shouldn't she? Tony was serious about his architecture, had a degree from somewhere, and was going to climb in his profession. Robert could not imagine a more ardent suitor than Tony, if Tony were only given a chance. Tony had had a girlfriend when Lee and Robert had moved into their house, but after three months or so (Tony had been doing some carpentry work for them, and had brought the girl once or twice), Tony had dropped her. Tony had fallen in love with Lee, that had been plain. Robert remembered mentioning it, early on, to Lee, and Lee had shrugged, uninterested.

Robert had been doing portraits, heads as he called them, for two people or clients in Bloomington, and for one in Chicago. They brought in money. Only middle-aged and well-to-do people could afford the luxury of having themselves or their wives cast in bronze at three thousand dollars each. Robert had had to work in rather conventional style to get a likeness that pleased the client. He tried to be as free as he could in his style, but still it bored him.

Lee had begun to bore him. Incredible realization! One day he had driven back from a sitting in Chicago, nervous, unhappy, and he had said to Lee, "What if I just disappeared?"

She had turned from the stove where she was cooking something. "What do you mean?" Her smile was almost her former smile, amused, cool, showing rather pointed white teeth between her rouged lips. She wore white sneakers, a pair of girls' maroon corduroy jeans. She couldn't wear boys' trousers, because she had a waistline and hips, though she was not plump.

What had he replied? Robert tried to remember now, because it was important, because he had really been trying to make the right suggestion. "I don't see that you need me anymore." Robert was sure he had said that. What else could he have said? "If I went away, I'd send you money to live on, you can be sure of that." Then he had blurted out the truth: "You're not the same girl as before. It's not your fault, I think. It's *my* fault. I should never have asked you to marry me. Somehow I'm destroying *you*. And this situation or whatever it is is bothering my work. It depresses me."

"But I *am* the same person. Sure I have to spend a lot of time now with Melinda, but I don't mind that. It's normal." And at that moment hadn't she run across the kitchen to stop Melinda from poking a finger into an electric outlet? Melinda crawled around a lot, because Lee was against confining her too much in her crib. "When she's really tired, she'll sleep better," Lee often said. What else had she said? Maybe, "I thought you were working rather well. Aren't you?"

And her dressing table, its top covered with little boxes of pins, lipsticks, perfume bottles, lotions, cologne. Robert had used to look at all that with a smile—mystifying objects, but Lee knew what to do with them. She made herself prettier, different. She amused herself, she amused other people. Boys and men looked at her when they went to restaurants. But Lee didn't invite attention, never had, didn't need to. Maybe men took as flirting one glance from her, but Lee could hardly go around with her eyes shut all the time. No, she hadn't flirted, and once she had decided she liked him, Robert had been the only man for her, he knew that.

One Friday morning, one of the mornings when he had to get up at seven at the latest for the Chicago art school, Robert had quit the house. He had left Lee a note saying that he was going to telephone Tony. *Try it,* Robert had written. *See if you can't love Tony as much as he loves you. You know where to reach me, at the art school. Try it for maybe a month, please? You might find yourself happier.* Robert had taken a furnished room not far from the school. If Tony didn't work out, Robert had thought of acquiring a second-hand car for himself and giving Lee the car he had taken, their car. She was able to drive. Robert envisaged a divorce, of course. He felt a divorce would be better for both of them. Some other Tony would come along. Meanwhile he missed his workroom at home, his clay, a couple of works in progress.

Tony had said on the telephone, "But what happened, Bob? A big quarrel? You sound serious."

"Just look after her. We didn't quarrel, no. It's like a trial. I want to try it." Shocked silence at Tony's end. "She may like you better."

"Oh, no." Tony defensive now. "You've got me wrong, Bob."

"Try it. I invite you." Robert had hung up.

The following Sunday evening around eight, Robert got a telegram from Lee: CANNOT UNDERSTAND YOU. PLEASE COME HOME. I AM SO UNHAPPY. LEE.

Robert had sent his furnished-room address to Lee on Friday, so she would have got his note Saturday morning. He had not sent the name or telephone number of his landlady, so maybe it had been easier for Lee to send a telegram straight to the address. Robert had found it under his door, when he got back from supper.

And that had been that. After a minute's debate Robert had driven back home. He had not been able to bear the thought of Lee *unhappy*— either because of being alone, or because of not liking Tony, or of being bored or annoyed by him. Robert had been willing to leave his week's rent with Mrs. Kleber, but she gave it back to him except for a charge of one extra day.

Lee's first words to him had been, "What is the matter, Bob? And Tony! What're you trying to do? I never said I liked Tony."

Tony had not been there when Robert got home. Tony had been polite, helpful, it seemed, but Lee did not want him.

Robert fell on his cell cot exhausted, and had to be awakened for his early supper. Hours ago they must have poked lunch at him. He couldn't remember, he must have been daydreaming then.

"God, I wish I had a radio," he murmured to himself. He would have switched on anything just to take his mind off Lee and himself. It grew dark early, because it was December. He walked and walked around his cell, deliberately tiring himself so he could sleep.

The next day at one-thirty P.M. his parents came. Robert was allowed to go into a side room with table and chairs and to talk with them. There were no other prisoners in the room, and only two other cells in the place, as far as Robert could see.

His mother was nervous and looked as if she had been weeping. She was blondish, wore a green tweed dress and a sheepskin coat. His father was as tall as Robert, six feet, a man of fifty, a logical man. Robert recognized the downturning of his father's strong mouth. His father was displeased, he didn't understand, was going to be stubborn. Robert remembered that look from his childhood, for his minor misdemeanors. His father now had reason to be grim.

"Bobby, you must tell us what happened," said his mother.

"What they said happened," Robert replied. "It's the truth."

"Who's they?" asked his father.

"The police, I suppose. I called the police," said Robert.

"We know that," said his mother. "But what happened at home?"

"Nothing." He stopped, having been about to say that he must have had a moment of irrationality, of anger. But that wasn't it.

"You had a quarrel? You'd had a few drinks?" asked his father. "You can tell us the truth, Bob. We're in a state of shock, I can tell you that." His father was making an effort to get his words out; he glanced at Robert's mother, then looked back at Robert. He said quietly and earnestly, "It's not *you*, Bob. You worshiped Lee, that we know.—Can't you talk to us?"

"Was there another man in the picture?" asked his mother. "We thought of that. This Tony you mentioned in your letters—"

"No, no." Robert shook his head. "Tony is a very polite fellow."

"Polite, well," said his father tolerantly, hoping for a lead here.

"No, it's got nothing to do with Tony," Robert said.

His mother asked gently, "What did Lee do?"

"Nothing," Robert answered. "She just changed."

"Changed how?" asked his father.

"She turned into a different person from the one I married. She didn't *do* anything.—Maybe she was just herself, after all. Why not?" He tried to sound reasonable. What they were talking about was perhaps not susceptible to reason, not to be understood in logical terms. Also Robert had never been intimate with his parents, or tried to talk with either of them about his moods, his crushes and loves in his adolescence. They had been sympathetic about his wanting to go to art school, though Robert knew his father had considered it impractical, somehow "easy," undemanding and unrewarding. He was an artist, therefore more sensitive, Robert supposed they thought, so what he had done must be all the more unbelievable to them.

"Changed how?" his father repeated. "Neglecting you maybe, paying more attention to the baby. I've heard of that happening, but—"

"It was *not* that." Robert was suddenly impatient, wanted to end the useless conversation. "I've been absolutely unreasonable," Robert said, "and I deserve everything they're going to give me or do to me."

His mother's hand shook as she reached in her pocketbook for a tissue, but she was not weeping now. She gave her nose a pinch. "Bobby, we've talked to a lawyer by telephone, one who knows the state laws here, and we'll see him this afternoon. He says if there had been a quarrel about anything, if you'd been angry about something, it would help you when—"

"I refuse that," Robert interrupted, "because it's not true."

His parents exchanged a glance, then his father said calmly, "We'll see you again, Bob, after we talk with the lawyer. When is it, Mary, four, isn't it?"

"Between four and four-thirty, he said."

"He's coming to see us at our hotel, and I know he'll want to talk with you tomorrow morning. His name is McIver. Good man, I'm told."

It was all less important to Robert than a stage play taking place at a distance from him. Lawyers, rules, putting everything into abstract phrases, more abstract than himself and Lee—which was difficult enough for Robert.

His parents got up from their chairs. Robert thanked them. They left, and Robert with them, walking quietly out of the room, into the hall, where a guard stood up to escort Robert to his cell. His mother pressed Robert's hand. The guard looked at Robert's hand afterward, as if to see if his mother had put anything into it.

Before the guard closed his cell door, Robert asked for some paper and a pen. The guard brought him three sheets of ruled paper (Robert disliked ruled paper) and a ballpoint pen. When he sat down at the little table, he realized that a pack of cigarettes was bulging his back pocket. His mother had produced the pack from her handbag, Robert remembered, saying something about having had to use a machine to buy them in a hurry or she would have bought a carton.

Robert closed his eyes, deliberately tried to make his mind go blank, and at the same time think about his theme, as he did with sculpture, but now his theme was Lee as a person. When he tried to think of Lee as a piece of sculpture, he often thought of the words *grace, strength,* sometimes one or the other, sometimes combined. Grace was easy to combine with Lee. She had never made a clumsy gesture that he could recall. She walked gracefully, as if she weighed nothing. But the strength? She had had it, all her own, a strength that he didn't understand.

Finally he wrote (it seemed to him a fragment, but he could go back or forward from here):

> *To see her wilt before my eyes like that was frightening to me, like a slow death in itself. People speak of blossoming with childbirth, love, all that. It was not true in Lee's case. But what I write here is by no means an effort on my part to excuse what I did.*

Did he have to add that awful last sentence? Well, he could cross it out later. For whom was he writing this, anyway?

> *She gave up her photography, except for some mediocre pictures of the baby. What can one do with a baby? At least in regard to Lee's former bent of character, intellect, tragedy in the human face—nothing.*
> *Instead of her good cameras, she might as well have been using a cheap pocket camera. She had stopped talking about the photography exhibitions in Indianapolis and Chicago. We used to go quite a lot. We knew some of the photographers who lived in those cities. They had gradually stopped visiting us.*
>
> *All this was so unnecessary! I can look back now on the work Lee did just before we married, just after. Terrific! And easy for her! Powerful! I thought I was the cause of all this downslide, this collapse*

really, so I offered to go away, support her from afar, as it might be,
until she found maybe another man to share her life with. She declined
this and

Here Robert stopped, seeing suddenly the living room that last
evening, Lee's photographs gracing the walls, blown-up, her old good
stuff, people, buildings. There hadn't been a quarrel, no. Lee had been on
her feet, talking about ordinary things—that there had been a telephone
call from Fred Muldaven, a friend of Robert's who lived in Chicago, a
painter. Melinda had been in her crib in the kitchen then. It was around six
or seven in the evening. Robert had been in a strange mood, he had realized, staring at Lee without listening much to what she said. He had just
driven back from Chicago, and maybe he had been drinking a cold beer
straight from the can.

"Beecham's has a sale of desert boots," Lee had said, "and you could
use a new pair. Those look awful."

That had been merely unimportant, boring. A couple of years
before, Lee would have paid no attention whether his desert boots were
worn out, or if his shoes needed a shine. Old falling-apart clothes had
their place, and it was nice to dress up sometimes, too, but why talk about
it? Why bother trying to please the public, or whoever might look at his
sloppy desert boots?

Yet nothing that evening had been what Robert could call the last
straw. Rather the atmosphere had been one of quiet gloom, hopelessness,
a slowing up as if something were coming to an end, like a train losing
momentum because the engine has been shut off. They had gone into the
kitchen. Melinda, symbol of the future, had for once been sleeping quietly. And had any vision of Lee at the Chicago art school danced before
his eyes as he watched her fussing at the stove? Had any of her enchanting air of "I don't care if I ever see you again or not," as in the days before
they married, come back into his head? Whatever, it was all gone now. He
had picked up the rolling pin, floury from something Lee had just made,
and that had been it.

Robert got up from the chair and walked around the cell. He moved
back to the table, his hand reached out for the cigarette pack, and drew
slowly back. He was thinking of something else—Lee dead, the baby at

Lee's mother's, himself dead, too. It was all abstract somehow. There had been no word from Lee's mother, or from Fred Muldaven (that was a new friendship and Robert supposed that Fred was now afraid of him), only from his parents, natural appurtenances, calling on him, because by blood they were linked, like a triple star floating around in space. And to be just a little more concrete, though the fact as such did not matter, Robert was going to spend the next fifteen years (with the lightest sentence) in prison, working if he worked at all in a prison art department, being told when to get up and when to go to bed, being reminded of Lee day after day by barred window and door, being reminded of the way she had been, which was even worse.

He wrote one more sentence: What a terrible shame I once loved her so much. I do think that ruined everything.

Then he did light a cigarette, and stood looking at the gray and rather rough wall across from his cot. And Melinda. Should he write one *more* sentence to that young creature of whose personality he knew nothing at all? He knew something, of course: she seemed to be cheerful by nature, but that could change by the time she was twelve or so.

He decided not to write a word to Melinda. She was in good hands. She would grow up to hate him. She would look at all the pretty, the beautiful photographs of her mother, and hate him. And his statues of Lee? Would Lee's mother have those thrown away, broken up?

Robert sat on his cot for a couple of minutes, finishing his cigarette. Then he put it out in the metal ashtray on his table. For no reason he lifted his left hand and looked at his watch: 4:37 in the afternoon.

Robert stooped by his cot, facing the wall opposite in the position of a runner about to take off. Then he ran forward with all the force he had, all the force, he felt, that he had ever put into his work, and very briefly with a vision of a statue of Lee, better than any he had ever made. His head hit the wall.

THE TROUBLE WITH MRS. BLYNN, THE
TROUBLE WITH THE WORLD

Mrs. Palmer was dying, there was no doubt of that to her or to anyone else in the household. The household had grown from two, Mrs. Palmer and Elsie the housemaid, to four in the past ten days. Elsie's daughter Liza, age fourteen, had come to help her mother, and had brought their shaggy sheepdog Princy—who to Mrs. Palmer made a fourth presence in the house. Liza spent most of her time doing things in the kitchen, and slept in the little low-ceilinged room with double-deck bunks down the steps from Mrs. Palmer's room. The cottage was small— a sitting room and dining alcove and kitchen downstairs, and upstairs Mrs. Palmer's bedroom, the room with the two bunks, and a tiny back room where Elsie slept. All the ceilings were low and the doorways and the ceiling above the stairway even lower, so that one had to duck one's head constantly.

Mrs. Palmer reflected that she would have to duck her head very few times more, as she rose only a couple of times a day, making her way, her lavender dressing gown clutched about her against the chill, to the bathroom. She had leukemia. She was not in any pain, but she was terribly weak. She was sixty-one. Her son Gregory, an officer in the R.A.F., was stationed in the Middle East, and perhaps would come in time and perhaps wouldn't. Mrs. Palmer had purposely not made her telegram urgent, not wanting to upset or inconvenience him, and his telegraphed reply had simply said that he would do his best to get leave to fly to her, and would let her know when. A cowardly telegram hers had been, Mrs. Palmer thought. Why hadn't she had the courage to say outright, "Am going to die in about a week. Can you come to see me?"

"Missus Palmer?" Elsie stuck her head in the door, one floury hand resting against the doorjamb. "Did Missus Blynn say four-thirty or five-thirty today?"

Mrs. Palmer did not know, and it did not seem in the least important. "I think five-thirty."

Elsie gave a preoccupied nod, her mind on what she would serve for five-thirty tea as opposed to four-thirty tea. The five-thirty tea could be less substantial, as Mrs. Blynn would already have had tea somewhere. "Anything I can get you, Missus Palmer?" she asked in a sweet voice, with a genuine concern.

"No, thank you, Elsie, I'm quite comfortable." Mrs. Palmer sighed as Elsie closed the door again. Elsie was willing, but unintelligent. Mrs. Palmer could not *talk* to her, not that she would have wanted to talk intimately to her, but it would have been nice to have the feeling that she could talk to someone in the house if she wished to.

Mrs. Palmer had no close friends in the town, because she had been here only a month. She had been en route to Scotland when the weakness came on her again and she had collapsed on a train platform in Ipswich. A long journey to Scotland by train or even airplane had been out of the question, so on a strange doctor's recommendation, Mrs. Palmer had hired a taxi and driven to a town on the east coast called Eamington, where the doctor knew there was a visiting nurse, and where the air was splendid and bracing. The doctor had evidently thought she needed only a few weeks' rest and she would be on her feet again, but Mrs. Palmer had had a premonition that this wasn't true. She had felt better the first few days in the quiet little town, she had found the cottage called Sea Maiden and rented it at once, but the spurt of energy had been brief. In Sea Maiden she had collapsed again, and Mrs. Palmer had the feeling that Elsie and even a few other acquaintances she had made, like Mr. Frowley the real estate agent, resented her faiblesse. She was not only a stranger come to trouble them, to make demands on them, but her relapse belied the salubrious powers of Eamington air—just now mostly gale-force winds which swept from the northeast day and night, tearing the buttons from one's coat, plastering a sticky, opaque film of salt and spray on the windows of all the houses on the seafront. Mrs. Palmer was sorry to be a burden herself, but at least she could pay for it, she thought.

She had rented a rather shabby cottage that would otherwise have stayed empty all winter, since it was early February now, she was employing Elsie at slightly better than average Eamington wages, she paid Mrs. Blynn a guinea per half-hour visit (and most of that half hour was taken up with her tea), and she soon would bring business to the undertaker, the sexton, and perhaps the shopkeeper who sold flowers. She had also paid her rent through March.

Hearing a quick tread on the pavement, in a lull in the wind's roar, Mrs. Palmer sat up a little in bed. Mrs. Blynn was arriving. An anxious frown touched Mrs. Palmer's thin-skinned forehead, but she smiled faintly, too, with beforehand politeness. She reached for the long-handled mirror that lay on her bedtable. Her gray face had ceased to shock her or to make her feel shame. Age was age, death was death, and not pretty, but she still had the impulse to do what she could to look nicer for the world. She tucked some hair back into place, moistened her lips, tried a little smile, pulled a shoulder of her nightdress even with the other and her pink cardigan closer about her. Her pallor made the blue of her eyes much bluer. That was a pleasant thought.

Elsie knocked and opened the door at the same time. "Missus Blynn, ma'am."

"Good afternoon, Mrs. Palmer," said Mrs. Blynn, coming down the two steps from the threshold into Mrs. Palmer's room. She was a full-bodied, dark blond woman of middle height, about forty-five, and she wore her usual bulky, two-piece black suit with a rose-colored floral pin on her left breast. She also wore a pale pink lipstick and rather high heels. Like many women in Eamington, she was a sea widow, and had taken up nursing after she was forty. She was highly thought of in the town as an energetic woman who did useful work. "And how are you this afternoon?"

"Good afternoon. Well as can be expected, I think you'd say," said Mrs. Palmer with an effort at cheerfulness. Already she was loosening the covers, preparatory to pushing them back entirely for her daily injection.

But Mrs. Blynn was standing with an absent smile in the center of the room, hands folded backward on her hips, surveying the walls, gazing out the window. Mrs. Blynn had once lived in this house with her husband, for six months when they were first married, and every day Mrs. Blynn said something about it. Mrs. Blynn's husband had been the captain of a merchant ship, and had gone down with it ten years ago in a collision with a Swedish ship only fifty nautical miles from Eamington. Mrs. Blynn had never married again. Elsie said her house was filled with photographs of the captain in uniform and of his ship.

"Yes-s, it's a wonderful little house," said Mrs. Blynn, "even if the wind does come in a bit." She looked at Mrs. Palmer with brighter eyes, as if she were about to say, "Well, now, a few more of these injections and you'll be as fit as can be, won't you?"

But in the next seconds, Mrs. Blynn's expression changed. She groped in her black bag for the needle and the bottle of clear fluid that would do no good. Her mouth lost its smile and drooped, and deeper lines came at its corners. By the time she plunged the needle into Mrs. Palmer's fleshless body, her bulging green-gray eyes were glassy, as if she saw nothing and did not need to see anything: this was her business, and she knew how to do it. Mrs. Palmer was an object, which paid a guinea a visit. The object was going to die. Mrs. Blynn became apathetic, as if even the cutting off of the guinea in three days or eight days mattered nothing to her, either.

Guineas as such mattered nothing to Mrs. Palmer, but in view of the fact she was soon quitting this world, she wished that Mrs. Blynn could show something so human as a desire to prolong the guineas. Mrs. Blynn's eyes remained glassy, even when she glanced at the door to see if Elsie was coming in with her tea. Occasionally the floorboards in the hall cracked from the heat or the lack of it, and so they did when someone walked just outside the door.

The injection hurt today, but Mrs. Palmer did not flinch. It was really such a small thing, she smiled at the slightness of it. "A little sunshine today, wasn't there?" Mrs. Palmer said.

"Was there?" Mrs. Blynn jerked the needle out.

"Around eleven this morning. I noticed it." Weakly she gestured toward the window behind her.

"We can certainly use it," Mrs. Blynn said, putting her equipment back in her bag. "Goodness, we can use that fire, too." She had fastened her bag, and now she chafed her palms, huddling toward the grate.

Princy was stretched full length before the fire, looking like a rolled-up shag rug.

Mrs. Palmer tried to think of something pleasant to say about Mrs. Blynn's husband, their time in this house, the town, anything. She could only think of how lonely Mrs. Blynn's life must be since her husband died. They had had no children. According to Elsie, Mrs. Blynn had worshiped her husband, and took a pride in never having remarried. "Have you many patients this time of year?" Mrs. Palmer asked.

"Oh, yes. Like always," Mrs. Blynn said, still facing the fire and rubbing her hands.

Who? Mrs. Palmer wondered. *Tell me about them.* She waited, breathing softly.

Elsie knocked once, by bumping a corner of the tray against the door.

"Come in, Elsie," they both said, Mrs. Blynn a bit louder.

"Here we are," said Elsie, setting the tray down on a hassock made by two massive olive-green pillows, one atop the other. Butter slid down the side of a scone, spread onto the plate, and began to congeal while Elsie poured the tea.

Elsie handed Mrs. Palmer a cup of tea with three lumps of sugar, but no scone, because Mrs. Blynn said they were too indigestible for her. Mrs. Palmer did not mind. She appreciated the sight of well-buttered scones, anyway, and of healthy people like Mrs. Blynn eating them. She was offered a ginger biscuit and declined it. Mrs. Blynn talked briefly to Elsie about her water pipes, about the reduced price of something at the butcher's this week, while Elsie stood with folded arms, leaning against the edge of the door, letting in a frigid draft on Mrs. Palmer. Elsie was taking in all Mrs. Blynn's information about prices. Now it was catsup at the health store. On sale this week.

"Call me if you'd like something," Elsie said as usual, ducking out the door.

Mrs. Blynn was sunk in her scones, leaning over so the dripping butter would fall on the stone floor and not her skirt.

Mrs. Palmer shivered, and drew the covers up.

"Is your son coming?" Mrs. Blynn asked in a loud, clear voice, looking straight at Mrs. Palmer.

Mrs. Palmer did not know what Elsie had told Mrs. Blynn. She had told Elsie that he might come, that was all. "I haven't heard yet. He's probably waiting to tell me the exact time he'll come—or to find out if he can or not. You know how it is in the Air Force."

"Um-m," said Mrs. Blynn through a scone, as if of course she knew, having had a husband who had been in service. "He's your only son and heir, I take it."

"My only one," said Mrs. Palmer.

"Married?"

"Yes." Then, anticipating the next question, "He has one child, a daughter, but she's still very small."

Mrs. Blynn's eyes kept drifting to Mrs. Palmer's bedtable, and suddenly Mrs. Palmer realized what she was looking at—her amethyst pin. Mrs. Palmer had worn it for a few days on her cardigan sweater, until she had felt so bad, the pin ceased to lift her spirits and became almost tawdry, and she had removed it.

"That's a beautiful pin," said Mrs. Blynn.

"Yes. My husband gave it to me years ago."

Mrs. Blynn came over to look at it, but she did not touch it. The rectangular amethyst was set in small diamonds. She stood up, looking down at it with alert, bulging eyes. "I suppose you'll pass it on to your son—or his wife."

Mrs. Palmer flushed with embarrassment, or anger. She hadn't thought to whom she would pass it on, particularly. "I suppose my son will get everything, as my heir."

"I hope his wife appreciates it," Mrs. Blynn said, turning on her heel with a smile, setting her cup down in its saucer.

Then Mrs. Palmer realized that for the last few days it was the pin Mrs. Blynn had been looking at when her eyes drifted over to the bedtable. When Mrs. Blynn had gone, Mrs. Palmer picked up the pin and held it in her palm protectively. Her jewel box was across the room. Elsie came in, and Mrs. Palmer said, "Elsie, would you mind handing me that blue box over there?"

"Certainly, ma'am," Elsie said, swerving from the tea tray to the box on the top of the bookshelf. "This the one?"

"Yes, thank you." Mrs. Palmer took it, opened the lid, and dropped the pin on her pearls. She had not much jewelry, perhaps ten or eleven pieces, but each piece meant a special occasion in her life, or a special period, and she loved them all. She looked at Elsie's blunt, homely profile as she bent over the tray, arranging everything so that it could be carried out at once.

"That Missus Blynn," said Elsie, shaking her head, not looking at Mrs. Palmer. "Asked me if I thought your son was coming. How was I to know? I said yes, *I* thought so." Now she stood with the tray, looking at Mrs. Palmer, and she smiled awkwardly, as if she had said perhaps too much. "The trouble with Missus Blynn is she's always nosing—if you'll pardon me saying so. Asking questions, you know?"

Mrs. Palmer nodded, feeling too low just at that moment to make a comment. She had no comment anyway. Elsie, she thought, had passed back and forth by the amethyst pin for days and never mentioned it, never touched it, maybe never even noticed it. Mrs. Palmer suddenly realized how much more she liked Elsie than she liked Mrs. Blynn.

"The trouble with Missus Blynn—she means well, but . . ." Elsie floundered and jiggled the tray in her effort to shrug. "It's too bad. Everyone's always saying it about her," she finished, as if this summed it up, and started out the door. But she turned with the door open. "At tea, for instance. It's always get this and get that for her, as if she were a grand lady or something. A day ahead she tells me. I don't see why she don't bring what she wants from the bakery now and then herself. If you know what I mean."

Mrs. Palmer nodded. She supposed she knew. She knew. Mrs. Blynn was like a nursemaid she had for a time for Gregory. Like a divorcée she and her husband had known in London. She was like a lot of people.

Mrs. Palmer died two days later. It was a day when Mrs. Blynn came in and out, perhaps six times, perhaps eight. A telegram had arrived that morning from Gregory, saying he had at last wangled leave and would take off in a matter of hours, landing at a military field near Eamington. Mrs. Palmer did not know if she would see him again or not, she could not judge her strength that far. Mrs. Blynn took her temperature and felt her pulse frequently, then pivoted on one foot in the room, looking about as if she were alone and thinking her own thoughts. Her expression was blankly pleasant, her peaches-and-cream cheeks aglow with health.

"Your son's due today," Mrs. Blynn half said, half asked, on one of her visits.

"Yes," said Mrs. Palmer.

It was then dusk, though it was only four in the afternoon.

That was the last clear exchange she had with anyone, for she sank into a kind of dream. She saw Mrs. Blynn staring at the blue box on the top of the bookshelf, staring at it even as she shook the thermometer down. Mrs. Palmer called for Elsie and had her bring the box to her. Mrs. Blynn was not in the room then.

"This is to go to my son when he comes," Mrs. Palmer said. "All of it. Everything. You understand? It's all written . . ." But even though it was all itemized, a single piece like the amethyst pin might be missing and Gregory would never do anything about it, maybe not even notice, maybe think she'd lost it somewhere in the last weeks and not reported it. Gregory was like that. Then Mrs. Palmer smiled at herself, and also reproached herself. *You can't take it with you.* That was very true, and people who tried to were despicable and rather absurd. "Elsie, this is yours," Mrs. Palmer said, and handed Elsie the amethyst pin.

"Oh, Missus Palmer! Oh, no, I couldn't take *that*!" Elsie said, not taking it, and in fact retreating a step.

"You've been very good to me," Mrs. Palmer said. She was very tired, and her arm dropped to the bed. "Very well," she murmured, seeing it was really of no use.

Her son came at six that evening, sat with her on the edge of her bed, held her hand and kissed her forehead. But when she died, Mrs. Blynn was closest, bending over her with her great round, peaches-and-cream face and her green-gray eyes as expressionless as some fantastic reptile's. Mrs. Blynn to the last continued to say crisp, efficient things to her like, "Breathe easily. That's it," and "Not chilly, are you? Good." Somebody had mentioned a priest earlier, but this had been overruled by both Gregory and Mrs. Palmer. So it was Mrs. Blynn's eyes she looked into as her life left her. Mrs. Blynn so authoritative, strong, efficient, one might have taken her for God Himself. Especially since when Mrs. Palmer looked toward her son, she couldn't really see him, only a vague pale blue figure in the corner, tall and erect, with a dark spot at the top that was his hair. He was looking at her, but now she was too weak to call him. Anyway, Mrs. Blynn had shooed them all back. Elsie was also standing against the closed door, ready to run out for something, ready to take any order. Near her was the smaller figure of Liza, who occasionally whispered something and was shushed by her mother. In an instant, Mrs. Palmer saw her entire life—her carefree childhood and youth, her happy marriage, the blight of the death of her other son at the age of ten, the shock of her husband's death eight years ago—but all in all a happy life, she supposed, though she could wish her own character had been better, *purer,* that she had never shown temper or selfishness, for instance. All that was past now, but what remained was a feeling that she had been imperfect, wrong, like Mrs. Blynn's presence now, like Mrs. Blynn's faint smile, wrong, wrong for the time and the occasion. Mrs. Blynn did not understand her. Mrs. Blynn did not know her. Mrs. Blynn, somehow, could not comprehend goodwill. Therein lay the flaw, and the flaw of life itself. Life is a long failure of understanding, Mrs. Palmer thought, a long, mistaken shutting of the heart.

Mrs. Palmer had the amethyst pin in her closed left hand. Hours ago, sometime in the afternoon, she had taken it with an idea of safe-keeping, but now she realized the absurdity of that. She had also wanted to give it to Gregory directly, and had forgotten. Her closed hand lifted an inch or so, her lips moved, but no sound came. She wanted to give it to Mrs. Blynn: one positive and generous gesture she could still make to this essence of nonunderstanding, she thought, but now she had not the strength to make her want known—and that was like life, too, everything a little too late. Mrs. Palmer's lids shut on the vision of Mrs. Blynn's glassy, attentive eyes.

THE SECOND CIGARETTE

George Leister, a New York tax lawyer age fifty-one, went into his kitchen one Saturday morning and was mildly surprised to see a long, recently lighted cigarette burning in an ashtray. George glanced at the cigarette in his own hand, also recently lighted, and reproached himself for absentmindedness. He had even vowed to cut down to ten a day. He wasn't doing better than fifteen. George put out the ashtray cigarette to save for a next smoke—he *was* counting—picked up the coffeepot and was about to refill his cup when he became aware of a figure standing in his kitchen doorway through which he had just walked. George jumped with shock, and some of the coffee splashed from the pot onto the floor.

The figure in the doorway was himself, as if a mirror were there, except that his effigy was smiling a little and George was not smiling.

"I smoke, too," said the figure softly, and in an amused way.

Now George, trembling, turned sideways and poured his coffee as steadily as he could. It was an auditory hallucination as well as a visual one, he thought. Was he going mad? Why? He'd had a quiet evening at home last night—no crazy food, no extra drink. Frowning with fear, his jaw set, George faced the apparition again.

The figure looked back pleasantly. It wore the same dark red dressing gown, hair as much gray as brown, George saw (like his own, he admitted), creases in the cheeks from middle age. George had no brother, had never seen a cousin who so much resembled him. George could have taken two steps and touched him, but George didn't want to. He noticed with disgust the slight yellowness of an eyetooth as the figure continued to smile at him. Disgusting! So this was the picture he presented to the world! Not even clean and healthy-looking!

"Not very proud of yourself, eh?" The figure picked up the stubbed-out cigarette, and lit it from the box of matches on the kitchen table. "Must be the fourth, this, even this morning. Are you counting honestly?"

George thought he had been. But now he had a clue. "If you're my conscience," George mumbled with a protective shrug, and at the same time his eyes slid away from the figure, "I'm not falling for that. Heard of it before. Visions." At the same time, George's morale was weakened, he realized, just because he had spoken out loud. Wasn't that the same as talking to oneself? "Other *self,*" George sneered. "Load of baloney!"

"Not your other self. *Your* self," replied the apparition, unperturbed.

The fleshly—even a bit overweight—figure in the doorway scared George all the way down his spine, but he determined to advance as if it didn't exist and return to his newspaper in the living room. George did advance, cup in hand, as if the cup were a lance with which he might run the apparition through if it did not get out of his way.

The apparition stepped back rather smartly into the hall, out of George's path.

George would have been more comfortable if he had been able to walk through the figure, because that would have proven that it was imaginary. George seized the *Times* like a life raft, and immersed himself in the financial pages. Good solid stuff. DOLLAR CONTINUES DECLINE VERSUS DM AND YEN. George read hungrily, concentrating.

He became aware of the figure in the dark red dressing gown strolling into the living room.

"No, not very proud of yourself.—Seen Liz lately?"

George glanced up with an air of annoyance, and was delighted to see that the figure appeared dimmer now, caught as it was in a beam of sunlight. Good! But George saw also the very real swing of the tassel of the dressing gown belt, as the figure came to a stop. "Liz doesn't want to see me," George said with conviction, in the same firm, polite tone he used in his office when he made an incontrovertible statement.

"Of course she does. She'd like to be on friendlier terms. She's not the one annoyed, though she ought to be. It's *you*—who're ashamed of yourself."

The old conscience game again. *I should take a cold shower,* George thought, *and get rid of this thing.*

"Doubt very much if you'll get rid of me."

Now George could see part of the bookshelves through the figure's torso. That was encouraging.

"Because I'm *you*—not your other self," the figure went on, and chuckled.

George recognized his own chuckle. He had, of course, recognized his own voice. *I don't even like myself,* George thought suddenly. He hadn't liked the chuckle, because it had sounded vaguely dishonest. But George didn't think he was dishonest, not basically. There had to be minor dishonesties in everyone—otherwise the social and business worlds would hardly function. But if he had been asked to rate himself, George would have said he was as honest or more honest than the average fellow. Until that chuckle. What did other people really think of him?

"Now, about Liz," said the apparition, in the tone of starting a speech.

"Quite happy with her new husband," George murmured, and picked up the paper again.

"More than one can say for you, eh? That was a mistake, George, a big one."

What was, Harrietta? George felt warmth rise to his face. Anger? Shame? George had had a girlfriend, Harrietta, for two years, and Liz had found out about her. It had happened almost simultaneously, Liz finding out because of a blabbermouth secretary in his office (George had managed to get her sacked on other grounds), and Harrietta asking George if he would, ever, divorce Liz and marry her. George had said yes to Harrietta. After all, they had got on well in bed and out, Harrietta had a brain, and George and Liz had only one offspring, a grown-up son who was married and doing well in California. When Liz found out about Harrietta, she asked George if he wanted a divorce, and he had said yes. The ironic thing was that Harrietta had then decided she didn't want to get married, after all, and Liz after only three or four months had met a recently divorced man in some kind of molasses-importing business and married him. George had met Liz's husband, Ed Tuttle, a couple of times, a really decent man, full of goodwill, and with an old-fashioned courtesy of the kind that George thought had died out. Yes, Liz had come out all right. And George, piqued by Harrietta's attitude, had broken with her. Harrietta wanted independence, didn't need any money from him, and adored her P.R. job with United Artists. Both Liz and Ed wanted to be friendly. It was George who kept his distance. Liz and Ed lived in a small town north of New York City, but in easy commuting range.

"You can't face them," the apparition said, interrupting George's thoughts. "You're the loser, alone in life—no Harrietta now to have secret midnight suppers with. . . ." The voice faded out.

George felt a stab in his breast, and it lingered as an ache. Yes, he'd lost. There were some compensations for living alone, but very few. George disliked preparing meals for himself, or even dining out alone, and felt especially lonely Sundays. He and Liz had often gone to a museum or a film Sunday afternoon, had had tea at a hotel or the Russian Tea Room, then a quiet evening at home and a snack before bedtime. That had been nice. But bedtime—George might as well have been sleeping with his sister or brother in the last decade of their marriage. It was almost embarrassing to look back on.

"Have another cigarette."

George had been looking at the silver box on the coffee table, thinking that if he took one, the figure would reproach him. George opened the box, hesitated, then decided not to smoke.

"Then I will."

Had George really heard it? George saw a translucent hand take a cigarette from the box, and reach for the table lighter. George heard its click.

". . . not your conscience," said the faint voice, "just you. You think I'm your good side? Have you got one? Ha!—But I think we've had some fun, don't you? In our long life?—Remember Maggie?"

George wasn't going to stand any more of it. He stood up, drank off his coffee, and walked to his right (which happened to be away from the figure) toward the hall which led to the bathroom. George took his cold shower, gritting his teeth, every muscle rigid, hating it. Then he scrubbed down hard with a towel. A brisk walk, that was what he needed. Thank goodness he'd done the supermarket shopping yesterday after work, because he wasn't in the mood for that boring chore. George shaved with his battery razor, and dressed in rather a hurry, because he felt that his recent tendency to slow up and daydream might have caused the vision. George was convinced it *was* a vision. What else? He didn't believe one bit in ghosts, or the supernatural, and when he read articles on extrasensory perception, it was with skepticism, a desire not to believe rather than to believe.

The ghostly figure did not reappear as George went to his door to leave, and George did not glance about for it.

Out in the sunlight, he felt free and safe. The honk of taxicabs sounded pleasant, reassuring. The sight of a black miniature poodle defecating in the gutter, leash securely held by a young woman, seemed normality itself. He breathed deeply, and felt physically rather fit. Hadn't he taken off about four pounds since Liz's departure? Yes. Now, as for girls, women—pretty absurd at his age. Maybe not absurd, but he couldn't act as if or pretend he was thirty any longer. If one of his friends or business associates introduced him to an interesting woman who was free, that was another matter. Free for an affair, maybe, free for marriage, even. That wasn't impossible, no.

"No?"

The voice in his ears had been his own. Rather that of the vision, but quite as clear as he had heard it at home. George quickened his steps, then slowed to the pace at which he had been walking before. He was not going to look over his shoulder. Funny to imagine the fellow—himself—striding along Fifth Avenue in pajamas and a dressing gown! Of course he might be wearing exactly the same clothes George was wearing now: a beige glen plaid suit and a blue polo neck sweater. George thought of other things. Monday was going to be hellish, with a conference in the morning starting at ten and another in the afternoon on the same subject, the Polyfax Company. Polyfax made plastics in all shapes and sizes, and had a Canadian branch called something else. What? They had been easing their profits by messing up their tax declarations, claiming Canada as source, or America when the situation demanded. Freer, Leister, and Foreman had had to go back over three years of Polyfax's tax reports.

"Polyfax, Polyfax," said George's own voice in his ear, in a mocking way.

George paid no attention. Best to go over the xeroxes again tonight, then another glance tomorrow evening, so he'd be well briefed for Freer Monday morning. "Must do the best for them—within the law," old Henry Tubman Freer always said, unnecessarily, as if thinking to himself.

George would have preferred to have a date for that evening, and remembered he'd declined an invitation from Ralph Foreman, their younger partner, to come to dinner tonight and meet a young man who was interested in joining the firm. So be it. George turned around and walked back in the direction of his apartment.

The vision did not appear that evening. George had been apprehensive, thinking it more likely that visions appeared at night. Silly and childish to think that.

Sunday morning, rather a duplicate of Saturday morning, brought no apparition, either. George felt better. Around noon he prepared his frozen chicken, which he had begun thawing at breakfasttime. He lunched, then rang his son George Jr. at three P.M. It was a Sunday ritual that George would telephone between two and three.

"G-*wamp*!" said the baby voice at the other end.

George heard his son's hearty laugh, and George Jr. continued, "Trying to teach Georgie to say 'grampa.' He can say it, but I think he's rattled by the telephone.—Want to say hello to Mary?"

Of course George did. Mary sounded energetic and cheery as usual, informed him that the sun was shining, that they were going to set up their new croquet wickets on the lawn later that morning, that Georgie was cutting another tooth. . . .

When George hung up, he felt a thick silence surround him, as if a dream had suddenly ended—noisily. There was such a thing as noisy silence, wasn't there? For a few minutes he had seen and heard the sunshine of California, the sound of forks and spoons clinking against breakfast plates—almost—the babbling of a year-old baby, the laughter of his son, a man happy with his wife.

He started to take a cigarette, maybe the ninth of that day? Then he did not. He was afraid he might conjure up the apparition again, smoking also. And *Maggie*. Why had the—what should he call it?—brought up Maggie, of all people? That story, finished thirty, no, exactly thirty-three years ago, when George had been eighteen. He'd done the right thing. Yes. With his father's help—money—to be sure, but still the right thing. He had been in love with Maggie and she with him, no doubt about that. And he had got Maggie pregnant, despite their both trying to avoid it. Marriage had been impossible. She wouldn't have put up with four more years of university for him. Would she have? No, Maggie was a simple girl, had been. A juvenile affair, that. . . .

This was a weak moment, George realized. He stood up, again thought of a cigarette and refused it to himself. Coffee, yes, and another swat at Polyfax. Be strong. George went to his kitchen to warm up the coffeepot.

His counterpart stood with back to the sink, dressed just as George was now in dark gray trousers, house slippers, the blue cashmere sweater. "Be strong. Ha-ha. You're your same old self." The apparition was smoking a cigarette, exciting both envy and shame in George.

"Out of my sight!" George said, and swung his right arm in a back-handed blow that would have caught the vision in the side of the head, if it had been solid.

The apparition ducked and laughed boyishly.

Had George touched something, even faintly? He was not sure.

"I see you're in a foul mood. Happy day to you!" said George's likeness, and strolled out of the kitchen.

George took an aggressive step toward the retreating figure, hands stretched out in the manner of a subway guard about to shove a last passenger into a crowded train. George felt nothing against his hands, and when he blinked, he saw nothing.

But the figure did not appear again that day, and by ten P.M., George was feeling better, even cheerful. He had gone over Polyfax, watched a little TV, listened to a Beethoven concerto on his record player as he defrosted his refrigerator and cleaned its interior. Nothing but an *illusion,* that duplicate of himself! George lay on his back now on his long sofa, thinking, daydreaming. It occurred to him, however, that all life was an illusion—of progress, of achievement, a fact obscured by absurd and constant movement—meeting appointments and deadlines, all the silly business of what the human race called "work." George had achieved— what? A respected business reputation and money. Money in the bank and in investments, which Liz had declined to share when they divorced. She had accepted some maintenance at first, and had given even that up when she married a year ago. He and Liz owned a cottage on Montauk Point which they had seldom used, but now Liz said it might be "his and hers" together, since they could always find out when either of them wanted to use it, and not conflict. George had been there only once since their divorce, and then merely to collect a few books and records and personal items. Money, yes, to do what with? His son was doing well, and didn't need his money. George Jr. was a lawyer, too. By the time he went to bed, George had thought himself into a vague depression. But at least the vision did not come back, even when George smoked his twelfth cigarette in bed.

The next morning, George found an envelope among his letters addressed in Liz's handwriting. He opened it as he waited for his bus down Fifth Avenue. Liz invited him to dinner tonight, Monday, and gave him Ed's office number (which George had somewhere) so he could arrange to meet Ed for the drive up.

> *. . . I know you don't like making quick decisions, so I thought I'd write you, and you should get it Sat. or Monday morning anyway. Please try to come, as Ed's son Willie is here for a few days recovering from broken ankle he got playing basketball. He is eighteen now. I think you met him once. . . .*

George put this out of his mind, or at least half out of his mind. He had to concentrate on Polyfax that day. George intended to telephone Ed just before three P.M. and decline politely, but the thought that his image, the apparition, might reproach him for cowardice kept intruding during the morning Polyfax conference. If the vision returned, mightn't he throw it at George that he hadn't had the guts, the civility to accept a dinner invitation from his former wife and her husband, who were really quite kind without overdoing their friendliness?

George rang Ed at two forty-five that afternoon and accepted with pleasure.

"Oh, good! Liz'll be pleased," said Ed with the usual smile in his voice. "Can you meet me at my garage, then, Forty-ninth and Sixth? Kammer's, it's called."

George said he would. He had met Ed at the garage once before. When George left his office, he walked two blocks north in order to buy a bouquet of multicolored carnations from a little old lady who was usually on a certain corner with her pushcart, weather permitting.

"How're you, sir?" said the old lady, all bundled up in sweaters and cape as usual.

George gave her double the price of the flowers. Many a time he had bought a bouquet on the way to see Harrietta, after phoning Liz to tell her he would be working an hour or so late.

By seven that evening, Ed and George with his bouquet were walking up the stone steps to the Tuttle house, which had four gables and a chimney now smoking against the darkening sky. Ed and George had conversed pleasantly during the thirty-five-minute drive. Ed's son Willie, his only child, was doing well at Columbia, but was a bit reckless, Ed thought, hence the basketball accident.

"Hello, George! So happy you could come! Ed phoned and told me." Liz kissed George on the cheek, pressed his hand. "Oh, thank you. Aren't these lovely!" she said, taking the bouquet. She wore a brown satin dress, and her ample breasts bulged against it. Her brown hair looked fluffy and shining, as if she had just been to the hairdresser's. She radiated happiness as she led George into the living room, one hand extended behind her, but not really reaching for George's. "You remember Willie, don't you, George?"

George did. Now Willie sat with plastered foot extended toward the fire, and said politely, "Evening, sir. Can't stand up so well because of this. But I will," he added, pushing himself up on the arms of the upholstered chair.

"Don't bother yourself, Willie! How are you—otherwise?" George shook the tall boy's hand, smiling, and steadied Willie until he had sat down again.

"Quite well, thank you, sir."

Liz served drinks, Manhattans for her and Ed, scotch and water for George. He smoked a cigarette. The conversation was easy, with a few laughs. George was conscious of the heavy Tuttle furniture, a bit rustic, no doubt already installed before Liz's advent. Her touch was probably the plain dark yellow drapes at the windows. George leaned forward to pick up his drink, then he looked at Liz, who was talking. Standing just to Liz's left was the specter—*himself*—now with slightly mocking smile, nodding his head as if to say, "Stupid ass, I suppose you think the evening's going fine?"

A few drops of George's drink spilled on the waxed coffee table, and George at once whipped out his pocket handkerchief.

The gesture snapped Ed out of his happy trance, and he said, "Oh, that's nothing, George!"

George looked at Liz, and past her, and saw that the vision was not there now. Also he had *not* heard the voice, only imagined the words. He was sure of that. It was all bound to be something inside his own head—like buzzing ears.

"Something the matter, George?" asked Liz.

"Not at all," said George. "Just clumsy today."

"*Busy* day," said Liz, inviting him to say more on the subject if he chose.

"I don't want to talk about business," said George with a smile. "It's the month of May. We might talk about vacations—something pleasant." He glanced at Willie. College kids always took an interest in vacations.

They did talk about vacations. The Montauk house, which Liz and Ed said they'd like for the third week in June, if George didn't want it then. George said he did not want it then. Then Venice: Liz and Ed and Willie were taking a boat from Naples which cruised to Sicily first. . . .

George half listened. Dinner. George feared the reappearance of the vision, wondered too if Liz sensed something odd about him tonight, because she knew him so well. They adjourned to the living room for coffee and brandy. Willie walked with two short crutches. The dessert had been Liz's homemade chocolate cake topped with ice cream.

"You're looking *well,* George," Liz said as he was leaving with Ed for the train station. Ed had offered to drive George to Manhattan, but George wouldn't hear of it. "Keep well, dear. We'll see you again soon, I hope."

Was Liz trying to make him feel better? George thought he looked all right, but he knew he had not been in the best of form.

Less than an hour later, George was home in his apartment, alone. Or was he alone? He seemed to be. But how long would it last?

It lasted almost a week. George had made no special resolutions to himself by way of keeping the specter at bay, and indeed wouldn't have known what kind to make. On Saturday around noon, just as George got home with a cart full of groceries that he hoped would last the coming week, he saw his own figure, again leaning against the kitchen sink rim, and dressed in old green corduroys, tweed jacket, desert boots, just as George was then. George blinked, his body went rigid, but he began to unpack his purchases as if the vision were not there. George neatly set the new sack of coffee at the back of a shelf, causing him to pass within inches of the standing figure.

Don't you say good morning?

George *thought* he had heard that. George did not reply. Seeing a new bottle of Haig on a shelf, George took it down and gave the top a twist. Irritation made George say out loud, "I suppose you'll . . . chide me if I take a drink?"

"No, no, might do the same myself. Have done many a time."

The bottle chattered twice against the rim of the glass as George poured. He was not deranged enough to offer the specter a drink, but would not have been surprised if the bottle had moved from the table and a glass had been reached from the drainboard. This did not happen.

"Ha-ha," said the specter mirthlessly.

George left the kitchen with his drink in hand. *Ha-ha.* Well, hadn't he often laughed at himself in the same manner? For taking a drink at noon when he had intended not to take one before six P.M.? And why take *that* so seriously? Neither Liz nor any doctor had ever told him he drank too much. Was it that he had nothing else to worry about?

Half-finished drink in hand, George frowned at the kitchen door, from which nothing emerged. He had something to worry about, all right.

That afternoon, George called his doctor, after three calls got Dr. Pallantz in person, and asked him the name of a reliable psychiatrist. The doctor gave him two names, recommended the first more highly, then inquired if anything was the matter.

"I'd rather not say just—I'm quite all right physically, I believe," George went on, glancing toward the kitchen. "Just thought I'd have a talk with a psychiatrist for an hour. Always less than an hour, I know." Here George gave a chuckle, which he hated.

That same afternoon, George succeeded in arranging a half hour visit with Dr. Kublick at six-thirty P.M. the coming Monday. George had mentioned Dr. Pallantz's name, and it had plainly carried weight. George was heartened to find that the weekend brought no further intrusions from the specter. This strengthened George's belief—the only logical thing to believe—that the trouble was due to some kind of lack of confidence in himself, and perhaps the mere appointment with a psychiatrist had done the trick.

On Monday at six-thirty P.M., George told all. It was amazing how much a man could tell in hardly ten minutes. All about his father and mother in Chicago (hardware store owners, and they had wished to see George go to a good school and enjoy a better life than theirs), George's marriage with Liz and the breakup. And of course George had begun with the strange visions which had started a couple of weeks ago, the last of which had been Saturday noon. That, specifically, was why George had come, he told the psychiatrist.

"I'm wondering if it's some kind of schizophrenia in myself," George added, as the doctor pondered, chin in hand, but with a pleasant, even entertained expression on his face.

Dr. Kublick looked about forty-five, was rather tall, and wore a brown suit with no sign of a crease in the trousers. Through black-rimmed glasses he kept steady eyes on George, and he made no notes. "Schizophrenia . . ." he said finally. "An old catchall. Are you sleeping well lately?"

"As usual. Like a top. I've always slept well."

"No dizziness in the morning? No feeling of faintness?" And at George's shake of the head, "Do you drink much?"

"Three or four a day. Scotch and water.—I honestly don't think that's it." As the half hour grew shorter, George felt that he had to hurry for an answer, for a bit of help. He repeated, "The reality of that red dressing gown was amazing to me. I could have *touched* it. That's the way I felt, anyway."

"Yet you said when you did swing at the . . . thing backhand, you didn't feel anything." The doctor was smiling in a friendly, reassuring way.

"I said I thought I didn't. But I saw the thing duck." And the *voice.* "And the voice," George continued. "Like my voice. I must admit I heard that. I *seemed* to hear it. I know it's an illusion, but I'm not the kind of man to have illusions," George said forcefully, and oddly his strong voice made the vision more real to him than before. Didn't the shrink believe him? George was telling the truth!

The doctor said calmly, "All this could be due to tension. Had a lot of strain in your office lately?"

Polyfax. That was a big job, but not one with tension, not even a tough deadline attached to it. "No." George said.

"Do you feel guilty—about anything?"

The clock on Dr. Kublick's wall jumped another five minutes. How vulgar, George thought, to have a five-minute-jumping clock in an office where time was geared to money, but thoughts and dreams were not, not even geared to time. Or was the clock, even beholdable by a patient who might be lying on the leather sofa to George's right, considered by Dr. Kublick to be somehow an asset to the patient? Something to bring him or her back to reality? Dr. Kublick had just asked him a big question, impossible to answer in a few words. Didn't everyone feel guilty about something or several things? Would it be normal to feel not guilty about anything? "I think I have the usual amount of guilt feelings. I wouldn't call them serious—or obsessive."

"About what, for instance?"

Two minutes to go. George pondered desperately, imagining suddenly a woman rummaging through a sewing basket, looking for a thread of a certain color. "I had a woman friend—as I told you—during two years of my married life. That didn't cause me to be less kind to my wife." He was not going to start the Maggie story, a teenage mistake. That was *not* on his mind. Neither was Harrietta, even. He and Harrietta had parted amicably, agreeing that they didn't care to see each other again. Somehow Harrietta's proposal of marriage and his agreement had extinguished even their affair. "I honestly think guilt is not the cause of these . . . hallucinations."

Ping!

It was like the end of a round of boxing. The doctor stood up. So did George, already thinking about paying. The doctor indicated that his secretary could take care of that, and George understood that the doctor wanted to be free at once for his seven o'clock patient.

"You're under a strain of some kind," the doctor said as George moved toward his open door. "Up to you to identify, if you can. And if you want to see me again . . ."

George signed a check for fifty dollars. He did not ask for another appointment, thinking he could make one in the next days, if he decided that he should.

He felt dazed, rather than enlightened. What had Dr. Kublick said, after all? And George had dumped all his problems into the psychiatrist's lap, confessed to some loneliness now. But just what were his sins, if he came down to it? Or rather, what had he done so wrong, in all his life, to warrant visitations from a specter which seemed (George couldn't get rid of the notion) to be bent on reproaching him?

The question was: Was he really deranged, to have seen that vision of himself? Or had he really seen it, meaning that it really existed (after all, some people believed ghosts existed), and had it some valid meaning in regard to his life? Was there some abstract judge who made an assessment of these things? The abstract judge in George's mind was not God, but some scale of value which perhaps not even a philosopher of highest rank had yet codified. Therefore one had to struggle and try to do it for oneself. George felt that he had not even tried as yet, and that therefore he was in a moral sense as low as an uneducated peasant anywhere, as low as any animal on four legs, though without that animal's innocence.

Maybe the vision wouldn't turn up again, George thought as he prepared a simple meal that evening. He was trying to take some fortitude from the fact that he had seen a psychiatrist and stated the facts. What else could a person do?

As he ate, George thought of something else he could do: speak to Ralph Foreman and say that he would be glad to meet the young man who was interested in joining the firm. Since this was more a social event than a business one, George decided to telephone Ralph now, even though he would see him in the office tomorrow.

Ralph's wife Nancy answered, spoke to George in a friendly way, then put Ralph on. George said he was sorry that he had not been able to make the dinner date the last time, and could they make another?

"I'd like you to meet Edna Carstairs, too," Ralph said. "I'll see if we can get her for Friday. I'm sure Pete can make it."

Pete was the young man. Had Ralph mentioned Edna Carstairs before?

George felt better, as if he had accomplished something, or at least set himself on a positive course. During that week, George kept to twelve cigarettes a day, counting them carefully. One had to make an effort. There was no "second" cigarette in the kitchen ashtray or anywhere else. Slowly but surely he would erase that apparition, that figment, and finally he'd laugh at the memory of it.

Friday after work, George came home to put on a clean shirt before going to the Foremans'. He chose another tie. As he was putting his jacket back on, he became aware of a dismal depression, as if he were exhausted, or had just heard a piece of bad news. George straightened up, even tried to smile at himself in the mirror. It did not help. He could have collapsed on the bed and stayed there all evening. He deliberately strode toward his apartment door, thinking that extra physical effort would wake him up. He glanced aggressively toward his kitchen, walked into it to prove to himself that it was empty.

In the round white ashtray on the kitchen table lay a lighted cigarette, half burned. Had he come into the kitchen when he got home? He didn't think so. He looked in the direction of the sink. Nothing there.

"Ha-ha." It was a soft, dry laugh behind him, and George turned.

For an instant George saw himself beyond the kitchen door, in the hall that led to the living room. Then the vision vanished.

The laugh and the figure were *both* imaginary, George thought. But the cigarette? Well, he must have lit one when he came in, thinking of something else, not counting this cigarette, and it would have been half burned, as it was, by the time he had changed his shirt. Was he conquering, winning, just because the vision had disappeared so fast, because the laugh hadn't been so audible as before? George stared boldly into the empty living room, as if defying the thing to reappear. But he did not feel in a conquering mood. The depression still clung to him, and he could feel the corners of his mouth turning down, a frown clamping his brows.

"Damn it to hell and gone!" George said. In that instant he felt that his half hour with the psychiatrist had netted him nothing. George squared his shoulders, and smiled in order to erase the frown. He had an obligation to be pleasant this evening, because he was a guest. He took a taxi to East Eighty-fourth Street.

"George! Welcome—finally!" Ralph Foreman slapped George on the shoulder. "Come in and meet—Edna Carstairs."

A pretty woman in a longish black and gold dress sat on the sofa, smiled at George, and said, "How do you do?"

"And Peter Buckler—from New York."

A young man with reddish brown hair and a beaming smile got up and extended a hand to George. "How do you do, sir? Ralph says New York because I'm from upstate. Troy."

"Graduate of Cornell Law," Ralph added to George.

Ralph gave George a scotch and water, rather a strong one. Nancy had said hello, but excused herself to go back to the kitchen. The woman called Edna had lovely brown eyes whose lids seemed to turn up at the corners, probably due to makeup, but the effect was beautiful. For this reason George avoided looking at her often. She did not talk much, and laughed only when a laugh was appropriate. She was an editor somewhere, at a publishing house. Ralph maneuvered the conversation so that he could state Peter Buckler's qualifications: a promotion—recently, too—in a firm in which he was not happy, however, for reasons that Ralph made sound valid. George listened, but felt oddly rattled by the heavy colors—dark red with a bit of blue—of the floor-length window curtains, now drawn, opposite him at the street windows. Were they the street windows, or windows on a court? Did it matter? No. Why should he care what was behind those curtains? Did the dark red remind him of his dressing gown?

"We might speak to old Tub. What do you think, George? Introduce Pete. Old Tub can always think of a reason to say no, but I think we could use some new blood.—You with me, George?" said Ralph.

"Yes, why not?" said George. No harm in introducing Peter Buckler, who did look bright and promising. At this moment, the red and blue curtains behind Ralph whirled in a kaleidoscopic way, and formed an image, much vaguer than the others George had seen, of himself in his red dressing gown, with a hint of pajamas at the top. George blinked and looked down at his drink. George was determined: he was not going to countenance the vision tonight, not going to acknowledge its presence. Nancy came in to summon them to dinner, and George was the first to stand up. George felt he had won that round with his hallucination. The vision had been paler. If it ever appeared again, George thought a bit wildly, maybe he should try to seize it, crush it in his arms, join it somehow, or prove to himself that it was nothing but thin air. If there was a next time.

The dining alcove off the kitchen presented a different atmosphere, and George intended to be pleasant, alert, outgoing. The merry faces around him cheered him. And the red wine tasted delicious. Should he invite Edna Carstairs to something? Dinner? The theater? She looked about thirty-eight. Why was she single? What had happened? Well, what had happened to him? Was it a disgrace?

Edna was the first to leave. George thought that Ralph might want to talk a bit with Pete, so George got up also—by this time they had had coffee in the living room—and asked if he might drop Edna off somewhere in a taxi.

"West Sixty-ninth and Broadway?" said Edna, as if she weren't sure it would be convenient for George. "You don't have to, really."

"A pleasure," George assured her, then said his thanks to the Foremans for the evening.

In the taxi George asked Edna if she liked going to the theater. All kinds of theater, she told him, except stupid sex comedies. In answer to George's question, she said she was free next Tuesday evening, and George said he would see what he could do about either of the two plays Edna had mentioned. She gave him her card. It had her home address, plus the downtown address of the publishing house where she worked. George said he would telephone her Tuesday to confirm, and he would pick her up around seven P.M. George saw her into her apartment building, then returned to his waiting taxi. He felt happy.

His good humor lasted over the weekend. He and Ralph saw that Peter Buckler got an interview Tuesday with Tub, the outcome of which George did not ask.

George was home before six P.M. on Tuesday, took a shower and changed into a suit fresh from the cleaners. He felt optimistic and sure of himself, even thrilled by his first date with Edna. It was not that he had any intentions in regard to her. She might merely like him as a friend, as the saying went, but this kind of success, even the prospect of it, picked up George's ego. And she *was* pretty, the kind of woman he would be proud to escort anywhere. George was about to leave his bedroom when he saw the awful self-image standing to his right, in front of the tall windows, dressed also in the same handsome suit and dark blue bow tie that George wore now. George's shock turned at once to anger, to a desire to erase the vision, to walk out on it, so he started for the door.

"Optimistic," said the vision cynically.

George stood up straighter. "There is such a thing as joining me. Joining me, physically," George said, and moved toward the vision, arms outspread, thinking either to make the vision vanish by reaching for it or—or what? Press it into his own body? "What did I do that was so wrong?—I find you *fuzzy*—as fuzzy as you look!"

"Ah, the fuzziness of life," said the vision in an amused way. It moved backward, arms also outspread. "What did you do that was so wrong? That's the question and that's for you to answer, isn't it?"

"*Join* me," George repeated. "What's this joke all about?" George might as well have been talking to himself, but he felt full of courage at that moment. And as he came close, he could feel a slight resistance in the half-solid figure, as if he were finally touching something. He wanted to press the thing into his own body, and to get rid of it in that manner.

The vision seemed to rock in his arms, and George had the impression that it had several arms instead of two. George's frustration made him angry in a matter of seconds. He opened the French window with his left hand. There was a balcony too narrow to walk out on, and a rail waist-high.

"I'll throw you over if you *don't*!" George meant, if the vision refused to merge with him. George lifted his knee, but his knee hit nothing. Who was pushing or pulling whom? He seized the jacket front in his right hand and lifted, his left hand under the vision's right arm. "I'll get rid of you!" George said between his teeth, tugged the thing toward the balcony and lifted. He was hardly aware of a weight, yet there was *something,* enough to make George lose his balance, and the bulk of his weight in chest and shoulders pulled the rest of him over the rail.

George felt space, a quick sense of release. Then there was an instant's time for terror, and the realization that he had made an awful mistake. He hadn't meant to fall out the window himself, not at all!

He fell from the eleventh floor. George's death was attributed to accident, and the psychiatrist Kublick and the doctor Pallantz both suggested "dizziness."

AFTERWORD

by Paul Ingendaay

I

Patricia Highsmith's emergence as a writer is shrouded in mystery, perhaps unnecessarily so. If we look at her earliest stories, published between 1939 and 1949, we cannot but wonder why they were kept under lock and key for half a century. Highsmith herself may have been one of her harshest critics, as demonstrated by her decision on her twenty-fourth birthday to abandon a novel of almost three hundred pages, "The Click of the Shutting." In a conversation with Austrian writer Peter Handke she characterized the fragment as "quite different from my later books" and "an odd stylistic mixture of Thomas Wolfe and Marcel Proust."

Highsmith did not judge her early stories as harshly, and there was no need to reject them so formally. Since her school years she had been experimenting in this genre, so that by her middle twenties she commanded a considerable repertoire of narrative techniques. Among her favorite authors at that time were not only psychological realists such as Dostoevski and Joseph Conrad but also the canonic masters of the short story form: Poe, Stevenson, Henry James, and Hemingway. "What I like best when I write is economy," she commented in her notebook at nineteen, "and that's why I like Maupassant. What an incredible satisfaction it must be to fashion a story like that!" She then goes on to explain why she uses the term "to fashion": because in her eyes the technical process of shaping is far superior to simply writing. Because, she adds, it resembles the work of a sculptor, who only liberates his conception by reducing mass—chipping and chiseling away.

This idealism, which was largely based on an economy of means, was from the beginning a component of Patricia Highsmith's artistic thinking. Hardly less urgent was the far more prosaic problem of keeping her head above water in New York. After graduating from Barnard College in 1942, Patricia Highsmith found a position writing texts for comic books. On the side she had the time to do some minor editing and got assignments to write essays for which she was poorly paid. It was apparent from very early on that writing was her "*Lebensmittel*," her means of living, as she noted in her diary in curious but appropriate German. But why, one wonders today, did it take her a good thirty years, until 1970, to first publish her stories in book form in *Eleven*? And why did she, with few exceptions, leave out her stories written between 1938 and 1949, which comprise the present Part I of her uncollected and mostly unpublished stories?

There is no clear answer to these questions; there are at best hints that require interpretation. Highsmith, who was born in 1921, strove to be independent, worked freelance, and therefore needed money. Whatever she aspired to had to be struggled for. Even when she was a student, we can assume that she had a sharp sense of the commodity value of literature. What she wrote, however, did not always turn out to be marketable, and her native land remained an unreliable partner throughout her life. It may even be guessed that the need for profit and the "impure" conditions under which she wrote her stories—repeated workings of drafts to satisfy editors, shortening the stories, changing the titles, not to mention countless rejections—may have vitiated her own perception of the quality of her writing. The present volume amply proves that her early work contains some remarkable stories.

Highsmith published her first important stories in the student magazine *Barnard Quarterly*, of which she was editor in chief in her senior year (1942). During her college years, she found the time to work with communist youth groups; read avidly in literature and philosophy; and take courses in Latin, Greek, German, and zoology, as well as writing courses on the short story and plays. She was curious, ambitious, and restless, her schedule always on overload. Surprisingly, the Second World War seems not to have entered her consciousness: Roosevelt's death in 1945 is noted in her diaries, but no details of the global earthquake that resulted from World War II. Private concerns, on the other hand, are a major theme. Frequently expressed is her sense of oppression, compounded by her need to return every evening to the constricting apartment of her mother and stepfather on the Upper East Side.

Not that she dutifully returned there every night. As a student Patricia Highsmith had an active social life for which she ultimately put even politics aside, and one can deduce from the earliest surviving entries that her mother was pleased neither by the company she kept nor the "masculinization" of her appearance. Remarkably, despite an imposing sequence of lesbian friendships and brief affairs, Patricia Highsmith could not summon up the courage to tell her mother (who suspected something but did not know) the truth about her sexual orientation. She even submitted for a while to psychotherapy in order to be "cured" of her "condition." It is fortunate that the travesty of a bourgeois marriage, which she and a friend were considering for a long time, was never celebrated.

There is an obvious connection between her writing and her friendships. On the one hand, Patricia Highsmith wanted to earn money with her typewriter; she saw herself—correctly—as the "strong" half of all her relationships. Yet on the other hand, after a successful so-called conquest, she quickly became bored, jealously defending the time she reserved for writing, and complaining in her diary that she needed to endure the adventure of writing by herself. In 1943, after she was hired by the comics publisher Fawcett, she rented her first apartment, on Fifty-sixth Street on the East Side, quite near her parents.

We know from these first few months away from home a number of things about Patricia Highsmith: that she cleverly painted walls and furniture and in the evenings read Kafka; what she ate, how much money she spent; with whom she socialized, with whom she slept and how often. The picture is more diffuse if one tries to grasp her aesthetic ideas, not because they are unclear but because the insights that pour forth incessantly are not always coherent. Patricia Highsmith had not even decided whether she wanted to be a painter or a writer, a question that was not resolved until 1944.

She experimented with both short and long forms. At twenty she already realized that she was not interested in mere storytelling for the sake of plot and tension. Since she had become more reflective, she felt she would need to write less. Moreover, she was more inclined to the novel than to the short story, because she saw no value in even the best stories. Six months later, however, in August 1941, she is "very, very happy" and dreamily thinks of spinning out short stories as delicate as smoke rings. With these kinds of entries, her thinking seems to have drifted completely away from economic considerations. At twenty-six, she comments on her hope to reconcile at some future stage "commercial" and "artistic" writing, an idea that strikes us as profoundly American.

Commercialism as such, in any case, might have discouraged the author in later years from carefully reviewing the stories of this period and selecting some for book publication. She might have been similarly hesitant given the stories' multiplicity of tones, themes, and stylistic registers. The stories assembled here from posthumous papers in Part I are not mere detective or suspense or animal stories but complex psychological tales—about little girls, middle-aged women and middle-aged men, about accepted and illicit morality. They follow no pattern, no single method. In some cases, they do not even seem to emerge from the same hand.

Looking for the type of character most frequently encountered among the fourteen stories collected in Part I, the reader is in for a surprise. While her novels are mostly about men in their early thirties—the typical Highsmith hero is sensitive, cultivated, well bred, not necessarily handsome but not ugly either, and in no case fat—the young, twenty-five-year-old author finds her most interesting figures in fading women who have to assert themselves in dreary, boring lives. Three stories, which are among the strongest in the collection, present unattached, rather agitated heroines who risk the danger of being run over by the trauma of what has become everyday life. "Where the Door Is Always Open and the Welcome Mat Is Out," "Doorbell for Louisa," and "The Still Point of the Turning World" offer three small portraits of souls, written with a mercilessly precise sense of daily routine, surroundings, and weather.

When Mrs. Robinson in "The Still Point of the Turning World" accidentally witnesses a scene on a park bench, she does have an intimation that because of her conventionality and narrow-mindedness she has missed out on much of life. Overcoming her curiosity, she takes her spruce, neatly combed son by the hand and walks past the pair of lovers out of the park. Her last glance as she leaves is the instant in which her character is momentarily revealed: a mixture of envy and pride, longing and self-righteousness.

Patricia Highsmith commented extensively on this story, one in which she repeatedly changes perspective in a way that she otherwise spurned. For one thing, "The Still Point of the Turning World" was written just after the author had separated from an important woman friend. The kiss of the lovers in this story, she wrote, is the kiss of this friend, which she, the author, will no longer experience (and the jealousy that she depicts so brilliantly was at the moment of writing already her own). But she was also happy with her work, and expressed this time and again—in German—in her diary: "God! I feel my power—if I can only maintain the good condition of my mind, my mood!" (This in August of 1947.) And a day later: "Am very happy and full of peace."

Despite her own sense of accomplishment, *Harper's Bazaar* rejected the story. That October, *Today's Woman* expressed interest. In November, however, she heard from an editor at the magazine who advised "smoother transitions." In the pages of her diary the author explodes: "Just what I did *not* want!" But she reconsidered and revised the text. In December, the story was sold to *Today's Woman* for eight hundred dollars. It appeared sixteen months later, in March 1949, under a different title. Quite a few compromises for eight hundred dollars.

In a certain sense, the two other stories about middle-aged women—"Where the Door Is Always Open and the Welcome Mat Is Out" and "Doorbell for Louisa"—can be read as complementary interpretations of one and the same observation: What happens when a person gives herself over to the dictates of her compulsive work and organizing delusions? If she collapses, who notices it? If she holds out, who rewards her? "Where the Door Is Always Open and the Welcome Mat Is Out" describes a minutely detailed defeat in a struggle against the big city, circumstances, and the clock. But here the woman, who in spite of the best of intentions makes a mess of everything, prefers to hang on to the life she has chosen for herself. Like a hamster on its wheel she will remain frantically in motion until her heart gives out. Louisa Trotte, the main character in the other story, is of a similar stripe. But here, in a story about sacrifice and solidarity, everything turns out well: Louisa's work is not in vain, but useful and appreciated. At the end, her employer even invites her out for dinner, which Louisa hopes will be at the Plaza Hotel— more than just a hint of a happy ending. And yet the two stories do resemble each other in that their final sentences are totally open to possibility, a kingdom in which the happy are apparently no happier than the failures.

The middle-aged women in Part I have a male colleague and comrade in misery, as in the story "Magic Casements." Highsmith's male characters are somewhat more passive and melancholy. Such a person, sad and worked over by life (but not lacking for money), meets a woman who attracts and fascinates him. They start talking in his favorite bar, have a few drinks, seem to understand each other in some intuitive way, make a date on which their exchange seems to reach a note even more intimate. At the next rendezvous on the following day, in a museum, the woman doesn't show. The man finds out that she has left town. He stays behind, alone.

This is a recurrent theme throughout Highsmith's stories. Yet their desolate sense of daily routine, briefly interrupted by an enchantment brought on by a meeting of like-minded souls, only to be followed by disappointment—the deadened steps of a figure abandoned to mourning—has been captured in exquisite detail. "Magic Casements" is one of those stories sketched in the notebook with great precision, almost overelaborated, and the actual writing seeks to free the story from a plot that has become too complicated. There is no doubt that Patricia Highsmith's ambition in her early short fiction was to be a craftsperson, without regard to commercial success.

Some of Highsmith's older stories slumber in a dim past; others seize a later generation more strongly than they did their first readers, such as they were. The latter is the case with "A Mighty Nice Man," written about 1940, a story from Highsmith's college days, and "The Mightiest Mornings." At the center of both stories is the relationship between an adult man and a small girl he does not know. But the theme of pedophilia (in the 1940s one spoke of the "bad uncle") plays no role on the surface of "A Mighty Nice Man." Patricia Highsmith seems above all interested in what the little girl—and later, her clumsily flirting mother—sees in the stranger who owns the fine car. In this sense the story is quite radical. For with her innocent gaze, the child "recognizes" something that adults at best deduce as subtext: the conditions of sexual transaction.

In "The Mightiest Mornings" (1945) several themes are superimposed. There is a rumor that the town's new arrival, Aaron Bentley, might be having forbidden relations with ten-year-old Freya, herself a social outsider. When the contempt from the town becomes tangible, Aaron and Freya retreat to an attitude of "arrogant innocence." Aaron soon notices that the notion of guilt directed at him is actually taking root in him. In an almost masochistic form of acceptance, he internalizes the view that the muted majority has of the minority (himself) and he leaves the small town: Aaron imbibes a guilt that is not his and allows it to drive him into action. In the notebook draft, Bentley was sketched as an ambiguous man; in the final story, however, he becomes the early model of all Highsmith heroes who have less to fear from others than themselves.

Given the prevailing views of the era, it does not come as a surprise that the story was rejected several times, first by *The Atlantic Monthly*, then by *Mademoiselle*—an example of inspired writing that misses its target market. The present edition offers the first publication ever of "The Mightiest Mornings." In any event, as far as we can see, Patricia Highsmith enjoyed working on it. "Read Proust," she noted in her diary in November 1945. "And of course—my story."

II

Like the stories in the first part of this collection, those in the "Middle and Later Stories" transcend the time in which they were written. It is difficult to fathom why Highsmith did not seek to publish them or what caused her reservations about her own work. Still, the stories managed to survive and were not among the roughly three hundred pages of short fiction that she destroyed after a process of meticulous inspection.

The stories in Part II are collected from the fifties, sixties, and seventies, the decades in which Patricia Highsmith earned a reputation in Europe as a "literary" suspense writer, a category that was highly unusual at the time. Any attempt at greater precision would only obfuscate matters, because she is essentially a writer who defies easy categorization. The texts that appear in the "Middle and Later Stories" encompass the entire range of Highsmith's writings—psychological narrative, prose farce, crime or suspense story, and ghost and animal story. Moreover, they might also have had a role in helping Patricia Highsmith cope with personal conflicts that unsettled her apparently serene secluded life. They can therefore be read on several levels: as literary narratives, as a testing ground for recurrent motifs in her writing, and sometimes even as encoded diaries, if we couple our readings of the texts with scrutiny of the documentary evidence—the author's diaries and notebooks—housed in the Swiss Literature Archives in Berne.

It is not very likely that Patricia Highsmith herself would have compiled and prepared for publication such a diverse volume spanning all these decades. However, the work is hardly a violation of her will; on the contrary, *Nothing That Meets the Eye* can be seen as a liberation—from the self-doubts assailing her as a writer and the conditions under which she earned her living. We may therefore feel justified today in rescuing undeservedly unknown or forgotten texts of considerable quality from the paper grave of her literary estate. Despite their consistent literary mastery, their central motif can be summed up in a single word: *failure.*

For reasons that I am at a loss to explain in detail, "The Trouble with Mrs. Blynn" strikes me as the jewel of Part II. Readers might be puzzled to find it marked with the Highsmith tag. Nothing uncanny, odd, or abysmal occurs. There is neither quirk nor anomaly to marvel at. Certainly nothing on the order of a murder takes place. The story simply centers on a small, mean-spirited calculation that offers the reader a quick glimpse into the much greater and incorrigible mean-spiritedness of the world.

An old lady is dying. The house in which she lies, a small cottage on the English east coast, has been rented for only a few weeks. Likewise rented: a housekeeper and a nurse. This nurse, the widowed Mrs. Blynn, was herself a former resident of the house. Now, she is watching Mrs. Palmer die. Her steely eyes pass through the text as a leitmotif. Her gaze alights on everything that the dying woman has gathered around her, including an amethyst pin. In Highsmith's notebooks, we find the following exquisite, solemn statement, dated July 24, 1964: "The world widens when death comes near, all that lies in us is apparent—our lens has widened, and certainly it is too much for the average person."

The notion that the world "widens" as death approaches and that everything presses to the surface so as to shock those who are not dying unfolds almost imperceptibly in the story. The pattern strikes us as natural as calm breathing. Quite likely the author experienced little difficulty in identifying with the old lady who lies down to die far from home. Patricia Highsmith herself, shortly after completing the first draft of the novel *The Glass Cell* in December 1963, moved from Italy to Aldeburgh in Suffolk, in the south of England, to be with a girlfriend. Visiting the place half a year earlier, she described the dreariness and the stormy climate of Aldeburgh in her diary: "It is hard to imagine anyone wintering here by choice, for Aldeburgh alone. For the people here, it is different: they are married to it and cannot get away."

This inability to get away—because of disease or death—is exactly what underlies "The Trouble with Mrs. Blynn." The motionless body and the widened lens focus the situation with complete clarity. Everything happens as it is bound to happen. As Highsmith's notebook reveals, Mrs. Palmer sees in the face of the nurse "a cosmic vision of life and of everything that went wrong with life. The nurse is like misfortune, a failure of understanding, a misreading of goodwill, the shutting of the heart" (November 22, 1963).

The pure, defenseless Mrs. Palmer is joined by another equally virtuous soul in the title story "Nothing That Meets the Eye," which may have been written at about the same time. This character, however, is altogether different. Whereas Mrs. Palmer sinks into her cushions and shrinks in stature, Helene Sacher-Hartmann seems to bloom in the Austrian winter resort and to make the whole world fall at her feet. The aura she generates deludes everyone she meets. Helene, healthy and sociable, seeks out death with a determination that we might almost call cheery.

In *Plotting and Writing Suspense Fiction* (1966), Patricia Highsmith uses this story to illustrate the question of how a writer can "feel the story emotionally." She explains that it was difficult for her to project herself into the mind of a woman contemplating suicide because she herself had never been near the edge of suicide. "So I took the easy way out," she writes laconically, "and did not explain her state of mind. (Never apologize, never explain, said an English diplomat, and a French writer, Baudelaire, said that the only good parts of a book are the explanations that are left out.)" Her strategy certainly worked. In the stories collected here there is no suicide that makes more sense than this one, although it is the only one that is neither explained nor justified.

The gallery of exceedingly Germanic names in "Nothing That Meets the Eye" (Helene Sacher-Hartmann, for example, and Gert and Hedwig von Böchlein, who are all lodgers at the Hotel Waldhaus in

Alpenbach) may startle regular Highsmith readers. The writer was somewhat conversant in German, having learned the language in high school given her father's German heritage. On occasion, she even composed her diary entries in German. During her trip through Europe from 1951 to 1953, Highsmith wrote an additional story, "The Returnees," which also has a strong overlay of German local color.

"The Returnees" chronicles the disintegration of a couple's relationship over the course of several years, with attention being paid to both partners, a feature uncommon in Patricia Highsmith's writing. Moreover, the story, with its postwar ambience and repeated suggestions of German anti-Semitism, is one of the rare examples of historical-political references in her books. The diaries reveal that the author met in Munich in December 1951 a Jewish friend of a friend, whose rapid financial ascent in the postwar era clearly provided the model for the figure of Esther Friedmann in "The Returnees." Ten months after this encounter, in a Paris hotel room, Patricia Highsmith began to compose her "German story," which she finished some three weeks later, on October 21, 1952.

It is striking how often the word "failure" occurs in the notes and plot sketches. Considering that most of the stories in the last half of the book revolve around the idea of a bungled and shattered life, they share a common outlook. Patricia Highsmith was a tough-minded writer who believed man capable of extraordinary evil, and she took a dim view of man's capacity for self-knowledge and self-improvement. Several of the stories included here, however, veer in the opposite direction. They are unexpectedly comforting, uncharacteristically Highsmith, the exceptions that prove the rule. Paradoxically, it is one of these stories, "Born Failure," that features "failure" in its title.

Patricia Highsmith actually comes close to creating a parable in this story, written in 1953. Winthrop Hazlewood, a small-town retailer, has made pitifully little of his life. He toils away until late into the night to earn a meager income. His good-for-nothing brother robs him, all of his business ventures peter out, and his wares get ruined in a dank basement. Then he inherits one hundred thousand dollars, of which he is entitled to keep eighty thousand. All he has to do is pick up the money at his lawyer's office in New York. On the ferry that brings him home, his money stashed in his briefcase, Winthrop Hazlewood looks back. The phases of his life flash before his eyes, all marked by ignorance, ineptness, and bad luck, and it seems to him that his only success in his life is in tracking down failure with the sure touch of a divining rod. A merchant who has accomplished little (although he has a happy marriage, and his wife Rose does not find fault with him), Winthrop Hazlewood realizes that the theme that characterizes his existence is failure, in a way the suitable expression of his personality. He comes to believe that the money in his briefcase is almost obscene: "He didn't deserve it." While he contemplates his new prosperity and the opportunities now open to him and Rose, tears well in his eyes. He reaches for his handkerchief, and in doing so inadvertently lets the briefcase slip overboard. It falls into the water with a soft thud and sinks.

The story does not conclude here. Nonetheless, this is a critical juncture that enables us to understand the author's deepest motivations. Highsmith was preoccupied with the theme of failure since her earliest recorded notes. Undated entries in her second notebook, which she kept from November 1939 to July 1940, broach an idea for a novel, namely the "story of a failure." Failure, according to the young woman recording these notes, "inevitably" occurs more often than success. She then remarks: "A good man, thoughtful, sensitive, eternally optimistic at last sees himself honestly after middle age." That, in a nutshell, is the portrait of Winthrop Hazlewood, who is capable of self-knowledge and assesses the circumstances of his existence without any self-deception.

I am not suggesting that the author's early reflections inexorably led to a story that she wrote a full twelve years afterward, but rather that "Born Failure" is the outcome of a similar concern. Her actual plan to write a novel about a failed artist did not materialize. On September 14, 1940, Patricia Highsmith wrote in her notebook that she was exasperated about the "vagueness" of her prose as soon as she prepared to put her ideas into words. She realized what the problem was: Since she was still young, and every depiction of an artist in one way or another contains a self-portrait within it, she simply could not project herself into the role of an aging artist looking back. On September 19, 1940, she gave up on the idea of the artist figure ("too weak and vague") and determined that she needed to model her characters on real life. In the same note, she quotes her professor at Barnard College, Ethel Sturtevant, who advised her that the ability to create literary characters by invention comes "with experience."

Regardless of how Patricia Highsmith gained her new self-awareness—

her unambitious stepfather, for one, provided a dismal example from an early age—by the time she was thirty-two years old, she wrote a story about the failed Winthrop Hazlewood, depicting his trials and tribulations with precision and economy, and unexpectedly giving an upward turn to his destiny instead of racing it down into the abyss. Far from being mocked and detested, Hazlewood is celebrated and hoisted up onto the shoulders of several men in the cheering crowd. This moment is important. It is less about poetic justice in the conventional sense, and certainly not about the question of whether Hazlewood has truly "deserved" the love of his wife and the friendship and recognition of his neighbors. (Of course he has.) But haven't other Highsmith figures deserved more than they get? And if so, why do their paths so often lead downhill?

The turning point of "Born Failure," where she must turn the story into a tragedy or a tale with a happy ending, is critical to our understanding of it. At this moment, readers' expectations need to be satisfied or disappointed, genre conventions fulfilled or violated, interpretations offered or withheld. In this case, the author opts for a finale that recalls fairy tales: The immense material loss no longer matters; it is nothing compared to the self-reflection that the hero has undergone. And the woman whose husband has just allowed eighty thousand dollars to slip through his fingers pronounces herself happier than ever. Something in Winthrop Hazlewood's life has apparently been fulfilled.

Likewise, several stories in this volume have what I might call an either/or situation, and they can just as easily conclude with positive or negative outcomes. One example is "A Bird in Hand," an undated story to which neither the notebooks nor the diaries contain any reference. Placid, harmless Douglas McKenny enhances his meager income with chronic deceit. When a reporter gets wise to him, his very existence is threatened. Highsmith, however, gives a didactic twist to the story. McKenny makes people who have lost their parakeets happy by bringing them new birds and deluding them into thinking that the replacement birds are the ones that had taken wing. The fact that he amasses substantial monetary rewards for his efforts is beside the point. McKenny is friendly to his neighbors; he is a philanthropist of small gestures. "A Bird in Hand," then, proves didactic in the sense that the basic decency of the man—coupled with his love of animals—greatly outweighs the significance of his deceit.

Another story, "Man's Best Friend," written in July 1952, also lets the hero off the hook and allows him to establish a quiet, austere happiness. What matters most in this farcical story of a spurned lover is his ability to reclaim his squandered life. More clearly than in other stories, "Man's Best Friend" provides us with a clearer understanding of how Highsmith devised her narrative structure. The author remarks on two occasions in her notebooks that the hero, a dentist named Dr. Fenton, who is driven into a corner by his unbearably civilized dog, ultimately commits suicide to throw off the yoke of his absurd moral servitude. The version finally put down on paper, however, goes no further than two suicide attempts, both of which are thwarted by the dog. (Douglas McKenny, in "A Bird in Hand," also considers taking his life, before rejecting the idea as ignoble.) At the last second, the author shifts the motif of failure from one character to another. The story does not culminate with Dr. Fenton's demise. Instead, the ending focuses on the woman with whom the dentist was so desperately in love years earlier. Now she has aged badly and become, in Dr. Fenton's eyes, a caricature of her former self.

In switching back and forth between self-preservation and suicide, between salvation and devastation, Patricia Highsmith is concerned with the total picture, not with narrative components that can be inserted randomly, and most assuredly not with playful calculation. Yet, this existential gravity does not make every conclusion a successful one. Some appear to be deadly serious and rather leaden.

What we learn from the diaries and notebooks, on the whole, strips away any illusions about Patricia Highsmith's commercial success as a writer. On December 30, 1963, she notes that the sale of the story "The Hate Murders" (retitled "Music to Die By" in this collection)—which she claimed not to "love very much"—to *Ellery Queen's Mystery Magazine* marked the end of a seven-month phase of utter financial drought. That was a bitter pill for her to swallow, because the 1960s were a phase of intense, wide-ranging work that included essays and reviews. In ten years, after all, she completed seven novels among which we find some of her best work. However, even fine books like *The Two Faces of January* and *The Glass Cell* were first rejected in America, and not until 1968, as Patricia Highsmith stated in an interview, did she begin to find herself in reasonable financial shape. If we keep in mind the emotional turmoil surrounding her stay in England—her girlfriend had a husband and child in London and made only rare appearances in Aldeburgh—the potential for failure in the author's everyday life takes on daunting dimensions.

A similar turn of events threatens the hero of the story "Variations on a Game," which was outlined in 1958 but not published until 1973 in *Alfred Hitchcock's Mystery Magazine*. The misogynistic lines in the story's conclusion show a certain similarity with the novel *The Cry of the Owl*, which was written some four years later. In both cases, fingerprints appear on the knife that was used as a murder weapon, and in both instances, the main character succeeds in getting out of a tight spot. The women in both texts have unpleasant fates that await them. In view of the malice with which several of Patricia Highsmith's female characters are abused and punished, it seems quite plausible that she was taking literary revenge on unreliable friends.

The diaries do not contain a single word about the remarkable story "A Girl like Phyl." We know next to nothing about it apart from the simple fact that it first appeared in 1980 in the German edition of *Playboy*. There is occasional mention in the notebooks of the name "Phyllis," denoting a certain type of young, conservative, and distinguished upper-class woman. Perhaps it is sufficient to say that the story is one of the most impressive in the volume. What it shows us is how disappointments in life create their own framework, and how the unresolved past informs and corrodes the present. The long passage describing the night in the hotel, in which the businessman Jeff Cormack vacillates between curiosity, longing, reticence, and shock, is the product of a consummate author.

—First section translated by Burton Pike,
second section by Shelley Frisch

The recipient of the prestigious Alfred Kerr Prize in literary criticism in 1997, Paul Ingendaay is one of Germany's most influential and respected literary authorities. Born in 1961 in Cologne, he wrote his dissertation on William Gaddis, and is regarded as one of the leading voices of a younger generation of German critics. Given that the scholarly work on Patricia Highsmith is only in its infancy, Ingendaay is at the forefront of this field. Since 1998, he has been a cultural correspondent for the *Frankfurter Allgemeine Zeitung* in Madrid.

NOTES ON THE STORIES

by Anna von Planta

The files of Patricia Highsmith are so massive that when spread out they are 150 feet in length. The literary papers in a narrower sense contain typescripts of short stories, essays, poems, plays, television scripts, radio plays, workbooks, novels (fragments and manuscripts withdrawn by Patricia Highsmith at the time of their composition as not intended for publication), travel reports, and children's stories. The author preserved this material in a total of fifteen accordion files. The files "Oldest Short Stories 1945–1955 c.," "Middle Short Stories," "Short Stories 1972–74–78–80–81–82," and "Short Stories 1983–88" contain over 120 short story typescripts and print versions. Some fifty of them are typescripts or first printed versions of stories that were later included in the seven story collections she published during her lifetime. Of the more than eighty other surviving stories, more than half have presumably never been published worldwide. Hardly any of them have ever appeared in book form.

Patricia Highsmith published her first story at seventeen in *The Bluebird*, the Julia Richman High School magazine. Until the appearance of her first published novel, *Strangers on a Train*, she earned her living from short stories, along with writing texts for comics, and secretarial work. For her, these stories were in a double sense a necessity. This was so even if until 1965, when she presumably spoke about it publicly for the first time, she was known only as a writer of novels: "And short stories are absolutely essential to me, like poetry: I write a lot of both. Only a fraction of the stories I have written ever appeared in print." (Interview with Francis Wyndham: "Sick of Psychopaths," in *The Sunday Times*, London, April 11, 1965.) Yet her first volume of short stories, *Eleven*, which appeared five years later in 1970 after she had published thirteen novels, contained only stories that had previously been published in magazines or anthologies, and which moreover (with few exceptions, like the story

"The Heroine," first published in 1945), had all been written or first printed in the 1960s.

The author's handwritten notes and assessments on the typescript pages of the unpublished stories indicate that in 1966, Patricia Highsmith was first examining the unpublished typescripts of her short stories. Maurice Richardson wished to include her in an anthology, and her American publisher, Doubleday, was interested in publishing a volume of stories (later, in 1970, to be published as *Eleven* in Britain and as *The Snail-Watcher* in the United States, with a foreword by Graham Greene). In 1973, the author was again revising, or discarding, unpublished typescripts: "Lately—last couple of weeks—I am clearing out old files, incredible 300 pages or so of useless, rotten old short stories bit the dust. Good riddance." (In a letter to her friend Kate Kingsley Skattebol, July 9, 1973.)

Yet hardly any of the short stories she retained were included in her subsequent collections. One reason might be that the volumes that appeared in 1975 and 1977—*The Animal-Lover's Book of Beastly Murder* and *Little Tales of Misogyny*, as coordinated cycles of short stories dedicated to a central theme—did not lend themselves thematically to the inclusion of the "Oldest" or "Middle Short Stories." But the next collection, too, the short story volume *Slowly, Slowly in the Wind,* contains only more recent stories that had been first published in the 1970s, and the subsequent collections also almost always contain her most recent productions.

Part I of this volume of stories from Patricia Highsmith's papers contains the majority of the short stories preserved in the archives and written between 1938 and 1949. Excluded from the start were those stories that had remained fragmentary, as well as those clearly left in the state of preliminary draft or those that Patricia Highsmith herself called unready or unsuitable for publication. Also not selected were commissioned pieces or detective stories that Highsmith called purely "commercial stories," which moreover are often only variations of other stories that already appeared in book form. From the remainder fourteen short stories have been chosen for the first part of this book, and fourteen of the best or most representative of the later period 1952–1982 appear in Part II. Most of the unpublished stories are undated. With the exception of the three earliest—"Quiet Night," "Miss Juste and the Green Rompers," and "A Mighty Nice Man"—which appeared in the *Barnard Quarterly* and whose handwritten or typescript versions were not preserved, all the stories in Part I were found in the file "Oldest Short Stories 1945–1955 c.," to which belong also five stories of Part II ("The Returnees," "Born Failure," "Man's Best Friend," "A Bird in Hand," and "The Trouble with Mrs. Blynn, the Trouble with the World"). Most of the stories of Part II, however, are from the file "Middle Short Stories," with the exception of "The Second Cigarette" and "Two Disagreeable Pigeons," which are from the file "Short Stories 1972–74–78–80–81–82." Because of Highsmith's many travels, moves, and change of agents, the publication history of many stories is obscure, compounded by the fact that there remains so little secondary literature. In addition, the author herself often provided incomplete, false, or contradictory information about the individual stories.

The editors were able to rely on documents in the Highsmith papers and archives, recently made extensively available, in the Swiss Literary Archives in Berne, for the Afterword and the following record of the publication history. The notebooks and diaries there, which amount to about 8,000 handwritten pages, were particularly useful.

The distinction between notebooks and diaries in Patricia Highsmith's case is by no means absolute. Many diaries contain working notes, while the notebooks record not only ideas for books but also places, names, (encoded) meetings, ordinary daily routines, poems (by herself and others), notes on her reading, quotations, and thoughts about American and world politics. There are thirty-seven notebooks that the author kept between 1938 and 1992, nineteen from the period before 1950, the year of publication of her first novel, *Strangers on a Train,* and eighteen diaries (1941 to 1984), which contain only sporadic entries after 1954. Altogether, the diaries are far less important than the notebooks, for Highsmith worked these notebooks continually, while the diaries expanded for years without being drawn upon for new projects.

PART I: EARLY STORIES, 1938–1949

"The Mightiest Mornings." 31 pp. TS (typescript), undated. Written (first as "The Mightiest Mountains") between July 10, 1945, and February 15, 1946. Unpublished.

"Uncertain Treasure." Written November–December 1942, first published in *Home and Food* (New York), August 1943, vol. 6, no. 21, pp. 15, 27, 32–34.

"Magic Casements." 19 pp. TS, undated, written under the alternative titles "The Magic Casements" and "The Faery Lands Forlorn" between ca. December 1945 and the end of February 1946. Unpublished.

"Miss Juste and the Green Rompers." Written in 1941, first appeared in *Barnard Quarterly*, vol. XVII, no. 4, Spring II, 1941, pp. 19–26.

"Where the Door Is Always Open and the Welcome Mat Is Out." Two versions, both undated, both unpublished; the first version of 22 TS pp., second, shortened version (titled "The Welcome Mat") of 17 TS pp., written between February 1945 and April 1947, revised in 1949. This edition is based on the first, longer version.

"In the Plaza." 28 pp. TS, undated, written in Taxco, Mexico, in April 1948. Unpublished.

"The Hollow Oracle" (untitled by PH, title provided by editor from PH text). 14 pp. TS, undated. Presumably written between September and November 1942. Unpublished.

"The Great Cardhouse." 19 pp. TS, written August/September 1949. First published in *Story*, vol. 36, issue 3, no. 140, May–June 1963, pp. 32–48.

"The Car." Two undated TS versions, both 22 pp., one (presumably later) version with corrections of Spanish phrases. A first draft was written in March 1945, which PH revised in December 1962. This edition is based on the corrected (presumably later) version. Unpublished.

"The Still Point of the Turning World." 20 pp. TS, undated, written between August and November 1947, first published as "The Envious One" in *Today's Woman*, March 1949.

"The Pianos of the Steinachs." 41 pp. TS, dated by PH 1947, written between ca. December 1946 and May 1947. Unpublished.

"A Mighty Nice Man." Written in ca. 1940, first published in *Barnard Quarterly*, vol. XV, no. 3, Spring 1940, pp. 34–40.

"Quiet Night." Two versions; the first version presumably written in New York in 1938 or 1939, first published in *Barnard Quarterly*, Fall 1939, pp. 5–10; twenty-seven years later, in February 1966, PH revised and lengthened the story, which was published as "The Cries of Love" in *Woman's Home Journal*, January 1968, and in book form in PH, *Eleven*, London: Heinemann 1970 (U.S. edition titled *The Snail-Watcher and Other Stories*, published by Doubleday, 1970).

"Doorbell for Louisa." 26 pp. TS, with a handwritten 1973 note by PH, "Cosmopolitan 1948?" while her diary tells of having sold the story to *Woman's Home Companion* on September 3, 1946. Unpublished.

PART II: MIDDLE AND LATER STORIES, 1952–1982

"A Bird in Hand." 19 pp. TS, undated. Unpublished.

"Music to Die By." 15 pp. TS, written in Aldeburgh, Suffolk, between December 1962 and August 1963. First published as "The Hate Murders" in *Ellery Queen's Mystery Magazine*, May 1965, pp. 11–22; first published in book form (in French translation) as "Une logique folle" in PH, *Le jardin des disparus*, Paris: Calmann-Lévy 1982. (New title applied by editor from PH text.)

"Man's Best Friend." 16 pp. TS, undated, written between July 3 and 9, 1952. Unpublished.

"Born Failure." 18 pp. TS, undated. Written between May 22 and 29, 1953. Unpublished.

"A Dangerous Hobby." First story outline in June 1959. First published as "The Thrill Seeker" in *Ellery Queen's Mystery Magazine*, August 1960, pp. 10–21; handwritten note by PH on magazine copy, "A Dangerous Hobby." First published in book form (in French translation) as "L'amateur de frissons" in *Les cadavres exquis*, Paris: Calmann-Lévy, 1989 (as "The Thrill Seeker" in PH, *Chillers*, London: Penguin, 1990).

"The Returnees." 24 pp. TS, undated, written in Munich and Paris between September and October 1952. Unpublished.

"Nothing That Meets the Eye." 22 pp. TS, undated. Presumably written in April 1964. Unpublished.

"Two Disagreeable Pigeons." 9 pp. TS, undated, first story outline December 21, 1973. Unpublished.

"Variations on a Game." 19 pp. TS, undated. First story outline February 1958. First published in *Alfred Hitchcock's Mystery Magazine*, vol. 18, February 1973, pp. 22–35. First published in book form (in French translation) in *Photo à l'arrivée*, Paris: Calmann-Lévy, 1995.

"A Girl like Phyl." 29 pp. TS, undated. First published (in German translation) as "Ein Mädchen wis Phyl" in (German) *Playboy*, vol. 8, 1980; first published in book form (in French translation) as "Le portrait de sa mère" in PH, *Le jardin des disparus*, Paris: Calmann-Lévy 1982.

"It's a Deal." 14 pp. TS, undated. First story outline in October 1963, first published (in German translation) as "Quitt" in *Tintenfass* 24, Zurich: Diogenes, 2000.

"Things Had Gone Badly." 17 pp. TS, undated. First story outline in June 1978. First published in *Ellery Queen's Mystery Magazine*, March 10, 1980, pp. 64–78. First published in book form as "Un meurtre" in PH, *Le jardin des disparus*, Paris: Calmann-Lévy, 1982.

"The Trouble with Mrs. Blynn, the Trouble with the World." 11 pp. TS, undated. Probably written in Aldeburgh, Suffolk, in 1963/1964. First published in *The New Yorker*, May 27, 2002.

"The Second Cigarette." 19 pp. TS, undated, written (under alternative titles "Twin Story" and "Poynters") between April 1976 and January 1978. First published (in French translation) as "La deuxième cigarette" in *On ne peut compter sur personne*, Paris: Calmann-Lévy 1996.

Anna von Planta, an editor at Diogenes Verlag in Zürich, was Patricia Highsmith's primary editor from 1985 until her death in 1995. She continues her work with the literary estate.

ABOUT THE AUTHOR

Born in Fort Worth, Texas, in 1921, Patricia Highsmith spent much of her adult life in Switzerland and France. She was educated at Barnard College, where she studied English, Latin, and Greek. Her first novel, *Strangers on a Train,* published initially in 1950, proved to be a major commercial success and was filmed by Alfred Hitchcock. Despite this early recognition, Highsmith was unappreciated in the United States for the entire length of her career.

Writing under the pseudonym of Claire Morgan, she then published *The Price of Salt* in 1953, which had been turned down by her previous American publisher because of its frank exploration of homosexual themes. Her most popular literary creation was Tom Ripley, the dapper sociopath who first debuted in her 1955 novel, *The Talented Mr. Ripley.* She followed with four other Ripley novels. Posthumously made into a major motion picture, *The Talented Mr. Ripley* has helped bring about a renewed appreciation of Highsmith's work in the United States, as has the posthumous publication of *The Selected Stories of Patricia Highsmith,* which received widespread acclaim when it was published by W. W. Norton & Company in 2001.

The author of more than twenty books, Highsmith has won the O. Henry Memorial Award, the Edgar Allan Poe Award, Le Grand Prix de Littérature Policière, and the Award of the Crime Writers' Association of Great Britain. She died in Switzerland on February 4, 1995, and her literary archives are maintained in Berne.